BAD BLOOD

R.D. NIXON

This edition produced in Great Britain in 2023

by Hobeck Books Limited, Unit 14, Sugnall Business Centre, Sugnall, Stafford, Staffordshire, ST21 6NF

www.hobeck.net

A CIP catalogue for this book is available from the British Library.

ISBN 978-1-915-817-06-8 (pbk)

ISBN 978-1-915-817-05-1 (ebook)

Cover design by Jayne Mapp Design

Printed and bound in Great Britain

Are you a thriller seeker?

Hobeck Books is an independent publisher of crime, thrillers and suspense fiction and we have one aim – to bring you the books you want to read.

For more details about our books, our authors and our plans, plus the chance to download free novellas, sign up for our newsletter at **www.hobeck.net**.

You can also find us on Twitter **@hobeckbooks** or on Facebook **www.facebook.com/hobeckbooks10**.

*In loving memory of Eddie Deegan, whose love for his family
was only ever matched by his love for Scotland.*

Prologue

Castle Stuart Golf Links, Inverness. March 1998

CHRIST, could today get any worse?

Blissfully unaware that it could, and would, Andrew Silcott squinted irritably at his companion, who was taking an age to line up his shot off the eleventh. It was obvious this Bradley clown had wildly exaggerated his prowess as a golfer; he was hamstringing Silcott's own game, and pretty soon they'd be faced with the embarrassment of the next pair asking to play through. Silcott wished he'd never agreed to take the upstart copper around the course to begin with.

'You've used up your extra seconds already,' he pointed out. 'And the lighthouse looks pretty from here, right enough, but there's only so long I can stare at it before my eyes fall from my head.'

'It's a tricky shot on a par three,' Bradley muttered.

'Go short, and to the right.' Silcott stifled a yawn as he looked at his watch. His daughter was flying back from her mother's today, and there'd be hell to pay if he wasn't there to pick her up at the airport. There would be anyway though, he conceded with a bitter little grimace. It was widely known now that he'd sold on a Mercanti painting that had subsequently been proved a fake, and he wasn't the one who'd lost the money, but even so he could just imagine his ex-wife Amanda's reaction, and she'd be right for once; you didn't come back from something like this. Who would buy from him in the future? No-one and their sodding neighbour, that's who. It was over.

Unlike this game, which had been going on for what felt like weeks. Silcott tapped his fingers on the handle of his club, as if expending his own energy could speed Bradley up some-how, and turned to look back the way they'd come; the next players were already making their way towards them.

'Step it up,' he urged, and lifted a hand by way of apology to the approaching group. Then he groaned as he saw who it was, and his hand froze mid-wave. *Of all the shitty luck.* 'Forget it,' he muttered to Bradley. 'Let's get back to the clubhouse. The flight's due in at—'

'Hang on, I've got it lined up now.'

'We're out of time!'

'They can always play through.' Bradley followed the direction of Silcott's gaze. 'Ah, Matthew Sturdy. That's the bloke you sold the dud painting to, isn't it? I didn't even know he was a member here.' He gave Silcott a sly grin. 'Don't see how he can afford it, to be honest, especially not now.'

'Fuck off.' Silcott slid his own club back into his bag. 'I knew nothing about the fake; they proved that.'

'Oh, aye. You had all the *paperwork*.' Bradley punctuated the word with a single set of air quotes, his club still in position beside the ball. He turned back to re-align his shot. 'Don't worry, we'll be out of his hair in a minute.'

Sturdy had clearly recognised Silcott at the same time, and

stopped walking. There was a long, tense pause in which nobody spoke, or moved, then Sturdy slowly withdrew a sand wedge from his bag and began walking again. Silcott watched him through narrowed eyes, but Sturdy wasn't making for the bunker, he was walking straight towards Silcott, and he had left his bag behind. Silcott's stomach did a slow twist as he stepped back, telling himself he was going to look pretty stupid in a minute, when Sturdy simply located his ball and took the shot. He heard Bradley give a soft, mocking laugh beside him, but there was something coldly purposeful about Sturdy's stride, and Silcott couldn't *quite* shake the idea—

'You bastard,' Sturdy said in a flat voice.

Silcott spared Bradley a quick glance, still not ready to believe that a respectable art collector, and fellow member of Castle Stuart, as it turned out, would actually dare to *assault* anyone in front of a policeman. Not even over a multi-million pound cock-up. It just wouldn't be worth it.

Nevertheless he tightened his grip on the five-iron in his own hand. 'Look, Matthew, I swear I didn't know.' But his voice came out thin and unconvincing-sounding. 'The paperwork—'

'*Bastard.*' Sturdy stopped in front of him, leaning on the wedge and breathing hard. He looked as if he was having trouble keeping himself steady, let alone planning a confrontation, and Silcott's fingers loosened on the iron.

'I understand, Matt. It came as a shock to me too. Let's talk about some recompense, okay? A goodwill payment, from me to you. Off the books, of course. Half a mil? I'll write you an IOU right now.'

He took his eye off Sturdy only long enough to swap the iron into his other hand and reach for his wallet, but that was all it took. He heard Bradley's shout of alarm a split second before he felt the fiery pain as the sand wedge thudded into his upper arm. His fingers instantly went numb and he dropped his club, thinking dimly, *I deserved that*, then the wedge swung again, this time catching him on the side of the neck and sending him stumbling sideways to fall on the grass. The twanging agony of abused tendons gave way to the sudden, horrified realisation that Sturdy didn't give two shits whether there was a policeman there or not.

There were more shouts: Silcott only knew none were his, because the shock and pain had robbed him of the ability to draw breath. He twisted to look up from where he lay on the beautifully kept green and saw someone grab Sturdy's arm and try to wrestle the club from his hand; he saw Sturdy's face, twisted with hate and unthinking rage, and then the club was arcing towards him again. There was an explosion of white light, something inside his ear erupted and he felt some kind of fluid, maybe blood, coursing down his jaw and neck.

Sturdy spun around, swinging the club in a defensive circle around himself that forced the others back a couple of paces, and Silcott tried to use the time to scramble backwards on his hands and feet, but they wouldn't work. His left elbow buckled, his feet wouldn't co-ordinate, and as the sand wedge swung towards him, the metal catching a ray of sunlight and firing it directly into Silcott's streaming eyes, he knew there was no escaping it.

Chapter One

14th April 2019

BOTH THE BEAUTY and the downside of a four-hour ride home from a bike rally was the time to think. Hazel Douglas swiped the side of her glove across her visor, watching the rain flick satisfyingly off and enjoying the few seconds of clear vision before the beads appeared again and left trails snaking down the plastic. The tail lights of the bike in front flashed brighter as its rider braked, then faded back to their previous dull glow as the bike settled into its new, lower speed to match the road they had turned onto. Thank God they'd left the motorways behind now and were onto the A82 – it felt like the home stretch. Speaking of stretching... Thirty-five was getting on a bit for this rough camping malarkey, and Hazel rose on her footpegs for a moment, letting her lower back enjoy a moment of decompression, before settling back into the saddle and once more wiping at her rain-channelled visor. Time to think, yes. Far too much of it. She didn't want to, but perhaps she owed it to them both now, her father *and* her mother.

This time of year was always tough, but it was harder than ever now, without her father to help her get past the memories. It was his bike she was riding, and this was the first time he hadn't been there to hear the talk amongst the other bike clubs as they made their usual leisurely, Saturday morning tour of the rally field, clutching steaming coffee cups and clustering around anything faintly interesting. Her own club, the Caledonia Road Riders, had arrived late, missing Friday night's party, and in the morning she'd lain in her sleeping bag, a sad but reflective half-smile on her face as she'd listened to the familiar chatter outside her closed tent.

'There he is! Bike's still looking good.'

'Can't go wrong with a classic Kwak.'

'Not seen him since the Wanderers' do, three years back.'

'I thought he was ill. Good to see he's made it here after all though. Got his girl with him again?'

'Oi, Gray!' A hand rattled the tent, making Hazel jump. 'Get up, ya lazy bastard!'

A quick zipping sound came from across the way, and then Dave Griffin, her own club chairman, spoke quietly. 'Um, mate, I'm sorry, but Graeme died. Hazel's got the Zed now.'

There had been a momentary, shocked silence, then some muttered oaths and condolences, and the voices had drifted away. Hazel had lain there for a while longer, getting her hot, choked tears under control, before sitting up and readying herself for public viewing; she was going to be the focus of a lot of attention this weekend and she had to be braced for that. She reached inside her shirt for her necklace; an irregularly shaped lump of silver that her father had made for her out of her mother's rings, knowing Hazel would never wear the rings but would treasure this unique, mis-shapen nugget. She wrapped her fingers around it and closed her eyes, sent him the *thank you* she always did, and crawled out to face the day.

In the end it had been a surprisingly comforting experience; her father had been hugely popular among the bike clubs that gathered regularly at these rallies, but then Hazel herself had been coming with him since she'd been old enough to reach the pillion pedals, and was as much a fixture at these events in later years as he had been. She'd been greeted with warmth and sympathy, but a good deal of Graeme-related banter too, and there had even been a tribute to him shouted out over the tannoy at the start of the games on Saturday afternoon. He'd excelled at crank-throwing, particularly, and Hazel had been touched to learn that the host club were naming that prize the *Graeme Douglas Award*, for that year at least.

But comforting memories of her father were always going to be intertwined with dark, frightening and confused memories of her mother. As she rode now, in the middle of the pack of sixteen motorcycles heading back towards Abergarry, Hazel's thoughts were tugged reluctantly from the somewhat life affirming weekend of reminiscences and nostalgia, and pushed back into the home she'd known when she was fourteen: into the afternoon in 1998, when the world had splintered, taking her childhood with it.

It had been a couple of weeks off her dad's big fortieth birthday, and she'd just got off the school bus. Home in those days had been a place called Druimgalla, out in the sticks, and

7

as she walked up the punishingly steep lane her mind had dropped its pondering on what she could buy her dad, and occupied itself with whether or not she'd be able to persuade her mum to drive her back into town that night for the end of term disco. By the time she'd pushed open the front door she was already framing the query in terms of how dangerous it would be to walk it, because *for sure* she was going anyway. But the words never left her mouth.

Her mother was usually in the kitchen at this time of day, having spent the day in her studio, but as Hazel glanced into the open sitting room as she passed, she could see bare feet hanging over the arm of the sofa. Her mother never went bare-foot, ever. Not even in summer; she was paranoid about insects and spiders. And she was so...still. The banging of the front door hadn't woken her, and neither had the gust of cool spring air that had followed Hazel into the house.

Hazel cleared her throat. Nothing. She called out, in a voice oddly lacking in strength; still nothing. She felt a cold, crawling sensation down the back of her neck and between the layers of clothing, like a chilled finger asking a silent question, to which the only possible answer was a scream. But if she let that scream out she knew she'd never stop, so she just moved closer to the still form, keeping away from those awful white, dangling feet, and focusing instead on the other end of the sofa... She wished to this very day that she'd never done that.

The face she'd last seen smiling vaguely but affectionately at her, as she'd left for school that morning, was now purple and swollen; the tongue protruded a little way from between lips that had, just last night, pressed against Hazel's temple in a casual goodnight kiss, and were now cracked and caked with dried blood. The yellow dressing gown was gaping open in a way that would have horrified the very private woman Yvette had been, showing the soft, pale flesh she had always taken great pains to hide away. As if it had mattered.

Hazel pressed the back of her hand to her mouth and bit the skin there as hard as she could. Nothing changed. Her eyes went to the rest of the room, and only then did she take in the mess: the overturned magazine rack; the way the easy chair by the window had been shoved aside, presumably to allow access to the cabinet behind it; the bureau with its open lid, and the drawers removed. The front door hadn't been locked, but then it never was when Mum was home. Even when she was in her studio.

Something about the dressing gown kept pulling Hazel's attention back, and she realised then that her mother must have been lying there like this all day; she hadn't even had time to shower and dress before whoever had invaded her home had killed her. Would she have stiffened by now then? With her feet dangling, and her hands still clutching at the terry-towelling tie around her neck?

A low cry rose in Hazel's own throat. Her knees shook, then failed her, and she sank to the floor with the back of the sofa now mercifully blocking her mother from her sight. She never knew how long she'd sat like that, but it gradually dawned that her father was away in Stirling, and no-one was expected at the house. She realised no help was coming, there was no comforting neighbour to take charge; it would fall to her to call...who? The police, ambulance? Her father's hotel? Yes, all of them. But who first?

Somehow she had made her way to the phone in the hall, and called 999. After that everything had become a tangled mess of voices, sirens, questions, rustling suits and the awful, final zipping sound of her mother disappearing forever into the hands of people who'd never known her. Hazel had been taken into the kitchen but she'd heard it all. Blue and white tape had gone up around the house, the sitting room had been photographed and examined, and all the while the gentle but probing questions had kept coming: Where was her father? What time had he left? What time had *she* left that morning, and had she come home for lunch? What time had she come home from school? Where was her father? Had anyone seen her? Had *she* seen anyone? *Where was her father?*

That was when she'd passed into the system for the first time. Placed with a foster family she'd rebelled against, and had not really given a chance, taking comfort instead in new, brittle friendships; kids like her, with their wild ideas for savage thrills that momentarily made her forget everything else; adrenalin-pumping, high energy stuff, leaving her breathless and exhilarated by a chase, or, as time went on, a chemical high. A spell or two in custody, and before long she was utterly gone. She'd welcomed the void as a haven.

When she'd finally returned home, her father's quiet pleading had irritated her beyond belief; what the hell did he know? By the time *he'd* been allowed to see her mother—acccompanied by the police, who'd only really wanted to see his reaction to his wife's cold, still corpse—she had been somewhere you expect to see shit like that. All laid out nice and straight, in a cool room, in an atmosphere and with knowledge that at least prepared you. It fucking...*prepared* you.

Not like coming home from school ready for your tea, and thinking only about how great you were going to look in your new lycra mini, and how much Ben Cameron was going to eat his heart out over your long, skinny legs. Not like looking into the comfortable, familiar room where you usually watched TV, did your homework and tried out your new nail varnish... looking into *that room* and seeing your mother half naked, stiffened into a grotesque dummy with the wrong head attached to it; a head that had been torn from some horror story and sewn onto the body of the woman you'd known and loved all your life.

What did *he* know of that?

———

She rode the winding roads now, remembering that time only as a tunnel of darkness, with patches of light that were the Caledonia Road Riders MCC, the only thing she and her father had still shared at that point. He must have sensed that the rallies and camping weekends had been the best way back for her, helping her to balance the thrills with the solid, unwaveringly loyal companionship that went with it. It had done more than bring her back, it had saved her.

She waved absently as another rider peeled away from the group to take their own road home, and wiped her visor again. On top of the fact that her mother had died around this time of year, today would have been Graeme Douglas's sixty-first birthday. His room and all his belongings were exactly as they'd been the day he died, and even Linda, the woman he'd been seeing for the past few years, had somewhat nervously broached the subject of clearing it out. Hazel had to consider that she might be right, and perhaps even that there was no better day than his birthday to do it. But she couldn't do it alone.

Around twenty minutes later she pulled up alongside Griff and signalled to him that she was taking the turning up ahead, so he wouldn't worry when he didn't see her in his mirror. She turned off at the junction, lifting one gloved hand to the remaining riders, and once away from the pack she suddenly felt very lonely. The low thrum of bikes behind and in front had felt comforting and protective, but now, on this steep, rain-swept stretch of road that wound up to the ridge and her childhood home, she began to wonder if this was a good idea after all. Perhaps it would be better to stop and call her aunt instead, and arrange for her to come to Hazel's home... But she pushed that thought to the back of her mind and kept going, remembering how the school bus had laboured up here, hissing and protesting all the way, to tip her out at the foot of the even steeper lane that ultimately led to Druimgalla.

She puttered slowly up over the rise, and the house came into view. Squat and ugly, made more so by the driving rain, and by the memories that lay beneath the grey slate roof, it sat in a large yard that was bare, except for Isla's Toyota and the garage by the trees. It had never been used as a garage when Hazel had lived there, either; it had been the little studio where her mother had created her sweet cottage scenes, and flowery offerings that she'd felt had never held a candle to her husband's richly detailed painting. Yvette had been quite happy to acknowledge that though, and content with her separate studio space where she needn't compare the two. Still, Hazel had loved to watch her work; she'd been so much more relaxed about it than Dad, who'd always felt he had something to prove.

Now the garage had lost that sense of magic and was just a brick-built square again, its roof brushed by the weight of the sodden tree branches that scraped and dripped on it from above. Hazel turned back to face the house, and saw a movement inside the sitting room as her aunt crossed to the window to see who was visiting. It was too late to change her mind now, so she switched off the engine and climbed stiffly off the bike, rolling her shoulders to bring them back to life after the long ride from the Borders.

Isla opened the front door and beckoned her in. 'What in God's name are you doing up here on a day like this?'

'I'll tell you in a minute.' Hazel pulled off her helmet and rubbed a hand through her flattened, smoky-smelling hair. 'Sorry, I stink a bit. I've not been home for a shower yet.'

'Never mind that.' Isla grimaced once more at the filthy weather. 'The rain's due to pass off soon; you could've come out later.'

'Everything okay with the house?' Hazel asked, her eyes automatically roaming the ceiling and walls. Although she'd had her own place in town for years, the family home had passed to her after her father's death, but she hadn't been able to bring herself to move back. Since Isla's divorce had left her floundering financially, it had made more sense to rent it to her and her son at a reduced rate, and Hazel's landlady senses were always on higher alert when the weather was bad.

'Fine, thanks,' Isla said, moving quickly past and pulling the sitting room door closed before Hazel reached it. 'Go through.'

When Hazel was settled in the kitchen, with a hot chocolate sending sweet-smelling warmth into the air around her, she was able to turn her mind away from the thoughtfully closed sitting room door and bring it back to her reason for visiting.

'I thought it was time we went through my dad's things,' she said. 'I know there's some stuff of Mum's still in there, so I thought maybe you might like to—'

'No,' Isla said at once, then she caught Hazel's expression. 'Sorry, that sounded blunt. I just meant... Well, I'll let you look at it. You can always pass over anything of hers you think I might like to see.'

'Okay.' Hazel sipped at her drink, noticing how Isla's gaze travelled the room restlessly, as if looking for something else to comment on, to change the subject. 'I just wanted to give you the chance, you know.'

'Aye, thanks. Good of you to think of me. So, how's work going, up at that new place? Glencoille, is it? How's the building coming along?'

Hazel would normally have been amused at the quick-fire questions, but she was distracted by the way Isla's demeanour had altered. 'What's up?' she asked, borrowing some of her aunt's bluntness. 'Is it my dad? You always seemed okay with him when he was alive.'

'I've got no issue with him now,' Isla said carefully, after a moment. 'I just don't want to spend what little free time I have going through a bunch of old clothes and vinyl records.'

Put like that it did seem reasonable, and Hazel nodded, though she was still not wholly convinced. 'Fair enough.'

'I'm glad you have that job to focus on,' Isla said, pushing one of her many snap-lid containers towards Hazel, this one full of custard creams. 'Do you still see that woman you made friends with on your community payback? The investigator?'

'Maddy Clifford,' Hazel supplied, taking a biscuit. 'Aye, we see each other a lot. She's the one who got me the job, and thank God she did.'

Working with Ade Mackenzie and his father, on the new Highland Experience centre at Glencoille, was never dull; they were also building a family home up there, and Hazel's work varied between ordering building supplies, keeping Ade's calendar under control and refereeing discussions between Ade and his father, Frank, over the layout of the house or the distillery. Sparks often flew, which made for interesting times, but she enjoyed every minute.

'The work's been good for you, too,' Isla said, 'since Graeme died, I mean.' Her tone had changed again, and it was fairly obvious she was referring more to Hazel's coping mechanism than to the bereavement itself.

Hazel closed her lips on a defensive comment and just nodded. 'I wasn't as bad as when Mum was killed, but it could have gone that way. Thanks to Maddy, it didn't.'

'Your mum was a whole different thing,' Isla said, frowning. 'You were only a kid, and it was so sudden. So *violent*. I only wish I'd been here for you instead of halfway across the world.' She paused, then pushed on. 'You know, I still can't believe the police were so convinced it was a burglary—'

'Of course it was a burglary!' Hazel scowled. 'What else would it have been? Mum didn't have any enemies.'

'They didn't always think that,' Isla reminded her. Her gaze fell on Hazel's necklace, and her lips thinned. 'They questioned your dad pretty thoroughly, didn't they? I know,' she held up a hand, 'he was exonerated. I'm just saying. The whole thing wrecked you, Haze, you know it did, but I think them suspecting your dad was actually worse than what happened to Yvette.'

Hazel was about to argue but subsided, because ultimately Isla was probably right. She might, with the right help and guidance, and with a conviction brought for her mother's murder, have been all right eventually. The burglary that the police had at first suspected of being staged, was accepted to have been real, and Yvette's undignified and brutal fate had been filed away as unsolved; no doubt infuriating for those working the case, and not satisfactory by any means, but tidily squared away so they could move on to the next priority.

But those weeks and months while the investigation had kept her apart from her father had shown her that the system really didn't have what it took to protect her; the nightmares had been eased only by sousing her senses with cheap vodka, and then by the pills she'd been offered by one of the other girls being fostered at the same house. The smoking had come a little later, but the relief it had brought her was undeniable.

Hazel became once more aware of where she was, and which room lay next door; she saw again those white, dangling feet, and the blackened tongue peeping out through swollen lips. She gulped her chocolate too fast, and cursed as the scalding milk took a layer of skin off the roof of her mouth. Isla ran cold water into a glass and passed it to her.

'Do you want me to ask Griff to come up and sort out those trees by the garage?' Hazel asked, after taking a cooling slug of water. In response to Isla's puzzled look, she went on, 'He's a tree surgeon. Won't take him long.'

'Oh, this is your friend from the bike club?' Isla nodded. 'Well yes, if he's got a free slot. Thanks. I'll be busy at work though,' she added. 'The gallery's got a big summer exhibition this year, and stuff's already coming in for it.'

'Make sure they don't work you too hard,' Hazel said. 'You know Dylan doesn't need any excuses to get into bother.' She saw immediately she'd spoken out of turn; Isla bristled.

'What's that supposed to mean? You think I neglect my own son? He's *fourteen*, Hazel. I can't watch him every minute. And I don't need to.'

'No need to get prickly,' Hazel said, and blew on her hot chocolate warily. 'I'm not saying anything like it. You do work really long hours, and that's not your fault, but he's the type to play on that.'

Isla looked as if she was about to argue, then subsided and gave a wry smile. 'Aye. Little chancer.' There was affection in her voice, but also acceptance, and Hazel gave a small sigh of relief. Dylan was sort of lovable, but he really knew how to push buttons when he wanted to, as well as how to wrap people around his little finger. That had a lot to do with the floppy blond hair and the wide, innocent-looking blue eyes. He reminded Hazel a lot of herself at that age. She'd cultivated an innocent persona to deliberately clash with her post-punk fashion style, and it had got her out of all kinds of trouble, but she hoped her young cousin wouldn't push things too far; people tended to be easier on a girl who'd lost her mother than on a boy with a stable, even privileged, some might say, home life.

She finished her drink, pretty sure she'd burned off all the nerve endings in her mouth, and rose to leave. 'I'd better get back and stick a load of washing on so I can get it dry for work tomorrow.'

'Will you be all right, going through Graeme's things on your own?' Isla asked as she accompanied Hazel to the door.

'I won't be on my own,' Hazel said, pulling her wet gloves out of her helmet. 'I'll ask Linda to do it with me.'

The surprise melted into distaste. 'Linda *Sturdy?*'

'Well she was Dad's girlfriend for his last four years,' Hazel pointed out. 'She did help me nurse him through the worst of it.'

'Still, I didn't think you were particularly close.'

'We aren't, not really, and I haven't heard from her in a bit, but we still get on okay when we do meet.'

Isla changed her tack and became solicitous. 'I heard she had her own health scare recently. I hope she's all right?'

'She's fine. She had the mole removed, and it *was* cancerous, but they got it all.'

'Well I'm glad to hear it.'

'It was good to have her around when I needed someone,' Hazel said, straightening her helmet straps ready for fastening.

'I'd have helped you,' Isla said. She sounded put out now. 'If I hadn't been—'

'Halfway around the world, I know.' Hazel touched her arm. 'It wasn't your place though. No-one would have expected you to come back for that. Dad wasn't really your family; you were only connected through Mum.'

'Aye, but I could have been there for *you*.' Isla's emotions were clearly getting the better of her. '*You're* still my family.'

'And now you are here.' Hazel smiled and lifted her helmet over her head, wincing as the wet interior mashed her drying hair flat to her head again. 'Which is why I wanted to give you the chance to look at any of Mum's things that Dad had held onto. But I'll let you know if we find anything, okay?'

'It's not that I don't want to,' Isla said quickly. 'I just... It's been twenty years but I still feel the anger of it all. I'm afraid that if I look at all that old stuff it'll come flooding back and I'll say something...indiscreet.'

'About my dad?'

Isla shrugged, and wiped unnecessarily at a drop of rain on the glass panel of the door. 'Go safe, love. Call me if you'd like to meet in town for coffee or anything.'

Hazel looked at her for a moment longer, then nodded and turned to walk across the puddle-strewn yard. She kicked the bike's side-stand back into place with a rare vigor, and pushed herself backwards with her feet until she could turn the Kawasaki back out to face the road. Then she wiped her visor with her glove, took one final look behind at the house where her life and family had been shattered over twenty years ago, and started on the last leg of her ride back home.

Chapter Two

JAMIE BOULTON STEPPED into the air-conditioned cool of the convenience store midway up the main Abergarry high street. If he'd been back in Liverpool he'd have been just starting the Easter break, instead of at the end of it, but he realised he was *almost* glad now; he'd been beyond bored, and had been spending most of the time in the library, avoiding jobs at home and wondering if that would put a crimp in his designs on getting a dog. He was on his way home now, after another mammoth library session in the company of his current favourites, the Three Investigators, but first there was this little detour to take care of.

He made his way down the snacks and confectionery aisle, trying not to look like someone about to steal something; he always felt as if the cameras would automatically swivel towards him when he was alone in a shop like this, drawn by some kind of tech magic, to single out eleven-year-old boys with guilty consciences. He didn't even have to try; it just seemed that everyone assumed he was just waiting for them to look the other way so he could pocket a pack of chewie, or a Creme Egg.

It was embarrassing. Jamie waited until the cashier turned his reluctant attention back to his customer and his card reader, and pocketed a Creme Egg.

He picked up a packet of crisps too, and wandered over to pay for it, his heart hammering in case he'd been seen after all. He resisted the urge to pat his jacket pocket in case the small bump showed, but the cashier just took his money and kept a stony, suspicious eye on him until he'd left. The relief Jamie felt stepping out into the sunlight was completely out of proportion to the cost of what he'd taken; he felt like a jewel thief who'd just made off with a million-pound necklace, and had narrowly avoided being chased down by twenty coppers into the bargain.

'Well?'

Jamie fumbled in his pocket and pressed the chocolate egg into the reaching hand of the boy who'd appeared at his side. 'Happy now?'

'You stood exactly where I told you to stand?'

'Opposite the multi-pack crisps and to the left of the 99p bags.'

'Good. Cameras wouldn't have got you, then.' Dylan Munro peeled the foil wrapper and bit off half the egg in one go, making Jamie's own mouth water. 'Next up, something more expensive. A bottle of whisky?'

'Get lost,' Jamie protested at once. 'I'm not even doing the egg again, I feel sick.'

Dylan laughed and punched Jamie's shoulder lightly. 'Don't worry, I was just kidding. I hate whisky anyway.'

At three years his senior, Dylan Munro was putting his considerable reputation at risk just being seen with a kid Jamie's age, never mind palling up. It might have been tougher if they'd gone to the same school, but Dylan went to Lochaber

High, while Jamie still languished at Abergarry Juniors like a baby. In September though, he'd be going to Lochaber and it would be a massive help to already be mates with one of the big kids; best to keep Dylan on side, for sure.

They'd met when Jamie had been knocking around at one of his favourite places: the construction site up at Glencoille. His mum's boyfriend, Mackenzie, had taken him up there while he was visiting his brother, and while Jamie had been sitting around outside, watching the builders, a woman had arrived with her son, a boy of fourteen or so. She'd asked to speak to Ade's office manager, Hazel, and it turned out she was Hazel's aunt, so Jamie was, predictably, instructed to take Dylan and show him around while they talked. Jamie had complied, albeit reluctantly, certain the older boy was going to rip into him just to prove how popular he was. He seemed that type.

But surprisingly, Dylan had actually appeared a little bit awed to be talking to Jamie. He said he'd remembered seeing him on the news last summer, 'the missing Liverpool tourist boy', and kept asking him to say things like *bucket*, and *shirt*. In return Jamie had made Dylan exaggeratedly repeat *Curly Wurly* and *murder* until they'd both forgotten their age difference and were hooting with laughter. Dylan had been doubly fascinated by the fact that Jamie was now living with an *actual* private investigator, and moreover one who'd been involved in an *actual* armed siege; he'd also found it both funny and cool that Jamie and his mum both called the investigator by his surname.

In the weeks that followed, Dylan had, to everyone's surprise, but not everyone's delight, stepped into the gap left by Jamie's best friend Ethan, who'd had to move away last year. Jamie and Ethan had shared a love of detective shows, books and games, and it seemed Dylan had recently become just as fascinated.

Today's little exercise in the shop was apparently Dylan's way of looking at things from the other side. 'If you know how the mind of a thief works,' he'd explained, 'you'll know how to get the better of them, see?'

'I know how a thief's mind works,' Jamie had told him. 'My real dad's in prison, for car theft and GBH.' He immediately wished he'd not said anything, but Dylan's raised eyebrows had registered approval. Jamie had realised he'd unwittingly scored yet another point, and sighed. 'Okay, I'll do it.'

He was a bit peeved that Dylan had scoffed the whole prize, but on the whole he was just glad it was over, and that he'd avoided being caught; the thought of how his mum would react made him go cold from head to foot, and he said so now, as he caught Dylan up. Dylan looked at him in surprise.

'She'd really mind that much?'

'You don't know my mum.' Jamie sighed. 'She'd go absolutely batshit.'

'Bit strict, is she?' Dylan raked his blond hair carelessly back from his face, and it fell neatly to the side. Jamie tried to imitate him, but his own hair stayed where he put it, and his face felt too naked, so he brushed his own dark fringe hurriedly back down.

'She's the worst,' he said, affecting a glum tone. 'You're lucky your mum's out so much.'

'Your mum works most days,' Dylan said. 'And didn't you say she's doing a college course as well? She must *always* be out.'

'You'd think so, but somehow she still manages to have her hand on my collar.'

It was true that she had always been deeply protective,

especially when it had been the two of them against his horrible, controlling father, but he also knew she'd been trying hard to loosen her maternal grip, so he felt a bit disloyal talking about her like this. 'She's okay though,' he added, to mitigate his comments. 'What's your mum like?'

Dylan shrugged. 'She's okay too. 'She lets me do what I want, and she's at the gallery all the time. Like, *all* the time.'

'Lucky you.' Jamie pulled out the phone he'd been given for Christmas, after much wrangling, feeling that little tingle of self importance he got each time it buzzed in front of any other kids. He checked the text, trying to look blasé about it. 'I've got to get back soon.'

'You ought to tell your mum to let you alone a bit more,' Dylan said, a little note of contempt creeping into his voice. '*I* don't get texted every five minutes.'

Jamie frowned. 'I'm younger than you,' he pointed out. 'And after what happened—'

'Yeah, yeah.' Dylan sounded bored now, which was irritating, considering he was the one who always wanted to talk about it. 'Better get back to your exciting life with your private detective friends.'

'You don't have to be a dick about it,' Jamie snapped back. 'Not my fault you've got a boring life, is it? You've got chocolate in your teeth,' he added, turning to leave.

'Hey!' Dylan grabbed his shoulder and pulled him back, but to Jamie's surprise there was no annoyance in his face now. 'Want to hear something about my life that *isn't* boring?'

Jamie shrugged, affecting a half-interested expression and not wanting to admit how relieved he felt that he hadn't messed up this new and influential friendship. 'If you like.'

Dylan looked around him in a way that made Jamie want to copy him; ridiculously theatrical, but hard to resist. 'I'm not supposed to say anything, but someone was murdered at my place.'

Jamie's interest kindled at once, but he kept his voice casual; after all, he was an old hand at murder now. Or at least he liked to pretend so. 'Who got killed?'

'My mum's sister.'

'She was murdered in *your house*?' Jamie could feel his own eyes widen despite his determination to appear unimpressed. 'How come you've never mentioned it before? Were you there?'

Dylan shook his head. 'I wasn't even born. It was *way* back, at the end of the nineties. Mum told me when we moved in, because I found her crying. But she didn't go into details. I had to find it all out by myself.'

'Well? What happened?'

Dylan grinned suddenly, and Jamie had the sense that he'd been neatly hooked by an expert fisherman. 'I told you, I'm not supposed to tell anyone.' He winked. 'But if you promise to keep your trap shut I might tell you later. *If* you get me a bottle of that Glencoille whisky I saw in my cousin Hazel's office.'

Jamie's heart sank. Just when he'd thought they'd moved onto an equal footing. 'I thought you didn't like whisky?'

'Not for me, for my dad. It's his birthday soon, and it'll save me a packet.'

'Forget it,' Jamie said. 'I don't need to know that badly. I'm not nicking stuff from Ade Mackenzie. He's a decent bloke.'

Dylan shrugged. 'No can do, then.'

'Fine.' Jamie turned away again. 'See you around.'

He didn't look back as he started up the road, but deep down he knew he was ready to do just about anything to keep Dylan Munro on his side. When his phone pinged, and he saw that Dylan had sent a winking face emoji and two whisky tumblers, he smiled, but only texted back a single, expression-less face and put his phone away.

They lived a short way out of town now, since Jamie and his mum had moved in with Mackenzie, but as yesterday's torrential downpours had given way to thin sunshine, Jamie ignored the bus stop and made his own way up the hill and out onto the open road. By the time he arrived home he was hot from walking and went straight to the sink for a glass of water, yelling his arrival up the stairs as he went. A moment later there was a thundering of feet on the stairs and his mother came into the kitchen, a look of mingled anger and relief on her face; not for the first time Jamie wondered how someone so tiny could fill an entire room.

'I walked,' he began, as an explanation, but he could see that was cutting no ice.

'Which way did you go?' she asked, sarcasm on full throttle. 'Via Glasgow? What else did you do?'

'I just went into McColls for a packet of crisps.' He showed her the crumpled pack, before throwing it into the bin. 'Got chatting with...some lads.' He didn't want to mention Dylan by name, since she'd made no secret of her disapproval, but he knew she was keen for him to make new friends now Ethan had moved away.

She subsided, and he could see she was battling with wanting to hug him and needing him to realise how worried she'd been. And he did understand, he truly did, but it was like Dylan said: she needed to stop being so clingy. He realised he hadn't actually replied to her text, and felt a guilty flush touch his face.

'Where's Mackenzie?' he asked, to deflect the issue.

'Out the back, kicking the car or something. I was about to send him out looking for you.'

Jamie looked at her in dismay; as cool as Dylan thought Mackenzie was, for him to turn up looking for Jamie would have been the worst. 'There was no need for that,' he said, knowing he sounded sulky and that his mum would hate that.

'Well no, there wouldn't be,' she agreed, with exaggerated patience, '*if* you replied to your messages.'

The back door opened and Mackenzie came in; a tall, wide-shouldered man with messy dark hair and a stern face. He was wiping his hands on his jeans. 'All fixed.' He looked from Jamie to Charis, and sighed. 'Everything all right, then, I take it?'

'Ticketty boo,' Charis said brightly. 'Except I *think* Jamie's phone is broken.' She held out her hand, waiting.

'Mum—'

'Better check, hadn't we?' Charis said, and Jamie could see the dangerous glitter in her eyes. He loved her, a lot. She was better than anyone he knew: mostly kind, and occasionally funny; clever too, though she hid that well; but if she thought she was being messed about, she switched into this whole other mode and there was no arguing with her. He dug into his pocket and handed over his phone.

Mackenzie quietly went about the job of washing oil off his hands, evidently knowing better than to interfere. He too was fair-minded, and rarely lost his temper, but Jamie sometimes wished he'd persuade Mum that she was overdoing things a bit.

'Ah.' She handed the phone back after a quick scroll. 'I see it's allowing you to answer cryptic little messages from that Munro boy, but not to tell your mum you're going to be a bit late because you're walking. What a very silly phone. What a waste of time and money.'

'I'm sorry,' Jamie said, and despite his annoyance at his mother's tightly sarcastic tone, he genuinely was. She looked hurt, as well as angry, and that wasn't something he ever wanted to cause. 'Really,' he added earnestly. 'I'll answer next time, promise.'

Charis sat down at the table and patted the place beside her. 'You know why I get like this, Jay,' she said in a gentler voice, 'and I know why you hate it. But please, just remember everything we've been through, and humour me for a bit longer. Okay? It won't be forever.' He nodded and gave her a faint smile, and she returned it with a slightly bright-eyed one of her own. 'Good. Thanks.'

She had started to loosen up a little last year, when his dad had finally been put away after presiding over his family through years of emotional torture, and had brought him to Scotland last summer for a holiday that marked the start of their new life. But the events that followed had pushed her protective armour right back into place around them both: a dangerous misunderstanding, leading to Jamie's kidnap and incarceration without his asthma medication, and then the near death of the man who'd been racing to save him.

He looked at Mackenzie now, remembering how he and Mum had risked everything, including their lives, and he felt a wash of shame that he had dismissed them both to Dylan as clingy and annoying, just for cheap brownie points... The thought of Dylan reminded him.

'Mackenzie?'

Mackenzie stopped rummaging in the freezer and looked at him over the door. 'Aye?'

'Did you ever hear about a murder up at Dylan's place? Back in the nineties.'

'No idea. Where does Dylan live?'

'That place that Hazel Douglas inherited,' Charis supplied. 'Up by the edge of the forest.'

Mackenzie considered, then shook his head. 'Not that I remember, but I was still working on the rigs at that time, so wasn't home an awful lot. Maddy might know, or more likely her dad or her brother.'

'Did Dylan say who was killed?' Charis asked.

'His gran. No, his aunt.' Jamie frowned, remembering. 'Yeah, his mum's sister, he said.'

'Poor kid. Did he say anything else?'

'Just that he wasn't supposed to talk about it.'

Mackenzie sprinkled frozen potato wedges onto an oven tray and turned to him with a raised eyebrow. 'He won't thank you for bringing up the subject here, then.'

'He said he wouldn't tell me any more,' Jamie complained, deciding at the last second to leave out the conditions under which that might be reversed. 'So since you're a detective I thought I'd ask you instead. Aren't you curious? I am. Mad curious.'

'He might not want to tell you because he doesn't want to talk about it,' his mother pointed out. 'It's his family, after all.'

Jamie shrugged. 'Dylan didn't seem upset though. He never knew her, and it was ages ago. But that would mean she was related to Hazel Douglas too, so I can ask her next time I go up to Glencoille.'

'No you can't,' Mum said quickly. 'It's not nice to go poking around into people's family history.'

'Maybe Ade can bring it up then, since they work together.' Jamie saw his mother's expression and gave up. 'Okay. No asking.' But he was still itching to find out what had happened up at that house. It seemed he'd have to try and get it out of Dylan after all, but he wasn't going to do it by nicking booze off Ade Mackenzie. He pondered for a minute; there might be something about it on the net, but he doubted there would be much more than Dylan had already told him, not from back in the olden days. Did they even *have* internet in those days?

He tuned back into the conversation now going on between his mum and Mackenzie, and perked up; they were talking about Ade's latest acquisition; a second-hand quad bike he'd bought both for his own use, and for that of any of the workers who needed it.

'It's pretty nippy,' Mackenzie said. 'I took it up the lane and across in front of the old house. Handles really well.'

'Are you getting ideas?' Charis asked him, and Jamie heard the tension in her voice though he could tell she was trying not to show it. The bike accident had left its mark on all of them, knowing how close Mackenzie had come to dying, but a quad bike was totally different, even Jamie knew that.

'D'you think Ade would let me have a go on it?' he asked eagerly, before Mackenzie could answer. 'You could give me a lesson. I'd be dead careful,' he added to his mum, who was busying herself getting cutlery from the drying rack.

'You'd have to ask Ade,' Mackenzie said. 'It's not for fun, it's for work. There's a lot of ground to cover on an estate like that, and the jeep can't always get where he'd need to go.'

'Like where?'

'Like up the narrow lanes past the distillery and along by the river, or down the valley, where I took it today.'

'Is it fun?'

Mackenzie's eyes had lit from inside, and he looked as if he was about to launch into just how much fun it was; then he looked at Charis and instead just smiled gently. 'Aye, it's okay. It's strange though, being back there.'

He emptied beans into a pan, and now it seemed as if his mind was straying somewhere else. Or some*when*. As Jamie understood it, the new estate was actually created from the neglected bottom halves of two really old ones, one of which had belonged to Mackenzie's own family years ago, before they'd lost everything. It must be weird, Jamie thought. It would be like him and Mum going back to their flat in Liverpool and buying up the whole block, then turning it into something entirely new. Imagine being able to zoom round *there* on a quad bike... A little grin surfaced as he thought about what his old mates would think of that, and how envious they'd be.

'Go and wash your hands, Jay,' Charis said, cutting into his thoughts. As he trudged up the stairs his mind kept coming back to that notion of appearing in front of his old school friends on a massive, bright red quad bike, then he transferred their awe onto Dylan Munro's face. Like Mum kept telling him, it was good to have goals.

Chapter Three

After work on Tuesday, Hazel gathered everything that had belonged to her father and brought it into the sitting room of the rented home they'd shared. His bedroom looked horribly bare now, everything clean and neat, ready for charity shop or recycling centre. While she waited for Linda to arrive, Hazel picked over a few bits and allowed herself to shed the tears that rose again, catching her unawares but leaving her a little easier in her heart.

The ring of the doorbell came earlier than she'd expected, but it was Griff, not Linda, who stood there. He was smartly dressed, and his long-ish grey hair was tied neatly back; this was weekday professional, drives-a-van Dave Griffin, a sidestep away from weekend, anything-goes Griff, and it was always faintly unsettling the way these little things made a difference.

Hazel led him into the kitchen for a cuppa. 'What brings you here?'

'Crappy news, unfortunately.' He sat down. 'You look a bit red around the eyes. Are you okay?'

'I'm fine. Just getting ready to go through Dad's things with Linda.'

He gave her a sympathetic look. 'I'm sorry. That'll be hard for you both. I'll get out of your hair when she gets here.'

'So? The crappy news?' Hazel could have done without it, but it was clearly enough to have brought Griff here in person rather than texting her.

'It's about the rally.'

'Oh?' The Caledonia Road Riders' own rally was just a couple of weeks away, and the arrangements had been plagued with niggling issues, to the point where one or two of the club had suggested ditching it altogether. 'What's happened now?'

'The big one, I'm afraid. The field's been sold on, and no-one bothered to let us know until now.'

Hazel's already low spirits plummeted. She put the drinks on the table and slumped into her own chair. 'This has been—'

'Hang on, don't count us out yet.' Griff pulled his mug closer. 'I emailed the new owner this afternoon and explained the situation. He's promised to think it over.'

'Well he can't be doing that for too long,' Hazel said. 'We'll need time to find an alternative.'

'So you're not giving up just yet, then, after all.' Griff smiled. 'I knew I could count on you not to be a Jackie.'

Hazel couldn't help smiling back: Jackie, who ran the club's event calendar, didn't have the cheeriest of outlooks at the best of times, and had inevitably gained the role title *antisocial secretary* as a result. 'No, I'm not giving up,' she said, on a sigh. 'It just seemed like...I don't know. One thing after another has a way of wearing you down.'

'If anyone's got the resilience to bounce back, it's you.' Griff spoke quietly, and Hazel saw that his blue-grey eyes were more serious now. 'After what you've been through, and the way you came out on the right side of it all... You could just as easily have been lost.'

'I'm not exactly pleased with the way I coped,' Hazel pointed out. 'I did some pretty awful stuff.' But the drugs, the thieving, the damage to property – it all seemed to have been part of someone else's life now, and she even had to keep reminding herself that she had done it at all.

Griff shifted his direct gaze away from her. 'We've all done stuff we'd rather forget. But it's where we are now that matters; we can't do anything about that other shit.'

Hazel guessed he was talking about his time with his former bike club, the one he'd run with before finding the mellower side with the Road Riders. He too was a changed person, and that was thanks, in large part, to her father. Her eyes found the curled-edged and sun-faded photo, which had been pinned to the kitchen cork board since the last rally Graeme had been well enough to attend. She saw that Griff's gaze had followed hers, and had to change the subject back to the matter that had brought him here, before emotion got the better of her again.

'So,' she said briskly, 'this new owner then. Do you think he'll honour the club's arrangement?'

'No idea.' Griff shifted his own attention back. 'He said he'd let us know by Saturday, before the Easter bank holiday, so that's something.'

'And what if he says no?'

'Then we've got about a week to find somewhere, before we'd have to cancel and refund the ticket money.'

Hazel pulled a face. 'Do you have anywhere in mind?'

'A couple of possible places, but I reckon they'd charge at least double, especially when they realise how close we are to the rally date. They'll know we're desperate.'

'Could we postpone?' Hazel looked up as she heard foot-steps on the path. 'That'll be Linda.'

'Okay.' Griff took a gulp of his coffee and picked up his van keys. 'I'll be off. And no, I don't think postponing will work; there's hardly a weekend free that we can jump into, as far as I can tell. And this one's such a long way out for most people.' The doorbell rang, and Griff stood up. 'I'll call you as soon as I hear anything.'

'Better text,' Hazel said, accompanying him to the door. 'I'll probably be at work.'

'Text then. Fingers crossed, eh?' He gave her his usual kiss on the cheek. 'See you Friday night?'

'Friday...' Hazel had to think for a moment. 'Oh yeah, the Easter bash. I'll be there.'

'Twisted Tree at seven-ish then.' He gave the new visitor a perfunctory smile as he stepped past her outside the door.

Linda Sturdy came in, wafting the faint smell of her menthol cigarettes with her and looking uncomfortable as her gaze swept what had once been such a familiar place. As it was Hazel's own rental, she'd never actually moved in, even after Graeme had done so, but she'd been given her own key to come and go as she'd pleased. She hadn't been back since his funeral.

She took off her light jacket and hung it on the newel post. A neat, trim woman in her mid-fifties, she embodied Hazel's idea of what a university lecturer ought to look like: earnest, curious, a little bit solemn but with the possibility of a smile never too far away. She offered one to Hazel now – a shy, hesi-tant one – and Hazel returned it with as much warmth as she could muster, given the circumstances.

'I've done the clothes; everything else is in there.' She gestured to the sitting room. 'Go through and I'll bring drinks in. The kettle's not long boiled.'

It didn't take long for the two of them to pick through what remained of Graeme Douglas's belongings. As with his clothing and his paperwork, he had been able to tell Hazel what to do with most of the things he'd accumulated over his sixty-one years, and all that remained now were the things he'd kept close to him during the final weeks of his illness. Records, which Linda agreed Hazel should take to the vinyl specialist shop in town; CDs to be boxed up and given to the charity shop, once Linda had removed Eric Clapton's *Crossroads* box set and the Jethro Tull and Eagles albums; and the few letters and photos Graeme had kept. These, Linda looked through with a tight little smile and handed back to Hazel.

'I never wrote him any letters, never had a need to. But there are some here from your mum from the early days. And the photos are ones you took, I think.'

'There's another box,' Hazel said, and pulled it towards her. A dark green box she'd seen in wardrobes and on shelves, in the two different houses she'd shared with her father, but had never bothered to look into beyond a brief glance.

Slightly larger than a shoe box, and with a dark, paisley-like pattern, the edges were frayed and the corners split, but beyond that it had held together reasonably well. Hazel opened it now and saw, as she had done before, the stack of paperwork: her parents' marriage certificate; another copy of her own birth certificate, this one with only the barest details on it; National Health Service cards, with wonky, typewritten names and numbers; and a copy of her mother's will. That must have hurt him so much to look at, as necessary as it had been at the time, and no wonder the box had remained more or less ignored over the years.

'A watch,' Linda said, taking it out. 'Rather a nice one actually,' she added, turning it over.

'Do you want it?'

'Oh, no. But thank you. I don't remember him ever wearing it, to be honest.'

'He wore the one you gave him,' Hazel pointed out, 'so he probably just put this one aside as a backup in case the battery went. This is a proper wind-up one.'

'And some more photos.' Linda took out a brightly coloured envelope and pulled out a few glossy snapshots. 'I don't know why he kept these, they're just...' Her voice trailed away, and Hazel looked up from her examination of the watch to see her peering at one particular photograph: three people in a line, posed for the photo in the yard up at Druimgalla.

'Is that Mum and Dad?'

Linda nodded and pointed to the third person, standing nearest the camera; a bearded man, of around Graeme's age, with a lot of curly dark hair blown back from his face by what would seem to be, from the fully leafed oak tree in the background, a summer breeze. 'Who's this?'

Hazel took the photo from her and tried to cast her mind back. 'I remember him being here sometimes, and that he was a friend of Dad's, but he died not long after...after Mum was killed. His name was Leslie something. It'll come to me.' She handed the photo back, for Linda to replace in the envelope, but instead Linda stared at it again.

'Are you sure?'

'About which bit?'

'Both bits. The name and the fact that he's dead.'

'Aye, it was definitely Leslie something. I remember because I had a friend called Lesley, so I kept telling him it was a girl's name. And he definitely died in 1998.' Hazel thought back, remembering her father's distress at the tragedy, coming so soon after the murder of his wife. 'It was a boat fire; the lifeboat couldn't get to him in time.'

'And they found his body, presumably?'

Hazel fell silent for a moment, digesting this question. 'Why?' she asked, at length, already knowing what the answer was going to be, but not the details.

'Because he told me his name was Michael, and yesterday I interviewed him for a job.'

After Linda had left, some twenty minutes later, Hazel sat quietly, thinking everything over. The man's full name had come to her as soon as she'd stopped trying so hard to remember it: Leslie Warrender. He'd been an artist too, of course; her parents had rarely mingled with anyone who wasn't part of that world in some small way, but he'd been more successful than her father, and certainly more than her mother. Linda had insisted she'd seen documentation and academic certificates that proved his name was Michael Booth, and Hazel had, somewhat hesitantly, offered the theory that she was simply mistaken.

Linda had been adamant, however, and pointed out similarities the two men had shared, which made it clear it was the same man. 'I do know someone who'd recognise him,' she'd said. 'Would it be okay if I borrowed the photograph, to show him?'

'Someone else who was in the interview with you?'

'No. My dad.'

That had stopped Hazel in her tracks for a moment: Linda Sturdy's father was currently serving a life sentence for murder. 'But even if he did recognise the picture,' she said after a moment, 'that wouldn't confirm it was the same bloke you interviewed.'

'Oh, he's definitely that.' Linda remained absolutely firm. 'I only want to ask him if *this* is actually Leslie Warrender. He commissioned a couple of Warrender's paintings back in the day, so he'd know him.'

'It is him!' Hazel was growing exasperated. 'I told you!'

'But you were a child,' Linda said, more gently now. 'You can't have even been in your teens, and memories can get distorted when you're that age. If it's all right with you, I'll take this and show my dad, without giving him any names to latch onto, and see what he says.'

'Why though?'

'Because,' Linda said patiently, 'I was about to recommend "Dr Michael Booth" for a job. He's very well qualified, and I want to be absolutely sure of my reasons if I'm going to turn him down.'

She'd taken the photo with her, leaving Hazel surrounded by everything her father had left, only lighter to the tune of a few CDs; it would all probably end up in Isla's garage, along with the shrouded paintings of her mother's that she'd been unable to part with. For another few years, at least.

She had put the papers and the remaining photos back in the green box, and pondered for the rest of the evening what had prompted this Warrender bloke to disappear, and whether her father had known he wasn't dead after all. Which would mean all that grief at Warrender's death would have been an elaborate and horribly convincing lie.

It was an unsettling thought.

Thistle Inverness. Friday 19th April

Linda Sturdy excused herself from her group and left them arguing over dessert. She made her way to the toilets, but Breda, her friend and the manager of the restaurant, caught her eye and tapped two fingers to her lips, nodding towards the kitchens. Linda nodded back and made her way around the side of the building instead, to the cluttered area at the back of the restaurant, where she lit up while she waited. She was dying for that wee, but she had to be fair to Breda, who had very little choice when she could take her breaks, and it'd been a while since they'd caught up so she didn't want to miss this chance.

The noise drifting out into the yard was to be expected on any busy bank holiday night; the clanging of pans, the shouts, the occasional quick burst of laughter, the release of steam under pressure... Thistle was at full capacity for Good Friday and it was clear Breda was grateful to escape for five minutes; her Irish eyes were definitely not smiling as she emerged, and her expression was one of heat and harrassment. She gave Linda a relieved look as she turned her face to the cool night air.

'Thanks for coming around to the dark side; it means I can keep my ear open for shenanigans from in there.' She indicated the kitchens, then patted her pockets and sighed. 'Feckin' Max.'

'What's he done now?'

'He's *assistant-managed* my cigs out of my office and into his pocket. Again.'

Linda chuckled. 'Here you go.' She offered her own pack, but Breda shook her head.

'I've not got long enough to smoke a whole one. I'll take your one that you've started, if that's okay?'

'I didn't think you liked these. S'cuse the lippy.' Linda passed Breda her own half-smoked cigarette and took a fresh one from her pack. 'So, what shenanigans are you expecting, then?'

'Who knows? One meal too many returned to the kitchen, the chef throws a wobbly...' Breda shrugged. 'With this lot you can never tell.'

'You have my sympathies. Not that I expect many meals get returned here.' Linda put her lighter back into her bag and readjusted the strap across her shoulder. She leaned against the wall, not too bothered about the wet stone on her thin jacket; at least it wasn't raining any more. 'What time will you get to your bed tonight then?'

Breda drew deeply and gratefully on the cigarette, and held the smoke in for a lung-bursting length of time before sending it skyward into the darkness. 'About four, if I'm lucky. Not before six if anything goes wrong.' She coughed. 'God, these menthol things are appalling! Sooner they ban them, the better. Anyway, are you and your friends enjoying your meal?'

Linda laughed. 'You don't have to be the perfect hostess with me, not after all these years.'

'You looked a bit tense when you came in,' Breda said, and smiled at Linda's look of surprise. 'I might be run off my arse in there, but I still notice when my friends come here to eat. I've not seen enough of you since I took this place over from Donna. God rest her soul.'

'I'm fine,' Linda assured her. 'It's just that Graeme's birthday was a few days ago, and it's a bit tough.'

'I'm sorry. Give his daughter my best, when you see her again.'

'I will. And we'll fix up a night round at mine sometime. *If* you ever get a night off,' she added.

Breda huffed softly. 'I must be due one. I'll get Max to take over if needs be. He's forever telling me to give him a shot.'

'Good. Let him.'

'Sundays are usually best, but not this one coming. I promised to show my face at a birthday bash.'

'Okay.' Linda looked around at the cluttered yard, with its crated bottles awaiting washing and recycling, and the empty boxes not yet broken down; the bags of peelings and other food-related rubbish... All this would no doubt be tidied away before Breda would allow herself to leave the restaurant for the night, but for now it made the small yard a more homely place. A comforting glimpse of the chaos behind the perfection.

'We sorted through Graeme's things, finally,' she said at length. 'Hazel said she was ready, and it's been around six months now.'

'God, yes, I suppose it must be,' Breda mused. 'I don't mind saying, I was worried when you told me the poor girl went off the rails again. I'd hoped she was over all that.'

'Well, they were close,' Linda said. 'And when you think how her poor mother died too, it was understandable she'd relapse. Inevitable, even.' She sighed. 'Anyway, I'm glad it was her decision. I could never have told her to do it, I could only suggest it. I was just her dad's girlfriend, after all.'

'For four years, love.' Breda put a comforting hand on her arm. 'Must have been difficult for you both. How is the girl, really?'

The unspoken question, *is she likely to go on another bender?* hung between them, but Linda shook her head. 'She's got a job on that estate they're developing up at the old Glen-lowrie place, and she wants to keep it, so it's no fags, no booze, and definitely no drugs. As far as I can tell. That'll be tough though, with her lifestyle.' She hesitated. 'We found something, you know, in with Graeme's things.'

'What sort of something?' Breda had finished her inherited smoke and stubbed it out in the tall, brushed-aluminium bin fixed to the wall. 'Nothing bad, I hope?'

'No, it was a photo of her parents, with someone who looks a lot like Leslie Warrender.'

Breda posted her cigarette butt through the grill and turned back, frowning. 'Who?'

'He was an artist. Had a few exhibitions around the region in the nineties. You were still here back then – you don't remember him?'

'Don't know the name,' Breda confessed, 'but then you know I'm not really into art, like you lot. I was always more about the hospitality trade.'

'Well his work was well known, but he really wasn't that "out there" as a person. The weird thing is, I saw him a few days ago—'

'Really?' Breda seemed to think the word sounded dismissive, and now put on an overly interested face that was even more embarrassing. 'Where'd you see him, then?'

'At the college, actually. He was interviewing for an associate lecturer's position.'

'Ah, that's grand, isn't it? Nice to find an old friend.' Breda gave her a distracted smile and glanced at the time on her phone. 'So...have you told anyone else you've such famous connections?'

'I'm not absolutely certain yet that it's him,' Linda said. 'The thing is... Never mind. It'll keep. '

Breda was straightening her jacket now, and Linda could see her attention was already preceding her back into the fray; this clearly wasn't the time to delve into the complicated questions the photo had raised. 'I'll let you get back,' she said instead. 'I'll give you a ring, all right?'

'Right, so.' Breda turned back. 'Aren't you going in?'

'I've only just started this.' Linda held up her cigarette and flashed her friend a grin. 'Some bastard nicked my other one.'

Breda chuckled, and as she pulled open the door to the short passageway the noise grew distracting and jarring again, making Linda wince. But at least she herself would be going around to the dining room, where there was an altogether different kind of buzz: the warm, low-key thrum of voices and cutlery; the rich smells of good food; unobtrusive, ambient music; and the swift, sure movement of highly trained staff flitting between the tables. Her group would have ordered their desserts by now, Linda had given them her choice to order on her behalf so there was no rush, and even her full bladder had stopped bothering her for a minute; her mind was once more occupied with that photograph Hazel had found. A puzzler for sure, and a disturbing one at that.

Linda took one final pull on her cigarette, then dropped the half-smoked stub into a nearby puddle, where it fizzed for a heartbeat and died. She gave herself a mild ticking off for not following Breda's example and using the bin on the wall, then grew distracted again; if she was right about the photo, she and Hazel needed to have a good long conversation about what the girl thought she knew about her father... And what she herself knew about Leslie Warrender.

She fished out a packet of mints, and paused to shake one into her hand before starting along the path that led around the side of the restaurant. During that pause she heard the scrape of the footstep behind her that would otherwise have been lost, and it was loud enough to make her turn and peer behind her into the shadows. She couldn't see anything, but her heart slid uncomfortably against her ribs, and she faced forward again and walked faster. A more overtly sinister sound reached her: an empty wine bottle sliding out of its plastic crate. A muted splintering sound...

Linda instinctively broke into a run. Before she had taken more than three steps she was jerked backwards by the strap on her bag. Her arms snapped out to the sides, seeking purchase on something. Anything. She found only a cardboard box, and it peeled away from its miniature tower, spilling her to her knees where she felt the sting of the paving stones cut through her tights.

A punch in the side of her neck stole her breath, and for a second she wondered dumbly at it; why hadn't her attacker hit her in the face, or the head? Then the sickening wash of warmth spilling down across her shoulder told her what had really happened, and at the same moment the wrenching, searing pain burst into life as the broken bottle was yanked free, leaving Linda kneeling on the sticky path, with one hand groping in horrified wonder at the side of her neck, the other hanging limply at her side.

She heard the hesitant scuffle of footsteps once more, and she tried to concentrate on the sounds, but she couldn't tell if they were fading, or if she was. She heard the gate swing shut, and a hot tear found its way from the corner of her eye onto her icy cheek. The crash of falling cookware, followed by a yell of derisive laughter, came from the kitchen, and Linda's growing terror was abruptly replaced by cold inevitability and a deep swell of utter loneliness. She tried to lift her head towards the sound, a last attempt to rejoin a place where life and laughter were still real and reachable, but she couldn't. Through a wall of roaring sounds, deep in her head, she heard a familiar voice, first crying out her name in horror, then raised in a piercing scream for help, but it was all too late. So much too late.

She simply stared down at the spreading pool of her own blood, where she saw an ant had become mired and was even now struggling to free itself. To survive the unsurvivable. *You and me both*, she thought tiredly, as the tears fell faster and the world faded away. *You and me...*

Chapter Four

Glencoille. Saturday 20th April

HAZEL PUT the office phone back in its charging cradle and tried not to swear too loudly. Ade wasn't going to be happy to find out there was going to be a delay in the delivery of the cask washer, but his father was going to be even more annoyed; the distillery was Frank's baby. She made a note in her calendar and stood up, ready to go and break the news to her boss, but before she had rounded the desk, the portakabin door opened and Ade popped his head into the office. His usually sunny, open expression was sombre and troubled, and Hazel frowned.

'What's up?'

Ade didn't answer, but he stood back and ushered in a man and a woman who Hazel immediately pegged as CID officers, and her entire body instinctively tightened. Ade followed them in, looking at Hazel with ill-disguised suspicion. Standing behind the officers as they took the hard plastic seats Hazel indicated, he caught her eye and mouthed, *What have you done?* Hazel didn't react outwardly, but she felt a twist of anger and disappointment that this was where he'd gone, without even waiting to see what the coppers wanted.

'Miss Douglas?' The woman eyed Hazel's scruffy shirt and the leather jacket that hung on the back of her chair. 'I'm DC McAndrew, this is DC Byrne.' She twisted to look up at Ade, then back to Hazel. 'Are you happy to talk to us with Mr Mackenzie present?'

Hazel nodded, still mystified and unsettled. 'What's happened?'

'We'd like to talk to you about a Miss Linda Sturdy,' McAndew said. 'I understand you know her quite well?'

'She was my dad's partner.'

'Was?' The officers flashed each other a look.

'He died last year.' Hazel's feeling of dread deepened. 'What's happened?' she asked again, more firmly this time.

McAndrew lowered her voice. 'I'm very sorry to tell you that she died last night.'

It didn't matter that Hazel had realised it was coming, she still felt the words like a heavy blanket falling over her, muffling everything. 'Died,' she said slowly, then looked point-edly at the officers' clothing. 'You're CID, so I'm guessing she didn't have a heart attack.'

They exchanged another look, and McAndew shook her head. 'Can you tell us where you were last night?'

'Me? Why?'

'We have to eliminate everyone who might have had a motive,' DC Byrne said.

'Motive?' Hazel blinked. 'What motive could I have had?'

'That's what we're working on.' He took out his notebook and flipped it open. 'If you could start by telling us where you were, we can work from there.'

Hazel took a deep breath, feeling the room recede around

her. 'I was with the club. The bike club,' she added, seeing Byrne's pen pause over his paper. He nodded and continued writing. 'We were having a sort of Easter party at the Twisted Tree in Abergarry. A couple of other MCCs were there, too.'

'Cricket clubs?'

Hazel stared at him. 'Motorcycle clubs,' she said patiently. 'MCCs are non-back-patch clubs.'

'As opposed to?'

'MCs. The likes of your Hell's Angels and so on.' He nodded for her to go on, and she shrugged. 'That's it. That's where I was.'

'All night?'

'From about seven-ish until about two this morning.' Hazel could see Ade's dark eyebrows go up, telling her quite clearly that he now realised why she'd been in zombie mode since she'd got to work. 'Linda said she was going out to dinner with some of the lecturers from the college... Oh my God, did something happen at Thistle? Some kind of attack?'

McAndrew shook her head. 'Nothing like that.'

'How did she die?'

'We're not ready to divulge that information yet.'

'We'll need to check your alibi, Miss Douglas,' Byrne said. 'Would you mind giving us the names and contact details of anyone who can corroborate your story?'

'It's not a...' Hazel sighed and closed her eyes. 'Okay. There were loads of us there, but you can start with Griff. Dave Griffin. He's the club chairman.' She pulled out her phone and gave Byrne a list of names and numbers, and after a few more questions, mostly about Linda's relationship with Hazel's father, the officers rose to leave.

'We're very sorry.' McAndrew said. 'We'll probably need to

talk to you again at some point though, so if you intend to leave the area at all, please let us know.'

Ade saw them to their car, guiding them through the chaos that was a Saturday on the building site, then came back, looking both shamefaced and sympathetic. It was an odd combination on a man with his infectious energy and sense of fun, and it pulled the usually square shoulders down until he was almost stooping.

'I'm sorry about Linda,' he said quietly. 'That was such a shock. Feel free to take the rest of—'

'Why did you want to know what *I'd* done?'

'It was just...well, your history and all.'

'I might not be squeaky clean like you,' Hazel said hotly, 'but I didn't *kill* anyone.'

'I didn't know they were here about a death!' Ade straightened a little, and the animation came back into his face. 'And don't even think about giving me that crap about people looking at you and judging you because of your clothes either, or because you ride a sodding motorbike; you forget I know what you *did* do! If Maddy hadn't put in such a good word for you I'd never have taken you on. Though I'm glad I did,' he added. A hot temper didn't sit well with him for more than a minute; it was one of the reasons she liked him. But he'd pissed her off severely this morning, and shock was making everything worse.

'And did Maddy tell you why I did those things?'

'No. It was enough for me that the two of you got on like a house on fire when you were doing your community payback. And,' he gave her a brief, grim smile, 'that you were the one who taught her that little trick that got her away from the bastard who attacked her. Thank you for that, too.'

'There you go, then.'

'So why did you? Do those things, I mean.' Ade sat down and linked his hands on the desk in front of him. His voice was quieter now, and the angry flashes in his eyes had faded, turning them back to their usual sludgy green.

Hazel shrugged. 'I'll tell you sometime, but not now.'

'You ought to take the rest of the day off,' he said, sitting back. 'Go on, I can manage here.'

'No, I want to work.' She almost smiled as she saw his poorly disguised look of relief. 'But I also want to find out exactly what happened to Linda,' she added. 'I still can't believe it.'

'Were you very close?'

'Not as close as you'd think, even when she was with Dad. But she was wonderful when he was sick.' She shook her head. 'It's just...awful. I can't understand why anyone would want to hurt her.'

'Perhaps it was a chance attack, and nothing to do with her personally.'

'That's even more frightening,' Hazel pointed out. 'If some random killer's out there just targeting people who turn up in the wrong place at the wrong time, how are we supposed to protect ourselves?'

'Aye.' Ade pursed his lips. 'Someone has to know what happened. It might help if we found out how she died, at least. Whether it was premeditated or not.'

Hazel thought for a moment. 'Maddy might be able to find out,' she said at length. 'I wanted to call her anyway, about something else...' Her voice faded as she considered what she'd just said. *Was* it something else, or was it connected? 'Would it be okay if she came up to the site today? I don't want to wait until she's picked up her boy after holiday club.'

Ade paused with his hands braced on the desk, ready to

push himself to his feet. 'You want to call and ask Maddy to come here?'

'Yes.'

'Maddy Clifford?'

'Yes.'

'Today?'

'If she's free.' Hazel felt her reluctant smile returning. 'I take it you've no objection, then?'

Ade wiped his grubby hands on his shirt and dragged them through his hair, tugging it as flat as it would go. 'Go on then. If you absolutely must.'

As he reached the door, much cheered, Hazel realised there would be no better time to break the news. 'There's something else.' He looked at her questioningly, and she gestured to the phone to remind him that she was only the messenger, and not to shoot. 'Wilsons called. The cask washer won't be here for another three weeks.'

He sighed, no doubt as he considered the imminent joy of telling his father, then he shrugged, and his old, sunny grin returned. 'Ah well, can't be helped. What time's Maddy coming up?'

The Clifford-Mackenzie office was at the top of a narrow flight of stairs leading up from the main street that bisected Abergarry, and as Maddy Clifford climbed the steps she could already hear Paul's voice rumbling around the stairwell; he was usually quietly spoken, so it was a fairly safe bet he was talking to his father. She straightened the ever-slipping sign on the door, told herself once again that she was going to fix the damned thing before she went home tonight, and went in.

Paul held up one finger and pulled a face at the landline handset he was holding, and Maddy smiled and went to her own desk. She opened her laptop and whipped her way through a few email replies while Paul finished his conversation with his dad, but the moment he did, her own phone buzzed.

'Hazel, hi.' She gestured at Paul to put the kettle on, and stuck her tongue out when he shook his head. 'How are you?'

'Not great,' Hazel said. She sounded far from the chirpy woman Maddy had befriended so easily last year, and Maddy frowned. 'What's wrong?'

Paul immediately stopped messing about and went over to make the coffee. Hazel was quiet for a moment longer, then asked if Maddy had seen the news that morning.

'Local?'

'Aye. But it'll probably make the nationals.'

Maddy propped her phone on the desk and switched to speaker, then checked her laptop. A story popped up that made her wince. 'This woman who was killed at Thistle?'

'Yeah, she was Dad's...partner, I suppose you'd say. Girl-friend. Whatever.'

'Oh, God. I'm *so* sorry.'

'Don't worry about me.' Hazel hesitated again. 'I don't want to explain over the phone. Can you come up to the site some-time today?'

'Of course.' Maddy signalled to Paul to forget the drink. 'Do you know something about how she died?'

'No.' There was a long silence, then Hazel spoke again, her voice quieter than Maddy had ever heard it. 'But I think it might have something to do with my dad.'

Maddy was jolted, but kept her tone calm. 'Okay. I'll be with you in around an hour.' She ended the call and looked over to where Paul was splashing milk into his mug. 'I want to pick your brains, as puddled as they are.'

'Good luck,' he said amiably. 'About what?'

'Did you hear what Hazel said?'

He pulled a face. 'I'd be lucky to hear a bomb go off, over the racket that kettle makes. Is she okay? You sounded concerned.'

'She's fine.' Maddy drew her notepad closer and picked up her pen. 'Have you heard about the woman who was found dead at Thistle?'

Paul nodded. 'I had a quick read first thing. Apparently she was a lecturer at the same college Charis is doing her access degree through.'

'GCAP?'

'Gee what?'

'Glenside College of Art and Performance.'

'Ah.' His expression cleared. 'That's the one. The woman—'

'Linda Sturdy.'

'Linda Sturdy,' he agreed, 'was found outside the kitchens by her friend. Breda someone.'

'Kelly. The restaurant manager.'

Paul closed the fridge and glared at her. 'If you know all the answers, why did you ask?'

'I've only read up to that bit,' she said, smiling at his aggrieved look. 'Go on.'

'That's pretty much it,' he admitted, setting down his Everton FC mug; a deliberately provocative gift from his girlfriend, who knew he was Scottish rugby to the bone. 'Oh, yeah, and she was the daughter of Matthew Sturdy, who was jailed in the nineties for murder.'

Maddy stopped scribbling and stared at him. 'Well that's a pretty big *just one more thing*, Columbo.'

He grinned. 'I've only just remembered, to be honest.'

'Do you still think it was random then?'

'Probably. It's been twenty-odd years. But what's that got to do with us, anyway? The police'll make any connections they need to.'

'She was Graeme Douglas's girlfriend.' Maddy told him the cryptic little thing Hazel had said about her father. 'I'm going up to Glencoille so we can talk about what she meant.'

'Oh?' Paul's hazel eyes lengthened in a sly smile she knew very well indeed. *'That's* why you're going up there then, is it?'

Maddy ignored the comment; if he wanted to fixate on a non-existent romance between her and his brother he was free to waste his time. 'Who did Sturdy murder, anyway?' she asked.

'Can't remember. I'd have to look it up.' Paul sipped his drink. 'Seriously though, Mads, what does it matter? The police will do all this, and if you go in there armed with all this info, and throw it at Hazel, she might even think you're accusing her dad of something. That'd be the quickest way to lose her trust, you know that.'

Maddy subsided. 'All right. I'll just listen. Speaking of dads, is everything okay with yours? You sounded tense on the phone.'

Paul sighed. 'He was asking, *again*, when he could get out of the Heathers and go and live on the estate.'

'But the house isn't even built yet.'

'I know that, you know that. Even *he* knows that.' Paul caught her look, and shook his head. 'He does. He's angling for an invitation to live in Ade's caravan with him.'

'Up in the woods? He'd go mad in five minutes.'

'It'd be a race to see who kills who,' Paul agreed. 'Dad just likes to remind me how he's stuck away up at the nursing home, while all the exciting stuff's happening without him.'

'Exciting?' Maddy gave a little snort. 'I take it he's not sat and watched a bunch of architects staring at a plan for half an hour straight without speaking, or listened to the ground clearing team arguing about whose turn it is to make the tea, and whose to wash the mud off the digger. Right.' She grabbed her coat again and headed for the door. 'I'll see you later.'

'Oh, Maddy?' Paul smiled that knowing little smile again. 'Give my love to Ade, won't you?'

'Away and raffle yer doughnut.'

When she arrived at Glencoille she saw it had in fact regained a little of the excitement that Frank Mackenzie craved. The diggers had moved further up the site, clanking and groaning as they broke the ground that would become the footprint of the Mackenzies' home, but the main clearing, which would eventually hold the permanent office and car park, was deserted. Ade Mackenzie's tatty jeep was conspicuous by its absence, but Hazel's bike was parked next to a red and black quad bike, alongside a portakabin not much bigger than a small mobile home. Maddy parked her faded red Corsa alongside the Kawasaki and tapped on the office door, which had been propped open with a bucket.

'Hiya.'

Hazel looked up from her laptop, then at the clock on her screen. 'Blimey. Either time flies, or you're going to get a speeding ticket.' She smiled encouragingly. 'Don't worry, I hear you're great at cleaning graffiti.'

'Ha ha,' Maddy said as she came in, but Hazel's humour had eased her concerns a little.

'Thanks for coming,' Hazel said, getting up to pour coffee from the pot on the side. 'Ade's just had to nip into town.'

Maddy chose not to question why she should care where Ade was, and instead sat down in the squashy seat by the door. 'What did you want to tell me?' she asked, and stopped prodding at the foam poking through the torn vinyl, to accept a steaming cup from Hazel. 'You said it was to do with your dad, and Linda Sturdy?'

'It's not so much her I want to talk about, but something she said.' Hazel kept glancing out of the open door, as if keen not to be overheard. 'Just for a bit of background,' she went on, moving the bucket away and closing the door, 'I was at this bike rally in the borders last weekend. First time I've been anywhere since Dad died, and a lot of the other clubs didn't know about that yet. They were all so nice though, telling me how they'd miss him. Something felt...sorted, just by talking to those guys. Almost like a sort of proper farewell, even more so than the funeral. D'you get what I mean?'

Maddy nodded. 'That was his world, and yours. Of course it would feel right. And funerals are usually so soon after the death that it's all still raw.'

'Aye. Anyway, I was thinking about it all on the way home, and I decided it was finally time to go through Dad's things.'

Maddy gave her a sympathetic look. 'That must have been tough. I'd have been with you if you'd asked.'

'I know. And thanks. To be honest though, the first person I thought about was my Aunt Isla, my mother's sister, but she said she didn't want to. Then I thought that, actually, if I called anyone it should be Linda. I'd not seen her for ages, but she came over. It was mostly records, books, bike memorabilia, rally trophies, you know, and some of Mum's old bits too, but we got it all sorted pretty quick. There was this little box, with a few odds and ends in it, including some photos. One of them was of Mum and Dad, with this bloke I remembered from when I was a kid. Beardy bloke, part of my dad's arty crowd.' Hazel broke off and started playing with her phone, tipping it end over end and tapping it thoughtfully.

'What bloke?' Maddy prompted after a moment, resisting the urge to pull the phone out of Hazel's hands and drop it into her coffee.

'Leslie Warrender, he was called. He used to come around quite a lot as I remember. He died in a boating accident.'

'Okay.' Maddy paused. 'You said earlier that you were worried Linda's murder might have something to do with your dad, but I don't understand how it could be. Is it actually something to do with this Warrender person then?'

'Maybe. Linda asked about him, so I told her he'd been friends with Mum and Dad.' Hazel shrugged. 'I thought she'd think it was pretty neat that they knew him back in the day, what with her being an art historian. Not that he'd have been on *her* radar, not being 400 years old.' She gave a faint smile. 'Not worthy.'

'I take it she didn't know him or your parents back then?'

'No. She only met my dad later, when he gave up his own painting and started teaching at the same place as her. She kept staring at the photo, then she asked me if that was definitely Leslie Warrender. I said I could remember him being around the house a lot. Then she told me she'd seen him.'

'Well, if they moved in the same circles, then—'

'No, she saw him last week, at the college. She actually interviewed him for a job.'

Maddy felt a tingle of real interest, but spoke carefully. 'So...if she's right, then he staged his own death.'

Hazel put down her phone at last. 'He must have. She said he doesn't have a beard now, and he's lost all that really long, thick hair; he's practically bald. He's using the name Booth.'

'I see.' Again keeping Paul's warning in mind, Maddy went on, 'I'm not doubting her word, but if your mum's in the picture it has to have been taken at least twenty years ago.'

'Twenty-one.'

'Right. So if he looks that different, how could Linda be so sure it was him?'

'That's what I wanted to know.' Hazel sat forward. 'Okay, so the photo was taken in our front yard up at Druimgalla, right? And Warrender was on the left of the three of them, closest to the camera. It's pretty windy up there, and his hair was lifted back a bit in the picture so you can see a mole behind his ear. Booth had the same one, only it's permanently on show now.' Hazel evidently read the immediate cynicism in Maddy's face, and shrugged. 'I know, but Linda's a bit mole-conscious at the moment. She had one taken off a few weeks back and it was a dodgy one. She remembered wondering whether she ought to tell this Booth bloke, and advise him to get it looked at.'

'Two moles can look the same,' Maddy pointed out.

'True enough, and that's what I said. But when Linda spotted the one in the photo she started looking more closely, and could see other, less obvious similarities. Weird earlobe shape and so on. She's got a well-trained eye for detail, goes with the territory. Anyway, she swears...' Hazel caught herself, '*swore* it was him.'

'And presumably you want me to try and find out for sure, rather than involving the police, in case your dad was the one who helped him fake his death?'

'If you have time.' Hazel lowered her voice. 'I couldn't afford to pay you much.'

'For crying out loud, you saved my life!' Maddy held up a hand. 'And don't argue with me,' she added, over the ringing of the office phone. 'You know it's true. Answer that.'

Some of Hazel's tension faded, and when she turned to answer the phone Maddy picked up her drink, reflecting on the change in her friend since they'd met last November.

On paper they should have struck sparks off one another right from the off: Hazel had shown herself in the larger group to be bolshy and quick-tempered, always on the defensive, her eyes fierce and her tongue fiercer, while Maddy was well aware that she herself could come across as snobbish, or superior. Paul had said it was to do with the way she automatically withdrew a little when she met someone new, combined with the way she carried herself... Well, what he had actually said was, 'You're too tall, too posh-looking, and too bloody bossy.'

So when Maddy and Hazel had been paired up and Hazel had given her an unexpectedly friendly smile, Maddy had been so relieved she'd responded with a smile of her own instead of immediately questioning the woman's motive. Hazel's casual factoid, delivered with inarguable authority over a cheese and salad cream sandwich, had, as Maddy had said, undoubtedly saved her life. *Fifteen pounds of force, that's all it takes to dislocate a knee from the side.* And she'd been right; Ian George had gone down screaming. But not before he'd sliced her face open... She kept her hand away from the still-livid scar beside her left eye, but with an effort.

'Have you got the photo here?' she asked, when Hazel had ended the call and made a note about it on her laptop.

Hazel gave her an apologetic look. 'Sorry, no. I gave it to Linda. She was going to take it to her dad and get him to confirm it's definitely Warrender. He'd bought one or two of Warrender's paintings, apparently, and knew him a bit.'

Maddy sighed. 'So if she still had it in her bag that night, the police'll have it now. It'll be ages before you get it back.'

'There's bound to be a half-decent photo online you can use.'

'Aye, but yours would have been better, so we can see that mole and so on.' Maddy sat forward, frowning. 'Warrender must have pissed someone off hugely though, don't you think, to have needed to fake his own death? Why did you say your dad might be involved?'

'All I can think is that Warrender was frightened for his life when he left.' Hazel's voice tightened. 'Presumably not anymore though. But if Dad *was* the one who helped him escape, he'd have recognised him straight away, because he'd be the only person alert to the fact that it could be him. He would have been the only barrier to Warrender coming back, if he wanted to. And he clearly did.'

'Warrender didn't have family who'd recognise him?'

'Not around here, apparently, and Matthew Sturdy's going to be banged up for the rest of his life. It's the picture I keep coming back to; Dad must have had dozens of photographs of the two of them, or the three of them, taken during the years they were all friends, so why would he get rid of them?'

Maddy pondered. 'If he'd helped Warrender double-cross someone by escaping, that someone must have been dangerous. He probably wouldn't want to hang on to evidence they knew each other that well.'

'No, that can't be it.' Hazel frowned. 'People will know they went to uni together; they'd expect *some* photos. But there's nothing at all in any of the family albums. It's like Dad was trying to erase any suggestion to himself that they'd even known one another. Which is mad. Futile, even. Yet there's this rogue one that ties all three of them, and it's clear when you look at it that they were close friends. I just don't get why he kept it.'

'What happened to Warrender's boat?'

'It caught fire off the coast of Peterhead. Dad told me his mayday call said something about an electrical fault, but by the time the lifeboats were able to get there, there was next to nothing left.' Hazel picked up her phone again, checked it, put it down. Maddy thought her friend seemed to be growing more twitchy the more she spoke, rather than less, and was probably searching for distractions.

'And I'm guessing no body was ever recovered,' she probed.

'Not even one they couldn't identify?' Hazel shook her head. 'That's one good thing. At least it means there isn't another dead person involved.'

'Maybe not.' Hazel looked troubled again. 'But if Dad was the one who helped Warrender escape, that'd still make him a criminal. And he's not here to argue his case.'

'What if Warrender forced him, somehow? He disappeared sometime in the nineties—'

'Ninety-eight. Declared dead the year after, given the state of the boat and the fact it was out at sea.'

'You seem very certain of the date, considering you must have only been about twelve.'

'I was fourteen. And it can't have been long after Mum was killed; I was still in care.'

'So... No-one's heard anything from, or about, this bloke for twenty years. Then he shows up again, and at the very same time, *you* find a photograph of him with your dad.' Maddy raised an eyebrow, and Hazel sighed.

'I know how it sounds.'

'Hell of a coincidence. Is it possible Linda might have planted the photo herself?'

'She was a damned good actor if she did. She looked gobsmacked when I told her he was dead. Why would she try to involve me, anyway?'

'Maybe...' Maddy spoke slowly, still thinking it through, 'if your dad had told her what he and Warrender had done, at some point, she would be an accessory. If she didn't report seeing him now, she could get sent down for fraud.'

'So she'd want to shift the onus for that onto me.'

'It's possible. It'd be useful to find out who else knew he was back. Do you think Linda saw her dad, between finding the photo and last night?'

'I don't know.' Regret touched Hazel's expression. 'I didn't see her again.'

'Hmm. Be bloody hard for me to get to talk to him and find out,' Maddy mused. 'Paul told me Sturdy was put away for murder,' she explained, 'but we don't know any more than that. Did Linda tell you about it?'

'No, but Dad did, after they started seeing each other; he didn't want me finding out from someone else.' Hazel flipped her phone over, glanced at it, and then turned her attention back to Maddy. 'It was over some fraudulent art deal. The dealer sold Sturdy some famous painting, for a couple of million or something, but it turned out to be a dud, so Sturdy went mental and bashed his face in with a golf club. I don't exactly blame him, but I don't get why he didn't just prosecute the dealer and get his money back.'

'There was probably nothing to prosecute,' Maddy ventured. 'If the seller's paperwork was all in place and he made the sale in good faith, Sturdy wouldn't have had a leg to stand on. It was down to him to get it evaluated before he bought it.' She chewed at her lip thoughtfully. 'There does seem to be an obvious link with Warrender, him being an artist, and maybe he *did* paint the fake. But this isn't getting us any closer to working out why he's back here right now. Unless...' She paused, and when Hazel's hand reached for her phone again she put her own over it firmly. 'For God's sake! What's so important anyway? Is it to do with Linda?'

Hazel looked slightly shame-faced. 'No. And I know it seems trivial now, but I'm waiting to find out if our bike club's going to be able to stage a rally this year.'

'What?'

'They've sold off the field we usually use,' Hazel explained, 'and the new owner's been mulling it over as to whether he wants the land chewed up by a hundred or so bikes.'

'Well, that can wait. For a few minutes at least. Right, what sort of artist was Leslie Warrender? Is his work online?'

'Probably. I think he did old-timey stuff, like Rembrandt kind of things. He wasn't as good as my dad though.'

'I'm sure.' Maddy assumed a polite expression, and Hazel gave her a wry smile.

'It's not just me saying that. Everyone knew it. They both did their degrees at the same time, then Dad got married and went into teaching. Warrender had family money, so he was able to indulge himself for a while, and zipped off to Europe to make a name for himself, but everyone knew Dad was more naturally talented.'

Maddy had taken out her own phone and now tapped Warrender's name into a search. 'Hmm. Not that much to see, but...' she zoomed in on the screen, 'was the painting Sturdy bought like one of those Old Masters kind of things?' She showed Hazel the screen, on which a chubby, ivory-skinned child glowed up at his saintly looking mother. 'Like that?'

'Sort of. But this one wasn't people, it was a building. A cathedral, I think.'

Maddy cleared the screen and tried again, this time putting *Matthew Sturdy, Inverness* and *fake painting* into the search. 'This would be it, then: *Florence Cathedral*, by Fabrizio Mercanti. The dead man was an Andrew Silcott, and the painting was being exhibited at Waterfront when it was investigated.' She saw Hazel's hand inching towards her phone again, and gave in. 'Go on then. And good luck.'

A rumble outside signalled the arrival of Ade Mackenzie, whose jeep rivalled Maddy's Corsa for the title of Abergarry's Tattiest Vehicle. Hazel's groan of disappointment as she checked her phone coincided with Ade's cheery greeting as he ducked into the portakabin, and Maddy focused on the smilier of the two.

'How's it going? Your dad's champing at the bit to move up here, by the way.'

'No change there, then.' Ade shucked off his jacket and dropped it in the corner, and Maddy suppressed a smile; he and Paul were alike in more than just looks. Both were dark-haired, both tall, though Paul was taller and more heavily built, and both were just as likely to trip over their belongings as put them somewhere sensible.

Ade's recent return from life as an engineer in New Zealand had put a solid foundation beneath his younger brother's feet, and Maddy was deeply grateful on Paul's behalf, but he had also been instrumental in bringing to justice the man who had almost killed Maddy last year. He had then thrown himself into this project, and despite Maddy's earlier assertion that it was all mindnumbingly dull at the moment, no-one could deny that his presence and enthusiasm lent the atmosphere an undeniable buzz. As if something huge was just on the horizon, and that he only had to give the nod and it would erupt into life.

She saw his eyes graze the scar beside her eye and move on, but she was relieved to see no pity in his expression, just a flicker along his jaw that told her he'd never forgive the person who'd inflicted the wound.

'You've heard about Hazel's dad's girlfriend then?' He tilted the coffee pot, pulling a face at the dregs that were all that remained. He checked to see that Hazel was still bent over her phone, then mouthed, *is she all right?*

Maddy nodded. 'She's fine. Shocked, and sad, but they weren't that close.'

'Then what are you looking so grim about?' he asked Hazel, who glanced up with a frown.

'The rally's a no-go.'

'Bummer.' He clearly already knew a lot more about this crisis than Maddy did. 'Got any alternatives?'

'Nope. And hardly any time to go looking. I'm going to text our antisocial secretary and let her know, so we can get the word out on Facebook.'

'Hold on, before you do that.' Ade folded his arms and studied the wall chart. Covered with massive crosses, ticks, scribbles and arrows, it was a wonder he was able to make head or tail of it at all, but he gave a small grunt, then his mud-grimed finger landed on Friday 3rd May and he turned back to Hazel. 'For whatever you were paying your other bloke, you can have the bit of land behind the dry stone wall up as far as the tree line. That big enough?'

Hazel's eyes widened, and she looked at Ade as if he'd given her the keys to an ice cream factory. 'More than! It's a small rally. We don't have—'

'Great. We're not getting the diggers on that spot until early June.' He grabbed a marker pen. 'What's the rally called?'

'Soggy Socks,' Hazel said, her thumbs already busy on her messenger app, the phone's light making her face glow almost as much as her relief.

Ade exchanged a brief grin with Maddy and printed the name in the box. 'Sog-gy socks. There.' He drew an arrow through Saturday and Sunday as well, and tossed the lid-less pen onto the desk, then he peered at the lid in his other hand and threw that after it. 'Better give me some details when you've done that. Contacts and so on. So,' he turned to Maddy, 'how's the prettiest detective north of the border?'

'Bloody cheek. Who's prettier south of it?'

'I've definitely got a bit of a thing for Miss Marple,' he confessed. 'It's the hats, I think.'

She couldn't help laughing at that, as she stood up and straightened her jacket. 'Right, Hazel, I'll give you a call later. I'm going to investigate the possibility of getting a look at that photo.'

'Okay. Thanks again for coming up here at short notice.'

'You in a hurry to get off?' Ade asked, as Maddy fished her car keys from her pocket.

'Not particularly. Tas is at holiday club until six, and woe betide me if I try to pick him up early.'

'Good.' Ade bent and snatched up his own jacket again. 'Come with me. I'd like your opinion on what we've done in the distillery. Got a fantastic site up by the weir, and it's coming on great.'

'Okay, I was planning on a bit of a walk anyway.' Maddy gave her neck a little stretch and rolled her shoulders. 'I've been sitting down so much lately, I've lost about three inches.'

Hazel put her phone down, and now her smile was

showing echoes of Paul's knowing grin as she looked from Maddy to Ade and back again. 'You kids behave on your own out there, all right?'

'Belt up,' Maddy said cheerfully, and as she followed Ade down the steps and back out into the afternoon sun she pushed thoughts of art forgeries and mysterious photographs to the back of her mind, just for a while. She'd earned a bit of fun.

Chapter Five

'Not bad for seventy.' Patrick Ross straightened his tie in the mirror and accepted the clothes brush from his wife in order to brush the dog's hairs off his trousers. 'I'm beginning to wonder if it was a good idea to have the party at Waterfront though. Even on a Sunday.'

'I think so,' Julie said, plucking another of Pica's ginger hairs off his sleeve. 'It's not as if you're twenty-one; you won't have to worry about your guests throwing up on the Reubens, or drawing flying ducks on the Mercanti.'

'No, I suppose you're right.' Ross turned and kissed her cheek, then handed back the clothes brush. 'Are we ready then?'

'We are. I hope you're braced; there'll probably be several people who've heard about Christie's, and will be keen to take advantage of the proceeds.'

Ross rolled his eyes. News of the gallery's recent success at auction had hit the internationals a couple of weeks ago, accompanied by the usual glamorous photos of himself and Julie, with Picasso, their adorable springer spaniel, and their impressive home on the outskirts of Inverness. The publicity was great for the gallery, but it had also brought the expected flurries of phone calls and emails, and offers 'too good to refuse'.

'I'm sure you'll keep the charities under control, as usual, while I keep the investment invitations at bay.' Ross flattened a tuft of white hair and sighed when it popped up again. 'I've had one suggestion I'm actually interested in though,' he added. 'A small investment in a new venture in the hills.' He flashed her a grin. 'Whisky might be involved.'

'Of course,' Julie said drily, and he laughed.

'Well, we'll see. I'm going up tomorrow night to look the site over. Beyond that, I'd rather keep my money where I can see it, for now."

He picked up his car keys and looked at them for a moment, before handing them to Julie. 'Just make sure I don't throw up on the Reubens, eh?'

The Waterfront Gallery, on the west bank of the River Ness alongside the cathedral, might have been small and unobtrusive, but it glowed this evening with warm lights at its windows, through which it was easy to see that plenty of guests had already arrived. Music spilled onto the street, mingled with voices raised in high opinion, laughter, or simply in efforts to catch the attention of others.

Ross, arriving late enough to guarantee an entrance, offered Julie his arm and passed through the open door and into the entrance hallway. He was quickly noticed and cheered, and drawn into the gallery proper, where his guests milled and admired the exhibits, offering opinions both learned and otherwise, and making Ross smile as he moved among them.

'Look over there,' Julie said, nudging him as they accepted drinks from a passing waiter. She pointed to a table placed against the wall, on which was piled an array of beautifully wrapped gifts and a stack of coloured envelopes. 'Your director's told everyone who's brought something to leave it there, so you're not inundated with eager gift-bearers.'

'Thank God for Isla.' Ross made his way over to the table and picked up the stack of cards. 'I think I'll leave the presents for later, when everyone's gone. Last thing we need is a stampede of one-upmanship.'

'I'll keep them off you for a bit.' Julie left him to it, wandering off to press the flesh and thank their friends for making the effort tonight, and Ross arranged each opened card on the table after he'd read it. About two-thirds of the way down the pile, however, his life turned inside out.

The card itself was unremarkable. Generic. An old-man's card in muted colours, featuring a rickety-looking shed, outside which stood what was presumably a retiree's dream: an easel and palette, a cup of steaming tea with biscuits on the saucer, and a snoozing dog. Ross grunted at the queasy sentiment of the image, threw the envelope into the bin and opened the card.

Does this bring back memories of Florence? I hope so!
Have a special day, my friend. See you very soon for a proper
catch-up, we have a lot to talk about!!!

I'll be in touch!

LW

Ross stared numbly at the neatly printed words for a moment, not registering why they struck him as sinister, and then the feeling came back into his fingers and a pain started needling at his temple. He lifted a hand absently to massage it away but didn't take his eyes from the card's message, which counteracted the inoffensive blandness with what looked like almost hysterical good cheer. Those exclamation marks felt like slaps.

'I didn't know you'd been to Florence,' Julie said, almost making him drop the card as she appeared at his elbow. 'When was that?'

Ross somehow found a laugh. 'Even before I met you,' he said, trying to slow the frantic pounding of his heart, and to suppress the urge to burst into the crowd and find the person who'd left the card on the table. Unless... He turned to the bin, stooped to snatch up the envelope, and smoothed it out. No, hand-delivered. Julie was watching him with guarded amusement.

'Are you alright, Tricky?'

The use of the old nickname she'd long ago coined for him, having affirmed her dislike of the name Pat, brought him back to some kind of calm. 'Perfectly,' he smiled. Or was he beaming? Was it too much? He dialled it down, just in case. 'Just someone I hadn't realised was here. I might go and find him.

'Nice handwriting, whoever it is. Obviously an artist.' Julie took the envelope off him and dropped it back into the bin. 'Go and mingle, then – your public awaits. The new manager of Thistle's even taken the time to show her face. What's her name now? Kelly, isn't it?'

'Breda, aye,' he muttered. 'Nice of her.'

'Her mother brought her up to show respect,' Julie said, 'which just goes to show *you're* well respected.' She squeezed his arm, and he thought once more how lucky he was that she wasn't the clingy, demanding type, who'd want to know all about Florence, and who LW was. And whether they were female. He dropped a kiss on her temple, stuffed the card into his pocket and moved back into the crowd, his eyes burning as he scanned the faces that smiled at him and wished him many happy returns. But there was no sign of the one face he both hoped and dreaded he'd see, and he realised he was wasting his time; the gallery was small, there was nowhere for someone to hide and watch. The guest had dropped their little bomb and was long gone. Ross finished his drink and took another, and he knew what he had to do, but not yet how to do it.

He spotted Breda, the manager of the elite restaurant that was his favoured dining spot. A rounded, friendly looking woman in her middle years, she was soft-spoken, easy-going, and smiled a lot; nevertheless, he knew her to have a razor for a mind. And often for a tongue, too. But she always ensured he, and whoever he was entertaining at her restaurant, received the very best attention, so he had cultivated the kind of rapport that enabled him to drift over to her now and strike up a conversation.

'Miss Kelly. Thanks so much for coming.'

She turned and smiled, dimples forming high in her cheeks and making her look much younger. 'I wouldn't miss it, Mr Ross. Many happy returns, and please call me Breda.'

'Thank you, Breda.' He was careful not to return the invitation; rapport was one thing, but over-familiarity wasn't to be encouraged. He quickly came to the real reason he'd spoken to her. 'Is Mr Kilbride here?'

'He was.' She turned to look around for her boss, then pointed, with a hand wrapped in a neat crepe bandage. 'Over there, talking to someone I've no doubt will turn out to be extremely beneficial to him at some point.'

'Ah yes. No doubt.' Ross lifted his own hand in the direction of a distinguished-looking man in a wheelchair, who nodded back and raised his glass. Then he turned back to Breda. 'I was very sorry to hear about what happened at the restaurant at the weekend.'

Breda looked more stricken than he'd expected. 'It was pretty awful,' she said quietly. 'I was the one who found her.' She lifted her bandaged hand. 'Cut myself on the glass, trying to revive her.'

'God, I hadn't realised. I'm doubly sorry then, it must have been terrible. Did you know her?'

'I did, yes. We were friends.'

'I'm *so* sorry.'

'Thank you.' Breda took another drink from a passing tray, and Ross could see that her hand was shaking. He looked over at Kilbride and tried to maintain his sympathetic tone, while moving on.

'If you'll excuse me, I just need a word with Mr Kilbride. Again, my condolences.'

He reached Kilbride in a few steps, knowing he'd left Breda feeling wretched, but unable to spare her any further thought now. 'Will. Thanks for coming.'

Kilbride accepted the polite farewell of the person he'd been talking to, then turned to look up at Ross. 'Happy birth—'

'I need to talk. In private.'

Kilbride blinked. 'That sounds nice and celebratory.'

Ross checked the room and saw that Isla Munro was deep in conversation. 'Come to the director's office in five minutes?'

'All right.' Kilbride looked mildly curious, and Ross wondered if he'd rushed into this, but only for a moment; there was no-one else he could ask, after all. He grasped Kilbride's shoulder briefly, smiled too broadly, and made his way across the room to the office.

As soon as Kilbride had wheeled himself through the door, Ross pushed the latch and locked it. He automatically headed for the chair behind the desk, but changed his mind and instead sat down on the small two-seater couch, so he was at a lower level than Kilbride. It seemed more correct that way, given he was about to ask a favour.

'Who do you have?' he said, without preamble, but Kilbride seemed to know what he meant, anyway.

'I don't "have" people any more,' he said carefully, his eyes never leaving Ross's. 'What do you need?'

'Look, I understand you're out of...of all that stuff you used to do, but—'

'I'm out of the loan business, if that's what you mean.' Kilbride looked around the room, almost as if he suspected a lurking law presence. 'I don't plan to go back to it, so I don't need...collectors anymore.'

'Obviously I appreciate that,' Ross said quickly. Late last year Kilbride had lost first his son-in-law, his top enforcer, and then his daughter, who'd set out to avenge her husband's death. He had since gone what he referred to, with a grim smile, *as straight as a non-bendy thing with no corners.* At least, on the surface. There were those who had their doubts, and Ross still wasn't sure which side he came down on, but he was about to find out.

'What's the problem?' Kilbride asked now, shifting his attention back to Ross. 'It's your birthday. You should be out there enjoying being king of all you survey.'

'I'm going to tell you something,' Ross said, sitting back and wiping his damp hands on his trousers. Something still hissed at him to shut up, but he needed help, and Kilbride owed him: when he'd woken from a coma thirty-odd years ago, with money, ambition and the hide of a rhino, but nothing else, Ross had helped get him his first business deal setting up weekend retreats for city executives. Kilbride had always said he would return the favour if he could, and Ross had believed him, but now it was time to put it to the test.

Kilbride watched him calmly. 'And when you've told me, you're going to ask me again,' he surmised.

'Yes.'

'Then fire away.'

'Drink first.' Ross wasn't sure if he was suggesting it as a host, using it to delay the moment of truth, or just vocalising his immediate need. Either way, he was on his feet again and moving around his desk before the words were fully out. He took out the bottle of single malt he kept in the bottom drawer, sloshed generous levels into two cut crystal tumblers and passed one to Kilbride, who took it but did not drink. Instead he rolled the glass between his hands as if it were brandy, his expression curious but not at all disturbed.

Ross sat down again and searched for the best place to start. 'You remember Andrew Silcott?'

'Of course. I met him at a party, the same night this happened.' Kilbride tapped the arm of his wheelchair. 'His sportswear company was in the market for an executive weekend, but I lost the deal. Hardly surprising. When I got back on my feet – metaphorically speaking, of course,' he spared Ross a brief grin, 'you re-introduced us.'

'And you know how he died.'

Kilbride grimaced. 'Matthew Sturdy went nuts with a golf club, as I recall. About ten years later.'

'And you remember why.'

'For God's sake, man!' Kilbride sounded irritated now, which Ross definitely didn't want.

'Okay, sorry. So you remember he sold Sturdy a Mercanti original, *Florence Cathedral*, for a couple of million, but it later turned out to be fake?'

'Hard to forget that,' Kilbride said. 'I also remember that this gallery's the one that got it authenticated...or rather, not. It's no wonder Sturdy took a nine iron, or whatever it was, to Silcott's face. I'd have done the same.'

'The purchase ruined him.' Ross was coming to the difficult part now, and he paused. Kilbride took a sip of his drink and waited, saying nothing, and eventually Ross went on, 'He just saw Silcott living it up at Castle Stuart, and lost it.'

The guilt must have been clear on his face because Kilbride shook his head. 'Hardly your fault if Sturdy's got more money than sense when it comes to art. If he couldn't spot a fake, he should have had it authenticated himself before he bought it. For insurance purposes, if nothing else.'

'He did. And it had full provenance,' Ross pointed out. 'All the auction inventories, signatures and so on, going back to its very first exhibition in Rome. He'd no reason to suspect anything was wrong with it.'

'So what *did* prompt you to get it re-authenticated, anyway?' Kilbride asked. 'And why on earth have you still got it hanging out there?' He gestured to the closed door, and the gallery beyond it.

'Let's go back a bit.' Ross finished his drink and got up to pour another. Kilbride had barely touched his, so Ross didn't offer a top-up, and instead of returning to the sofa he sat behind his desk; bugger subservient, he felt more in control there. 'Silcott sold the painting to Sturdy, for a bit under three million, and Sturdy offered to loan it to Waterfront as part of the exhibition we had going on. A Renaissance season.'

'Naturally.'

'We accepted, and arranged for the loan of it for three months. While we were advertising... Oh, sod it.' Ross had been about to trot out the official line, purely from habit: *While we were advertising, a Mercanti scholar noticed something about the way the light fell on a part of the canvas, and queried it...* But this was Kilbride he was talking to. 'Okay,' he said, 'so there's this bloke called Leslie Warrender. You know him?'

Kilbride gave it some thought, then shook his head. 'I don't think so.'

'He's, *was*, an artist. Renaissance style, but mostly contemporary subjects. I used to exhibit his work sometimes; in fact there are one or two smaller ones on the walls in the side gallery now. Anyway, he had a bold suggestion.' Ross linked and unlinked his fingers, wondering just how non-bendy Kilbride was now. 'He reckoned he could do an exact and faithful copy of the Mercanti before the exhibition started.'

'Why would he want to do that?'

'I started out thinking it was just a challenge, to stretch himself, you know?' Ross took another drink; he was starting to feel a pleasant buzz now, and it helped. 'But then I remembered he'd been seeing Silcott's niece, or daughter or someone, and there was a bit of an age gap. Silcott put the kibosh on the whole thing, so it was a revenge thing, clearly, even if he never came right out and said it.'

'And you saw no reason to let that stand in the way of a good profit.' Kilbride gave a faint shrug. 'Don't blame you. Neither of you could have seen where it was headed.'

'Exactly. Anyway, I told him to have at it, but he'd have to get his hands on the painting, which meant stealing it from

Matthew Sturdy. Next thing, wouldn't you know it, there's been a robbery at Sturdy's place.'

'Imagine that.'

'Quite.' Ross shared his dry tone. 'Bunch of stuff's taken, some of it valuable, some of it not. Some of it looks expensive, but isn't. So basically this is someone who has no idea what they've taken.'

'Including the Mercanti.'

'Everyone assumes the robber just struck lucky choosing it. Sturdy claims on the insurance, but after about three months the painting turns up in a charity shop. Left there as part of an anonymous donation, and spotted the same day by none other than—'

'Leslie what's-his-name.'

'Warrender, aye. He "recognises it for a Mercanti", reports it, and accepts a modest reward from Sturdy, who buys it back from the insurance company.'

'Doesn't Sturdy spot it's a fake?'

'It's not though. It's the real thing.'

Kilbride was looking a little perplexed now. 'You'd better get to the point before someone comes looking for you.'

'The point is this: everyone's thrilled the painting's back. Sturdy, us, everyone. We exhibit it, as planned, and then a couple of days in, someone comes in and publicly says they're convinced it's a fake. We put up an argument to the contrary, but by then the press are involved, so we remove it from display and agree to get a reputable company in to assess it. I forget their name but they're the real thing, arranged by the insurance company. Anyway, they declare the one *we let them look at* to be a forgery, painted within the last ten years or so. Which it is. And which meant Silcott must apparently have known it too, since he'd sworn blind he'd owned it for at least thirty.'

'Hence the golf club incident.'

'Hence, as you say.' Ross gave a little shudder, and drank again. 'We issued a public apology, of course, for displaying a forgery. You might remember that?'

Kilbride shrugged. 'If I saw it, it went over my head. I can see the gallery didn't suffer from it though.'

Ross shook his head and smiled slightly at last; he was beginning to feel lighter for having unburdened himself. 'We bought it from Sturdy at the price it was valued at. Which wasn't to be sniffed at, incidentally. I mean it was still an incredible work of art.'

'Nowhere near three mil, though.'

'Of course not. But it gained a bit of its own provenance with all the press it got. It just wasn't a genuine Mercanti.'

'You keep using the past tense.'

Ross fidgeted with the pen pot on his desk. 'It was destroyed when Warrender tried to do a runner with it. His boat caught fire halfway to Norway.'

'So the one you've got out there,' again Kilbride gestured at the closed door, '*is* actually the real thing?'

'It's as real as that whisky you're staring at. That'll evaporate, you know, if you don't drink it.'

Kilbride ignored him. 'I remember the news story about the boat fire. You never let on you knew the bloke who died though.' He sounded faintly accusatory, and Ross wanted to believe that was because he considered him a friend, not because he'd kept him out of the loop when it came to a potential money-maker.

'You were busy with other stuff around then; we didn't see each other much... Why are you grinning?'

'I was just thinking about all the twats who still stand in front of it, twenty-odd years later, pointing out how it's clearly a fake because of this or that, and how they don't know why anyone didn't spot it before.'

Ross pulled a face and affected a pompous tone. 'The canvas is too thick, the light's wrong, there's obviously a painting underneath it... That one's probably true, though, Mercanti was never rich.'

'I'd imagine it's still pulling in more interest than it would if they knew it was the original.'

'Immeasurably more. Profits about tripled when the story broke, and they've stayed way up on what they were before. I suppose, in a weird way, it actually made us what we are now.'

In fact there was no *suppose* about it; before *Florence Cathedral*, and the scandal of its origins, Waterfront had been just another gallery on a river bank, ticking over but not exactly setting the art world alight. Now wall space and exhibition time were both at a premium, and new director Isla Munro had the ear of every art magazine editor who mattered.

'All with the added bonus that your insurance premiums are a lot lower.' Kilbride gave him a shrewd look. 'I'm also assuming you'll get it re-assessed at some point, say, when you retire, or if you sell the gallery, and it'll, oh-my-gosh-who-knew, turn out to be genuine after all.'

'That was the plan.'

'But not now?'

Ross drew the bent card from his pocket and passed it wordlessly across the desk.

Kilbride opened it, a puzzled little half-smile on his face, and read the inscription. 'Who's Florence?'

'Cathedral!'

'Right. LW... Ah.' Kilbride looked up as comprehension dawned at last. 'The boat fire was a *bit* less fatal than he let on, then.' He tossed the card onto the desk, and Ross pocketed it again, wanting it out of sight.

'So he's back,' he said, 'and this is the first contact he's made. Presumably he's here to blackmail me over this whole crappy mess that wasn't even my idea to begin with.' He was aware he sounded self-pitying, but the shock of all this was enough to do that to anyone.

'And that's where I come in, I take it?'

'You know people.'

'There's an agency in Abergarry I can recommend—'

'No.' Ross spoke in a low voice, but firmly. 'Nothing on paper. I can't risk anyone else knowing he's here; they'd probably be obliged to report it.' He took a deep breath, knowing his next words might well change everything, and send even Will Kilbride to the police. 'That woman who was killed at your restaurant was Matthew Sturdy's daughter.'

'Aye, I recognised the name. But there's no reason to suspect any connection to this Warrender bloke.'

'The coincidence is a bit hard to ignore though, don't you think? Warrender comes back to a place that thinks he's dead, and the next thing we know, the daughter of the only person with an axe to grind with him is killed.'

'But...Sturdy doesn't know Warrender's the one who painted the fake. He still thinks it's all down to Silcott. Doesn't he?'

Ross had told himself this many times in the years since Silcott had died, and it was true; there was nothing to connect the gallery to any of the events leading up to the murder, beyond an honest mistake on the gallery's part. Warrender being the one to find the painting had been natural enough, understandable even, given his credentials, and *his* only connection to the gallery was as a sometime exhibitor. He hadn't known Andrew Silcott, who had only ever been a casual buyer with more money than knowledge or passion, and was on no more than nodding terms with Matthew Sturdy.

But no matter how much he reminded himself of this now, Ross knew, deep down, that Leslie Warrender had killed Linda Sturdy, and the most obvious reason was that Linda had seen and recognised him. He put this to Kilbride now, trying to suppress the fear that came with it.

Kilbride listened without interruption, then frowned. 'Seems an extreme length to go to, even if she did recognise him. Being done for murder's a bit different to being done for fraud. Hell of a risk.'

'Then there must be something else she knows about him that could bring him down,' Ross said firmly. 'But you can't ignore the coincidence, can you?'

'Yes,' Kilbride said, sounding impatient now. 'You can. It might be a bit risky him being seen, but he's got no reason to be that scared that he...he *kills* anyone who recognises him. Why would he come back at all, if that were the case? Come on, Pat, think about it.'

Ross subsided as he accepted the logic. 'Maybe I've just panicked.' He sighed. 'But this card really spooked me. It was hand-delivered, so he's been here tonight.'

'A party full of artists, where anyone might have recognised him.' Kilbride drove his point home, and shook his head. 'Look, you just need to sit tight and find out what it'll take to get him out of your life again.'

'Except he'll never be out, will he? Not if he's still got that painting, and can prove it led to Silcott's murder.'

'They can't lay that at your door,' Kilbride protested tiredly. 'You're being paranoid now. You didn't know Sturdy was going to lose his shit like that, no-one did. Not even him! It's not like it was planned.'

'No, he's never been violent as far as I know. It was totally out of character.'

'Well, three million's a lot to lose,' Kilbride pointed out. 'He saw the guy playing a cheerful round at the links without a care in the world, and it would have felt like a kick in the teeth.' His eyes narrowed. 'So...if you don't believe he'll ever be out of your life, even if you give in to whatever blackmail's coming, what *exactly* are you asking me to do?'

Ross wasn't sure what Kilbride meant for a moment, then he realised, with a nasty jolt. 'Not that! God, no. Not that.'

Kilbride visibly relaxed, but his frustration still showed. 'Well, what then?'

'I need someone to find out where he's keeping that painting,' Ross said. 'Destroy it before he can use it to destroy me.' He saw Kilbride's almost-eyeroll, and shook his head. 'I'm *not* being paranoid here, Will – just think about it. Fraud charges at that level will ruin me, and put me behind bars right along with Sturdy. And once Sturdy finds out who was really behind that fraud, which he will, I'm dead. I can't be sure Warrender *is* going to blackmail me, but even if he does, that's the best case scenario I can think of here.'

'The best?'

'The alternative being he's got that hold over me for the rest of my life. And if he has a heart attack, or walks in front of a bus and carks it, someone'll go through his stuff and find the painting. It'll all come out, and that's me in jail anyway, with a man who's lost everything, including his daughter now, because of me.'

'Put like that,' Kilbride conceded. 'But if you don't want to use the agency I suggested, how do you know you can trust anyone else I can dig up for you?'

'Because anyone *you* dig up will have their own issues they don't want raised.'

'Jesus!' Kilbride barked a short laugh. 'I came here to wish you a happy birthday, and maybe get stuck into a quiche, and here I am talking about double-blackmail.'

Ross shook his head quickly. 'I wouldn't do that to someone helping me out. I just mean they're more likely to understand my need to keep this under the official radar.'

Kilbride considered him for a moment, then sighed. 'Let me give it some thought, okay? I told you, I don't move in those circles anymore.'

'But you still—'

'Aye, I still know people.' Kilbride looked at the hardly touched whisky in his glass, then put it carefully on Ross's desk. 'I think I'll call it a night,' he said. 'Thanks for a lovely party.'

Ross's heart sank. 'You understand I had to ask.'

'I do. And I told you, I'll give it some thought. I'm not ruling it out.' Kilbride turned his chair around and buzzed smoothly towards the door. 'I'll call you in the morning,' he promised. 'And we need to discuss that investment I told you about, too.'

'I thought I'd go up there tomorrow evening.' Ross opened the door for him, letting in the party sounds from the gallery; they made the conversation he'd just had feel slightly surreal by comparison. 'Thanks for coming, Will.'

'Oh, you know me, I love a good party.' Kilbride looked down at his wasted legs. 'Shame they keep turning out to be less fun than I'd hoped for.'

Chapter Six

For a Monday evening, the Twisted Tree pub was pretty busy. Hazel dodged her way through the clusters of people chatting and playing darts and pool, and managed to deliver the tray of drinks to the corner booth without spilling too much. The rally committee had pulled together an emergency meeting to discuss potential new sites, and Griff had his laptop open and had been typing furiously into it; Jonah, his business partner as well as club vice-chair, was tapping on his phone's calculator, and Greg and Jackie had their heads together over a list of attendees they'd pulled from the Facebook group. When Hazel was seated again, Griff looked at her, eyebrows raised; she'd been deliberately vague when she'd texted him, looking forward to breaking her news face to face.

'Spill,' Griff demanded, but there was amusement on his face at the excitement on hers.

'Okay. So you know I'm working up at what was the old Glenlowrie Estate?'

'The one where that kid went missing last year?' Jonah broke in, wiping foam off his beard.

She nodded. 'Ade Mackenzie, the new—'

'Wait.' Griff pushed his long hair away from his face and flexed his fingers over his keyboard. 'Let's get all this down. Glenlowrie Estate.'

'It's called Glencoille now. Double l, e,' she added, watching him typing it in. 'The Mackenzies are building a new Highland Experience centre there.' The mild scoffing sounds from around the table weren't unexpected, and she rolled her eyes. 'It's not as tacky as it sounds,' she insisted. 'Anyway, they've said we can use a plot of land that isn't due to be worked on until June.'

Greg and Jonah high-fived one another, and Griff rubbed his hands together.

'Fantastic.' he said. 'Who's "they" though? Contact?'

'Ade himself. I'll have to make sure he's happy for me to give you his number, but I've given him yours already.'

'Typical.' Griff shook his head. 'One rule for the toffs, aye?'

'He's not a toff! Far from it. Anyway, there's nothing to stop us taking a ride up there tonight and looking the place over. It'll be light for a couple of hours yet.'

'To be fair, what choice have we got?' The social secretary's tone was predictably glum. 'The other place was perfect, but it's a bust. So...' She shrugged.

'This place is pretty good.' Hazel took a swig of her lime and lemonade. 'Ade lives on the site usually, but it's his brother's girlfriend's birthday so he won't be there tonight, A quick look around wouldn't hurt.'

'Right,' Griff said. 'Let's draft the social media stuff now, then we'll go up. All okay with that?'

Talk moved onto what Jackie should say on the Facebook page, assuming the Glencoille site proved suitable, and Hazel's attention wandered until her gaze landed on a fifty-ish woman coming out of the toilets. At the same time, the woman saw her, smiled in surprised recognition and changed direction to approach their table. Normally anyone interrupting a meeting would have been asked to wait, but Hazel was curious enough to fling a quick apology at Griff and meet the woman halfway.

'Hazel Douglas, isn't it?' The woman looked relieved when Hazel nodded cautiously. 'I'm Breda Kelly. A good friend of poor Linda's.'

Hazel relaxed. 'She mentioned you a lot. It's nice to meet you.'

'I've seen your photo, of course, but you're much prettier than it gave you credit for.' Breda's accent was Irish, southern, and her clothes bright and cheery, almost hippie-like. She gave the impression of a primary school teacher...or at least what Hazel recalled her own to have been like, back in the early nineties. They probably didn't dress like that now. Breda's sympathetic smile gave her the same aura, but her hand was firm as she shook Hazel's.

'I'm *so* sorry for your loss, you poor girl.'

'Likewise,' Hazel said. 'I know you two were close. It must have been such a shock finding her like that.' She almost added that she knew how it must have felt, but closed her lips on the words; this wasn't about her.

Breda's eyes filled and she blinked quickly. 'I can't even describe it. So much *blood*...' She raised her left hand, which Hazel now saw was bandaged. 'I tried to help her, but ended up messing up the crime scene and just got ticked off for my trouble.'

Hazel winced in sympathy. 'Easily done, I should think. This is a long way out from Inverness; I'm surprised to see you here.'

'Who'd have believed it? I was visiting an old friend up at

The Heathers this afternoon, and got caught short on my way back through. I knew this would be your local, and I must admit it crossed my mind to look you up, but Linda said...' She looked embarrassed and lowered her voice a little. 'I just didn't expect to see you in a pub, if I'm honest.'

'It's for a bike club meeting,' Hazel said quickly. 'No booze. I'd ask you to stay so we can chat, but we're heading up to Glencoille to see if it's a suitable place to hold our rally. Ade's offered it for our use.'

'That's kind of him; he's a nice fella. But I couldn't stay anyway, thanks, I've to be at Thistle in a little over an hour. Let me give you my number though, and you can call me anytime.'

Hazel added the number into her phone, and Breda gave her an unexpected hug before she went, leaving her feeling strangely comforted, considering they'd only just met. She returned to the table, where discussion had returned to the rally venue, and picked up her glass without sitting back down.

'Shall we drink up and go then? We can talk about the details later.'

'If we still think there's any point after we've seen it,' Jackie said, and Hazel sighed.

'There will be,' she said, striving to keep her tone patient. 'It's near a river, there's plenty of wood for a bonfire, and it's not so far off the road that people will get lost looking for it.'

'Size?' Griff said, fingers once more poised over his keyboard.

'You'll see for yourself in twenty minutes.' Hazel saw his expression and gave in; being a business owner he did love his paperwork to be organised. 'Only a wee bit smaller than our old site. But plenty big enough for the silly games, and there's room for the marquee if the band doesn't mind slumming it a bit.' She sighed, looking at Griff's face again, and condensed it. 'Adequate.'

'Adequate,' Griff muttered typing it in. 'Come on then, you lot.' He closed his laptop. 'Looks like we're going for a ride.'

The site met with universal approval, as Hazel had known it would. Jonah and Greg paced out the area just north of the low stone wall, while Jackie got straight onto the club's Facebook page and finished drafting the new venue information for everyone who'd registered to attend. Griff shoved his hands into his jacket pockets and joined Hazel sitting on the wall.

'So, I didn't want to talk about it in the pub, but the police came a-calling about Friday night.'

'Aye. I told them where I was, and who else was there. Sorry I didn't get around to giving you the heads up.'

'Probably better that way, so my surprise wasn't faked. Can't believe they'd think you had anything to do with what happened.'

'They didn't.' Hazel shrugged. 'But with my history... Well, you know.'

'Blimey, you never *killed* anyone!'

'That's what I said. Still, I'm never going to be Mary Poppins, am I?'

'Good thing, too. The woman's a freak anyway.' Griff was silent for a moment, then changed the subject, waving up towards the field. 'The marquee will be okay in that top corner, if we can run the cables up that far.'

'We can,' Hazel confirmed, and looked around. 'I like this place a lot. Pity we can only have it for one year.'

Griff nodded, and re-tied his pony tail after the yanking it had taken in the wind. 'You're well in with the owner, then?'

'I told you, he's a good boss. And,' she added, 'the land further up the estate actually used to belong to my family in ye olden days.' She saw the incredulity on his face. 'Way back,' she clarified, 'long before I was born. Maybe even before *you* were.'

He snorted. 'I'm only about ten years older than you, ya cheeky bitch.'

'Surely not?' Hazel laughed. 'No, a great-great uncle or something, on my dad's side, used to live on a little farm called West Glenlowrie before he moved down to Cornwall. It doesn't exist anymore, but we've...*I've*, got a painting he did of it.'

'Another artist in the family then, along with your mum and dad.'

She nodded, and in danger of becoming emotional now, she looked away at the trees by the gate posts swaying in the evening breeze and remembered something else she'd meant to ask.

'Work busy at the moment?'

'Fairly, aye. Why?'

'My aunt could do with someone who knows their way around a chainsaw.'

'Wow. Someone must have *really* annoyed her.'

Hazel gave him a look. 'For her trees.' He chuckled, and she smacked his arm. 'If you've got some time I'll take you up there and you can quote a price, okay?'

'Yep, fine. Just let me know when you're free, and I'll see how I'm fixed.' He looked over at Jackie, who waved her iPad in the air to indicate she'd updated the club page. 'Looks like we're all set.'

'Hard to find a good place for a signal,' Jackie said, joining Hazel and Griff on the wall. 'Had to walk around for a bit. That'll piss off some attendees, I reckon. I don't know how you cope with that every day,' she added to Hazel.

'Ade's getting it sorted for when we open,' Hazel said. 'But it won't be done in time for the rally.'

Griff pulled a face. 'Who cares? It'll be good not to have everyone glued to their phones all weekend. If we're going old-school, let's go totally old-school. Trad rallies are the best.'

'The only place I could get the update to send was by the office,' Jackie said. 'Lucky for you, eh, Hazel?'

'That's *why* the office is right there,' Hazel pointed out patiently, feeling Griff's arm shake against hers, and avoiding catching his eye; Jackie could ride like a demon, but she was prone to the occasional short-circuit in the thinking department.

'Anyway, I've said no-one'll have access prior to the rally,' Jackie went on, as if Hazel hadn't spoken. 'Your boss won't get inundated with recce parties, so tell him not to worry.'

'Okay, good work.' Griff stretched, ready to leave. 'Better get some signage organised then. Want to give me a hand, Haze? You're the one with all the arty credentials. We'll design something together, and I'll get it printed off. Meet in the Tree tomorrow evening, yeah?'

'Only if you're buying.'

'Tight arse,' he said amiably, and Hazel grinned.

Greg and Jonah had finished their examination by now, and after they'd given a favourable verdict and pointed out a couple of minor and fixable pitfalls, the five of them walked back to where they'd parked the bikes, by the stone pillars that marked the entrance to the estate. 'Who was that woman you were talking to in the pub, Haze?' Griff asked. 'She looked a bit familiar but I can't place her.'

'Breda Kelly.' Hazel pulled her gloves out of her helmet. 'She's not from round here though. She lives in Inverness.'

'Really niggled me,' Griff said thoughtfully. 'Inverness...' He fished in his cut-off pocket for his keys, then stopped. 'Thistle! *That's* where I've seen her. Is she a waitress or something?'

'The manager,' Hazel said, amused. Griff's rangy, craggy appearance didn't seem to go with Thistle, somehow. 'Go there a lot, do you?'

'I've been once or twice.' He raised an eyebrow. 'What?'

Hazel shook her head and pulled her helmet on, smiling to herself. 'Nothing. See you in the Tree tomorrow at seven. More your scene, aye?'

The others had already taken off, and she had her thumb poised over the electric start button when an unfamiliar car bumped its way between the gateposts and stopped. Hazel peered at it in surprise; such an expensive-looking vehicle was a rare sight up here. The passenger side window buzzed down, and she relaxed and removed her helmet.

'Hello, Mr Kilbride. Ade's not here, I'm afraid.'

He beckoned her over, and she suppressed a sigh and put the kickstand back down. Kilbride gave her a wide smile and she knew she was about to be asked a favour, but she owed Ade a few minutes of overtime, at least, for the way he'd jumped to the bike club's rescue.

'What can I do for you?' She leaned down to speak to him through the window, and looked across to see who'd driven him up here, surprised and a little awed to see the owner of Waterfront behind the wheel.

'This is Mr Ross,' Kilbride said, unnecessarily. 'I brought him up here so he could have a look at the place. But since you're here maybe you wouldn't mind showing him the plans too? Potential investor; I've spoken to Ade about it.'

'Um.' Hazel looked from one man to the other, unsure. 'Would you mind if I give Ade a call first?' She felt closer to twelve years old than thirty-five at this moment, daring to argue with a teacher, but Kilbride waved a hand.

'Of course. I'd expect nothing less.'

Hazel dug in her jacket pocket for her phone, then grunted in annoyance. 'I'll have to go back there to do it.' She gestured up the wide path towards the portakabin office.

'That's fine, I'll wait here. More trouble than it's worth, getting out.' Kilbride sat back in his seat and closed his eyes, and Hazel gave him another speculative look before hooking her helmet over the handlebar of her bike and stomping back up to the office.

She wasn't entirely surprised to find Mr Ross following closely at her heels, but she did feel uneasy about it. She knew him by reputation, of course, but he was still a stranger, and while she actually trusted Kilbride, he would be no help to her sitting back in the car, if Ross turned out to be some axe-wielding nut job.

She kept an eye on her phone as she approached the office, and as soon as the signal bar appeared she pressed to call Ade. She could hear laughter in the background and recognised one of the voices that cut through it as Ade's younger brother.

'If that's Maddy, tell her to shake a tail feather, would you? We're waiting to eat.'

'It's Hazel,' Ade called back, before lowering his voice again. 'What's up?'

'I'm up at the site. Mr Kilbride's here, and he's brought Patrick Ross, you know, from the gallery?'

Ade hissed in irritation. 'What do they want at this time of night? And what are you doing there anyway?'

She told him briefly why she and the others had come up, then looked over her shoulder at Ross, who had his hands firmly behind his back and was keeping his distance, as if making a very defensive point. She was damned if she'd apologise though. 'Mr Kilbride says can we show Mr Ross the plans for the estate, something about an investment, and he's spoken to you already?'

Ade paused, and Hazel couldn't help smiling as she listened to Paul's girlfriend in the background, telling someone to stop buzzing around like a demented wasp; presumably her eleven-year-old son Jamie, but with Charis you could never be sure.

'Well?' she pressed, wanting nothing more than to get this over with and go home.

'Okay. Just show him the estate layout plans, not the main house. And don't let him take pictures.'

Hazel unlocked the office and led Ross inside, where she rolled up the top layer of plans that lay on Ade's desk and put it back in its cardboard tube. Beneath it were detailed drawings of the estate, and she spent a few minutes pointing out the various features.

'Why are you interested in investing, anyway?' she asked bluntly, standing back to let Ross take a closer look. 'Doesn't seem to gel with an art gallery.'

'On the contrary,' Ross said. 'These cabins and the main reception will all act as extra gallery space. Ade's agreed to hang paintings by my artists, and provide contact and sale information at the front desk, should anyone ask for it. There's more to it, of course, but that's the gist.' He seemed to think he'd explained more than enough to a lackey, and turned away again, tracing the route of the river through the estate.

'What sort of paintings?' Hazel asked, her interest piqued now.

'All sorts.' He glanced at her, clearly taking in her shabby leathers, scuffed Docs and faded black jeans, and then dismissing her. 'But nothing that would interest you, I'm sure.'

'Oh, so not the one with the dogs playing snooker then? Damn. That's my favourite.' A flash of anger had made it hard not to react more strongly, but she kept both her tone and her expression bland; she couldn't risk screwing this up for Ade.

Ross looked at her again, this time a little more shrewdly as her sarcasm struck home. '*Are* you interested in art then?'

Hazel's immediate reaction to any kind of probing question had, for many years, been to either shut down and change the subject, or to respond with a cutting remark designed to raise a cheap laugh. But since becoming friends with Maddy she had learned to open up a little. *If* she trusted someone. Patrick Ross was a well-respected man, someone her father had rated highly, and, at least in the news articles she'd read, he'd displayed a genuine passion for art along with the more cynical aspect of buying and selling.

'My dad was a brilliant artist,' she said, deciding to go for the truth. 'Mum too, though she dropped out of uni.' She cleared her throat. 'They're both gone now. But loads of relatives on Dad's side have been artistic in one way or another.'

'You seem young to have lost both your parents already.' Ross sounded genuinely sympathetic now. 'Would I have known any of your father's work?'

'I don't know. His name was Graeme Douglas.'

'It doesn't ring any bells,' Ross said, and he looked a little embarrassed, but Hazel shook her head.

'He didn't sell much, and he went into the academic side after a while. His friend did better; someone said he was actually quite well known, but I was too young to know really.'

'And *his* name?'

'Leslie Warrender.'

Ross had been poring over the plans again, and Hazel saw his finger pause in its tracing of the river, but only for a moment. 'Oh. Aye, Mr Warrender showed at Waterfront several times, back in the nineties. I was very sorry to hear of his death, but he'd have been glad to know his paintings made good prices at auction.'

Hazel was keener than ever to let Ross finish looking at the plans and go, but it seemed he wasn't ready to let go of that subject just yet.

'You said you'd *heard* he was known locally,' he said, straightening. 'Who told you that, then?'

'Dad's girlfriend.' Hazel met his eyes, which were brown and friendly, but fixed on hers with a disturbing intensity. 'She died last Friday; you probably heard about it.'

'The woman who was killed at Thistle?'

Hazel nodded. 'We found a photo while I was clearing out Dad's things, and she told me his name, and that he was sort of famous, locally at least.' Something had stopped her from mentioning Linda's suspicion that she'd seen Warrender alive and well, and while she didn't understand it, she obeyed it; Ross's reaction to hearing Warrender's name had been slight, and if she hadn't been focusing on him so hard she might have missed it. As it was, she just filed it away to tell Maddy.

'Have you seen everything you want to?' she asked, keeping her tone polite. 'Ade will be happy to talk you through anything else, I'm sure.'

'He lives up here, doesn't he?'

'He's got a caravan on site. His brother lives in town though, and that's where he is at the moment. You'd probably have caught him if you'd come up any other evening.' Hazel didn't know why she felt it necessary to make it clear that the place was rarely unattended, but again, she obeyed her instincts. She hovered by the door, hoping Ross would get the hint, and to his credit he did, but not until he'd given the office a very slow visual sweep. His gaze lingered on the massive wall planner, and she could tell the moment his brain registered the scrawled words *soggy socks* from the way his eyes widened, just a fraction, and a flash of mild but puzzled amusement crossed his face.

'Thank you for accommodating me,' he said, turning back to Hazel. 'You're clearly dedicated to your job, to be up here so late.'

Talk about fishing... Hazel didn't correct him; she just smiled, looking deliberately distracted. 'You're welcome. Shall we?' She pushed open the portakabin door and preceded Ross down the steps. 'Ade'll give you a ring tomorrow.'

Ross followed, then, while she locked the door behind them he let that unsettlingly thorough gaze travel again, this time around as much of the estate as was visible from the yard. 'So the distillery's going where?'

'A bit further up there,' she pointed, 'where the river widens.' She remembered his interest in the flow of the river through the estate. 'Do you have an interest in whisky then?'

'It's where I understand the larger part of my investment will go.' Ross looked around for a moment longer, nodded, then held out his hand. 'Thank you again. I'll be sure to pass on my appreciation to Mr Mackenzie when we speak.'

Hazel saw him back to his car and returned Kilbride's gesture of farewell; when Ross had turned the car and headed back out through the stone pillars, she lifted her helmet off her bike's handlebar and watched until the road was empty once more. She turned to look at the estate behind her; its sprawling acres of largely untouched land, the hills that rose steeply either side of the river, and the forest that flanked the boundary, and she wondered if Ade really knew anything about these two businessmen he was getting involved with. Because she was beginning to feel a prickly unease about the whole thing.

Chapter Seven

Paul Mackenzie woke early on Tuesday morning, when it was barely getting light. He snatched joggers and a T shirt from the chair and left Charis snoring softly while he went downstairs, where his brother was lying on his back on the sofa, also snoring. It was like comparing a kitten with a buffalo. Mackenzie grinned and, leaving Ade to his slumber, dressed quickly, took his water flask from the fridge and set out on his morning run.

Listening to the rhythmic slapping of his trainers on the road, he thought back to the months when he'd been unable to do this, thanks to the horrific motorcycle incident – he couldn't really call it an accident; he'd been deliberately run off the road by Charis's insanely jealous ex-husband. It had taken him a long time to get back not only the strength, but the inclination, and now it felt good to have the air flowing through his lungs again, and to know his new family was waiting for him at home. He felt a smile touch his lips as he ran; he still couldn't quite believe Charis had finally agreed to move in, and Maddy had given him one of her particular looks when he'd told her, but even she had to admit it was working. Charis's photography course was giving her a real interest in something since she'd left her old life behind and moved to Scotland, but he was glad it hadn't knocked her sharp edges off; he wouldn't recognise her without them.

Most people never saw the quiet side of Charis Boulton, the thoughtful, inquisitive side that Jamie had inherited. They saw the funny, drily sarky version, heard the unrestrained bellows of laughter that sounded as if they'd come from someone three times her size, and they practically glowed if they managed to earn her approval – it was like being chosen by a cat among a roomful of prospective laps. You felt special. But there were a select few to whom she'd opened herself fully, and most of them had been at Mackenzie's place last night to celebrate her birthday. Himself, Maddy, Ade and Jamie had spent the evening determinedly forgetting absolutely everything that had gone before, and simply enjoying one another's company for what was probably the first time since their troubled paths had collided, rather than crossed, last year.

Ade had been a huge part of that. His return to Scotland, after so many years, had changed something fundamental in Mackenzie; he had remembered what it was to have people. Not just a friend, like Maddy, though she had pulled him through some horrific times, and not even a tentative new love that had turned him inside out with conflicted emotion, before he'd accepted it in the deepest part of him. But for the first time since the death of his wife and son, Mackenzie had begun to feel part of the wider world again. Ade had even managed to build a bridge between him and his stroppy, acerbic father, and now that Glencoille was a real, growing project, and his father was set to join the general population again after so many years at the nursing home, it felt as if the family had been dragged back from the edge of a cliff. They had a future, and it was filled with possibilities.

Mackenzie arrived back home, sweating and breathing hard, in time to hear Charis just switching off the shower upstairs. He found Ade slathering Marmite onto his toast in the kitchen, and ran cold water and splashed his face before putting another two slices into the toaster.

'Good run?' Ade asked around a mouthful, as he sat down.

'Pretty good. Going to be a warm day though. Got much heavy work planned?'

'Not too bad; mostly meetings today. I need to call Patrick Ross about a potential investment in the centre.' Ade had evidently noted Mackenzie's expression; he averted his eyes. 'How about you?'

Mackenzie ignored the question. 'Ross? Kilbride's friend?'

'They know one another, aye,' Ade said vaguely. 'I showed Maddy the site for the distillery yesterday, and she came up with a couple of ideas for the visitor centre. She's got a good eye.'

Mackenzie could tell his brother was angling for a humorous comment about Ade's compatibility with Maddy, if only to take the conversation in a different direction, but there was more to unpack here. 'Have you even met this bloke?'

Ade's sigh was barely audible, but it was there. 'No, and it's not even a definite yet. Will's only put it forward as a suggestion, and the two of them went up to the site for a chat last night. But I was down here, so Hazel showed him the plans.'

'So, just to be clear,' Mackenzie persisted, 'William Kilbride, who contacted *you* originally about a partnership with his restaurant, is now getting his friends in on it as well?'

'In on it?' Ade's voice had lost its mellow tone. 'In on what, exactly?'

'Come on.' Mackenzie snatched his breakfast from the toaster and threw it onto a plate. 'You know Kilbride's reputation; he's been doing dodgy deals since the eighties.'

Ade spoke carefully. 'I know Maddy says you've always disapproved. And I know why,' he added, as Mackenzie opened his mouth to inform him of a few choice facts, 'but I also know he's changed since his daughter died.'

Mackenzie's gut tightened as he recalled exactly how that had happened, and how close he'd been standing from her when it had... He'd had to throw his shirt away, and sometimes still thought he could smell the hot blood that had spattered across his face. But Donna Lumsden's death, at the hands of a police marksman, had no bearing on what he knew of William Kilbride's dealings over the years; the man would still have a grubby finger in a pie or two. People like him didn't change.

'He's had people beaten for their debts,' he said patiently. 'Seriously beaten and, for all anyone knows, maybe even killed. He's scum, Ade.' He concentrated on spreading his toast. 'I hate that he's got his claws into Glencoille, but that's your baby. Yours and Dad's. It's not up to me to scupper your business deals.'

'So why the downer on this one?'

Mackenzie considered; if he was being honest it was just a feeling he hadn't really thought through until now. 'Kilbride, on his own, I could sort of see where the mutual benefit with somewhere like Glencoille would sit.' He gave Ade a narrow look. 'Even though I've had my suspicions for a long time about that restaurant of his, and why he'd give it over to his daughter but still keep such a tight rein on the business side of it.'

'It's what he does! It's his expertise, where Donna's was the hospitality angle.'

'Granted, I suppose. And if Ross and Kilbride weren't pals

I'd probably not bat an eyelid about you getting into bed with Ross either. But two of them, and before the estate's even built? These are two of the wealthiest men in the area, and both approaching *you*?' He shook his head. 'I don't like it.'

'Thanks a lot,' Ade said, with a dry humour that sounded forced. 'Vote of confidence noted.'

'You know what I mean.' Mackenzie dropped his knife and began ticking off on his fingers. 'You've not been back in the country more than five minutes. You've got no track record in business, in *any* country. Your family has a piss-poor reputation when it comes to losing money. You're building this dream resort in a country already crawling with them, so you're going to be fighting for customers with places that have been trading for decades, and—'

'All right!' Ade had lost what remained of his good humour now, and his face was stony. 'You think they're planning on using Glencoille as a place to launder money, is that it?'

'It's likely, yes.'

'Money from what? Drugs?'

Mackenzie shook his head. 'I'm not saying either of them is involved in that, although what do we know? But Kilbride used to charge astronomical interest on the loans he handed out, and he had a stable of absolute bastards who were only too keen to help him make sure he got it. He'd have had to clean it somehow.'

'Which means he already has something in place.'

'Had.' Mackenzie kept his frustration in check, but barely. 'Once his bag man was beaten to death, and Donna died too, anyone doing that kind of business with him would have been mad to stick around through all the police interest. He'd need to look again.'

'And that could be the only reason he's interested in Glencoille, of course.' Ade's voice was flat. 'Never mind that it's actually his business to put places like mine in touch with customers *looking* for places like mine. That he's been doing it for thirty years.' He pushed his plate away. 'I know you've got a problem with him, and I'm not asking you to share a pint with the man, or even to trust him. But I hoped you'd at least trust me.'

'I do,' Mackenzie said. 'But you don't know—'

'Yes, I do! Maddy's told me, Dad's told me, *you've* told me, and believe it or not I'm capable of keeping an ear to the ground myself, and I know he's barely kept one step ahead of the law for the past however many years. But I've also talked with him, and listened to him. He's changed since Donna died. Maybe not all the way yet, but he's getting there.'

Mackenzie bit back the heavily sarcastic response that rose to his lips, and nodded. 'Okay. If you're sure.'

Ade gave him a faintly suspicious look at the way he'd backed down so quickly, but after a moment he nodded. 'I am.'

'Good.'

'Great.'

'That's all right then.'

'Aye.' Ade pulled his plate back towards himself and gave Mackenzie another wary look, then seemed to relax again. 'Thanks for putting me up last night.'

'Don't mention it. Thanks for coming over.' Mackenzie remembered the easy cameraderie of the evening before, and he deliberately softened his stiffly polite tone. 'It was a good night.'

'It was. Let's hope some of those photos don't end up on Facebook; your credibility will be out the window.'

'And you can kiss goodbye to any reputable investors,' Mackenzie added, unable to resist stressing the word *reputable*.

Ade flipped his middle finger up as he bit into his toast, and Mackenzie grinned, but the banter had a fragile edge to it and he wasn't fooled for one moment into believing Ade was comfortable with his interference.

Charis came in, dressed now, but with her short dark hair sticking up and still wet. She looked as shyly urchin-like as always, despite the late night, and her blue eyes were huge in her small, delicate-featured face as she looked at the two men tucking into their breakfast. Anyone who didn't know her might have expected her to murmur a quiet greeting and generally behave as if she felt she'd intruded. She opened the bread bin and looked back at the two men at the table, her eyes wider than ever.

'You pair of greedy guts leave any bread for the rest of us?' The Liverpool accent was strong, the words harsh, but the voice was just a little bit husky with sleep, and it all rippled over both Mackenzie brothers without leaving a smudge of resentment; Mackenzie felt, on days like this, that he could forgive her any insult she could throw at him. Mostly.

'Who're you calling greedy?' he demanded. 'Ade, remind us: who was it that snort-grunted her way through an entire tube of Pringles last night without drawing breath?'

'It was my birthday!' she protested, before Ade could respond. 'And I've told you before about buying them ones. They're me favourites.'

'Well, your real birthday meal should be even better,' Mackenzie said; he'd booked dinner at Thistle, at huge expense, for later in the week. 'So no shovelling *that* down your neck at a mile a minute.'

'Will if I like,' Charis said, throwing him a smile that lit him up inside, despite the flimsiness of the current peace in the house. She went to the freezer and dragged out a loaf. 'What are you lads up to today?'

'The usual,' Ade said. 'Listening to contractors, sub-contractors and actual tractors. What about you, working?'

'Yep. And then coursework. But this time next week I'll actually be in the college.' Charis's face brightened. 'I can't wait. We get campus days on this online course I'm doing,' she added, 'and I get to use the photography equipment, and talk to the academics who run the actual degree courses at the uni.' She slammed the frozen loaf onto the counter top, to loosen a couple of slices for the toaster, and the horrendous bang made Ade wince and rub his temples. 'Sorry,' she said, sounding anything but.

Jamie wandered blearily in, but brightened when he saw Ade was still there, and once again Mackenzie hoped he hadn't alienated his brother by his suspicions; his family was too important to risk losing all over again. He listened to Charis's animated chatter, and Jamie's chipping in with questions about absolutely everything but what they were talking about, and knew he couldn't bring up the subject of Ross again without spoiling the mood.

But that didn't mean he was happy to let it go. As soon as he'd dropped Jamie off at the library he'd head into Inverness and pay a visit to Waterfront. Patrick Ross wouldn't be at the gallery himself, he had people to run that for him, but there would be someone there that Mackenzie could talk to about him, questions he could ask. And he intended to, for the family's sake.

The gallery sat on the next road over from St Andrew's Cathedral, on the west side of the River Ness. Mackenzie nosed his Mazda down the narrow terraced street, wishing yet again that he was back on two wheels, especially for this kind of work. There were double yellows all the way down one side, but there was a recessed parking bay with meters in front of the buildings, and he was able to nudge the car into a spot right at the end.

He looked up at the narrow-fronted building, with its discreet sign over the door, and wondered how this place could have made such a name for itself compared to the glossy images he'd seen of other galleries. But it was the same as Thistle, he supposed; that too was understated and plain looking from the outside, but once you crossed the threshold you were left in no doubt as to the quality of what was on offer. For a moment his resolve wavered, but only until he noticed the wheelchair ramp alongside the steps, which reminded him of Kilbride. He climbed the steps to the open door and stepped into the reception area. Yes, there was the same calm elegance here, the same air of *exclusive, yet welcoming*. The same sense that he was never going to be quite smart enough... Or perhaps he just had an inferiority complex; the Burnside Hotel in Abergarry had always made him feel like that too.

The woman at the reception desk gave him a bland, professional smile and offered him a glossy leaflet filled with thumbnails and short blocks of text.

'No, thanks,' he said. 'I was wondering if I'd be able to talk to the gallery manager?'

The woman immediately assumed a regretful look; perhaps she thought he was a hopeful artist and was internally rolling her eyes. 'Miss Munro's in a meeting with Mr Ross at the moment. Would you like to look around while you wait?' She proffered the leaflet again, and this time Mackenzie took it; he didn't know whether he was glad or not that Ross was on the premises after all, but it meant he would have to alter his line of questioning, and it would be good to have a few minutes to consider that. He pushed open the gallery door and found himself in an unexpectedly spacious area, where quiet music played and the lighting varied in every corner. There were pillars and screens, giving the impression of lots of little pockets of something close to privacy, but it was clear he was the only person browsing this early in the day.

He wandered around, staring blankly at the paintings while his mind worked through his possible excuses for being here, but when he came to the now famously fake *Florence Cathedral*, he stopped, temporarily distracted without knowing why. After a moment of letting his mind wander again, he remembered Maddy explaining what Hazel Douglas had wanted from her, which was to find this bloke who'd turned out to have faked his own death, and who she thought had probably painted this very picture.

He looked closely at it, trying to spot anything that might mark it out as modern, but he had no knowledge of art, or even any real interest in it. Besides, if this Warrender *had* painted it, he was damned good, and unlikely to have done it just for shits and giggles. This painting, as beautiful as it was, had been the cause of Andrew Silcott's death, and the reason Matthew Sturdy had been behind bars when his daughter had been killed equally brutally. Somehow it looked less attractive in that light, and Mackenzie turned away.

As he did so he heard a door open at the far end of the gallery, and two people emerged, still talking earnestly. The woman looked vaguely familiar, and Mackenzie took a moment trying to think where he'd seen her before, but when he couldn't he turned his attention to Patrick Ross.

He knew Ross had just celebrated his seventieth birthday here at the gallery; it had been enough of a public event to have made some of the local online news stories. Waterfront's owner was trim and grey-haired, and he looked ten years younger than he was. He turned keen brown eyes as Mackenzie moved forward, and frowned slightly.

'Can I help you with something?'

'Mr Ross,' Mackenzie began, with a quick, apologetic look at the director, 'forgive me for interrupting. My name's Mackenzie. I was just—'

'Ah!' Ross's expression cleared and he turned to his director. 'I'll leave that with you then, Isla. The deliveries are still coming in, but there's plenty of room downstairs and the thermostat's already set.'

Isla nodded, threw Mackenzie a faintly curious look and went back to her office. Ross smiled and held out his hand to Mackenzie, who shook it, realising what had happened; it was on the tip of his tongue to correct the mistake, but he reasoned that as long as he didn't come right out and *say* he wasn't Ade, he was doing no harm, and he might learn something that would kick his own suspicions into touch. He'd much rather that, than be proved right.

'Your assistant said you'd call,' Ross said, 'but it's good to meet face-to-face.'

Mackenzie nodded vaguely. 'I gather you had a look at the plans last night. What did you think?'

'It all looks very well laid out. Not that I'm an expert, of course.' Ross laughed. 'I'd like you to send your architect's copies over, so I can look in more detail and get a professional opinion. You understand I'd have to be sure any business has got the best chance of success, if I'm going to commit to it.' He gestured Mackenzie ahead of him, back into the heart of the gallery. 'Are you knowledgable about art, Mr Mackenzie?'

'Not in the least,' Mackenzie said, glancing around. 'It's that old cliché with me.'

'You know what you like.' Ross smiled. 'Aye, well, that's what it's for, when it comes down to it, isn't it?'

'For some. I gather you've had some success recently at auction.'

'And you're wondering if that's why I'm looking to invest?' Ross asked. 'It's part of it, yes.'

'And the other part?' Mackenzie heard the hard note in his own voice, but reasoned Ade would have every right to ask, too.

'Our mutual friend Will Kilbride made the suggestion. When he said you were reviving the Drumnacoille single malt, I couldn't resist looking into it.'

'You're a whisky man, then?'

'Naturally. I've always wanted to get in on the ground floor of a really good distillery, and this one has the advantage of actually producing a tried and tested product. Will it keep the old name?'

'I believe so,' Mackenzie said carefully. He'd heard his father and Ade discussing it, and that had seemed to be the agreement. 'And that's all?'

Ross stopped meandering among the artwork, and turned to face him with a speculative look. 'What else? I have money; I'm looking to invest it. Your project was recommended by a business partner of yours, and I want to be part of a distillery. Isn't that enough?'

Mackenzie had to admit it sounded pretty straightforward on the surface, but he had to be sure. 'Glencoille's all my family has,' he pointed out. 'It's taking every bit of our money, and more besides.' He had finally persuaded Ade to borrow against the family's biggest asset: Mackenzie's own Lightning Ridge black opal, which they'd recovered last year, but Ade hadn't been happy about it, and their father still didn't even know. 'Kilbride's not actually putting any money into the place,' he went on, 'so of course we're keen to attract investors. But we have to be sure any partners we bring in are—'

'Excuse me,' Ross said, holding up a hand. 'My pocket's ringing.' He gave Mackenzie a brief, but much cooler, smile and fished his phone from his pocket. 'Ross.'

Mackenzie politely turned away while Ross took the call, but Ross simply listened for a moment, then said, 'Brilliant. Can I call you back in five minutes? Perfect, thanks.'

He put his phone away and gestured to the door. 'You needn't worry about any ulterior motive on my part, Mr Mackenzie. Now, as you'll appreciate, I have a lot of work to do. As I'm sure you do.'

'Of course.'

'I hope I've allayed your concerns?'

Mackenzie side-stepped that one. 'You do appreciate why I had to ask?'

'Of course.' Ross was almost beaming now; it was faintly unsettling. 'I'll be in touch over the next week or so, and if you could have those plans sent over?'

'I will.'

'Or rather, ask Ade to send them.'

Mackenzie felt his expression freeze in the shape of the obliging smile he'd pasted onto it. 'Right.'

'That was him on the phone,' Ross explained, his own smile vanishing. 'I don't *appreciate*, as you put it, being taken for a fool. Who are you really?'

'My name *is* Mackenzie, but I'm Paul, Ade's brother.' He

shrugged. 'I was going to introduce myself properly, but you just assumed, and I thought this might be a good chance to...to look out for my family's interests.'

'By which you mean, to pry into my business dealings in an attempt to find out if I'm worthy of buying a stake in a ten-a-penny little camp site?'

'No.' Mackenzie could just imagine how the conversation with Ade would go over this, and it wasn't a pleasant thought. 'But the fact that my brother's an unknown quantity for you, with no track record, and that you've been introduced by a known embezzler and loan shark, has to give rise to certain questions, don't you think?'

'What's *your* business, Mr Mackenzie?'

'I'm an investigator. I have an agency in Abergarry.'

'Ah.' Ross's expression was one Mackenzie could cheerfully have wiped off with a wet flounder. 'That's why you think you can just wander in off the street and start interrogating me.'

'I've not done anything of the kind. I introduced myself, you jumped to a conclusion without letting me finish, and I decided that might be useful. I'm not here in a work capacity in any case,' he added. 'I'm here as a member of the Mackenzie family, in whose estate you're showing an unsolicited interest. And I've not lied to you once.'

'You might not have lied in the literal sense,' Ross said, his voice hardening, 'but you've been pretty bloody sly in the way you've gone about things. Downright underhand, I'd call it. Why not just come straight out and ask?'

'I didn't want Ade to know I've been poking my nose in,' Mackenzie admitted. 'I've already pissed him off about this today. But he's been living in New Zealand for years; he doesn't have the same knowledge as I do about your friend Kilbride.'

'That he's an embezzler and a loan shark? Hearsay.'

'He's a violent... Look, I don't want to get into what I know about him, but I've never trusted that bastard, and I never will. Ade though, he's so eager to get this estate built, he assumes everyone else has nothing but that in mind too. And as a result, he...takes a lot at face value.'

Ross tilted his head slightly, and his eyes narrowed. 'Are you saying he's naïve? He doesn't strike me that way.'

'No, not naïve.' Mackenzie hesitated, searching for the right words. 'He just sees things through a...a big lens of optimism and trust.'

'Like I said, naïve.'

'Jesus!' Mackenzie sighed. 'All right, in a way. But he's not stupid. He's a quick study with people, and he has a long memory for arseholery.' He stopped, realising he was probably doing more harm than good, but Ross, surprisingly, now had a faint light of amusement in his eyes.

'If you keep going, you're going to talk me right out of an investment that could speed up the development of your brother's business by about fifty per cent.'

Mackenzie shrugged. 'Noted. But I had to check into your reasons for wanting to be part of it.'

Ross folded his arms and studied him carefully. 'I don't object to you looking out for your family's interests. I actually applaud it in a way.' He wasn't quite smiling, though his frame and expression had relaxed. 'But unless you're directly involved in both the funding and the running of the Glencoille estate, you need to keep your trunk out. Okay?'

'Ade would say exactly the same.' Mackenzie chose not to mention his own contribution.

'Are you older, or is he?'

'He is. By five years.'

'Then listen to him,' Ross advised. 'And by the way, Will Kilbride isn't involved in the loan business anymore.'

'So Ade says.'

'Then again, listen to him.'

'I'll listen to anyone who can convince me.' Mackenzie turned to leave, then looked back. 'I was looking at that forged Italian painting you've got hanging over there.' He nodded in the direction of *Florence Cathedral*. 'Buggered if I can see how it's a fake. Would you mind showing me?'

'Why are you so interested in that?' Ross's expression closed down again, with startling suddenness. 'I thought you said you'd no interest in art. Or was that another lie?'

'Just curious,' Mackenzie said, keeping his tone mild, but feeling a prickling of curiosity at the swift change in Ross's demeanour. 'I know you're busy. I won't trouble you again.'

He stepped out into the sunshine, with a little wince of surprise after the selectively lit interior, and walked back to his car. It seemed he'd touched a nerve there; he'd have to find Maddy and have a chat with her about what she knew. Then he'd bite the bullet, confess his dubious morning's work to Ade, and hope he hadn't screwed things up too badly after all.

Chapter Eight

MADDY WAVED at Tas through her father's sitting room window, and left them to their day of lego and the left-over Easter chocolate – of which her dad had denied any knowledge. Tony Clifford might have spent his working life interrogating suspects, but he'd learned nothing from the best of them, she reflected with a little smile; as soon as she was out of sight there would be a Cadbury explosion in that kitchen of his, and he'd enjoy it every bit as much as Tas would.

She was reluctantly preparing to catch up on some much-neglected paperwork, and had just fitted the key into the ignition when her phone buzzed. 'Paul. Hi.'

'Are you in the office?'

'Just dropped Tas off, and heading there now. What's up?'

He sounded cagey, and a bit nervous. 'I did something a bit stupid.'

'Oh?'

'I pretended to be Ade, and went to see Patrick Ross.'

Maddy closed her eyes as he explained everything,

knowing full well how Ade would react to that. 'You're an idiot. What are you?'

'Tall, dark and handsome.'

She couldn't help laughing. 'Charis might think so, but she doesn't know any better, bless her. Your *brother*, now—'

'Ah, shut up.' But she could hear the grin in his voice. 'Anyway, now I've met Ross I wanted to talk to you about what you've found out from Hazel. It feels like we need to pool our knowledge.'

'I didn't know you were going to get involved.'

'Well, we've not much on, and to tell the truth this one's got me curious. Ross is definitely hiding something.'

'Okay. I was going up to Glencoille later. Why don't we both head up there now, and talk to her together? That'd save anything getting lost in translation.'

'Great. See you there.'

'I'll probably get there before you.'

He gave a light snort. 'The way you drive, that'd be true even if you were back in Glasgow. That poor car.'

'Have fun telling Ade what you did,' she countered, and ended the call before Paul's expletive could melt her phone.

She could hear the racing engines and clanking sounds from the bulldozers even before she reached Glencoille, and as she drove between the gate pillars she saw Hazel in the yard, talking to Ade and someone who was presumably a foreman. All three were wearing ear defenders, Ade was holding up a plan and gesturing, and the safety-helmeted foreman was standing by with his arms folded as Hazel made notes.

According to Hazel, the site office would remain as a

portakabin until everything else was built, and then would be removed to make way for a single-storey stone building, which would then be the permanent estate office. It appeared to be this that Ade was discussing, and he was too involved in it to pay attention to the arrival of another vehicle, but Hazel looked over and raised a hand in greeting.

She was dressed, as always, in her scrappy-looking jeans and jacket, worn with the familiar don't-give-a-damn insouciance, but she still gave off an air of confidence and authority though Maddy knew she didn't feel it. Even when she'd been wearing the humiliating community payback bib she'd managed to look as if she was the person you went to, to ask questions. The dark hair had been shorter then, and had blown around her face in a mass of curls, whereas today it was pulled back into a haphazard ponytail secured by a scrunchie. But her manner still marked her out as someone important. Ade certainly didn't protest as she abandoned their conversation and came over to meet Maddy at her car. He didn't even turn his head to see where she was going.

'All right, face-ache?' Hazel shouted over the sound of the diggers as she came over. 'Have you found...' she looked around, a little nervously, 'him?'

Maddy shook her head, wincing at the loud drilling, and waited for it to stop. 'Not yet. Paul and I thought maybe we could have a chat with you, if Ade doesn't mind?' She looked past Hazel, but Ade was still deep in discussion. 'He won't be long.'

'I told you,' Hazel said, looking worried now, 'I can't afford to pay you, and if you're both getting involved—'

'You haven't asked us to do any of this. Paul just... Well, I'll let him fill you in when he gets here. He'll have questions though, so if you don't mind it'll be better if we go inside.'

'You can forget that.' Right on cue the drilling sound started again, making Maddy's fillings rattle, and Hazel grimaced. 'The office isn't sound-proofed,' she shouted. 'I can't even answer the phone while that's going on. But we can take a walk up to the distillery if you like?'

Maddy nodded. 'I'll text Paul and let him know where to find us.'

'I'll go and tell Ade where we're going.'

Maddy watched her cross to Ade and touch him lightly on the arm to get his attention. He lifted one of his ear defenders, and when Hazel leaned in close to speak to him Maddy was half amused and half alarmed to find herself reacting with a little pinch of jealousy. *Come on, Clifford! For God's sake!* But when Ade turned to follow Hazel's pointing finger and his eyes met Maddy's, the unguarded smile on his face was enough, and she had to accept that she and Ade were definitely unfinished business. While Hazel explained things to him, Maddy wandered over to the office to send a brief text to Paul: *gone up to the distillery where it's quiet. Join us there.* She added, *when you've come clean to Ade*, but backspaced over that part. It was nothing to do with her.

Hazel led her away from the noisy yard and up the narrow path for a couple of hundred yards. It wasn't until they reached the place where the river widened, and the rushing sound of the weir drowned out the distant rattle of diggers, that the distillery was really noticeable; a low building designed to look something like an old bothy, to suit its surroundings.

'They've got on well with it,' Maddy observed. 'Even more so than the other day.'

'Frank's priority. He wants to get this part of the business up and running before anything else.'

'Naturally. Yet he's the one bellyaching about not being

able to move into a proper house yet.' Maddy shook her head. 'He could always move in here, I suppose. Once the lock's fixed, that is,' she added, as Hazel pushed open the door. 'He's a bit paranoid about his privacy, after living so long at The Heathers.'

'It'll be fitted as soon as the equipment arrives.' Hazel led Maddy into the cool interior. 'Decorators are still in and out all the time, at the minute, since there's a bit more to do in here. None of the walls are done yet; they're all bare concrete, but that one's going to be faced with stone to give it that authentic look inside as well as out.' She pointed. 'They're anticipating visitors just as much as they are direct business.'

Maddy looked around. It was very much what she had expected from a building in the final stages of completion; there was a small table, on which stood an open bag of sugar, a jar of instant coffee and a kettle, beside a box of tea bags and a couple of irredeemably stained teaspoons. Camping chairs were dotted here and there, along with hand tools, rolls of masking tape and paint tins where decorators had left them at the end of their shifts. Apart from this usual building site debris, the main room was very neat and square, but Maddy could see that the rooms leading off it were small and low-ceilinged, with built-in cubby holes and a short, sloped passage-way. Until Hazel pointed it out, she hadn't even noticed there were no steps, and that the passageways were, deceptively, wide enough to accommodate wheelchairs.

'Ade wanted to give the impression of tradition and age,' Hazel said, 'but it needs to be accessible too. No doubt Mr Kilbride's checked the plans, just to make sure.'

'Kilbride hasn't invested, has he? As far as I knew he'd just drawn up some kind of mutual promotion contract between here and Thistle.'

'He's been up here once or twice. That Patrick Ross bloke came up with him last night, too, and I had to show him the plans.'

'Really?' Maddy was unable to hide her reaction, and Hazel frowned.

'Why?'

'That's one of the reasons Paul wanted to talk,' Maddy said. 'He went to see Ross this morning. Look, I don't want to get ahead of myself. Let's just wait until he gets here.' She noted Hazel's suddenly nervous look. 'Why don't you fill in the time by telling me what all this soggy socks business is about?'

'The rally?'

'Aye. Paul will know what you're talking about, and Ade seems to as well, but I haven't got a clue. I don't see that there's enough room for bike racing on that bit of ground you were talking about.'

'Oh, it's not that kind of rally.' Hazel brushed plaster dust off a deep window ledge onto the floor and sat down. 'It's just a weekend party really. The host club organises the site, and bands or a DJ, or both. A bar if necessary, but sometimes it's near a pub so there's no need to get a licence. Then they send out invites to a bunch of other bike clubs, everyone gets together and just...has a great time.'

'Sounds pretty good to me,' Maddy said.

'There's games late on the Saturday afternoon,' Hazel went on. 'After we've had a run out somewhere. Tug-o-war, crank-throwing, three-legged egg and spoon. Stuff like that. And on Saturday night they give out the prizes.'

'Prizes?'

'Best bike, oldest bike, longest distance travelled, and so on. Club turnout's a popular one; highest percentage of club members at the same rally. It's basically just a weekend-long piss-up, with music and camping. A bit like a mini-festival, if you like.' Hazel's expression turned a little sad, then. 'Dad and I had such a great time, every time we went on one of these together. The friendships, with people you sometimes don't see from one year to the next...it's hard to explain. But the club helped me through some...some *really* shit times. Especially Griff.'

'And that's how you met him? Through the club?'

'Aye. He used to belong to a back-patch club, but they got a bit...competitive with some of the other MCs.'

'Dangerously competitive?'

'It was heading that way,' Hazel said. 'It wasn't his idea of fun, so he left them. He met Dad at a rally down south, a few years ago. He's a bit of a magician when it comes to Japanese bikes, and Dad's Zed—mine now—was giving him a bit of bother on the Sunday morning when we were leaving. He fixed it up, and when Dad realised Griff was local he invited him along to a Caledonia Road Riders meeting, and that was it. Now Griff's our chairman.'

Maddy was about to reply when the door opened and Paul came in, looking grim-faced, and Maddy guessed he'd spoken to Ade. But when she gave him a questioning look, he shook his head briefly; his expression was evidently just in anticipation.

She felt a twinge of sympathy for him, knowing how quietly glad he was to have his brother back in his life, and how annoyed with himself he was. But the dark look vanished as he smiled at them both, and, as always, it transformed his face completely. When he smiled like that, he and Ade could be twins.

'I've only briefly mentioned to Hazel what you told me,' she said. 'I thought it was best to go back to the start. Talk about what we know, and what Hazel knows or thinks, and take it from there. Hazel, why don't you start? Tell Paul what we discussed after the police came up to speak to you.

Paul leaned against a wall and stared at the one opposite, while Hazel told him all about the connection between her father and Linda Sturdy, and about the photo they'd found amongst her father's belongings. She explained what little she understood about Leslie Warrender and his possible return, and he didn't interrupt, except to ask how Graeme had seemed when the news of Warrender's death had come back.

'He was a wreck,' Hazel said, then frowned. 'He seemed to be, at least. Especially so soon after losing Mum.'

'But now you believe he actually helped Warrender, so that was all an act?'

Hazel looked as if she was about to agree, then she paused. 'No, I don't think it was all an act,' she said at length. 'He *was* broken. But maybe for a different reason than I thought at the time.'

'Betrayal?' Maddy ventured. 'It seems fair to say that if Warrender killed Linda Sturdy because he realised she recognised him, his disappearance must have been over something a lot more serious than defrauding Andrew Silcott and worrying it'd come out. You skip the country for that, you don't fake your own death. Especially not when the victim of your fraud is already dead.'

'Shit.' Hazel stiffened. 'You don't suppose...' Her words dried up, but her expression as she turned to Maddy was drawn and sick-looking.

'Are you thinking that maybe *Warrender* was the one who killed your mum?' Maddy asked quietly. 'Is it likely she might have found out what he was doing, and threatened to tell someone?'

'I, I don't... Maybe.'

Paul frowned. 'But then why would your dad have helped him to escape?'

'Maybe he didn't find that out until later,' Maddy guessed. 'He might have thought he was helping him get away from someone else.'

Hazel spoke in a low voice, staring down at her hands, at her own short-nailed fingers twisting her heavy silver rings around and around. 'Maybe that's why he got rid of all the pictures of them together. Why he didn't tell the police when he realised, because then he'd have had to admit he helped Warrender escape.' Her hand went to her necklace, running it restlessly up and down the fine chain. 'He'd have gone to prison, and I was already halfway there.'

'He'd have lost you for good,' Maddy said. 'Haze, you're going to have to be *so* careful until Warrender's picked up.'

'You can't go to the police!' Hazel's head jerked up, her eyes wide and horrified.

'We can't not,' Maddy pointed out. 'If Warrender's a murder suspect, or we believe he might be, we can't just sit on it. He's dangerous. If he knows, or thinks, that Linda told you he's back, he'll be after you.'

'I don't know how he *could* know she recognised him,' Hazel said, her voice rising. 'She didn't even know his real name until I showed her the picture! And she didn't see him after that, so she had no chance to give anything away.'

'So you don't think he's the one who killed her.' Maddy chewed at her lip, still worried. 'We can't ignore the possibility though, especially if he really has killed before.'

'Did she visit her dad in prison?' Paul asked.

'We don't know,' Maddy said. 'It's going to be hard to find out, too, and until then we have to assume she did, which means *he* could have told anyone. Warrender's going to be lying very low if he suspects that's the case, which isn't going to make our job any easier.'

'So – *are* you going to the police then?' Hazel asked. 'It's an unsolved murder, so won't they be obliged to investigate?'

'It's a pretty safe bet they won't be able to do anything about it,' Maddy said, 'but yeah, we have to at least report it.'

'How do you mean, not do anything?'

'There's no new evidence,' Paul said, 'and certainly not enough to go pulling in some innocent bloke with a totally different name, who we can be pretty sure has all the right paperwork to prove he is who he says he is. I highly doubt Warrender's DNA is on file.'

'If we're wrong though, and they do approach him, we'll only alert him and drive him back underground.' Maddy scowled. 'How do we avoid that?'

'Worst comes to worst, we can't.' Paul shrugged. 'But they'll let him go again, and in a weird way that might actually make him feel more secure. Like he's passed some kind of test, and then hopefully he'll get careless. Either way wouldn't be a disaster.' He levered himself off the wall. 'At least if we do go to the police we can't be done later on for withholding evidence, or any of the other joyful little things they could throw at us. And while it's cooking away on their back burner, we carry on looking for him ourselves and getting together something stronger against him. And protecting you,' he added to Hazel. 'One of us will be with you the whole time, from now until we've found him. Okay?'

'Okay...' Hazel looked doubtful. 'But how? You've both got your own stuff to be getting on with.'

'Who else do you trust?' Paul took out a scrappy-looking notebook. 'Give me some names, and if you're not with any of those people, we'll make sure one of us is nearby.'

'Griff. That's Dave Griffin,' Hazel clarified, still looking uncertain about the whole thing. 'Pretty much anyone in the bike club, actually. Ade, of course; Breda Kelly, who was Linda's friend; and my aunt, Isla Munro.'

'Munro?' Paul looked interested. 'From the gallery?'

'Yes, she's Ross's director.'

'And her son must be the one Jamie's been hanging around lately. Charis is getting twitchy. Nothing against your wee cousin,' he added quickly, to Hazel. 'I've never met the lad. It's just that there's a bit of an age gap, and Jamie's...well, he's been through a lot, and Charis is kind of protective.'

Hazel nodded. 'Don't worry. Dylan might be a bit of a live wire, but he's a good kid.'

'Can you go and stay with your aunt?' Paul asked, writing the name down, and Maddy saw the look of panic cross Hazel's face.

'No,' she interjected. 'That's Hazel's old home. It was where...' She tailed away, not wanting to come out with a blunt explanation, but Paul had twigged.

'I didn't realise,' he said. 'I'm sorry.' He looked at Maddy. 'Can she come and stay with you instead, then? Just until this gets sorted?'

'Would you be happy with that?' Maddy asked Hazel. 'You could have Tas's room. I'll ask my dad to let him stay over for a few nights. They'll both be delighted, to be honest.'

Hazel nodded. 'That'd be great, actually, if you don't mind.'

'I'll meet you at your place after work, and help you pack up a few things.' Maddy gave her an apologetic look. 'You should leave your bike there though, sorry. You don't want to advertise where you are, and I haven't got a garage.'

'I'll lock it in the shed,' Hazel said. 'I won't need it for the rally either. Griff's taking his work van up with all the equipment in it, so I'll go with him.'

'So that's settled,' Paul said, sliding the notebook back into his pocket. 'You'll either be at work, where Ade can keep an eye out; with your club, in which case Griff's your man; at your aunt's place, or at Maddy's. And we're all just a phone call away, but we'll make sure you've got the landline numbers as well. My place, our office, your office.'

Maddy was glad to see Hazel looking easier in her mind now. 'We'll go to the police today,' she said, 'and tell them what we think. Once they've laughed us out of there, we'll get to work tracking this Warrender bloke down, okay?'

'Okay. And thanks, both of you.'

'We can start by thinking about how we might be able to get our hands on that photo,' Maddy mused. 'My brother might be able to help us there.' She caught Paul's look, and sighed. 'It can't hurt to ask, can it?'

'You know what he'll say. Better think of something else.'

Maddy turned to Hazel to explain. 'Nick's working on Linda's case, which would have been perfect, but he's not one for bending the—'

'Breaking,' Paul stressed. '*Breaking* the rules. Don't do it, Mads; it'll put him in a rotten position. Let the poor bloke do his job this time without risking it again, aye?'

Maddy nodded reluctantly. He was right, but it would put a serious crimp in things if she didn't even know what Warrender looked like, particularly that mole. 'Okay, I'll leave him be. Hopefully there'll be some photos online from some old exhibition or other. And now, Mr Mackenzie, I think you have some grovelling to do, don't you?'

It was Paul's turn to grimace. 'I suppose I ought to. He's going to kill me though.'

'In the light of what we've just been talking about, I think you going to see Ross is justified. He's bound to see that.'

'But I went to talk about money laundering, not art fraud and murder.'

'*Money* laundering?' Hazel stared at him. 'What the fuck? You don't think that's what he wants to do at Glencoille, do you?'

'The thought definitely crossed my mind.'

'Don't blame you, actually,' Hazel said, considering. 'He seems a bit of a creep if you ask me.'

Paul shrugged. 'There you go, then. But yeah, I need to have a chat with Ade before things get out of hand.'

'Good.' Maddy looked at Hazel. 'Thanks for filling me in about the rallies thing. Maybe I'll pop up when you put yours on. In my capacity as bodyguard, of course. I mean, it sounds like *no* fun whatsoever.'

Hazel laughed. 'God, I hope it's sorted by then. It's not for over a week yet.'

'On the bank holiday weekend then?' Paul asked as he pulled open the door and let the sounds and the light from outside flood into the bare little room.

'Aye. And with all those mystical celebrations of that sacred date,' Hazel intoned in a dramatic voice.

'Ah, yes,' Maddy said. 'Beltane. Celebration of Maia, a time for—'

'Star Wars day,' Hazel and Paul said together, and grinned at one another. 'May the fourth be with you,' Hazel added, then shook her head 'And you with a five-year-old, Maddy? I can see I'm going to have to educate you over the next few days.'

They reached the yard, and Paul groaned quietly. 'Oh, shit, here goes.'

Maddy followed his gaze to see Ade, in the office doorway, raising a hand to them and starting down the steps.

'Got a message for you, Paul. From Patrick Ross.' He looked annoyed as he approached his brother, and Maddy rested a comforting hand on Paul's rigid back.

'He'll be fine,' she murmured. 'It wasn't deliberate, was it? And he knows it was done with the best of intentions.' She saw Hazel looking curiously at them both, and shook her head slightly. This wasn't the time for explanations.

Ade reached them. 'Ross wants you to call him back, urgently.' He handed his own phone to Paul. 'Quicker if you just use this one. What's it about, anyway? I didn't know you knew him.'

'Tell you after.' Paul took the phone, and Maddy had to appreciate the irony of Ade's phone number popping up on Ross's phone, when Paul was the one using it. 'Hello, Mr Ross, this isn't Ade, it's his brother.' He paused and shot Maddy a quick look, and she read a welcome, though dark, humour in his expression. 'I know,' he said, 'I thought the same, and I've said I'm sorry. Anyway, what can I do for you?'

He listened for a moment, said his goodbyes, and handed the phone back to Ade. 'Text me his number, would you?' He turned back to Maddy. 'He wants to meet me, but at his place not the gallery. Must be something private.'

Maddy tensed. 'Want me to come with you?'

He shook his head. 'Let's keep our powder dry where you're concerned; it could be useful to have someone in reserve that he doesn't know.'

'Okay. I'm assuming he's calling because Warrender's got in touch with him.'

'That's my guess too.'

'In which case we should hold off on talking to the police.'

'Agreed. At least for now.'

'Good,' she said. 'Go and see what he has to say, and for God's sake be careful.'

Ade had been watching them in turn like a spectator at a tennis match, and she smiled at him as Paul jogged back to his car. 'I'll tell you everything,' she promised. 'Meantime, what kind of host doesn't offer his guests a Hobnob or two?'

She followed him and Hazel towards the office, but took one last look over her shoulder. Paul could be his own worst enemy sometimes; accusing Patrick Ross of money laundering had been a poor enough move, but including William Kilbride in the accusation had doubtless been a much worse one. He needed to keep a better guard on his temper and his tongue, or coming clean to Ade would be the least of his worries.

Chapter Nine

Earlier that morning, Patrick Ross had stared after the departing Mackenzie and muttered an oath even his easy-going wife would have flinched at. Despite the deception, he'd been feeling okay about the man until he'd professed a sudden interest in that bloody painting; what did he know about it? Ross didn't for one minute accept that he was *just curious*. He'd followed Mackenzie to the front door, though at a much slower pace and already pulling out his phone ready to return Ade's call, but as he passed the front desk his receptionist held up a finger to stall him while she finished her own phone conversation.

He drummed his fingers on the counter as he waited, and eventually, sensing his annoyance, she fumbled about one-handed and brought out an envelope. She held the phone against her shoulder and hissed, 'This came through the door while you were talking.'

Ross glimpsed the handwriting and snatched the envelope from her hands in his rush to pull open the door, but when he got outside he could only see Mackenzie's car rounding the end of the street, then disappearing. He went back into the gallery and looked down at the now crumpled envelope, pulled out the single sheet, and straightened it. The note was short, and left no room for misinterpretation.

Your place. 11:am. LW.

Half an hour's time. Ross's first reaction was anger, but that was followed very quickly by a cool trickle of fear; Warrender must know the house would be empty, which meant he knew Julie's routine. How long had he been back in the area then, and watching?

'Everything all right, Pat?' Isla had materialised beside him, as silent as her role required for moving unobtrusively around the gallery. Usually this was an admirable trait, but Ross's nerves were wire-tight and he nearly dropped the note. He shoved it into his pocket and hoped he sounded casual as he responded.

'Absolutely. I've just had a letter from an old friend. I'm going to nip into town and meet him for coffee, okay?'

Isla nodded. 'Of course, but we're expecting two more exhibits by courier today. Will you be back in?'

Ross nearly said he'd be fine, but it occurred to him that he didn't want people to assume he was, just in case it turned out not to be true. 'I hope so, but I'll call if not. If I don't,' he added, 'and I don't come back, you call me.'

Isla blinked in surprise, and dutifully nodded again, but didn't quite mask her resentment at his perceived swanning-off during this busy time. 'Of course. I'll sign for the paintings; you enjoy your catch up.'

Ross drove the short distance to his detached house near Culloden, on the outskirts of Inverness, as if the road were on fire; he only hoped he wouldn't wake up in a week or so to a bunch of speeding tickets on the door mat. There was a brand new red Volvo in the drive, and the man behind the wheel twisted in his seat as Ross drove up alongside. Ross had been trying to remember what Warrender looked like, and although he couldn't picture him exactly, he'd still expected to recognise him. He didn't.

He got out of his car and waited for Warrender to do the same, and even when they were face to face and his memory re-awakened, he could barely equate the shrunken man who stood in front of him with the burly, long-haired artist he'd known twenty or more years ago. He did remember the bushy eyebrows though, and when he mentally covered the almost-bald head with a mass of dark curls, he could believe they were the same person. But only just. He was sure Warrender could still only be in his sixties, but the man looked older than he himself did.

'Inside, quickly,' Warrender said. He was looking around them apprehensively, though there was no-one in sight and the house was shielded from its nearest neighbours by tall hedges on three sides.

Ross was already selecting his front door key, with fingers that refused to stop shaking. 'What is it you want?'

'I said inside.'

Ross got the door open and turned back to try and make a note of the Volvo's registration plate, but Warrender just gave him a tight smile.

'It's a hire car. I'm returning it as soon as I've left you. Rented legitimately, under the name Dr. Michael Booth, if you do bother to check.'

Once in his own home, Ross felt some of his confidence returning. 'This is about the painting, I take it?'

'I do feel you owe me something for keeping quiet about it for so long,' Warrender said, sitting down and making himself comfortable.

'Do I bollocks!' Ross didn't want to sit; instead he leaned against the closed door, as if he had the upper hand rather than Warrender. 'You were the one who instigated this whole thing. *You* were the one who stole it in the first place, and then created that fake. Which the insurers picked up pretty damned quickly,' he added, 'so it can't even have been that good.'

Warrender's fingers tightened on the arm of his chair. 'That was the idea, remember?'

'I'd still call it insulting, how quickly they identified it. Especially from a so-called Renaissance expert.' Ross could see his goading was having an effect, and although it helped his own state of mind, he dialled it down a bit. 'Anyway, here we are. And it's taken you twenty years to decide I owe you. I wonder what it can *possibly* be that's brought you back?'

'It's true, I heard about your little Christie's windfall,' Warrender conceded. 'Forty million, wasn't it?'

'Something in that region. Where have you been all this time?'

'Not that it's any of your business, but I live in France now. I used your payment to set up a new life, just as...just as I wanted to. But it left me broke again, and I'm a bit fed up with scraping a living now.' Warrender sat forward, his hands linked, and fixed his watery blue eyes on Ross's. 'I know the fragrant Julie is due home around lunch time, so let's move this on apace, shall we?'

Ross looked at the clock. 'Okay, let's get the main point out of the way. How much?'

'I'll not be greedy. Taking into account the profit you made on it, and are still making – I notice the original's still got pride of place in your gallery – and not forgetting inflation over twenty years, I'm willing to accept two million. You give me that, in cash, and I'll destroy my painting and never trouble you again.'

Ross almost laughed, but the situation was too absurd. 'Two million? How the hell do you plan to explain away that kind of money?'

'That's my business. But don't worry, I have a way of cleaning it.'

'Cleaning it! Jesus, I've stepped into a TV melodrama. And what if I refuse?' *Or arrange for you to disappear*, his mind added, but he shied away from that; it was a step too far in the *Ozark* direction.

'The painting's in secure storage,' Warrender said. 'I've given the entry code to a friend at home, the same person who owns the...the laundry, if you want to call it that. If I don't make contact at my regular time he's under instruction to gain entry to the unit. He'll find the forgery and a sworn statement attesting to everything, and he'll make sure the police do too. So I suppose it's up to you to make sure no harm comes to me, isn't it?' he added with a thin little smile. 'You're my own personal guardian angel. Who'd have thought, eh?'

'How long do I have?' Ross asked, in a tight voice. His anger was simmering, low and quiet at the moment, but Warrender's attitude was about to send it boiling. 'I can't just get that kind of money on demand; there'll be questions.'

'I'll be generous with my time.' Warrender sounded as if his words had slid out without forethought. 'I don't plan to return home after this anyway.'

'You're *staying* here?'

Warrender's guard had slipped, and now he let it drop altogether. He stood up and walked to the window to stare out at the impeccable shrubs beyond. 'I wasn't born here, and I have no family here, but I love the place, and I want to end my days here, eventually. This would allow me to do that.' He looked back at an incredulous Ross. 'I never wanted to leave in the first place, but I had no choice.'

'Which is exactly why this makes no sense! You thought I was that much of a threat that you faked your own death, so what's changed?'

'I didn't...' Warrender shook his head. 'I'm just tired of all this now. This can be an end to it, can't it? Our paths never need to cross, but if they do it'll be Michael Booth you're talking to. Leslie Warrender's dead, Pat. Surely we can let him lie.'

Ross still couldn't believe what he was hearing. 'How can you expect to just pick up here, where you left off? Even with a new name?'

'Sturdy's not getting out of jail, and no-one else here knows me, now Graeme Douglas has died.'

'He's got a daughter, for God's sake!'

'She's still here?' Warrender looked startled, then shrugged. 'She was just a bairn when I left; she'll never know me now. She barely took any notice of me when I was around, and she's hardly going to be looking out for a dead man anyway. Look, I even had a job interview with someone who should've recognised me, and she didn't.' He stopped pacing and shoved his face disconcertingly close to Ross's. '*You* were the one person, apart from Graeme and his wife, who knew me best, and you didn't recognise me either, did you? I could see that right from the start.'

Ross conceded the point, and another glance at the clock

told him he was running out of time as well as arguments. 'So how long have I got, and how do I contact you?'

'I'll give you until bank holiday Monday. You don't contact me, I'll call you from a pay phone, once a day, until you tell me you've got the money. Once you've paid up I'll get my friend to burn the painting and the memo, and they'll send me a video to prove it's been done.'

'And how do I know you've not spent the last few months painting another one?'

Warrender looked so startled at the idea that Ross believed him when he shook his head. 'I just... I haven't. You'll just have to trust me; he'll burn it, and then it'll be over.'

'And you'll have your cosy new life.'

'It's really not so much to ask for, is it?' Warrender's smile turned chilly, and the sad aura vanished. 'It's only what *you've* had, ever since Andrew Silcott and Matthew Sturdy got up close and personal with a golf club.' He extended a hand, which Ross ignored. 'I'll see myself out.'

As soon as he'd left Ross took out his phone and was about to call Kilbride, but hesitated, and instead hit Ade Mackenzie's number. 'Hi, it's Patrick. I don't suppose you'd let me have your brother's mobile number, would you?' Ade politely demurred, but offered to give him the office number, and Ross bit back a mild oath. 'No, thanks. Get him to call me, then, would you? It's business. And it's urgent.'

Julie had breezed in at her usual time, around half an hour later, and seemed to notice nothing amiss. She chatted to Ross as she moved about the kitchen putting together a light lunch, and he casually told her he was expecting someone, and might have to pop out for a quiet conversation.

'Someone from the gallery?' Julie turned a teasing look on him. 'Or one of those investors you pretend to hate so much?'

'The brother of one actually,' he said, returning her smile with an ease that surprised him. 'It's a family business I'm thinking of going into, so he has a few issues I can clear up for him.'

Julie didn't question it any more deeply, and she greeted Mackenzie with a polite smile when he arrived, before Ross took him off into the study and closed the door.

'Thanks for coming.'

'What can I do for you?'

Mackenzie's tone was even, professional and polite, but Ross remembered the holier-than-thou attitude he had shown when he'd demanded to know Ross's intentions; he'd been acting like the father of the bride. He wondered for a moment if he'd made a mistake, but there was something about Leslie Warrender that he didn't trust, and he was running out of options.

'Look,' Mackenzie said, evidently reading his mind, 'I know we didn't exactly get off on the right foot, but—'

'Wait, let me call someone,' Ross heard himself say. He wasn't even sure why he was doing this, his mouth seemed to be operating on a different plane to his logic, but he pulled out his phone and called Kilbride.

'That agency in Abergarry you were talking about,' he said, as soon as Kilbride answered. 'Is it run by someone called Paul Mackenzie?' He saw Mackenzie's raised eyebrows but didn't respond.

'That's one of the partners, aye. Maddy Clifford's the other.'

'And is he trustworthy?'

'Have you heard something from Warrender?' Kilbride said at once, his voice sharpening.'

Ross didn't want to say too much until he'd had a chance to talk to Mackenzie. 'He was here earlier,' he said carefully. There was a pause, then, when he'd made it obvious he wasn't going to say any more about it yet, Kilbride spoke again.

'Okay, I'd say you can trust Mackenzie, as long as you tell him everything. But don't try to fuck him over,' he warned. 'He's not overly fond of the police, but he won't hesitate to go to them, if you do.'

'He's not *overly fond* of you either,' Ross said, and Mackenzie looked questioningly at him again. 'Does that change your opinion of him?'

Kilbride gave a soft laugh. 'To be honest, I don't blame him. But he seems like a straight up bloke, and if he's anything like his brother you'll be in good hands. If you think he can help you, call him.'

'He's here,' Ross said. 'We had words earlier.'

'I see. And you're still thinking about asking for his help?'

'Like you said, he seems decent enough.'

'Aye, well, his partner's the one I've dealt with in the past, but she'll not have a word said against him. Besides...' He fell silent for a moment, and Ross was about to check that the connection hadn't dropped out, then Kilbride came back. 'His dad was an old pal of mine, years ago, when the two lads were just kids. I reckon they've both been brought up right.'

Ross looked over at Mackenzie again, trying to imagine the tall, powerfully built man as a child. He couldn't do it. 'Thanks. I'll call you later.' He faced Mackenzie again. 'Okay, I'm ready to talk.'

'Who was that on the phone?'

'Doesn't matter.'

Mackenzie's pleasant features remained polite, but there was a glint in the hazel eyes now. 'Kilbride.'

Ross didn't confirm or deny. 'If any word of this gets out to the authorities, I'm going to withdraw my offer of investment in the Glencoille distillery.'

'Threats now?' The glint became a flash. 'Then maybe you'd better get someone else to help you.' Mackenzie stood up, and Ross rose with him, a little dismayed at having overplayed his hand already, but trying to keep his expression neutral.

'I was given to understand you're no friend of the police,' he said, a little scathingly.

'I'm no enemy of them either,' Mackenzie said. 'The ones I had trust issues with before are... Well, they aren't problems anymore. If I feel like anyone's in direct danger, I won't think twice about it.'

'No-one's in danger except me,' Ross said. 'I need help, Mackenzie.' His desperation was embarassing, but it was too late now. 'Can I count on you?'

Mackenzie looked at him steadily. 'Okay. Here's my offer. You tell me what's going on, and I'll tell you if I think I can help.'

'And if you can't?'

'Then as long as it doesn't hurt an innocent, I'll just walk away.'

Ross considered for a moment, then nodded. 'Fair enough.' He indicated for Mackenzie to sit down again, and took his own seat. In a halting voice he told the investigator what he'd told Kilbride on Sunday night, and what Warrender had said today. Mackenzie sat quietly for a moment, processing it all.

'So,' he said at length, 'what do you want me to do? It seems like he literally just wants a quiet life, and the money, and you've got it to give him.'

Ross stared at him, appalled. 'Are you saying I should just pay up and shut up?'

'No.' Mackenzie leaned forward on the desk, and his voice reflected the sudden steel in his expression. 'Because things have taken an extremely nasty turn already, haven't they?'

Ross frowned. 'What do you mean?'

'Linda Sturdy. She recognised him, and now she's dead.'

'No.' Ross was adamant in this, at least. 'No, no, no. He swears she sat through an entire job interview and didn't realise who he was. Maybe never even knew him.'

'And you *believe* him? This man who stole, who committed fraud, faked his own death, and is now *blackmailing* you?' Mackenzie shook his head. 'It seems obvious he killed Linda to stop her telling anyone else he was back.'

The derisive snort was out before Ross could stop it. 'Bit disproportionate, wouldn't you say?'

'Precisely. Which means he's got a lot more to hide than some stupid, twenty-year-old fraud.'

'Like what?'

'Never mind that.' Mackenzie's face reflected a moment of real anger, just for an instant, but he didn't elaborate. 'But it also means anyone else Linda might have told about him is in danger. We think that probably includes her father, but there's nothing much we can do about him, given where he is. He's probably safer than anyone else, ironically enough.' He sat back, arms folded. 'So I want you to give me everything you know. *Everything*. Okay? *Then* we can talk about getting you out of this pathetic blackmail thing.'

Ross experienced passionate relief that the ferocious gaze was no longer focused on him, but pushing at his conscience now was how he'd reminded Warrender of Graeme Douglas's daughter; that scruffy, faintly bolshy, but rather nice young woman up at the building site. Warrender might have dismissed that, in the moment, but it would be sure to play on his mind once he had time to think, and she'd be easy enough to find – what would happen then? He sat on the information, hoping to Christ none of them ever had cause to find out.

'Look,' he said after a moment, 'maybe you're right, and you're not the one to help.'

Mackenzie nodded calmly. 'Okay. But you do realise that we're going to have to go to the police. We'd planned to anyway,' he added with a shrug, as Ross started to his feet again in dismay. 'I just wanted to hear what you had to say first, in case it was helpful.'

'You sneaky—'

'Don't worry,' Mackenzie held up a hand, 'I'll keep what you've told me out of it, as promised. But they'll be sure to pay you a visit, and good luck keeping a lid on what you've just told me, once they start digging.'

Ross hesitated. 'Are you saying that you'll keep them out of it, if I hire you?'

'Not completely. I'm just saying we could delay it. Look,' he went on earnestly, 'we need to find this bastard, and once we've got him he'll be in no position to go blackmailing anyone, will he?'

'But, like you say, once the police start digging into him they're sure to come up with a connection to me.'

'So deny it,' Mackenzie said. 'You've got the original painting; all he's got is a mad story no-one'll believe, and a fake picture stashed away somewhere with *his* prints all over it. With any luck we'll be able to bargain that code out of him, anyway, before we have to involve the police.' His eyes narrowed as he looked at Ross. 'What's that look for?'

'What look?'

'The one that says, *oh yeah, there was something else...*'

Ross sat back down and fidgeted with his pen pot. 'I was thinking of hiring someone. A...a heavy, I suppose you'd call it, to get the address and the entry code out of him.'

'A what? A *heavy*?' Mackenzie's incredulous expression cleared. 'Oh, aye. Kilbride again, I assume.'

'It wasn't his idea,' Ross said. 'He wasn't keen on it, kept reminding me he's out of that business.'

'People like him are never out of it,' Mackenzie said grimly. 'And where were you going to send this thug, in order to get the information?'

Ross looked away. 'I don't know yet,' he confessed. 'I hadn't thought it through that far, and I probably wouldn't have done it anyway. But you have to understand,' his voice rose again, 'if I got done for fraud, and ended up doing time in the same place as the bloke who killed—'

'Warrender won't bring it up, even if he gets pulled in,' Mackenzie said, dismissing it. 'He's not going to want to add to his list of crimes, is he?'

'But he won't be making those daily phone calls, either, to keep the painting hidden.'

Mackenzie didn't look convinced. 'Don't worry about that. Anyone seriously in the business of laundering money isn't going to risk getting involved in anything like that, for small fry like Warrender. Shouldn't be too hard to find the lock-up anyway, once we find our Dr Booth.'

Ross felt relief creeping tentatively though him. 'So... You're saying I've got nothing to worry about, provided you or your partner can get hold of him?'

'I'd be surprised. Now,' Mackenzie took out a messy, post-it stuffed note book, 'we can help each other. Tell me everything again. What you've already told me, plus dates, and anyone else who might be involved, however distantly. By that, I mean art suppliers, framers, the insurance company that did the original valuation, the lot. And then we can talk about how we can coax this blackmailing little rat out into the open.'

Chapter Ten

Jamie was back in the library, and deep into a brand new investigation with his new literary detective friends, when the voice filtered through the happy haze. 'You'll wear your eyes out, mate.'

He looked up to see Dylan Munro sliding into a seat at one of the computers across the way. 'All right?'

'Will be, once I've done this.' Dylan tapped quickly on the keyboard, then leaned across and hissed to Jamie, who'd already returned to his book. 'Hey!'

'What?'

'This is just an online shop for Mum, won't take more than half an hour. D'you want to come up to mine after?'

Jamie hesitated, but only long enough to remember what Dylan had told him about his house, and that if he played his cards right he might find out more. 'Is there a bus?'

'Aye, at twenty past. Let me crack on then.' Dylan disappeared back behind his monitor, and Jamie looked at the clock on the wall before settling down to his book again. After a moment his conscience prickled, and he picked up his phone to text his mum.

Going to mates, will be home by five. X. After a moment, he sent another. *Promise!* X

The bus dropped them off at the foot of another long, winding lane that took them up to a heavily wooded ridge. There was only one house up here, with *Druimgalla* carved into the stone gatepost. 'What does that mean?' he asked, as they passed through into the yard.

Dylan gave him a faintly wicked grin. 'The *galla* part is for *gallows*, apparently, so it's something like *gallows ridge*.' He laughed as Jamie peered around him in alarm. 'I'm pretty sure they're not here anymore, though.'

'Is your mum home?' Jamie couldn't see a car in the yard, but there was a garage across the way so it might be in there.

'No chance. She won't be home 'til way after tea time; never is, this time of the year.'

Jamie thought he sounded a bit sour. 'What does she do?'

'She runs an art gallery in town. She's the manager.' Now the dark tone had been joined by a touch of pride, and it was a strange mixture. A bit like Dylan himself, who gave off this big-man sort of image when there were others around, and sometimes when it was just him and Jamie too, but the rest of the time he seemed a bit...sad. He had no brothers or sisters; Jamie could understand how that felt, and the two of them shared a similar experience with divorce, but at least now his own mum had Mackenzie, who was better than his real dad by about a million miles.

'So no-one else is home?' he asked.

'Nope.' Dylan fitted the key into the lock and pushed open the front door. 'Want to see where it happened then?'

Jamie blinked in surprise; he'd expected to have to work for this, or at least promise some kind of payment. 'Okay,' he said, a bit warily. 'But I'm still not nickin' any whisky.'

'This has gone beyond whisky,' Dylan said, and put on a heavily theatrical, American accent. 'Thish time it's poisonal, my friend.'

Well, to be fair, you couldn't get much more personal than a murdered family member, Jamie conceded as he followed Dylan into the house, but he didn't say it out loud. It was a nice place, bigger than it seemed from the outside, and there were a few paintings hanging along the passageway wall. Some of them were even quite nice.

He looked nervously at the sitting room door as Dylan reached it, and wondered if he would sense the dark act that had taken place here, but once he was in the room there was nothing out of the ordinary. It wasn't dingy or mysterious in the slightest; in fact it was brightly lit, with a wide picture window that looked out onto the yard and the garage, and there was a decent view of the woods beyond. Jamie looked around, then questioningly at Dylan.

'Is this where she was murdered then?'

'Yeah, Mum said my cousin found... Hang on, who's that?' Dylan crossed to the window. 'Wow, posh car. Must be a friend of Mum's.'

Jamie followed his gaze. A dark blue Seat was pulling to a smooth stop near the garage, and a squat-ish bald-ish man climbed out and peered through the garage window, his hands cupping his eyes to cut the glare from the sun.

The boys watched in silence for a moment, while the man apparently satisfied himself that there was no-one home. Then he crossed the yard towards the house, giving the sitting room window a cursory glance as he passed, but evidently seeing nothing more than his own reflection, because he didn't seem to notice Dylan and Jamie staring back at him from across the room. Jamie expected a knock at the door, but it never came.

'Where's he gone?' he asked Dylan, who was looking as bemused as Jamie felt.

'Round the back, I think.' Dylan went out into the passage, and Jamie heard him open the kitchen door. 'Aye, he's here.' He pulled open the back door and called out, 'Hey, can I help you?'

Jamie hurried into the kitchen in time to see the man approaching and looking curiously around. 'Who is it?'

Dylan threw an irritated look at him and turned back to the visitor. 'Who are you looking for? If you're selling anything, I can tell you now that my mum won't—'

'Not selling anything.' The man held out a hand, which Dylan ignored as he kept the half-closed door firmly between them. The man's hand dropped. 'My name's Dr Booth. I've been away from the area for a few years, but I used to know someone who lived here at one time.'

'We've only lived here a few months. It was rented out before that. What's their name?'

Dr Booth smiled. 'It doesn't matter. I can see they've moved on. I was just in the area so thought I'd pop up anyway. I wondered if their car was in the garage, so I'm sorry if you caught me looking in there.'

'The garage is full of my cousin's stuff.'

'Aye, I can see there's no room for a car in there.' Dr Booth gave a little laugh and stepped away, leaning slightly to acknowledge Jamie's appearance behind Dylan. 'I'm sorry to have disturbed you and your wee brother. Enjoy the rest of the holidays, lads.'

'My mum might have their address,' Dylan persisted,

clearly eaten up with curiosity. 'We still get old post sometimes.'

'No, it's fine. Really.' Dr Booth raised a hand in farewell and followed the path back around to the front of the house. Jamie, running to the sitting room to watch through the window, saw him throwing one final look at the garage, and a minute later the Seat was gone, winding its way down the hill towards Abergarry again.

Jamie relaxed and went back out to the kitchen, where Dylan was locking the door. 'So. You were going to show me.'

Dylan gave him a suddenly crafty look, as if he'd only just remembered. 'What have you got for me in return?'

Jamie floundered. 'Nothing! You said it's gone past whisky.'

'Must be something,' Dylan persisted. 'Come on!'

'I could maybe get you a ride on a quad bike?' Jamie ventured at last. 'Ade's got one that he lets his workers ride around the estate. He might take you up the lane on it.'

'I've ridden one myself,' Dylan said, with some disdain. 'Don't need babysitting.' But he sounded interested, nevertheless, so Jamie went a step further.

'Well then, maybe I can get him to let you take it out by yourself? There's a spare key in the office.' He didn't think there was much chance of that, but it hardly mattered right now.

Dylan eyed him for a moment, pursing his lips, then nodded. 'Okay, deal.' He led Jamie back into the sitting room. 'Mum's sister, Yvette she was called, was at home on her own and someone broke in and burgled the place. He strangled Yvette with her dressing gown cord, and he was never caught. My cousin Hazel apparently found her after school.' Though he gave the words all the awe and mystery they deserved, something about his voice was flat; as if he had remembered that this had been more than just a gruesome story he'd read online. 'This place is so out of the way, no-one would have heard her screaming,' he added, 'or the burglar throwing the furniture around.' He looked towards the front door, and all his bravado had faded away now. 'I shouldn't go leaving the door unlocked.'

'Do you want to go back into town and...' Jamie stopped, realising that even in this new, vulnerable state, Dylan wouldn't react well to a suggestion that he should wait for his mother. '...get some dinner at the caff?' he finished, instead.

Dylan brightened a bit. 'Have you got money?'

'A bit. Enough to share some chips. But that means there won't be enough for the bus fare back into town.'

He'd expected Dylan to rummage around and find some of his mum's money stashed away somewhere, but the older boy surprised him.

'I'll give you a backie,' he said. 'It's all downhill so it won't be a problem. Then,' he added casually, though Jamie wasn't fooled, 'I could always wait in the library for Mum to drive back through. I've got some homework I can be doing anyway.'

'Will you tell her about that man? Doctor what's-his-name?'

'No chance. She'll not let me stay home alone ever again.' He looked almost relieved at that thought, despite the grumpy tone.

'Right then, let's go.' Jamie followed Dylan into the yard, and as the older boy locked and double-checked the door, he found his gaze wandering to the woods beyond the yard, and hoped that weird old bloke had actually gone back into town after all, and hadn't doubled back to lurk nearby.

Dylan pulled open the garage door and dragged his bicycle out, and Jamie waited while he pressed the tyres and checked the brakes. 'I haven't ridden this for a fair bit,' Dylan explained. 'Mum would kill me if I wrapped the two of us around a tree.'

Oh, great. Jamie gave him a smile he hoped looked more confident than it felt, but before he could say anything a knocking noise made his heart leap into his mouth, and he let out a grunt of shock as he whipped his head around to look back at the garage.

'Jesus, it's just the trees! You're a wee chickenshit really, aren't you?' Dylan swung his leg over the crossbar. 'Are you getting on, or not?'

Jamie crossed the yard to climb onto the back of the bicycle, where he gripped the sides of Dylan's jumper in his fists and raised his feet clear of the wheels. Dylan got them rolling, a little unsteadily at first, but by the time they reached the main road, or what passed as one up here, they were going at a fairly fast lick. They hurtled into the bends at what was rapidly becoming breakneck speed, and it was frighteningly obvious that one patch of wet on the ground would more than likely wipe them out; Jamie had to force himself not to yell at Dylan to slow down or, better still, let him get off and walk.

But it seemed his panicky grip on Dylan's jumper had said it all for him anyway. As the gradient eased off, and Jamie was finally starting to relax, they swept onto Abergarry's main street and Dylan took a quick glance over his shoulder. 'Crap your pants yet?' he yelled, and Jamie could feel the deep flush creeping over his skin as he saw heads turn nearby.

'Very funny,' he shot back. 'It'd take more than a little bike ride to make me do that.'

Dylan brought them to a stop and waited for Jamie to climb off before lifting his front wheel and pivoting the bicycle to face the library. 'Let me know when you've got that quad bike ride organised,' he called back. 'You can come too. Unless you're too chicken,' he added, and was still laughing as he rode off.

Jamie watched him go, feeling the shift in what was already an odd and tenuous friendship; he was going to have to prove himself properly, if he didn't want to be left out in the cold again. He turned towards home, knowing full well Ade wouldn't let Dylan anywhere near his precious quad bike, and wondering how long it would be before Dylan forgot about it.

Maddy used Hazel's laptop to do a quick image search for both Michael Booth—which had turned up nothing remotely helpful—and Leslie Warrender, and found a couple of pictures from the newspaper reports of Warrender's disappearance. They were poor quality, but gave her a vague idea of what he'd looked like back then: stocky, curly-haired and with tufted eyebrows that weren't quite Dennis Healey, but weren't far off, though Linda had apparently said they were less distinctive now anyway, either thinned naturally, through age, or trimmed. Probably the latter.

She decided to start by calling in person at the guest houses that seemed most likely; none of them would come right out and say if a Mr Booth was booked in, but at least face-to-face she could usually tell if she was being brushed off. She arranged to meet Hazel at her house at six that evening, to help her pack up what she needed, and then left Glencoille to begin her search.

Halfway down the hill her phone signal kicked in, along with a message from her brother asking her to meet him for coffee at their usual café in town. She sent back a quick response telling him to give her an hour, and all the way to

Inverness she turned over in her mind the photo that had been in Linda's bag, and the rights and wrongs of asking Nick to try and take a snap on his phone. If he was working on the case it would take no more than a moment, and if she swore to delete it as soon as she'd printed it...

Immediately she walked into the café and saw Nick, however, she knew Paul had been right to advise against it; not because Nick was already stressed or tense, but because, by contrast, he was looking more relaxed and happy than he'd been in ages. Maddy knew that was purely down to his relationship with Max Russell, who'd been a steadying hand for almost a year now, with only a minor blip, which they'd soon put behind them. At Christmas Max had been promoted to assistant manager at Thistle, and to mark the occasion, he had proposed. They'd already set up a new home together, so it wasn't entirely out of the blue, but that gesture seemed to have done something to conquer Nick's somewhat fragile sense of belonging – there was no way she could think about asking him to put his job on the line, not for this.

'How's it all going?' Nick asked her, after they'd ordered cakes to go with their coffee. 'Any word from Gavin?'

'He emails, and calls sometimes,' Maddy said. Her son's father had taken a job with a law firm further south, following their break-up, and although things had been difficult logistically for a while, Maddy had been surprised at how little she missed him once he'd gone. Part of her even wished he'd drop off her radar altogether, but there was still Tas to think about.

'So,' she said, 'what did you want to see me for?'

She could see he was dying to play it cool; she could practically see the words, *can't I just have coffee with my sister?* bubbling about on his lips, but instead he blurted, 'We've set the date. Seventh of September. '

'Ah, that's great news!' She reached across the table and briefly grasped his hand. 'Have you told Dad?'

'Aye, this morning.' Nick stirred sugar into his drink. 'He's pretty happy about it.'

'Where will you have it? Thistle, I suppose?'

'Max's boss wouldn't consider letting us have it anywhere else,' he admitted, though he sounded less enthusiastic now. 'So yeah, we're having a big posh do, by the sounds of it.'

Maddy smiled. 'As long as Breda's helping to pay for it. Max still getting on well in his job?'

'Loves it.'

'And the smoking?'

'He's down to a couple a day, mostly during his shift. He never smokes at home anymore, doesn't even buy any. He steals Breda's, and *she* loves him that much she pretends not to notice.' There was a note of pride in his voice that made Maddy smile.

'Good for him. And you? You're working a lot of long hours.'

Now Nick looked half-excited, half-nervous, and put down his drink. 'Max is quitting smoking, and I'm quitting the force.'

'*What?*'

He shrugged. 'You know I was struggling.'

'Aye, but I thought that was mostly down to Bradley, and all that crap he was putting you through. Are you sure this is what you want?'

'Deadly.'

'And what will you do?'

'Promise you won't laugh?'

'As if!'

Nick squared his shoulders. 'I'm going to train to be a

teacher. I've already applied for my PGDE, and I start in August.'

Maddy was momentarily speechless, then she thought back to all the times she'd watched him with Tas, thinking about what a great uncle he was and how it was sad that he might never be a father. 'It's perfect,' she said, and watched a broad, relieved smile cross his face. 'Teaching, eh? Does Dad know *that* yet?'

The smile faltered. 'Not yet. I was going to tell him later. I wondered...I wondered if you'd be there when I do?'

'Well, if you promise to let me get in my request that Tas stays with him for a few days first, I will be.' Maddy grinned. 'I'm not letting you put him in a bad mood before I ask a favour like that.'

Nick looked suddenly uncertain. 'Do you think he will be? Put in a bad mood, I mean?'

'No.' Maddy shook her head decisively. 'Think about what he's done for you, and how hard it's been for him to keep quiet about...' she glanced around, 'about what happened to Dougie Cameron.' She still found it hard to accept that Nick had killed the man, even knowing it was under the mistaken belief that he was protecting their father. And she knew that the strain the secret had put on the two of them outweighed even the strain she herself felt, and by an immeasurable amount. 'You being out of the force will be the biggest weight off his mind,' she said. 'Mine too, if I'm honest.' She gave him a little smile. 'Sure you don't want to join the agency instead? I've got a feeling Paul's getting more involved with his family business at Glencoille than he'd planned.'

Nick's eyebrows shot up. 'Are you serious?'

Maddy hadn't allowed herself to really think about it until now, but she had to accept it. Paul had always been an outdoors kind of man, and she'd seen the different looks on his face whenever Ade mentioned the jobs he'd be advertising, ranging from envy, to interest, to regret, and back to envy as Ade expanded on what those roles would entail. 'I don't know,' she said, on a sigh. 'But you go ahead and get your PGDE and we'll see where we are this time next year, shall we? Who knows, maybe your students would enjoy having a part-time private eye teaching them.'

'So, what are you working on at the moment?' Nick asked, tearing a piece off his Danish and picking out a sultana. 'If it's not classified, that is,' he added with a grin.

Maddy cleared her throat. 'I don't think you want to know.'

'Oh? Oh.' Nick dropped the danish with a groan. 'It's your mate Hazel, isn't it? I *knew* that name rang a bell when we were checking alibis. You're poking your nose into the Sturdy case.'

'I am not!' Maddy looked around and lowered her voice. 'You shouldn't be blurting stuff like that out, either, you know that.'

'So let's move this outside.' Nick picked up his Danish and found a lid for his coffee, and Maddy brought her own bun and followed him outside, where they found an empty bench. Nick stared straight ahead, every inch the DS again now, and reminding her strongly of their father.

'So what *are* you looking into?' he asked.

'If I tell you, you've to keep this—' She mimed zipping her lips. 'Okay? Not even Dad hears it.'

'Okay. Fire away.'

'I mean it, Nick. It could mean the difference between... well. You know.'

'I swear,' Nick said, 'it'll stay off the record, as long as you promise not to ask for my help.'

'Don't worry, I'd already decided not to.' Maddy began unwrapping the doughy layers of her Chelsea bun. 'Okay, you're right, it's Hazel. She came to me about someone who's meant to be dead, but isn't. Or at least he might not be.' She told him about Warrender, and how they'd planned to tell the police, but had decided to wait until Paul had spoken to Patrick Ross. His interest sparked at once.

'Do you like him for Linda Sturdy's murder?'

'Only if he knew she'd recognised him, or suspected it, but otherwise there's no connection to make there. And we haven't found out what Ross wanted Paul for yet, either, but we just... don't want you lot leaping all over Warrender yet.'

Nick frowned. 'Why not?'

'Because there *is* no obvious connection to Linda so you're bound to have to let him go, and then we'll have lost him for good. We need to get to him ourselves, to find out why he's back, and we don't want to frighten him away.'

'Why does it matter why he's back?'

'Because,' Maddy said, lowering her voice further, 'we think he *might* have killed Hazel's mother.'

'Christ, Mads!' Nick sighed. 'This isn't stuff I can just ignore!'

'But if you pick him up, and then decide he *is* just this Dr Booth character after all, Hazel's going to be looking over her shoulder for the rest of her life. Which might not be very long, incidentally.' Maddy gave him a pleading look. 'Any police attention on Warrender will just paint a sodding great target on her back.'

'But what can you do about it, if you do find him?' Nick persisted. 'Maybe I'm being dense, but this doesn't sound very logical to me.'

'We just need a bit of time, so we can work on uncovering the truth about Hazel's mother. Your lot won't even try.'

Nick looked stung. 'You keep saying that. What makes you so sure?'

'Going on what you've told me yourself in the past, you won't get the budget. You know you won't, because there's no evidence to support an investigation. There's just one woman – now dead, so you can't even interview her – who saw a photo of someone she might or might not have recognised.' She shook her head. 'All you'll do is spook him, and drive him underground so we lose our shot, too. On the other hand, *we* don't have to justify our investigation to anyone, in order to crack on with it.'

Nick spoke patiently now. 'But if he's a potential suspect in a murder we're currently investigating, which he would be, we've already got the budget. And we need to take samples. DNA. Fingerprints we can compare with those we've lifted from the back gate.'

'And I'd bet my last quid they'll come to nothing. How many people pass through that gate every day? Nothing's bringing Linda Sturdy back, but if you act too soon on what I've told you, you'll be putting lives at risk.' Maddy lowered her voice again. '*Please*, Nick! If your investigation leads you to him, fine. I can't stand in the way, and I won't even try. But this is privileged information, and you promised it was off the record.'

'Tell me about Hazel's mother,' Nick said after a moment's tense silence. 'I take it her case was not proven?'

'Worse, no-one was even brought to trial. Her name was Yvette Douglas, if you want to look it up. 1998. But it was put down to an interrupted burglary, and they didn't even turn up any evidence to solve that.'

'They might now,' Nick said. 'There's been a lot of advance in techniques in twenty years.'

'But not enough to guarantee anything.' Maddy was beginning to wish she hadn't said anything at all. 'It has to be a certainty, or as much of one as you need to hold him. So will you just give us a week, to make it one?'

Nick studied her for a moment, then sighed again. 'I wish to Christ you wouldn't put me on the spot like this.'

'Well, you asked,' Maddy pointed out. 'I wasn't going to say anything about Yvette, but you—'

'All right!' Nick began shredding his Danish and picking out the sultanas again. 'You know I could get fired for sitting on evidence?'

'It's not really evidence, is it? It's just...theory. But if you give us a week we might be able to turn it into something you can use. Look, I won't tell the others I've told you, and I'm not going to drop you in it with your job, am I?'

Silence fell between them again, but Maddy could feel the disapproval. She didn't dare beg him again for extra time; he would either agree or not and she'd probably do more harm than good. After a while he looked up from his mutilated snack.

'What was it you were thinking about asking me?'

'What do you mean?'

'You said you'd considered asking me to help you with something, then changed your mind.'

'Oh. Yeah.' Maddy coughed to cover her embarrassment. 'Well I was tinkering with the idea of asking you to take a photo of the photo. You know, on your phone.' She saw the look on her brother's face and held up a hand. 'I said I wouldn't!'

He gave her a sideways look as he took the lid off his coffee. 'When did you say this picture was taken?'

'Late nineties. Ninety-eight, I think, not long before Yvette died.'

'Most people still used analogue cameras for everyday use back then. Was it loose in the box, or was it in a developer's envelope?'

Maddy frowned. 'I don't know, why?' Then it clicked, and she sat up straight. 'Negatives!' She saluted him with a scrap of bun, before popping it into her mouth. 'You're a star,' she mumbled, wiping her hands on her shirt. 'Hazel's moving into mine tonight, for a few days. I'll check with her.'

She walked back to her car twenty minutes later, feeling a good deal less conflicted than when she'd arrived, and when Paul called her to tell her about his meeting with Ross and the blackmail attempt, and that he'd agreed not to tell the police anything until they'd got some information out of Warrender, she felt even more relief.

'So, what have you been doing?' he asked. She could hear him getting into his car, and swearing softly as he groped for his seatbelt, and she wondered if she could avoid telling him the whole truth.

'I've seen Nick,' she said.

'Oh?' His voice had sharpened a little. 'What did you talk about?'

She briefly closed her eyes. 'He and Max are getting married,' she said with false brightness, and pulled her own seatbelt smoothly across her chest. 'We didn't have time to talk about much else, as you can imagine.'

'That's brilliant news,' Paul said, with real warmth. 'Give him my best.'

'I will. Right, I'm going out to Dad's now, to ask him if he'll have Tas for a few days. I'll call you later.'

'Maddy?'

'Aye?' She stopped, one hand on the ignition key, wondering if he'd heard the tension in her voice beneath the brisk, light tone.

'She'll be okay,' he said, his voice serious. 'We won't let anyone hurt her.'

'No. Are you going back to speak to Ade now?'

His response came on a heavy sigh. 'Bollocks. I'd almost forgotten.'

She couldn't help smiling. 'He's your brother. He'll forgive you.'

'I hope you're right.'

'Of course I am. It's what brothers do.'

'D'you think we should bring him into what we know, too? It might make him watchful around Hazel.'

'I think that'd be a good idea,' Maddy agreed. 'The more people who can keep an eye out for her, the better. We'll tell him tomorrow, all of us together, so we don't miss anything out. Come up to Glencoille after nine. Hazel and I will be there by then.' She paused, considering. 'And maybe we should let her know she can tell that Griff bloke too. Not everything, but enough so that he can keep an eye out for anyone out of place at this rally of theirs. With so many strangers about, she can't be too careful.'

'Makes sense.'

She twisted the key. 'I'll let her know. Okay, speak to you—'

'Did you tell him about Warrender?' Paul asked quietly, and Maddy froze, then turned off the engine again.

'Yes.' The word was out, but the unsettling weight of the denial was gone too. 'He's not going to pass it on though, he promised me that.'

'For how long?'

'A week, maybe.' Maddy waited, her stomach in knots, but his answer was simple.

'Okay.'

'You sound surprisingly calm,' she ventured.

'You didn't ask him for anything but time?'

'Nothing. I swear.'

'I hope it doesn't get back to his team that he knew anything, or we'll both be looking for a brother's forgiveness.'

'Paul?' Despite the cars passing in and out of the car park, and the bright sunlight spilling through the windscreen, it felt like a private moment between them, and the right time to ask. When she couldn't see his face. 'Are you planning on giving all this up, to work with Ade and your dad?'

His silence might have been surprise at the absurdity of the idea, or it might have been him taking the time to find a diplomatic answer. She held her phone tightly, hoping she'd been wrong about this.

'I don't know,' he said eventually. 'And that's the whole truth as I know it, Mads. I just...don't know.' He spoke gently, like someone passing on bad news. 'I'll speak to you later.'

Then he was gone, and Maddy felt the unmistakeable snap of the first of the threads that had bound them in friendship and trust for fourteen years.

Chapter Eleven

'I've left all Dad's stuff back at mine,' Hazel said, when Maddy asked her about the photo that evening. 'Didn't seem any point bringing it here.'

'But do you remember if it was in one of those envelopes you get back from the developer?'

'It was, aye.' Hazel nodded. 'Dad only had one of those little 110 things, the pocket cameras. The chemist in Abergarry used to process them in twenty-four hours, and back then we thought that was super-fast.' She laughed. 'Imagine if we had to suddenly start waiting that long nowadays; that'd be the end of duck-face selfies and plates of artistic salad.'

Maddy nodded, a little impatiently. 'Those envelopes have a little pocket in the front, remember? They used to put the negatives in there. Any chance they might still be there?'

'Maybe. That'd make life a lot easier. I'll pick them up tomorrow, when I fetch my bike for work.'

'You're not riding to work,' Maddy said firmly. 'Sorry, but there's no way I'm letting you up that road on your own, not while Warrender's still out there.'

Hazel was about to argue, when she remembered what had happened to Mackenzie on his bike last year, on that very road. No wonder Maddy was twitchy. 'Are you going to give me a lift, then?' she asked. 'It's a bit out of your way.'

'I don't have a "way" at the moment,' Maddy reminded her. 'Tas'll be going to his grandad's for a bit, first thing tomorrow, so I can make Glencoille my office. Okay? I'm going to be your shadow for the next few days.'

'If you'll be my potty guard...' Hazel sang quietly, and gave Maddy a faint smile. 'Dad says he used to sing that to Mum, while she was potty training me and sat next to me for hours. Paul Simon would probably want to have words,' she added, and Maddy laughed.

'He'd be within his rights. Okay, that's settled then, as long as Ade doesn't mind.'

'Somehow I don't think he will.' Hazel flopped down into the chair nearest the window just as her phone went off. 'Hang on, this is him now. I can ask.'

'Ask him if he doesn't mind you being half an hour late too, so we can drop Tas over to Dad's first.'

'Okay. Hi, Ade.'

'Hi, I need a favour,' Ade said. 'Would you be free tonight? I've been summoned by Patrick Ross and Will Kilbride, and I could do with an ally.'

'Summoned for what?' Hazel asked, amused by the glumness in his tone.

'Dinner.'

'Well...that's good news, isn't it?'

'I hope so, but there'll be some wrangling even if it is. So, can you make it? I'll pay you overtime.'

'Aye, I can make it. But speaking of overtime, I'm going to be in a bit late tomorrow morning.' She looked up at Maddy to see her mouthing, *I said ask!* 'Only half an hour or so. Maddy's bringing me up. Oh, and she's also going to be sharing the office for a few days and working from there. Okay? Great.' She deliberately gave him no time to respond, and continued to ignore Maddy's increasingly agitated hand signals. 'Now,' she said, 'where do I meet you three wise monkeys tonight?'

'Um. I'll pick you up in about half an hour,' Ade said, still clearly recovering from the news that Maddy would be right there in his office for the rest of the week. 'We're going to Thistle.'

'What?' Hazel's good humour slipped a little. 'That's a bit posh for us, isn't it?'

Ade laughed. 'Speak for yourself. Besides, it's not that posh once you're in. Kilbride knows he'll get a table there, and there's no issue with wheelchair access. He always likes to meet there when he can, and why wouldn't he? It's free when you own the place, after all.' He fell silent, then spoke far too casually. 'Why not ask Maddy along, too?'

Hazel lowered the phone. 'Ade says do you want to join us for dinner tonight, at Thistle?'

'I can't,' Maddy said, glancing at the ceiling, through which thudded the sounds of a five-year-old boy at play. 'Who's "us" anyway?'

'Kilbride, Ross, Ade and me.'

'Sounds like a business arrangement to me. Besides, I'm not sure what Paul would think of me going off on a jolly with those particular gentlemen.'

'Hardly up to him,' Hazel retorted, and lifted her phone again. 'Hi, Ade. Afraid not; babysitting issues, at this short notice. But she said another night would be great,' she added, and calmly raised her middle finger to Maddy, who was miming wringing Hazel's neck.

She called Griff and arranged for him to pick her up on Thursday morning and take her up to Druimgalla, so she could show him the overhanging branches damaging the garage roof. 'I should get a commission for bringing him more work,' she said, as she ended the call. 'I must remember to mention it to him.'

'He's a good mate,' Maddy said. 'I'm glad you've got someone you can turn to.'

'Don't project,' Hazel said mildly, getting up from her chair.

'What's that supposed to mean?'

'Griff *is* a good mate, but that's all we'll ever be. Unlike you and my boss.'

'Absolute tosh.' Maddy buried her face in her coffee mug. 'D'you want a quick shower then? I've left your stuff in my room for now, but you can move into Tas's tomorrow if you'll be okay on the sofa for one night?'

'Perfect. Can I borrow something to wear though? I've only brought a few work clothes with me.'

'Take your pick.' Maddy gave a theatrical sigh. 'It's not as if *I'll* be needing to dress up anytime soon.'

'You look almost human,' Ade observed when he arrived, and Hazel punched him in the shoulder, screamingly self-conscious about the neat, but short, skirt and top she'd borrowed. He grinned and looked past her at Maddy. 'Wotcher, Cinders. Are you sure you don't want to get your glad rags on and join us?'

'Hazel's wearing the gladdest rags I have,' Maddy said, with theatrical mournfulness. 'All the others barely count as contented.' She shook her head as he laughed, and smiled back at him. 'Nah, thanks. I'll never get anyone to babysit. Dad's out with Farly tonight, and Nick's working really long hours now he's permanent CID.'

'Is he on this murder case?' Ade asked, and threw a quick, apologetic look at Hazel. 'Shit, I'm sorry. I didn't mean to sound callous.'

'Don't worry about it.' Hazel took her one and only smart jacket off the peg in the hall, sliding her phone into its pocket so she wouldn't have to embarrass herself by the state of her shoulder bag. She pulled on the jacket and flicked her hair out from under the collar, then turned to Maddy. 'Will I do, for somewhere like Thistle?'

'You'll do fine.' Maddy reached out and tweaked the collar straight. 'Now run along, kids, and don't get into any food fights.'

Ade gestured Hazel to walk ahead of him out to his jeep, and as she turned to wave goodbye to Maddy she saw he'd also turned back, and that there seemed to be a wordless conversation going on between the two of them. She couldn't see Ade's face, but she could see Maddy's, and her friend's clear, pale skin was now lightly flushed and her fingers were playing absently with the chain of her necklace. Hazel suppressed a smile and looked away again, waiting for Ade to follow her.

In the jeep, she fastened her seat belt and, when Ade didn't say anything, sneaked a quick, sidelong glance at him; he had one hand on the ignition key and one on the steering wheel, and was staring out through the windscreen, his moss-green eyes fixed on something she was certain he wasn't seeing. Dressed neatly tonight, for once, he cut quite the figure, she decided; the thick dark hair was trimmed, the jaw not too closely shaved but not scruffy either, and the suit fitted the square shoulders and showed an athletic frame she hadn't previously noticed beneath his baggy overshirts and combat jacket.

'We both scrub up pretty well, don't we?' she asked, bringing him back from whatever phantom was holding his attention; doubtless it was Maddy-shaped. 'I never knew you owned a suit.'

'I'm surprised it still fits after all the crap I've eaten lately.' He flashed her a smile and finally twisted the ignition key, and the jeep rumbled to life. 'Best do as we're told then, and not start lobbing bread rolls across the restaurant, not if I want to get this investment from Mr Ross.'

'Are you and your brother still at each other's throats?' she asked as they started up the street. 'Maddy told me what happened. He came to see you today, didn't he?'

'Aye. I couldn't believe it when he told me, the wee gobshite.'

'He didn't do it on purpose though.'

'He didn't impersonate me on purpose, no,' Ade said, 'but that wasn't what bothered me anyway. It was his assumption that the only reason anyone could possibly be interested in investing in me, is for...for...'

'Nefarious purposes?' Hazel supplied, with a little smile. Ade shot her a look before returning his attention to the road, and she adopted a less frivolous tone. 'Look, Mackenzie works in a business geared towards deceit and lies; it's bound to affect his everyday thinking. He's had some pretty nasty experiences from what Maddy's told me.'

'He has,' Ade allowed, 'but it's like I said to him, he doesn't have to trust Kilbride or Ross, he just has to trust *me*.'

Hazel nodded. 'How did you leave it?'

'We talked it through, and anyway he seems to have changed his opinion of Ross since he met him. Though he won't tell me what that was about, and he swears it had nothing to do with me.'

'It didn't.'

This time the look Ade gave her lasted longer, and she had to point to the road again. 'We're going to be eating hospital food in a minute, instead of Thistle's finest.'

'So you're not going to tell me what's going on?'

'Maddy says we can talk about it tomorrow morning, up at Glencoille. Your brother's coming up, sometime after nine, and we'll put it all on the table then. Provided you've forgiven him by then, of course,' she added, her smile returning. 'Not really still angry, are you?'

'He's...' Ade blew out a breath, then shook his head. 'Aye, I'm still angry. But it's hard to stay that way with the kid... What are you smiling about?'

'I always have trouble remembering you're the older one,' Hazel said. 'It's not just that he's taller, and bigger. But he's so *serious*, and you're...not.'

'Make no mistake,' Ade said, 'I can be deadly serious when I want to be. You'll see that tonight.'

'Interesting. I look forward to it.'

'And Paul,' he broke off again, and the smile that crossed his face was a mixture of exasperation and affection. 'He's got a sense of humour all right. He'd never have lasted five minutes with Charis if he hadn't. He just tends to keep it buried, until he knows you really well.'

'He and Maddy were an item, weren't they?'

'Aye, years back. Only briefly though, and it was a bad time for him. They work better as friends.'

'Lucky for you,' Hazel said mildly, and was amused when Ade gave her a look that she guessed was supposed to be puzzled. 'Oh, don't give me that, Ade Mackenzie! Just don't,' she added, as he opened his mouth ready to protest. 'Maddy's gorgeous, and brave, and clever, and if you even *tried* to tell me you weren't the slightest bit interested I'd know you were lying.'

Ade leaned forward and turned up the music.

Hazel had never been to Thistle; it was one of those places you hear about, and ordinary people have to plan weeks in advance and save up for, but they were greeted at the door by the Maître d', and whisked away to the reserved table near the back, having handed over their coats to a hovering attendant. It seemed they were definitely VIPs tonight.

Patrick Ross and William Kilbride were already seated, and there were handshakes all around, though Mr Ross seemed to disapprove of Hazel's presence, only pressing her hand briefly before dropping it and picking up his menu. She could already feel her annoyance building, frustrated with herself that he'd managed to make her feel out of place, just when she'd been starting to relax.

Mr Kilbride, however, made up for Ross's shortcomings as a dinner companion. He was charm itself, putting Hazel back at her ease and keeping the conversation on topics with which she felt she could join in; largely the Glencoille Estate and Ade's plans for it. Hazel gradually relaxed, taking less notice of Ross and more of her surroundings and her fellow diners. She was surprised to note that not everyone was dressed to the nines, and that she could probably have got away with her slightly shabby shoulder bag after all; there was old money here, which always came with comfortable attire and a lot of cheerful noise.

She was pleasantly surprised, too, when Breda Kelly made an appearance at their table, her tone muted but friendly as she assured them she'd be at their beck and call throughout the evening. Of course, with William Kilbride being her boss she'd be sure to make a point of that, Hazel realised, but it was nice to see a friendly face. Towards the end of dessert, before the real business of the evening began, Kilbride invited Breda to join them for a glass of wine.

Ross added his support to the request, and Hazel realised they knew one another too, and that Breda had been to Ross's recent birthday party at the gallery. She was surprised and gratified, therefore, that Breda turned the conversation on to Hazel and the people she'd been with when they'd met at the Twisted Tree.

'A bike club, then,' she said. 'I've never been on the back of a bike in my life, but Linda, God rest her soul, told me how your lot helped you through things after your poor mother passed.'

'They're having their rally up at Glencoille over the bank holiday,' Ade put in, looking at Ross, 'so don't be alarmed if you happen to come up there and see a load of bikes, and people in leathers. It's not a regular thing, just an emergency stop-gap.'

'I was hoping to come up in a week or so, actually, to see how the distillery's coming along,' Ross said, frowning. 'I hope you're not going to churn up the field with your racing all over the place.'

'Not at all, it's not that kind of rally.' Hazel briefly told him what she'd told Maddy, and added, 'We're arranging a long run out for them on the Saturday, to the Arctic Convoy Memorial at Poolewe. So the field will be mostly empty until late in the afternoon if you'd prefer to go up then.'

'No, thanks,' he said, still rather short. 'I'll leave it until after you've all gone.'

'I've never been out that far,' Breda said, turning to Hazel. 'Was it your idea?'

'Griff started it, I think, years ago, but we do it every year. It's a nice long run out, and a pub lunch on the way. Keeps everyone out almost all day, until it's time for the silly games.'

'Poolewe.' Ade smiled, a little nostalgically. 'I've not been out there since before I left Scotland. I must have been...I don't know. Maybe nine? Mum was still alive, and she died when I was ten, so, aye, must have been.' He gave a little laugh. 'Paul would have been five then, and just as much of a liability as he is now. He got into the defences by the memorial and nearly ended up drowning.' He looked at Ross. 'Look, Patrick, I've told Paul I wasn't happy about what he got up to on my behalf, and I know he felt bad about it. I hope you'll not hold it against him.'

Ross shook his head. 'I've had reason to speak with him since, and he's apologised.'

'Good.' Kilbride adopted a brisk tone. 'I think we're ready to discuss business then.' He gave Breda a pointed look, and she pushed back her chair.

'Of course. Let me know if bubbles are in order later.' She pressed Hazel's hand again. 'I hope you enjoyed your meal.'

'It was lovely, thanks.'

'Good. And it's grand to see you again. We must get together and have a little send off for poor Linda, since we can't have a funeral yet.'

Hazel nodded. 'I'd like that. You've got my number.'

'Indeed, I have.' Breda melted away into the busy dining room as if she'd never been there, and Hazel offered to do the same, but Ade shook his head.

'You're going to be Glencoille's assistant manager; you stay put.'

'Am I?' Hazel was startled, and Ade laughed. 'Well, I'd intended to go through the normal channels of making you interview for the role, but it hardly seemed fair to get a bunch of other people up, when I know you're the one I need around the place anyway.'

Hazel felt a flush stealing across her face, but it was a flush of pleasure and a new surge of excitement; she had no doubt she could do the job, but hearing Ade come out with the accolade so casually made her more determined than ever to prove him right. She saw Kilbride and Ross exchanging a look, and even Ross looked happier now he'd eaten a fine meal.

'Congratulations,' he said, raising his glass, and the others followed suit. 'Now, if we can get down to business? It's getting late.'

'Ready?' Ade said to Hazel, who belatedly realised that having no bag meant she had no notebook either. *Great. First mistake in a glittering managerial career, fuckwit.* But she nodded and, making it seem as if it had been her intention all along, went in search of her jacket so she could retrieve her phone and use the notepad app.

The meeting became intensely focused from that moment on. The three men discussed their vision for the new distillery and its distribution, and for Glencoille as a business. Kilbride had plenty to say on the matter of promotion, and Hazel was glad to see Ade push back when it seemed the older man was going down a route he didn't like; Glencoille had always been intended for the serious-minded experience-seeker, not for the lightweight executive getaways that Kilbride had envisaged back in the eighties, and Ade's easy-going manner vanished in the blink of an eye when the conversation started in that direction. Hazel could see Ross's appreciation take a step upwards then, too, and felt absurdly proud. Like watching your kid sticking up for himself in the playground, she mused, trying not to smile too broadly as she bent over her phone, tapping away at speed.

When the time came to wrap it up, she emailed the notes to herself, surprised to see how much time had crept by. Kilbride proposed brandies all around, but Ross declined, and Ade shook his head too. 'I've got to get this young lady back to her digs.'

'Digs?' Ross looked at Hazel, surprised. 'I thought you'd have had your own place at your age.'

'She's staying with—'

'I do,' Hazel broke in, appalled at how easily Ade had been about to give away her living arrangements. 'He's just taking the piss because it's rented.'

'Hardly anything to be ashamed of, this day and age,' Kilbride said, with a surprised look at Ade.

'Oh, he knows that; he's just winding me up.' Hazel pushed back her chair. 'I'll just pop to the ladies' before we go, if you don't mind. It's a bit of a drive back to Abergarry.'

Coming out of the toilets a few minutes later, she caught a waft of cool, refreshing night air as someone opened a door at the other end of the short corridor. She realised then that she'd barely given a thought to the fact that she'd been so close, all evening, to the place where Linda Sturdy had died; something about the atmosphere of the dining room managed to push such dark thoughts further back in the mind.

She opened the door and found herself on an artistically crafted crazy paving path, which led around the side of the building into an enclosed outdoor seated area. At the far end of this now deserted, but cosily lit space was a wooden gate that, by Hazel's reasoning, should lead directly into the yard behind the kitchens. The night suddenly seemed very lonely, and she hesitated; if she'd been watching herself on TV she'd have been yelling at the screen by now, but she took a deep breath anyway and pushed open the gate, seeing the pathway continue a short way between some stacked crates before it opened up to the yard.

A couple of waiters were taking a break by the open door, and looked at her impassively through the coils of smoke that curled around their heads. One of them muttered something to the other, and Hazel caught the words, 'morbid' and 'sicko' before he carefully stubbed his cigarette out on the grill in the wall, dropped the remainder into his pocket for later, and disappeared back inside.

Hazel's eyes were drawn to the path, and she wasn't sure if she was imagining there were darker spots there, or if it was just the way the shadows fell, cast by the crates and boxes ready to be either taken away or re-filled. The second waiter cleared his throat, and when she looked up he pointed to a spot behind her, closer to the wooden gate, which in fact looked cleaner than the rest.

'There,' he said, a dry note in his voice that told Hazel he'd pointed it out more than once before. 'Did ye know her then, or are you just one of those true-crime nutters?'

'She was my dad's girlfriend.'

The waiter looked abashed at that, and shuffled his feet. 'Sorry,' he said. 'Anyway, that's where Miss Kelly found her.' His gaze moved away from her and down another path that led to the gateway to the back lane. 'Don't hang around out here, aye? It's getting late.'

He shoved his own dog-end through the bin's grill and followed his colleague back indoors. Hazel stepped slowly back towards the place where Linda had fallen, trying to imagine how she must have felt in those last few, frantic moments: Warrender, if it was in fact him, would have watched her smoking alone, and waited until he was sure no-one else was coming out, before pushing through the gate from the lane, and...

She shuddered and jerked her head around, halfway to convincing herself that it was happening again, but saw only the two paths meeting by the door at right angles; no sinister movement, and no opening of the lane gate. She decided she'd seen more than enough and walked quickly back the way she'd come, but she wasn't entirely happy until she'd rejoined Ade and the others, who were now collecting their coats. She accepted her own, pulling it on with a haste that made Ade raise his eyebrows, though he said nothing.

As the three men said their goodbyes, Hazel's mind kept pulling her back to the yard, and her sleep that night was light and fitful, and dusted with dreams that left her sliding closer to the edge of the wagon than she'd been in months.

Chapter Twelve

MACKENZIE DROVE SLOWLY up to Glencoille on Wednesday morning to give himself time to think, but was unable to delve more deeply into the Warrender problem; instead Maddy's question marched around his head, demanding an answer: *are you planning on giving all this up, to work with Ade and your dad?* The bluntness of the words had come as a surprise, as had the direction from which they'd sprung, but once he'd heard them he'd felt something inside him settle. Something he hadn't even realised had been restless until that moment. He certainly hadn't realised Maddy had sensed it before he had, and he knew the question would be an undercurrent to everything until he was able to give an answer. Besides, Ade might not even want him; he'd hinted, when he'd been pitching the idea, that there would be a job whenever Mackenzie wanted one, but things were different between them now, and the seeds of mistrust lay uneasily on their shared ground.

The road led up towards where he'd had his near-fatal crash last August and he couldn't help picturing it; his bike flying off the side of the valley, and himself flying right alongside it. His hands tensed involuntarily on the steering wheel, and he was relieved to turn off before he reached the spot and take a lane that cut across the bottom of the estate, to where Ade had cleared the ground to begin building. The river wound through the land here, wide in places for the perfect fishing conditions, and narrow and fast-running in others. He was surprised by how the sight of it loosened some of the tension in his muscles, as he switched off his engine and sat watching it for a moment.

Ade's jeep was in the yard, but there was no sign of Maddy's car yet, and Mackenzie checked the clock on his dash; it wasn't yet nine. Around him the yard was coming to life; plastic sheeting was being pulled off stacks of bricks and mounds of sand and cement. A ready-mix concrete truck was turning into the yard behind him, and he started up again and pulled the car right up to the portakabin to allow it room to turn. The foundations for what would become the main house were already dug out, and Mackenzie felt a faint thrill of realisation; his brother's dreams were coming true right in front of him. It was really happening.

The portakabin door swung open and Ade stood there, his face impassive as he raised a hand in greeting. Mackenzie returned the gesture, but instead of following his brother into the office, he remained in his car and watched the builders, until Maddy's car crept between the gateposts a few minutes later.

Hazel went inside first, leaving Maddy and Mackenzie standing in the yard looking at one another; that loaded question was there in Maddy's eyes again, just as he'd known it would be. He shrugged and gave her a half-smile – the only answer he could give right now – then stepped back and gestured her ahead of him into the office, where Hazel was switching on her computer and Ade was filling the kettle.

'We've got some talking to do,' Maddy said, pulling the door closed. 'It needs to be kept between us though, okay?'

'Okay,' Ade agreed, and Mackenzie had the amused feeling he'd have said the same thing if she had suggested he stand on his head in the corner. He didn't bother suppressing his grin, and saw that it was echoed on Hazel's face as she disappeared behind her laptop screen. It lifted the tired, tight-mouthed expression she'd been wearing as she'd arrived, and now she looked less belligerent and more at ease in herself. Mackenzie, Maddy and Hazel quickly explained everything they'd discovered between them, leaving Ade visibly shocked and concerned.

'And you think this Warrender bloke disappeared because he killed your mum?' he asked Hazel, who nodded.

'I think Dad knew it, too, which was why he destroyed everything that connected them. Except the photo, which is really weird.'

'And,' Maddy added, 'we've got the negatives it came from.' She nodded to Hazel, who reached into her shoulder bag and withdrew a long, brightly coloured envelope with the name of a long-disappeared local printer splashed across it. She reached into the slit pocket at the front and took out the strips of thin brown plastic. 'You can see that the photo Linda found was one of these. There are a couple of other prints still in the envelope,' she added, and drew those out, too. 'They're just of some beach we went to. Roseisle, I think, judging by the forest.' She dropped them onto the desk. 'Nothing of any help. The rest will probably have been over-exposed, or covered in a thumb or something.'

'Do you remember anything about the day you took the other photo?' Maddy asked, picking them up.

'The one Linda had?' Hazel shook her head. 'I didn't take that one. I don't think I was even home. Looked like a sunny day, going by the photo, so if I wasn't at school I was probably in town with my mates.'

'So... Someone else knows that Warrender knew your parents.' Mackenzie frowned. 'It couldn't have been Linda, could it? Trying to distance herself from what happened to your mum?'

'No, Linda definitely didn't know him. Besides, she wasn't really on Dad's radar herself until after Mum died. Remember she was going to take it to her own father, and ask if he could confirm it was even Warrender.'

'I'll check with Ross,' Mackenzie said. 'He's the only link I can think of, though he said he didn't remember your dad.'

'Presumably you can get these printed in town, still?' Ade asked, leaning forward to pick up one of the strips. He held it up to the window, and Mackenzie could see blurred outlines, including one of a short line of people.

'We could,' Maddy said, 'but we don't want anyone else to see them.' She turned to Mackenzie with a big, cheesy smile, and he knew exactly what was coming. He sighed, and pre-empted it.

'I can ask her, but I can't promise anything.'

'Do you have a dark room set up at home?'

'No, the spare room's already being used for a studio, and there isn't room for a dark room as well. But she might be able use the equipment at the college.'

'When does she go in next?'

'Monday,' he said, 'but I don't know how much free time

she'll have to mess about with the equipment. It might take a few days before she can broach that subject with her tutor.'

'That's fine.' Maddy scooped up the envelope's contents and handed the whole thing to him. 'Sooner the better, obviously, but in the meantime we still have the newspaper photos of Warrender from when he supposedly died. That'll help.' She took an enlarged, inkjet-printed photo from her bag and handed it to Ade. Mackenzie could see she'd played with it a bit and done a fair job, for someone not conversant with Photoshop, of removing his hair. 'Keep this copy, in the meantime. If you see him hanging around, make sure Hazel's nowhere near him, and then call one of us.' She looked from Ade to Mackenzie and back again, and Mackenzie could see her frustration with the two of them. 'Doesn't matter which of us,' she added, 'but *not* the police. Not unless someone's about to get hurt, okay? We don't want him spooked.'

Ade nodded. 'And he's come back to blackmail Patrick Ross, but plans to stay? Seems risky.'

'Not if he believes everyone else who knew anything about what he did is dead,' Macknenzie said. 'He's given Ross until bank holiday Monday to get the money together.'

'And then what?'

'Presumably that's when he starts making threats to get hold of this pal he's got back home, who's ready to blow the whole thing wide open.'

Maddy looked at him, her eyes narrowing slightly. 'What's that?'

'What's what?'

'That tone in your voice.' She looked steadily at him for a moment, then her expression cleared. 'You don't believe he's got anyone back home, do you?'

Hazel looked up from her laptop. 'You don't?'

Mackenzie shrugged. 'He just...doesn't seem the type, from what Ross has said. I'm not basing that on anything,' he added, 'but something about it just doesn't ring true. I mean, Seriously. Casinos? Money laundering?' He shook his head. 'The bloke's strictly small-fry, with a strong homing instinct. I'm more inclined to believe he's got the damned painting here with him, but he's scared to admit that in case Ross finds out where he's staying and nicks it back, or destroys it. No painting, no proof of fraud, no blackmail. And no tearful homecoming.'

'How big's the painting?' Maddy asked. 'I've not been into Waterfront so I've got no idea if we're talking eight feet, or eight inches.'

'Somewhere between the two,' Mackenzie said. 'About three by two. Easily transportable, and probably cheap to courier, if you want to take the risk.'

'Have you mentioned this to Ross?'

Mackenzie shook his head. 'Not in as many words. I'd rather he went on thinking there's at least a credible threat, for the time being, in case he accidentally says something that sends Warrender scuttling back to France. This blackmail stuff is only muddying the waters as far as we're concerned, but at least it's a distraction and should hopefully be keeping Warrender's attention off Hazel.'

'What about your aunt?' Ade asked Hazel. 'Did she ever know Warrender?'

'No, she wasn't in the UK at that time. She got married in America and lived there for a while. She didn't start work at Waterfront until she moved into Druimgalla, after Dad died.'

'So they should be safe,' Mackenzie said. 'Good.'

'I'm showing Griff up there tomorrow,' Hazel said. 'He's giving me a quote to do some work on the trees before they crack the garage roof.' She hesitated. 'Can I tell him any of this?'

Mackenzie and Maddy shared a look. 'We'd said it would be a good idea,' Mackenzie said, 'but we need to know how sure you are of him. How well you can trust him.'

'He's my oldest, closest friend, and my dad treated him like a son, too. I trust him.'

'Okay then,' Maddy said. 'But be sparing with the finer details. He doesn't need to know about the blackmail, or about the link to Linda Sturdy's death.'

'So you do think it was Warrender then?'

'I do, aye. He must have been worried she'd tell someone. But,' she went on, 'Griff only needs to know that Warrender faked his own death, and now he's back, and that we think, we *think*,' she emphasised, 'that he might know something about what happened to your mother.'

'Not that we think he killed her?'

'No,' Mackenzie said, 'or your pal might get all protective and go off the deep end. Just tell him that Warrender's got mad theories and he's trying to drag you into them. You're trying to keep out of his way, and Griff needs to tell you if he's seen him. I know what bike rallies are like,' he reminded her. 'Even the close-knit ones will have strangers hanging around, and no-one bats an eyelid, so it's best he keeps an eye out for anyone not wearing this year's badge, or who looks a bit out of place.'

Hazel nodded. She looked uncomfortable, and Mackenzie privately had his doubts as to whether she'd keep to the agreement, but there was nothing he could do about it if she chose to tell a mate. He just hoped the man knew how to keep a lid on any anger issues he might have, or he might drive Warrender underground for good.

'Are we finished then?' he asked, standing up. 'If so, I'll

leave you to start going through those guest houses, Mads, and I'll go back and talk to Ross again. I also want a closer look at that painting.' He gave a short laugh. 'At least now I know why the bastard was so snippy with me when I asked him about it.'

Ade rose too. 'Before you go, come up with me to the distillery. See what your money's helping to pay for.'

'I saw it yesterday, it looks great.' Mackenzie frowned, then, as Ade's words registered. 'And it's not my—'

'Just come with me, aye?' Ade spoke quietly, and Mackenzie caught Maddy's eye. She gave him a barely perceptible nod of encouragement, and Mackenzie followed his brother outside into the rapidly warming day.

Together they walked up the narrow road to where work was continuing on their father's part of the Glencoille dream, and Ade pointed out various areas marked out for discreet development, and some for re-wooding. Mackenzie wanted to bring up the subject that still lay heavily between them, but he was loath to shatter Ade's quiet pleasure in what he was showing off.

The distillery door was propped open with a chair, and a man in overalls was inside using a screwdriver to lever the lid off a paint tin. Ade greeted him and introduced Mackenzie, and when the decorator took his paint off to the far end of the airy-looking room, Mackenzie wandered around the cool interior, feeling a blossoming pleasure as he spotted little suggestions he himself had made months ago, now come to life. He'd barely given his surroundings a second look yesterday, he'd been too intrigued by the conversation with Hazel and Maddy.

'You're facing the internal walls with that?' he asked, pointing to a pile of broken stones in the corner.

'Not all of them. Those will just do that wall around the

fireplace. Through there,' he indicated a bigger, plainer room next door, 'will be the actual distillery, but the cellars will be a visitor feature, so they're accessed directly from here too.'

Mackenzie followed where he'd pointed, and saw the ramp disappearing beneath a stone archway and leading away into cool darkness. He poked his head through the archway and sensed how the space opened up beyond it. 'It's going to look great,' he said, envy cutting away at him again a little. The whisky side of things had always been the shared pleasure of Ade and their father; neither he nor his brother had been born when Frank had distilled and casked the very first Drumnacoille single malt, but at least, when it had reached bottling age, Ade had been old enough to pretend to enjoy it, even if it had made his eyes water.

'Dad won't need a bedroom in the new house,' Ade said, a little smile softening his features. 'He'll practically live in here, I reckon.' He looked at Mackenzie, his expression turning speculative. 'I wanted to talk to you about something we said last year. When I first came back, and we talked about this place.'

Mackenzie put his hands in his jacket pockets; he had a feeling they might betray his sudden emotion. 'You said you wanted me to come in with you someday.'

'Aye, in a few years. You wanted me to keep a "nice outdoorsy job" open for you, just in case.'

'And you said you knew I was happy doing what I'm doing.'

Ade nodded. 'Is that still true?'

Mackenzie turned away from his brother's too-knowing gaze. 'I don't know,' he said at length. 'Sometimes I think so, when we get the results we're looking for. But I've been doing it for ten years now, and most of the other times, when all I seem to be doing is completing spreadsheets and tax returns, and arguing with benefits scammers...I just remember how much simpler it all was when I was on the rigs. But I'd never go back to that again.'

He thought of the times he'd left his wife and son behind and gone back to his engineering job, spending weeks at a time wondering what they were doing. Now they were gone, it was too late to claw back those years, and he wasn't going to risk missing out on his life with Charis and Jamie.

'I understand,' Ade said quietly. 'I'd be the same.'

'I keep imagining myself now, spending my days on the moor, or in the woods, and my nights at home with my family instead of following some arsehole around trying to uncover their seedy secrets.' He rolled his shoulder again; he was almost 100 per cent fit. 'Quad bikes don't argue back.'

'Don't you believe it,' Ade said, rubbing his calf ruefully. 'I ran over m'own leg two days ago. I swear the bloody thing's possessed by demons.' He took a deep breath. 'Look, Paul, just so you know, that business with Patrick Ross? I totally get it: you were looking out for me, for Dad, and for your own investment.'

'And it wasn't my fault he got the wrong end of the stick,' Mackenzie pointed out.

'Don't push it, *gille beag*,' Ade said. 'You still let him think it. But,' he held up a hand, 'Ross said you'd apologised, and since he's not holding a grudge, I won't either.'

'Thank you, O master,' Mackenzie said drily, and Ade gave a little laugh.

'Okay, that did sound a bit pompous. I just meant it's over, and I'm sorry for over-reacting. Am I forgiven?'

'As long as you stop calling me a little lad,' Mackenzie said, making a point of drawing himself up to his full six feet four, folding his arms and looking down at Ade's paltry six one.

'Deal.' Ade gestured Mackenzie ahead of him towards the door, and they stepped back out into the warm morning. 'My offer still stands. There's a nice "outdoorsy" job waiting for you, starting whenever you like. It'll change to a different one once we're up and running, but if you want to make the move sooner, you only have to say the word. Glencoille can always use a willing labourer with ambitions towards ranger.'

'Ranger, eh?'

'Head ranger, naturally. You'd have to do all the certificates, but I don't see any problem there, do you?'

'What about Maddy?'

'She'll find someone else, that's if she even wants to carry on herself.'

'What makes you think she won't?'

'I'm not saying that. But if you do leave, she's bound to re-evaluate, don't you think?'

'Oh, aye? Got a job for her too, have you?'

Ade laughed. 'I'd not insult her by offering. You're different,' he said, as Mackenzie shot him a look. 'In case it slipped your grasp, *I* wouldn't be giving you a job at all. You're family, and besides, you've put up your inheritance to get this place up and running. Ergo this is your business too. Equally,' he added. 'This is no magnanimous gesture; you have as much right to a share, and a job for life, as myself or Dad. We're all the Mackenzies of Glencoille now, aye?'

Mackenzie stopped as that truth sank home. 'I hadn't thought of it like that.'

'Then do it now.' Ade resumed walking. 'It's an exciting time.' He turned so he was walking backwards. 'Dad wants you to come in, too. He's told me. Anyway, let me know what you think. No rush.'

He spun away again, raising his hand in farewell and

leaving Mackenzie to look around him, first towards his old family home, across the river, and then at this new business, emerging out of the soil all around him. *Dad wants you to come in, too...* Ade had uttered those words almost casually, and he might never understand the emotion they had ignited.

The Mackenzies of Glencoille.

He liked it.

Chapter Thirteen

It FELT strange to Hazel to be climbing onto the back of Griff's bike, since hers was still locked away at her own home, but she told herself it might actually be quite nice to ride pillion for a change, and be able to look at the scenery instead of focusing on the road. It was tough at first to relax and remember she wasn't in charge, but the Speed Twin handled so much better than she'd expected, and after a few minutes she uncurled her fingers and stopped reflexively pressing nothing with her right foot when Griff got a bit throttle-happy.

The road up to Druimgalla took them out of town, past the turning up to Glencoille and up into the hills alongside wooded stretches and wide open moorland. In the distance, as they rose, Hazel could see the sparkle of sunlight on the waters of Loch Ness, and she remembered sitting in the back of her parents' car on their way home and staring back at it in just this way. What had she been thinking about, on those long ago days when everything was normal, and Mum and Dad would be there forever?

Feeling the beginnings of a wave of sorrow, she turned back

to face the front just as they came to the split in the road. She tapped Griff on the shoulder and pointed to the turning, and a few minutes later they were pulling into the yard. The weather today was very different from the last time she'd stopped here, and the branches were no longer weighed down with rain and hitting the garage roof, but Griff had clearly already spotted what she meant when she'd asked him for a quote.

He pulled off his helmet and gloves as he wandered over to the garage. 'What do you think of the bike then?' he asked, peering up into the tree.

'Actually quieter than mine,' she conceded. 'Torquey, too.'

'Aye, got a nice bit of pull in her. Good thing too, with that fuckin' hill we just came up,' he added, pulling a face as he looked back at her. 'So, this is what you wanted me to quote for, is it?'

'Mates' rates?' she asked, with a hopeful smile. 'Being a landlord's not cheap.'

'Then mates' rates it shall be. I didn't realise you were paying though. I thought the agreement was that your aunt had the place cheap off you, as long as she shelled out for the upkeep.'

'It is, pretty much, but, see, I know this *great* tree surgeon…' She gave him her best exaggerated coquette, twirling the toe of her boot incongruously in the dirt of the yard and looking up at him through her lashes.

Griff shook his head pityingly. 'You couldn't even pull that off in full Regency dress,' he said, and ignored Hazel's middle finger salute. 'Right, I'll get up and take a proper look, and you go in and put the kettle on.'

'I can't do that!'

'Why not? It's your house. Presumably you've got a key?'

'It's not my home though. I can't just wander in and out as

and when I like. It's against the terms of the contract, as much as anything else.'

'Bummer.' Griff lifted his head. 'Fear not, I hear a car approaching. All might not yet be lost.'

Hazel heard it too, and frowned. 'She's supposed to be at work today.'

'Who cares? Black and two sugars.' Griff gave her a disarming grin and disappeared around the back of the garage to boost himself off the fence and onto the roof.

Isla parked up and opened the back door of the car to lift out her laptop bag and handbag. 'I didn't expect you this early,'

'I didn't expect *you* at all,' Hazel said, following her to the front door. 'Why aren't you at the gallery?'

Isla grunted and hoisted the laptop bag onto her shoulder so she could unlock the door. 'Bloody Patrick can't seem to keep away from the place lately, unless there's actual work for him to do, and there's only one office for him to skulk in. Which is in fact mine,' she added, 'though you'd never think so.' She led the way into the kitchen and dumped her things onto the table. 'I've brought my work home with me; there's less chance of me swearing myself out of a job that way. Coffee?'

Hazel nodded. 'Griff's checking the job out now, and he'll have a quote for me in a minute. His is black and two,' she added as Isla filled the kettle. She sat down at the table. 'How's things? Apart from your job and your annoying boss, that is.'

'Fine. Glad Dyl's gone back to school though. He was starting to drive me a bit crackers.'

'To be fair there's not a lot for kids to do in Abergarry.'

'Aye, true enough. In fact he came into the gallery the other day to wait for me, he was that bored.'

Hazel sympathised. 'It's always been like that here. If your mates live in a different town you're buggered.'

'Speaking of mates, this Griff fella seems solid, from what you've said.'

'He's been a complete rock,' Hazel agreed. 'You'll like him.'

'As long as he knows what he's doing out there, that's enough for me.' Isla turned back as the kettle flicked off, and at the same moment Griff himself arrived at the back door, clearly loath to trail mucky bootprints through the nicely carpeted front hall.

'Come in.' Isla waved away his concerns as he peered at the soles of his boots. 'Sit down, I'm just making coffee.' She took an opened packet of biscuits from the cupboard and put it on the table.

'No biscuit box?' Hazel asked, taking one. 'I'd like to speak to the manager please.'

'Very funny.' Isla turned to Griff. 'So, what's the damage going to be?'

'It's only a few hours' work to trim and prune that oak, probably no more than half a day, with two of us. So, with mates' rates in play you're looking at a couple of hundred, tops, for Jonah and me. Sound okay?'

'Sounds great. Put it in writing for me and I'll pass it to my landlord.' Isla was smiling as she looked at Hazel, but Hazel couldn't help thinking she looked a little tight around the lips.

'When do you think you'll be able to do it?' she asked Griff.

'If it wasn't for the bike rally I'd make an exception and put you down for next weekend. How does the Monday after sound?'

Isla consulted the calendar on her phone. 'Bank holiday Monday? Are you sure you want to work then?'

'It's the only reason we're free,' Griff said, pulling his coffee closer. 'This time of year we're up to our eyes.'

'That okay with you, Isla?' Hazel asked, and her aunt nodded. Hazel tried not to resent the suddenly martyred look on her face, but it irritated her. 'Just say, if it's not,' she said, a little snappishly. 'We can always re-schedule.'

Griff's expression registered mild surprise, but he hid it as he took a drink, and Isla's own face lost that pinched look. 'No, that's fine. I'll be at work, since we've got this summer exhibition to arrange.

'Can you leave the garage unlocked, so they can use the electricity?' Hazel asked.

Isla frowned. 'I don't want anyone traipsing in there and knocking over my sister's paintings.'

'It's fine,' Griff said quickly. 'We use petrol saws.'

'I was thinking about boiling a kettle,' Hazel said. 'Won't you want a cuppa?'

'Don't worry, we'll bring a flask. We won't impose on your household fuel, Mrs Munro.'

Isla gave a small smile, and a faintly tense silence fell over them as they drank their coffee. Hazel nibbled at a biscuit, trying to put herself in her aunt's shoes; moving into her dead sister's house at the almost charitable rent offered by her niece; thrown out of her own office by her boss, only to come home and find said niece using her contacts to get a cheap price on some basic home maintenance. The same niece who had, just a few short years ago, been heading for prison and a wasted life, while Isla had done everything right: university, marriage, a fantastic job... She was sure to feel hard done by, but at the same time it was hardly Hazel's fault, and the price of being able to play Lady Bountiful now had been pretty damned high.

She found her gaze drawn to the kitchen door and the sitting room beyond, helpless to stop it. The conversation with Maddy and Mackenzie in the distillery had been playing on a loop in her mind; sometimes at the front, loud and jarring, other times all but drowned by the day-to-day stuff that kept her alive and functioning. Now, with the room where it happened no more than a few feet away, it was becoming deafening again.

'Did my mum ever mention someone called Leslie Warrender?' she asked suddenly, not realising she'd been going to.

Isla thought for a moment, then shook her head. 'Name doesn't ring any bells. Why, who is he?'

There was disappointment, but also relief that at least Isla wouldn't be in danger. 'Just someone she met at uni, a friend of Dad's. So she never mentioned him to you?'

'She didn't have a lot of time for us when she came up here to uni,' Isla said, her face taking on that faintly resentful look again. 'At least, not until she dropped out and told us she was getting married.' The underlying criticism was pretty obvious, and Hazel realised today wasn't going to be one of those happy, bonding aunt-and-niece days, not while Isla was still smarting and feeling embarrassingly second-rate. She finished her drink as quickly as she could, without scalding herself this time, and noticed Griff following her lead.

'Oh!' she said, as she stood up to leave. 'I forgot – when Linda and I went through Mum's things we found a few bits and pieces. I'll drop them round.'

'Thanks.' Isla visibly softened, and even smiled. 'I'll bet any money you like she still had that green box.'

'There was *a* green box,' Hazel said. 'Was that hers? I'd assumed it was Dad's.'

'About yea big.' Isla made a foot square with her hands. 'It does look a bit darker than her usual taste,' she conceded. 'Not a flower in sight.'

'Gold trim?'

'That's it!' Isla looked delighted. 'She pinched it from our grandad, so it's probably an antique in itself. Or I suppose you'd have to call it more of a relic,' she mused, 'considering it's probably falling apart by now. She used to keep her most private stuff in it when she was a teenager, and I was too young to be let near it.'

Hazel's skin had cooled as her aunt's words sank in, and she suddenly felt the need to talk to Maddy. She shook her head. 'Well, there's nothing very private in there now. Just some...some concert tickets,' she said, deciding not to mention the photographs, 'and some newspaper cuttings about local art exhibitions with people they knew. Oh, and a watch,' she remembered. 'That's why I thought it was Dad's; it's definitely a bloke's watch.'

'Might have been *our* dad's,' Isla said. 'A memento, you know? Aye, thanks. If you could just bring it up whenever you're next here, that'd be lovely.'

She saw them to the door, and Hazel could sense her eagerness to be back indoors and switching on her laptop, so she wasn't surprised or put out when Isla didn't wait at the door to wave them away.

'What was all that about?' Griff asked, with his back to the door and his voice lowered as if he thought Isla might still be listening. 'You looked pretty sick back there, and I don't mean that in a *down with the kids* sort of a way.'

Hazel chewed the inside of her lip for a moment, studying him. 'Okay,' she said at length. 'Drop me at work, and I'll tell you tonight, after the rally meeting.'

'Don't you want to go back and pick up your own bike?'

'No, Maddy can drive me. And I'm only stopping long enough to tell Ade I'm taking the rest of the day off anyway.' She took a deep breath. 'I need to think.'

Maddy looked up from the list she was compiling, as Hazel came into the portakabin and the chuntering motorcycle outside revved up again and took off. 'All sorted?'

'All sorted. And I have news about the photo.'

Ade appeared in the doorway before she could carry on. 'Ah, good, you're here. Could you call Wilsons again about the cask washer?'

'They said it wouldn't be—'

'I know what they said,' Ade broke in. 'But a nudge for confirmation of an exact date wouldn't hurt, would it?'

'Are you okay?' Maddy asked him, as Hazel obediently picked up the phone. 'You've been tetchy all morning.'

'*Tetchy?*' He grimaced. 'Aye, well, I suppose I have been. But Dad's coming up this afternoon. I'm going to pick him up after lunch. He's going to want to know every last detail about the distillery, even if he couldn't give tuppence for any other part of the build.'

'Except the house,' Maddy pointed out. 'He wants to move in last week, don't forget, so you'd better get onto that.'

Ade looked as if he didn't know whether to be cross or amused, but, as usual, amusement won. 'I don't suppose you'd like to show him around instead? He likes you.'

Maddy laughed. 'He sort of likes you a bit too, clot-heid.'

'Monday week,' Hazel reported a minute later, putting the handset back in its cradle. 'Apparently Griff and Jonah aren't the only ones who work on bank holidays.'

'Excellent! We'll clear out the last of the decorating crap on the Sunday.' Ade picked up his marker pen to scribble on the wall calendar, then paused. 'Your rally's that weekend. Will the place still be heaving?'

'Everyone'll be gone by lunchtime, except our club,' Hazel assured him. 'We'll still be clearing up, but I can help out if you need anything extra doing.'

'That's great, thanks.' Ade wrote *WASH!* in the square. 'You're a star.'

'Good,' Maddy said, 'then I hope you'll let me whisk your star away for a slightly extended lunch? To make up for you taking up her entire first night at my place,' she added, seeing him about to protest. 'I need to go into Inverness to check some things out, and you can't be around and watching her if you're picking up Frank. I'd be happier if I could take her with me, instead.'

'That's settled then,' Hazel said, employing her usual tactic of not giving him chance to answer. 'I'll get the emails up to date before we go, and divert the calls to my mobile.'

Ade's eyes met Maddy's with a hopeless *see what I have to put up with?* expression, and she responded with a look of wide-eyed incomprehension. *I don't know what you're making such a fuss about.* He snorted and ducked out into the yard again, and she heard his voice raised in a shout to one of his contractors.

'Around your little finger,' she said to Hazel in admiration.

'Right around,' Hazel grinned. 'Oh, and about the photo? It wasn't Dad's, it was Mum's.'

Maddy frowned. 'How did you find that out?'

Hazel told her what Isla had said, and her manner turned more serious. 'Do you think...' She let the thought trail away, and Maddy waited while she searched for the right way to say it. 'We couldn't figure out why Warrender would possibly want, or need, to hurt her, could we? Do you think...maybe they were having an affair, and she ended it?'

'Or even threatened to tell your dad?' Maddy considered.

'It's possible. But would that be enough to...' She stopped before she said anything too graphic, then went on, 'to do that? Enough for him to *kill* her?'

'It might only have been enough for him to get angry,' Hazel pointed out. 'He might not have intended to go as far as he did. Then he could have staged the burglary to cover it up.'

'She was still in her dressing gown,' Maddy threw a quick look at Hazel, in case she was causing her friend any pain, but Hazel's expression was hard now, rather than distressed.

'People have killed, accidentally or otherwise, for less,' she said. 'This might be all we need, once we've found him, to get some sort of reaction out of him when we show him the photo.'

'We could always intimate we know more than we do,' Maddy mused. 'Get him to give himself away.'

'And then what? They'd still need evidence to arrest him, wouldn't they? Or a warrant or something?'

'Not if they've got reasonable grounds to suspect he's done something. Other than Linda's word, I mean. Evidence can come later.' Maddy tapped her fingers for a moment. 'Besides, we wouldn't want him arrested until after the blackmail thing's sorted. Once that's done, and Warrender feels invincible, he'll be out there living it large. That's when we'll be able to get him checked out properly.' She stopped herself before she blurted out anything about Nick. 'Once we find anything out for definite, we'll make sure he's on the police radar.'

Hazel absorbed this, then nodded. 'Okay, understood. So, have you found some likely places to look for... Hang on.' She picked up her phone, which was vibrating its way across the desk, and her face broke into a broad smile. 'Breda! Hi.'

She listened for a moment, while Maddy jotted down the names of two further guest houses within easy reach of Inverness, then she lowered her phone. 'Can we meet Breda for lunch, seeing as we're going into town? She wants to talk about a memorial thingy for Linda.'

Maddy nodded and looked at the clock on her laptop. 'One-ish suits me. Thistle, I presume? That'll be a glass of water for me, then.'

Hazel grinned. 'No, don't worry, she wants to get away from there for an hour.' She made the arrangements, and ended the call. 'There's a place called Buchanan's, just down the road from Thistle,' she said. 'She'll meet us there just after one, when Max starts his shift.'

'Perfect. Meantime you've got about half an hour to get those emails done. I want to have a look in the gallery before we meet Breda, see what all the fuss is about with this painting.'

Buchanan's was packed on this late April lunch time, but Breda waved at them from a table by one of the windows; when Hazel led Maddy over she got to her feet, lifting her multi-coloured scarf clear of her orange boots, and embraced Hazel like a daughter.

'I'm so pleased you could come at such short notice, love.' She smiled at Maddy and held out her hand. 'Hello, Miss Clifford. Grand to meet you.' Her eyes touched, then slid discreetly away from, the scar beside Maddy's eye. 'Hazel's told me so much about you.' She eased her way back into her corner seat. 'Sit down, both of you, I know time's precious for all of us.'

Hazel picked up the menu and scanned it. 'Not a patch on Thistle,' she stage-whispered over the top of it, and Breda laughed.

'Prices aren't either,' she pointed out. 'Lunch is on me, so pick whatever you like best, and if they don't have your favourites, pick a couple and combine them.'

'Sorry, Haze, I don't know if they'll have squirty cheese and crisps,' Maddy said, and earned herself a protesting glare from Hazel.

'I can be sophisticated when I want to be!'

'Nothing wrong with a bit of squirty cheese.' Breda smiled. 'Now, while you have a think, I'd like to talk a little bit about poor Linda, and what we can do for her. Thistle's diary is fully booked for months, sadly, but I know a few other places we could try.'

'Did you know her really well?' Maddy asked, hoping it just sounded like a polite question rather than a fishing expedition.

'She was a friend of Donna's first,' Breda said. 'Lumsden, that is. You remember she was the manager at Thistle, before me?'

Maddy nodded; it would be hard to forget Kilbride's daughter. 'I met her a few times.'

'Linda was only a couple of years older than me, but maybe ten years older than Donna, so we got along a little better. Had more in common, you know?'

'And Hazel?' Maddy asked, looking from one to the other. 'How long have you two known each other?'

'Not long at all,' Hazel said. 'Breda was just really kind to me after Linda died, and we've agreed to try and cobble something together in lieu of a funeral. At least until we're allowed to send her off properly.'

'I know she'll have colleagues and students who want to pay their respects,' Breda added.

The waiter arrived to take their order, so Maddy took the

opportunity of the brief lull in conversation to send a quick message to Paul.

In Inverness atm. Check Linda history with Kilbride – was friend of Donna. Maybe L father worked for Kilbride? Back by 4pm, will call.

Breda and Hazel were already discussing dates and venues by the time she'd sent the text, and she kept any further questions to herself for the time being, only taking mental notes as the two women spoke about their mutual friend. The way Breda had immediately embraced the spiky, outwardly intimidating younger woman as someone who clearly needed a strong set of friends around her was touching, and Maddy felt it was time to put the connection to good use. By the time the food had arrived, and they'd unwrapped cutlery and were applying condiments, she'd decided on her best approach.

'I gather from Hazel that you're a friend of Patrick Ross?'

'An acquaintance really,' Breda said, accepting the black pepper from Hazel. 'My mother knew his wife, I think, back in the day, but I only know her by sight. Mr Ross comes to dinner at Thistle sometimes, and he's friendly with Mr Kilbride, so naturally he gets preferential treatment. I did pop in to his seventieth birthday party at Waterfront though.'

'Did you ever meet someone called Leslie Warrender?'

'Meet him? No. I've seen some of his pictures though. Mr Ross has a couple in the rear of the gallery still. Fine stuff.'

'You know he died though?'

'I do. Such a tragedy. I'm glad Mr Ross keeps those pictures up. Mr Warrender was very talented, but he died before my time here in Scotland.' She gestured at Hazel's lunch. 'That ham looks nice. Proper country ham, lovely choice.'

Maddy was somewhat irritated at having the conversation so abruptly re-directed, but realised she might have been sounding a little interrogatory, after all she herself was the third wheel here; Breda had asked Hazel to lunch so they could discuss their friend's memorial.

'Will you be bringing some of those friends you were with when I saw you the other night?' Breda forked up some spaghetti carbonara and twirled it expertly in her spoon; Maddy was glad she'd only ordered an omelette. 'They seem like a nice comfort for you.'

'They are,' Hazel said. 'They miss Dad, too.' Her fingers closed on the silver lump around her neck, and Breda smiled.

'That's a pretty necklace. I noticed it earlier.'

'My dad made it out of my mother's rings and stuff, after she died. It was the one way I could wear her jewellery all the time.'

'What a wonderful idea; he must have been a lovely man. I'm sorry I never knew him or your ma.'

Hazel nodded her thanks. 'To answer your question though, none of the club knew Linda really. She never got involved in that side of Dad's life, so we don't have to cater for any of them. Griff might come along though, if he's not working.'

'This Griff,' Breda said, giving Hazel a quizzical look. 'Is he a significant someone in your life?'

'If you mean a good friend, then yes. If you're thinking of anything else, the answer's no. He's like a brother, nothing more.' She applied herself once more to her ham, egg and chips. 'He recognised you, actually,' she went on. 'He couldn't think where from, then realised it was from Thistle. Does he go there a lot?'

'Not looking like that, he doesn't,' Breda said, then looked appalled. 'Lord, I didn't mean that the way it sounded! I just meant that if he comes to Thistle at all he probably doesn't stand out, the way he would if he was dressed in all his biker stuff.'

Hazel smiled. 'He dresses quite normally during the week. So you don't recognise him?'

'To be fair, love, it's like when you recognise your local shop keeper in a busy street, and they don't necessarily return the favour.'

'Did you ever meet Hazel's parents?' Maddy asked her.

Breda shook her head. 'No, never. My only link with Hazel here is through Linda. She was worried about the girl, I know that, so maybe it's partly out of respect for her memory that I've made it my little...quest, if you like, to make sure she's well cared for.' She smiled at Hazel. 'Though it seems from what you've said that you've plenty of people around you. I'm glad.'

'I'm not likely to fall off the wagon again,' Hazel said, frowning slightly. 'Don't worry about that.'

'It's not just that,' Breda said gently. 'You've lost your ma, your da, and now Linda. Anyone would be distressed by that. Anyway,' she went on, more briskly now, as she chased the last bit of bacon on her plate, 'speaking of Linda, we've got some possible dates now, so I'll have a ring around and see what we can come up with. Hopefully they'll release her body soon though, so we can do the whole thing properly.'

'Thanks,' Hazel said. 'It's really good of you to take the reins.'

'That reminds me,' Maddy put in. 'I meant to thank you too, for offering to host my brother's wedding.'

Breda looked at her in surprise, then her smile widened. 'Of course, you're Nick's sister.' She laid down her cutlery and patted her mouth with her napkin. 'It's my pleasure; Max has been such a godsend since I took over the running of Thistle, it'll be grand to see him married and happy, and I'm glad to be in a position to help.'

'The food there's gorgeous,' Hazel said to Maddy. 'Have you been?'

'Ade and I had lunch there with Frank, last year,' Maddy said, 'and Paul and Charis are going tonight, for Charis's birthday. I've told them to go for the beef Wellington; knocks Ramsay's into a cocked hat.'

'That's what Max and Nick have as one of their wedding dinner choices!' Breda was almost beaming. 'Chef will be delighted to hear it's made such an impact.' She pushed her plate away and turned to signal to an attentive server, who'd clearly been told to remain nearby. 'And now I must love you and leave you, but you stay here and order dessert if you like – it's on me.'

She gave her credit card details to the waiter, over protestations from Maddy and Hazel, and gave Hazel a squeeze as she left the two of them to the remainder of their meal.

'She's a powerhouse, isn't she?' Hazel said with a grin, as she picked up the dessert menu.

'Aye. No arguing with her, that's for sure.'

'You don't sound as if you approve.'

'Oh, don't get me wrong,' Maddy said quickly. 'Breda herself is great, I just think Nick would have preferred somewhere less fancy for his wedding do. But it'll save them a bit of money. And Max is her golden boy,' she added. 'Let's not forget that.'

'So you're already one of the highly favoured,' Hazel said. 'Enjoy it, there are worse things than a guaranteed table at Thistle anytime you want one.'

'Pity Paul couldn't have got a freebie tonight,' Maddy said, perusing the list of desserts.

'Maybe if he didn't so obviously have it in for William Kilbride he could have,' Hazel observed. 'Ade told me about the argument. About Kilbride and Ross being such a big part of the Glencoille Estate. So that's what you were talking about when you mentioned money laundering?'

'Not here,' Maddy murmured. She planted her finger on her menu and spoke normally again. 'That's what I'm having: salted caramel brownie and ice cream.'

'Sounds good. I'll have the same.' Hazel caught the eye of the server, though with noticeably more difficulty than Breda had done, and they gave their order. When the server had gone, she rested her chin on her hands and stared straight into Maddy's eyes. It was quite disconcerting, and Maddy found she had difficulty meeting the look.

'What?'

'I'm going to be Ade's assistant manager.'

Maddy blinked, and hoped she'd hidden a flicker of uncertainty. 'Wow, that's... It's brilliant news! Congratulations.'

'Which means I have a right to know everything that concerns Glencoille, don't you think?'

'I told you—'

'I know, not here.' Hazel sat upright again. 'But after lunch, I want to know what Mackenzie's concerned about, and what he's basing it on, and then *I* can keep an eye out for any reason Ade might have to listen to him. Because I don't know about you, but I barely know William Kilbride from a hole in the ground, and I don't trust Patrick Ross as far as I could throw him.'

Chapter Fourteen

MACKENZIE PULLED up outside Patrick Ross's house, after driving from Glencoille to Culloden on something worryingly close to auto-pilot; over an hour's drive, and he had no real idea how he'd got here. But here he was, and now he had to get his head out of all the possibilities the future suddenly held for him, and back in the game.

Ross had seen him arrive, and pulled open the front door. 'Come in,' he called, turning away and leaving Mackenzie to grab his notebook and his phone and follow him into his office. Ross closed the door as soon as he'd stepped in, and he seemed even more nervous and agitated than he'd been the last time Mackenzie had been here, two days ago.

'Have you heard from Warrender again?' Mackenzie asked.

'Only the daily phone call.' Ross sat at his desk and began playing with a folded piece of paper that lay there. 'He wants to speed things up,' he said. 'He's getting twitchy, and, get this, he told me he's not planning to settle here after all.'

'Not that surprising really; it's probably sinking in that he's actually killed someone.'

'You're still sure that was him? You said he was small-time. Small fry, whatever.'

'It was hardly an organised hit,' Mackenzie pointed out. 'Sounded like a panicky reaction more than anything else, and that kind of thing takes time to register if you're not used to it.'

'You've heard the details then?'

'I've heard enough. Look, I need you to do something.' Mackenzie leaned against the desk and spoke carefully. 'I need you to get hold of Kilbride again, and arrange for that...that, *heavy*, if you want to use that word. Don't do anything, just get some names at this point.'

Ross drew a breath to speak, then stopped, as if he had planned to say something quite different. He gave Mackenzie a shrewd look. 'How do I know you're not just going to use it against him? Or them? The blokes who used to work for Will aren't exactly playschool teachers.'

Mackenzie wanted to sigh, swear, and most of all to walk out. But he had a job to do, and as long as Warrender was around, Hazel Douglas's life was in danger. 'Look,' he said, as patiently as he could manage, '*we* need to find this bloke so we can protect...any innocent person Linda might have spoken to, and *you* need us to find him and stop him ruining your life. So can you just stop pissing about and trying to out-think me? I'm on your side here.'

Ross subsided. 'Aye, you're right.'

'So get on the phone to Kilbride.'

'No need.' Ross unfolded the sheet of paper on his desk. 'I've already got a list of names; Will just needs to know who I want to contact.'

Mackenzie was torn; he'd suspected that, despite declaring he'd turned over a new leaf, Kilbride wouldn't think twice about providing muscle he swore he no longer used, and it galled him that the proven liar was still going to be part of Glencoille. At the same time, that muscle was going to be useful, so, feeling like a complete hypocrite, he held out his hand for the list. It was short, and evidently outdated, showing as it did the names of the deceased as well as imprisoned. He took out his pen and put a line first through Craig Lumsden, then Ian George, and Neil George, his brother. Of the four names left, one stood out, and he felt a prickle of unease. He put an asterisk next to that one and handed the list back.

'Get him,' he said. 'And don't tell either him or Kilbride you've spoken to anyone else about it.'

Ross frowned at the name. 'Why him?'

'Never mind.' Dave Griffin was on two lists now: this one, and the worryingly short one of people Hazel trusted. It didn't necessary indicate conflict, but it was vital to check that her trust was justified.

'What do I tell him?' Ross asked.

'Nothing yet, we just want him in reserve. Meantime, my partner's working on finding out where Warrender's staying, and once we do that, we want you to call him and arrange a meeting. Tell him you have the money.'

Ross began to nod, then his eyes narrowed. 'Why do you need to wait until you've found out where he's staying?'

Mackenzie hesitated. 'Because we want to move in while we know he's out,' he said at length. 'We're not looking for anyone to threaten him, or beat him up.'

'Because you think he's got the painting here, in Scotland.' Ross gave a short laugh. 'I'm not a fool, Mackenzie.'

Mackenzie shrugged and gave in. 'Aye, well, we do think it's pretty far-fetched to believe he's got some dodgy casino behind him, prepared to risk everything to help a small time thief like him.'

'So you plan to send this...' Ross consulted the list, 'Griffin bloke in to get the painting while Warrender's meeting me.'

'It would keep our hands clean. And yours.'

'And what about this other thing you think he's hiding?' Ross asked. 'What will you do about that?'

'That's got nothing to do with you, or the painting.' Mackenzie rose to his feet and shoved his notebook away. 'We just want to get shot of this blackmail part of it, without spooking him into realising we suspect him of...of something else.'

'And of murdering Linda Sturdy to cover it.'

'That too. So it's imperative you don't give anything away. Wait for a call from us before you arrange to meet Warrender. Okay?'

'And when *he* calls, in the meantime?'

'Stall him. Just keep telling him you're working on it, getting closer and so on, and you just need a bit more time. Make up what you like. You can try and get any info on where he's staying, but for God's sake be subtle, or you'll send him running for the hills. He's going to be hyper-aware just now.'

'If I manage to get a clue, I'll let you know.'

'As long as he thinks you're too ashamed and embarrassed to have told anyone, he'll wait. One whiff otherwise, and lives'll be in danger.' Mackenzie looked closely at Ross. There was something about the way his eyes kept cutting away whenever there was a mention of putting someone else at risk; it didn't look so much worried, as guilty.

'I'll be careful,' Ross said, unfolding and re-folding the list. 'Thanks.'

Mackenzie had stood up straight to leave, now he leaned back again. 'What is it?' he asked, keeping his voice soft. He tilted his head to the side, his eyes never leaving Ross's. 'What aren't you telling me?'

'I've told you everything.'

'Now, see, I don't think you have.' Mackenzie fell silent again, and Ross's fingers began speeding up their nervous origami until Mackenzie felt like bellowing at him to stop, but he kept the urge in check. Waiting.

'I said something to Warrender,' Ross blurted at last, and dropped the list. 'He was banging on about how all he wanted was to be able to move back to Scotland, to Abergarry. That was when he'd mentioned that Linda had interviewed him and not recognised him, and I couldn't believe he really thought he could get away with it. He said he was safe here since Graeme Douglas died, and I...I might have reminded him—'

'That Graeme had a daughter,' Mackenzie finished for him, his heart sinking. 'Fuck's sake, man.'

'He said she'd never recognise him,' Ross went on, 'that she'd only been a kid when he left.' But his expression didn't match the hope in his words.

Mackenzie took a long breath, and let it out slowly while he thought about the implications. It was more important than ever now that Hazel stayed within the sphere of people she trusted, which meant Griff had to be vetted sooner rather than later. 'Get on the phone to Kilbride,' he said. 'Now. Tell him you want to meet with Dave Griffin as soon as possible. Today if you can.'

Ross picked up his phone, and while he made the call, Mackenzie stood silently looking out of the window. What if Warrender was out there now, watching? Just because there was no car didn't mean he wasn't lurking in one of the many hedges, or even somewhere inside the house... He mentally cursed the blasé way they'd been going about this whole thing, and wondered if they'd done the right thing by holding back on calling the police. But, he reasoned, as he heard Ross talking to Kilbride behind him, it would still be a bad idea to have spooked Warrender into leaving before they'd found something to tie him to Yvette Douglas's murder as well as Linda Sturdy's.

'Would he be free now?' Ross was saying to Kilbride, and Mackenzie turned back, eyebrows raised. Ross nodded. 'Get him to call me then, aye? Soon as. And thanks, Will... No,' he glanced at Mackenzie, 'and I'll make sure it's clear you've not been part of this.' He ended the call and placed his phone carefully back on the table. 'He's going to get Griffin to call me.'

'Good. If he's free, get him to meet you at the gallery, not here.'

'So we just wait now?'

'Aye. We wait. Meantime, I'm just going to have a little look around outside.'

Ross gave him a look of guarded amusement. 'Warrender's not here, you know.'

'Glad to hear it.' Mackenzie pulled open the office door. 'You'll forgive me for wanting to make sure.'

When he went back in, having satisfied himself that they were, indeed, alone, Ross was pulling on his jacket. 'He's finishing a job, but he'll be at Waterfront at three.'

'Right.' Mackenzie took out his own phone, checked the time and called Maddy. 'Where are you?'

'Just finishing up a very nice lunch, round the corner from Thistle. Hazel's with me.'

'Okay.' He lowered his voice. 'I want her back at Glencoille where it's safe, but I don't want her worried, and I *don't* want her going off anywhere with Griff.'

'I see,' she said carefully. 'I'll keep an eye on that for you.'

'Get Ade to text her to go back to work.'

'Ade's picking up your dad this afternoon,' she reminded him. 'I'll pass on the message.'

'We need to talk soon,' he said, 'and without her there. I'll call you sometime after three, so stay in signal if you can. Right,' he said to Ross, putting his phone away, 'get back to your gallery then. I'll leave it up to you how you get your manager out of her office. I'll text you when I see Griffin's turned up, and you can start recording.'

'Where will you be?'

'No idea yet. I'll have to see how the land lies when I get there.'

As it turned out he was able to take up a station in the gallery, in one of the more moodily lit sections. Isla had apparently already left the office, to work from home, so there was no need for explanation or argument, and when Griff's sturdy work boots sounded on the wooden floor, Mackenzie moved further into the shadow and sent the message to alert Ross. Then all he could do was wait.

After no more than five minutes, possibly less, the office door opened again and Griff strode back out to the reception. He was dressed in his work clothes, his T shirt and high-vis waistcoat startlingly out of place in this environment, and the few browsing art lovers and tourists gave him curious looks as he passed them, but he was clearly used to it.

Mackenzie waited for a few minutes after he'd left, to be sure he wasn't coming back, then knocked softly on the office door. 'It's Mackenzie.'

'Come in.' Ross drew his phone from his pocket and laid it on the desk. 'I don't know what you wanted from this, but there's not much of interest, I'm afraid.' He touched the play icon.

'Dave Griffin.' The voice came out muffled-sounding. 'I've heard you need someone.'

'Patrick Ross. Thanks for coming.'

'We shook hands there,' Ross supplied, and Mackenzie waved him to silence.

'So, what can I do for you?' Griff asked.

'Nothing, right now.'

A pause, Mackenzie could hear the rustle of fabric as Ross shifted in his seat, and then Griff's mildly amused puzzled voice.

'So... Why am I here?'

'I wanted to meet you. I'm going to need some help soon and I wanted to be sure you were the man to give it.'

A soft, derisive sound. 'Well you won't know that unless you tell me what kind of "help" you need.'

'Nothing violent.'

'Stop.' Mackenzie held up a hand. 'What happened there? Did he look relieved? Disappointed?'

'No reaction at all,' Ross said. 'Sorry.'

He tapped play again, and Mackenzie heard Griff ask, now clearly running low on patience, 'What, then? Anything illegal?'

'Would it matter?'

'I'm not playing games, Mr Ross. I'm a busy bloke, and I've already had to delay a customer to come here and speak to you, as it is.'

A chair scraped on the floor, and then Ross spoke again. 'We, I, might be asking you to break into someone's temporary accommodation and take something that doesn't belong to that person. Would you be available for that?'

'Take what?'

'I'll let you know if and when it becomes necessary to call you again.'

This time the pause was longer. Almost painful. Mackenzie looked questioningly at Ross, who shook his head briefly and pointed to the phone. Eventually, Griff said, cautiously.

'Possibly. Call me again if you've actually got something to talk about.'

'Just before you go,' Ross said, 'and purely out of interest, do you still work for William Kilbride?'

'I wasn't aware Mr Kilbride still had any requirements in that direction,' Griff said carefully. 'As far as I know he's no longer in the short-term loan business.'

'Okay, thanks.'

Presumably there was another handshake there, then the click of the door opening could be heard and the recording ended. Ross looked at Mackenzie, a little anxiously. 'Did you get what you needed from that?'

Mackenzie gave him a bland smile and offered his own hand. 'Thanks, Mr Ross. Wait for my call now, aye? It might be a few days.'

He made his way back down the road to where he'd left his car, away from the front of the gallery this time. It was true he hadn't liked the way Griff had shown up on Kilbride's list, which meant he had likely been guilty of some pretty vile behaviour in the past, but there was still nothing to say he was any danger to Hazel now. All they could do was make sure she was aware, and keep a close eye on him themselves. He sent Maddy a message of explanation, and asked her to put out feelers as to how much Hazel knew of Griff's past, then turned his thoughts to the other weighty matter that had been making inroads on his concentration: Ade's parting words up at Glen-coille. There would be a lot to talk to Charis about tonight at dinner.

His phone sounded, and it was as if the universe had heard him and sent its annoying little message in the mitigating shape of a text from Charis.

Max called. We're double-booked at Thistle. Gutted! If we switch to next Fri we get free champers to make up. Shall I say yes? x

Mackenzie swore under his breath and sent back, *Ok. Really wanted to talk tonight. Ask Jamie if he minds being banished to room with fish supper! I'll even bring coke. x*

Then he started slowly back home to Abergarry, weighing this job against whatever uncertain work and future Glencoille offered, and only vaguely aware of the faint smile on his face as he drove.

Hazel, once more settled in her office chair at Glencoille, had listened to one side of Maddy's phone call with Mackenzie, and then to her hesitant explanation of what Mackenzie had found out. She remembered Griff's comment on the day she'd sorted her dad's things: *We've all done stuff we'd rather forget...* and realised she had only assumed he'd been talking about his old bike club. But he was right in what he'd said, and just as he'd accepted what he'd known about her own past without judgement, she owed him the same understanding.

'Are you okay?' Maddy asked. 'I know it's not a nice thing to hear about someone you're fond of.'

Hazel gave her a wry smile. 'It's like Griff says,' she dropped her voice into a lower register and attempted to reproduce Griff's rumbly voice, 'it's where we are now that matters, we can't do anything about that other shit.'

Maddy returned the smile. 'He's not wrong. Will you tell him what you know?'

'I'm not sure how I can, without telling him everything that's going on, and how he was tricked and recorded.'

'Well, that second part's up to you,' Maddy said. She opened her laptop and switched it on. 'He might not have been one of Kilbride's violent ones, anyway, I'm sure Kilbride had people who just...looked the part and didn't use any of Craig Lumsden's methods.'

'Maybe, but I'm under no illusions either way. He's got a past, I knew that, but he can still be a loyal friend to me like he was to my dad.'

'Okay. I'll leave you to decide. What time do you finish?'

'We've got a rally meeting tonight at six, in the Twisted Tree, so I'll need to knock off at five if you can drive me back into town?'

'Absolutely. I'll drop in to Dad's and see Tas while you're doing that.' Maddy looked up from her screen. 'If you're okay with that, of course. Just say the word if you'd rather have me nearby.'

'No,' Hazel shook her head firmly. 'You go and see Tas, I'll be fine. I'll get Griff to see me back to yours after the meeting.'

The meeting ended by eight thirty, and Hazel wandered outside to wait for Griff at one of the picnic tables in the little road-facing beer garden. There were puddles on the wood from an earlier shower, and she wiped the seat with her sleeve but winced as her jeans still got a chilly soaking when she sat down.

'What's this?' Griff sat opposite. 'I thought you wanted to get home?'

'I'm not going home,' she told him. 'I'm staying at Maddy's. I wanted to talk to you, alone. And then ask you something.'

It was easier, in the half-dark, to tell him everything without getting emotional. He knew about her mother, of course, but not the details, and certainly not that it might have been a targeted murder rather than an interrupted burglary. When she told him their suspicions lay with Leslie Warrender, and that Warrender was alive and well, she could see his head come up in surprise, quickly followed by a scowl.

'I'll kill the fucker,' he breathed, and Hazel touched his wrist.

'Leave it, okay? I'm just telling you all this because we thought you ought to know what all the secrecy and security stuff's about. I'm being well looked after while Maddy and Mackenzie work on finding him, and we don't want him scared off. Or alerted in any way, right?'

'Who else is watching out for you?'

She told him about Ade, who would also know it all by now, and Breda, who didn't need to. 'And now you,' she added. 'But only because we think we can trust you not to go off the deep end.'

'You can.'

And...' she chewed at her lip. 'We know you went to see Patrick Ross today—'

'Ah.' Griff folded his arms. 'That's all part of it, is it? How did he know to contact me?'

'Kilbride gave him a list. When Mackenzie saw your name on it, he got a bit worried.'

'In case I was another Craig Lumsden?' Griff shook his head and leaned forward on the table again. 'Look, I know this'll be hard to believe, but I'm not. I promise. I never was. Well...' he stopped and took a deep breath. 'Me and Craig worked together once, and dealt out a bit of...rough justice, I suppose you'd call it. Not on a customer,' he added. 'I never did that, but on one of Kilbride's crew who been screwing him over. Even then Craig did most of the heavy stuff. Your dad knew about it.'

'You don't have to—'

'I'm not generally a violent bloke, Haze, I promise. That was a one-off.'

Hazel studied him as best she could, and saw only an earnest wish to be believed. 'Good,' she said. 'So now you know what it's all about, and why we're on the lookout for this Warrender creep, but also why you need to keep a lid on it if you see him. As long as he doesn't know I'd recognise him, I'm safe. But we really want to know where he's staying,' she added. 'It would get things cleared up a hell of lot faster.'

'If he's got any sense, he's not staying in the same place for more than a day at a time anyway,' Griff said. 'In his position I'd be hotel-hopping like crazy.'

'Good point,' Hazel said, her voice turning glum as she realised how much longer things could drag on. 'I'll tell Maddy to re-check some, thanks.' Something else occurred to her. 'That's why you recognised Breda Kelly then. From when you worked for Kilbride?'

He nodded. 'As a team we'd meet at Thistle quite a lot, back then, and whenever Kilbride was around she'd a habit of just hovering nearby in case he clicked his fingers.'

'She still does,' Hazel said, remembering the dinner with him and Ross.

'Come on, I'll walk you back.' Griff held out a hand, and she stood up, pulling her wet jeans away from her backside with a little shudder. She felt hugely better for drawing him into her corner, and her confidence in having surrounded herself with good people took another boost. Leslie Warrender didn't stand a chance.

Chapter Fifteen

IT WAS GETTING to the point where the moment his phone made the slightest sound, Ross felt his stomach drop. A full week had passed, with nerve-jangling slowness, since Mackenzie had given him that infuriatingly non-committal response to his question about Dave Griffin. *Wait for my call,* indeed. Well Ross had done enough waiting, and the team that Kilbride had been so keen to talk up had produced precisely nothing. They'd kept him up to date, and they did seem to be doing a lot of leg work, but they'd also admitted that they thought Warrender was skipping around daily, changing his plans at the last minute and travelling light so he could pick up and leave at a moment's notice. More than once Ross had been tempted to begin gathering the money together anyway, from different sources to avoid triggering any alerts or concerned calls from the bank; he just wanted to pay the blackmailing bastard and get him out of his life once and for all.

But up until now he'd been good. The obedient little blackmail victim. There was still whatever else Warrender might have done too, which had put Mackenzie onto him, and Ross's conscience had won out, so he'd sat on the impulse and left his money where it was. Now, with far too much time to think it through, he was wavering again; a spotlight on Linda Sturdy was a spotlight on her father, then that bloody painting, and finally Waterfront, and Ross himself. Sod that.

When the daily phone call came, Ross blurted, 'Okay, it's on.'

Warrender paused, then his voice came again, tense. 'You've got it?'

Ross knew it was wrong, but once he'd gone off-script there was no turning back, and besides, the sudden greed in Warrender's voice struck a spark of anger in him; so much for just wanting to retire to the place he loved.

'Aye. I've got it.' *You pathetic, grabby little wretch.* 'Now where are you staying?' Warrender's chuckle made him grimace and hold his phone away from his ear for a moment. 'All right, smart-arse,' he said, 'where can we meet, then?'

'The Burnside Hotel.'

'Where the hell's that? Is that where you're staying?'

'It's in Abergarry, and no, did you think I'd be stupid enough to tell you where I'm staying?'

'Why, what do you think I'd do? It's not as if I can break into your room and nick a painting that's sitting in a lock-up in France, is it?' Ross heard the challenge in his own voice and winced; Mackenzie would have fallen out of his tree if he'd heard that. But self preservation was a powerful instinct, and it had finally kicked in, along with his common sense.

There was a long spell of quiet, during which the wince became a knuckle-chewing desire to turn the clock back, and then Warrender spoke again, with exaggerated patience. 'I'm not telling you where I am, Mr Ross, in case you decide it would be a great idea to send someone round to beat the code out of me.'

'*Send* someone?' Ross gave what he hoped sounded like a derisive laugh. 'As if I'd want anyone else involved.'

'The Burnside,' Warrender repeated. 'Eight o'clock, in the bar.'

'Abergarry's miles away. Why are you all the way out there?'

'None of your beeswax, Ross.'

'And when I hand it over? When the painting's destroyed, and we're all done?'

Warrender was the king of the expectant pauses, and it once more took a moment for him to speak. 'Then I leave. Go back to France.'

'What happened to all that *settling down here* bollocks?'

'Pipe dreams exist to be extinguished, sadly.'

'Crap,' Ross said, his anger getting the better of him now. 'You're running, aren't you? You killed Matthew Sturdy's daughter, and—'

'No! I didn't.'

'And now you're hiding until you get your money. Well, what if I suggest to the police that they might like a word?'

'Michael Booth's got nothing to hide, remember?' Warrender's voice turned hard. 'And your own name will come under a bit of scrutiny if the police find out who I am; let's not forget that.'

'*I* didn't murder anyone,' Ross snapped back.

'Neither did I! But that won't stop you going to prison with Sturdy anyway, will it? He's pretty good at improvising when it comes to weapons, as I recall.' Ross didn't answer, and Warrender sighed. 'Look, this is a neat, clean transaction, or it could be. It'll all be over by tomorrow morning, I'll be out of your life and you can get that original painting re-valued and make your killing off it. Pardon my pun.'

Ross closed his eyes, thinking hard. If he could get Griffin out to this hotel in Abergarry tonight, they might just stand a chance of finding out where Warrender was staying. If not, he was on his own, but he was damned if this jumped up scribbler was going to hold him hostage like this any longer.

'Eight,' he confirmed at last. 'The Burnside.' As soon as he broke the connection he dialled Griffin's number. 'You said to call you if I had anything to talk about.'

'Aye. I'm listening.' The man's voice was unreadable; not eager, not reluctant, not even curious.

'Are you free tonight?'

'Some of it. What time?'

'Eight o'clock, but it's in Abergarry. A place called the Burnside, d'you know it?'

'Aye.' Again, no inflection in the voice, giving away nothing. 'I'll see you there.'

'But I haven't told you what—' Ross glared at his now-dead phone, as if Griffin could see his annoyance. 'Yeah, see you there,' he muttered, and rubbed his face. His resolve was already faltering; should he call Mackenzie and confess what he'd done? He too was based in Abergarry, after all. Then again, if it went pear-shaped and Warrender scarpered without waiting for his money, it was best if Mackenzie didn't know he'd had anything to do with it.

Julie was in the sitting room when he went through, kneeling on the floor and rolling a ball for Pica. She looked up in surprise as Ross scooped his car keys from the tray on the sideboard. 'Off out again?'

'I've got an appointment I forgot about,' he lied smoothly, feeling guilty as she just smiled and went back to playing with the dog. 'I won't be back late,' he added, 'but it's in Abergarry so a bit of a trek.'

'Drive safe, then,' she said. 'Call if it's going to be past midnight, and I won't wait up. Oh,' she added, ruffling Pica's coat, 'speaking of late, my coach isn't due back until around two on Sunday morning.'

'Coach?'

'And you're dropping me off at the station at six on Saturday morning,' she added, an amused lift to her eyebrow. 'You *had* forgotten.'

'Oh! The cocktail thing in Edinburgh.' He nodded. 'Don't worry, I'll get an early night tomorrow so I'm bright and early for driving duty.'

He paused after unlocking his car; with Julie away all day and most of the night on Saturday it might be better to postpone tonight's business until then, especially if it was likely to turn nasty. He took out his phone and looked over at the sitting room window. He could see Julie getting up to fetch the ball, all her attention focused on Pica, the child they'd never had, and a wash of affection for her swept over him. He had no number for Warrender, so it was hardly his fault he couldn't tell him he'd called off the meeting; instead he called Griff.

'Forget it,' he said. 'I'll call you on Saturday if you're free.'

'I'm not,' Griff said, still in that same, maddening no-tone. 'What's happened?'

'Doesn't matter. Something's come up, and tonight doesn't work for me, that's all. Thanks anyway, but I'll call again if anything changes.'

As he ended the call, Ross experienced a deep swell of unexpected relief; it had been a moment of madness, driven by frustration, but thank God he'd nipped it in the bud before it was too late; Mackenzie had been adamant they just wanted the blackmail thing out of the way, and, in his right mind again, Ross believed him. If the police did turn their attention to the gallery, Ross would just have to act his socks off, that's all. It wouldn't be the first time.

He went back indoors and threw his jacket onto the newel post at the foot of the stairs, then went into the sitting room and picked up Pica's ball.

'Change of plan?' Julie asked, easing herself up off the floor and onto the sofa.

'Wrong day.' Ross smiled and sat next to her, and tossed the ball across the floor. 'Just realised it in time.'

Mackenzie and Ade were quiet on the way back from visiting Frank at the Heathers. Their father had been surprised to see them on a Thursday instead of a Friday, and a little testy at being caught unawares, but when Mackenzie told him he'd had to re-schedule Charis's birthday dinner for tomorrow he'd mellowed at once; he'd had a surprising soft spot for Charis right from the start. But the visit had given Mackenzie a lot to think about, and Ade seemed to sense it and thankfully didn't bombard him with questions.

Ever since Ade had told him Frank was keen for him to come on board at Glencoille, Mackenzie had told himself not to get his hopes up; he and his father had had a difficult relationship for years, and it had only shown faint signs of softening late last year, when Ade had returned and begun to build bridges. But things had still been tense between them, awkward and uncertain, with neither prepared to entirely forgive the way they perceived the other had treated them over the years.

Tonight Mackenzie saw for himself that his brother had been telling the truth. When the subject of Glencoille came up, Frank's eyes had undeniably glistened as he'd looked from one of his sons to the other. Alike in so many ways, Mackenzie knew they both resembled their mother more strongly the older they got; Frank had clearly been particularly moved tonight, and had reached out and clasped a son's hand in each of his.

'We'll do this for Claire, aye? The three of us. In her memory.'

Mackenzie and Ade hadn't been able to look at one another for a moment; this was the deepest emotion either of them had witnessed in their father since his stroke, and the subsequent loss of the Mackenzie estate and their family. After a moment, Mackenzie had nodded, and they'd both spoken together.

'For Mum.'

Now he twisted in his seat as Ade's jeep passed his house and continued towards town.

'Hey!' He jerked his thumb over his shoulder. 'Aren't you forgetting something?'

'I thought we could have a quick pint at the Burnside. Seal the deal. What do you say?'

'I haven't properly decided yet,' Mackenzie pointed out. 'I didn't want to say it tonight, but there's a lot to think about.'

'Then let's talk it through a bit more while we're here, and with no other distractions.' Ade gave him a complacent smile as he pulled in to the car park. 'You know you want to.'

The hotel bar was busy, but Mackenzie found a small table out in the lobby while Ade went for the drinks, and sat down to think. He and Charis had already talked it through, and no doubt would do again tomorrow night, but deep down he knew his mind was made up; he'd had ten years of doing this job, and for the past three, at least, he'd been becoming more and more frustrated with all the invoices, spreadsheets, and hours of sitting in the car staring at people's closed front doors... It had grown stale, and the lack of exercise was starting to make him feel old before his time. Ade had five years on him, and moved with so much more ease and confidence, even taking into account Mackenzie's own recovery from the bike accident.

After what seemed like ages Ade came back with the drinks. 'It's mad in there. All right if I stay over tonight? I can leave the jeep here, and fetch it in the morning.'

'Aye, fine, if you don't mind walking back to mine.'

'I can just about manage that. Cheers.' Ade raised his glass. 'So then, what's stopping you from making the jump?' He took a sip and briefly closed his eyes in exaggerated bliss. 'Can't be the financial security,' he added, and Mackenzie shook his head.

'It's mostly Maddy, if I'm honest. I took over from her dad when he retired, and there's no-one else ready to step in yet.'

'Young Jamie would,' Ade observed with a little grin. 'In a heartbeat.'

Mackenzie gave him a wry smile. 'You're not wrong there...' He paused as the door swung open. 'Look who's here. Hazel's mate, Griff.'

Ade turned to follow his gaze. 'I didn't know you'd met him.'

'Not met, but seen. Around a week ago.'

'What's he doing up here?' Ade wondered. 'I got the impression he was more of a Twisted Tree sort of bloke.'

'He's looking for someone,' Mackenzie said thoughtfully,

watching Griff's gaze drifting across the lobby before he turned towards the door into the bar.

'Hazel?'

Mackenzie shook his head. 'Not here, I wouldn't have thought – bit posh for her too. Although he's dressed a bit smart tonight, come to think of it.' A nasty thought struck him. 'I wonder if this means he *is* still working for Kilbride after all, and they've got business here tonight.'

'Shit.'

'My thoughts exactly. He looks pretty angry about something, and I don't want to scare him away from whoever he's meeting. But I do want to keep an eye on him. Why don't you go and wait outside, by his bike?'

'What for?'

'Because you know him, and if he comes out in a hurry I want you to engage him in a nice little chat. Talk about the rally or something. The chances are he's seen your jeep already.'

'To be honest he didn't look as though he'd have twigged, if he had,' Ade pointed out. He took a slug of his drink, giving it a regretful look that make Mackenzie smile, despite his misgivings, and went back out to the car park.

Mackenzie made his way into the bar, which was heaving tonight, as Ade had said. His eyes automatically went to the booth where Charis had confronted him last summer, just before Jamie had been snatched from his room upstairs. His vivid memory showed him her blazing blue eyes, her scruffy jeans and spiky dark hair, and her absolute conviction that he was at least the second-worst person to stalk the face of the earth. The feeling had been very much reciprocated.

He felt another little smile touch his lips, then he looked away and found Griff standing at the bar, one large hand wrapped around a cut crystal tumbler containing what looked like whisky, keen eyes scanning the room. Mackenzie did the same, but could see no-one who looked as if they were, in turn, waiting for someone. His unease grew; if Griff wasn't expected, the list of reasons for his being here shortened considerably.

He remained by the door, ready to turn away if Griff came towards him, and after a minute or two he moved out into the lobby again, keeping his eye on the stairs and the front door. He acknowledged the pointlessness of it, since he had absolutely no idea who he was looking out for and didn't even know if it was a man or a woman, but a couple of minutes later he accepted that he'd subconsciously known all along; Leslie Warrender was coming in through the door, looking both nervous and excited, and staring around him with undeniable eagerness. Ross must have spoken to him, and sent Griff to meet him, but why? After all, the painting wouldn't be here.

Mackenzie's phone buzzed, and when he saw Ade's name flash up he knew it would just be the news that Warrender was here, so he ignored it and went back into the bar. He marched straight up to Griff, who looked startled but spoke first.

'You're Ade Mackenzie's brother, I take it?'

'Aye. Is Patrick Ross here?'

'No.' Griff turned back to the bar and threw back the rest of his drink. 'He was going to meet me here but changed his plans.'

'And he hasn't given you anything to hand over?'

'No. I came here to...see someone.'

'And I can guess who, and why. Look, Griff, you've to get out, right now. Go that way.' He pointed to the door at the far end of the bar, which led out to the side of the hotel by the small river from which it took its name.

Griff resisted, but Mackenzie had a good four inches on

him, and he used them now. 'The bloke you're meeting is in the lobby,' he said in a low, hard voice, 'and *you* need to get the fuck out before you take things too far, aye?'

He felt Griff tense as he stepped closer, before thankfully seeing sense, giving a quick nod and moving off towards the side door. Mackenzie followed him, and as soon as they got into the stone-floored passage he grabbed the collar of Griff's coat, pulled him back and shoved him against the wall.

'What the hell were you thinking?'

'Piss off, Mackenzie!'

Mackenzie released him with a sigh. 'Hazel told us what you said when you found out about him, and I get it. We feel the same. But that bloke in there gets wind that we're looking for him, or that we know *anything at all* about who he really is, and he's off. We'll have lost our chance to nail him for killing Hazel's mother. Tell me that's not what you want?'

'Of course it isn't.' Griff glared up at him. 'And if you thought I came here to beat him to a pulp, you're wrong, tempting as that is. I want to find out what happened to Hazel's mum just as much as you do, and killing the sod won't do that, will it?'

'So what were you going to do, ask him nicely?'

Griff shot him a filthy look. 'Persuade him that telling the truth is good for the soul, of course.'

'Very funny. Look, let him be for tonight, okay? Ade's outside; we'll see if we can follow Warrender when he gives up and leaves.'

'And what do I do?'

'You just concentrate on keeping Hazel safe during the rally, like we said. We'll figure out what to do when we hit Warrender's time limit on Monday.'

'He's not going to just give up then, is he?'

'Not a chance. But he might get more desperate. Become more accommodating.' Mackenzie stood back and allowed Griff to open the door. 'Just promise me you'll let him alone, okay? Let us deal with it.'

Griff studied him for a moment, then nodded reluctantly. 'But I reserve the right to pound an anvil up his arse if it looks like he's getting away,' he added, and Mackenzie could only shrug in agreement as he followed him outside.

Ade was leaning against his jeep, and as soon as he saw Griff he straightened and launched into a little prepared speech, but he'd only got a few words out before Mackenzie showed himself too and shook his head.

'Never mind. We've had a little chat. Which car's Warrender's?'

Ade pointed to a white Nissan Juke. 'Fancy.'

'Hired,' Mackenzie said. 'Ross says he was driving a red Volvo when he came to his place, but he's changing it every couple of days. Come on, get in. We need to be ready for when he realises Ross isn't coming. He's likely to be pretty annoyed.'

It didn't take long. Around five minutes after Griff had left, throwing one final, disgusted look over his shoulder at the hotel, Warrender emerged from the main front door looking equally deflated and angry. He took off at speed, as predicted, and it took a few minutes to catch up closely enough to follow without raising any suspicion. To their consternation Warrender took one of the narrow roads that climbed into the hills towards Glencoille, which made following unobtrusively a lot harder.

'At least the jeep looks like it belongs up here,' Ade grumbled, negotiating a steep turn that took them off the familiar road to the estate.

'Where does this lead?' Mackenzie peered ahead through the falling dusk, hoping to recognise a landmark. 'I don't think I've been up here before.'

'No idea. And I'm going to have to drop back even further, or we'll be too obvious.'

They kept the white car in view from several rises back along the road, but eventually it turned off, disappearing into the blanket of trees that stretched across the hillside. The jeep cruised slowly past the turning, and they saw a narrow, rutted lane leading along the back of the trees, between the forest and a fenced piece of land. Ade drew them to a halt and pointed to the glove box.

'SatNav's not a lot of good up here,' he said, 'but you can't beat a good old fashioned paper map anyway, when it comes to terrain like this.'

Mackenzie pulled out the battered atlas and laid it open on the dash shelf. 'We're at the top of the ridge here,' he said after a moment, putting a finger on the narrow white line that ran along the expanse of green. He looked closer, at the building at the far end of the unclassified track. 'Druimgalla...' He frowned, then the frown cleared. 'Christ, I think that might be where Hazel's mother died. Where that photo with Warrender was taken. Is he staying up here then?'

'Maybe Hazel's aunt's letting him stay,' Ade said. 'Shit. Hazel needs to know this, if so.'

'No, hang on. If he was staying on that side of the forest, he'd have taken the main road there.' Mackenzie lifted down the atlas and followed the track again. 'Yeah, look, dead end. You know what? I think he could be camping out here, in this part of the forest. Not moving around at all, just booking into random guest houses to throw off anyone that Ross might get looking for him.'

'Camping. Crap.'

'Aye.' Mackenzie sighed in frustration. 'Which means he's not likely to have the painting with him after all. Too much risk of damage.'

'Stashed then,' Ade said. 'But where?'

'Not in the cars he's been hiring – too visible. Could be anywhere though.'

'Maybe somewhere on Isla Munro's property, without her knowing?'

'Maybe. The garage in the photo could be a good bet.' Mackenzie looked at the dashboard clock. 'Better get back soon, but we'll come up here at the weekend, for a better look. Saturday morning, while Isla's at work? You won't be working, with that rally on... Wait, no.' He shook his head. 'Charis and I are out then, picking up some new stuff for her course, so it'll be closer to lunchtime. Sound okay to you?'

'Sounds great.'

'Best get back, then.' Mackenzie reached for his seat belt. 'Still want to stay over?'

'Damn right.' Ade gunned the engine, then shifted into gear. 'There's a cold pint waiting for me in the Burnside.'

'Then lay on, Macduff.' Mackenzie peered down the lane that disappeared into the trees, as they turned in a wide circle ready to head back. 'At least we can keep an eye on this little shite now, and when he comes out to take his money, we'll have him.'

Chapter Sixteen

'RIGHT,' Ade said late the next morning, one hand on the door handle of his jeep. 'We're clear then? No-one in the office but you. Not even your mate Griff.'

'Just me,' Hazel affirmed. Her rolled-up sleeping bag and backpack were on the torn vinyl seat by the door, next to the tent she'd no longer need, now that she'd promised to sleep in the office. She could hear shouts in the yard as the rest of the club started unpacking Griff's van, and felt herself twitching to get on with it. The rally didn't open its gates until four, but it would take most of the day to get organised. The large booking-in tent had just been dragged out of its bag by Greg and Jonah, and Griff was directing the truck carrying the marquee to the far corner of the field; everyone was doing something useful except her.

'...know when.'

Hazel turned back to Ade. 'Sorry, what?'

'I *said*, I'll be popping back up now and again over the weekend but I don't know when.'

'Don't you trust me?' Hazel widened her eyes in exaggerated innocence. 'Look, these things aren't nearly as rowdy or decadent as you seem to think.' She pointed to where Greg and Jonah were spreading a large piece of canvas on the grass, on the other side of the dry stone wall. 'See that? It's called a control tent. Which implies there *is* some.'

'I suppose.'

'We sit in there all weekend, on a rota, and check people in, answer questions, sort out issues, provide hot, non-alcoholic drinks... That's *our* office for the weekend, and you know I don't drink anyway.'

'Okay. But you reckon around a hundred or so others—'

'Limit's eighty this year,' Hazel said. 'And our club is in charge and liable for everything that happens here, which means we're not going to be letting anyone run riot. Seriously,' she went on, seeing the uncertainty still hovering around Ade's manner now that it was all starting to happen, 'you'd get more trouble from a cub scout group camping here for the weekend. We're all grown-ups. Well, mostly; some people's kids ride pillion, but not many. And it's just camping, music, some daft games and a ride out tomorrow. People will be drinking, so some of them will be drunk, and horribly so, but it'll be no worse than the Twisted Tree on a Saturday night. Now, babysitting head on, and get off to your brother's place.'

Ade got behind the wheel and pulled the door shut. 'No-one in the office but you,' he said again, through the open window.

'I promise.' Hazel turned away as someone called to her, and saw Jonah beckoning her over. 'I'm needed. Go on. I'll take care of the place, don't worry.'

She waved him off, then headed up to where the erected control tent would sit, just inside the gate, monitoring the comings and goings of bikes throughout the day. The electricity cables had been run out early that morning, and though there was no need for a heater yet, tonight it would be chilly for whoever was on duty, and Greg was unwrapping the cable of a convector heater he'd brought with him.

At the top of the field, the marquee staff were already busy, and Hazel set to work helping Jonah unfold the control tent's ground sheet. It wasn't too long before the tent itself had taken shape, and Hazel left Greg and Jonah to it and went off to help the rest of the club members gather wood for tomorrow night's bonfire. By mid-afternoon they were all ready for a break and gathered in the control tent, where Griff had boiled the kettle and was throwing bacon into a pan on the camping stove.

Jackie was pulling a face at her phone as Hazel ducked beneath the flapping canvas doorway. 'This is going to be a pain.'

'Bollocks it is,' Griff said cheerfully, flipping the bacon and leaning back as it hissed and spat. 'I've said it before, it'll be good for everyone to get away from the endless shit for a while, and it's only a quick walk to the portakabin.'

'Which no-one's to actually go into,' Hazel reminded them quickly. 'Ade'll have my hide. And probably my job.'

'It was good of him to let us have the place,' Greg said, handing her a steaming coffee in an enamel mug. 'We won't let anyone mess it up for you, don't worry.'

'It's too good to see you settled again,' Jackie added, and Hazel felt heat in her cheeks as they all looked at her and either nodded or smiled. Much as she valued them as friends and, yes, saviours of a kind, she wished someone could press a magic button and erase their memories. She strove to be just one of them, and most of the time she felt it, but all it took was one little comment like that and she was reminded that they would all be keeping a sharp eye on her to make sure she wasn't heading off anywhere stupid again.

She raised her coffee mug. 'To a bloody brilliant Soggy Socks, 2019.'

The rest of the club echoed the toast, and Hazel busied herself with looking at the rally ledger, already open on the rickety table awaiting the first arrivals. Several of the name slots had been filled in and were just awaiting ticks, mileage and bike registrations, and she saw a lot of familiar names that made her smile; it was going to be a great weekend, and a good time to put all thoughts of Leslie Warrender to the back of her mind. At least until Monday, when real life would be waiting to poke them all in the eye again.

By eleven o'clock that night, the party in the marquee was already starting to wind down. For most it had been a long ride up to the site, after an early start – many had been to work that day already – and they were ready to crash now, ahead of a packed Saturday. Two bands had been booked for tomorrow night; the bonfire would burn all night; the barbeque would run until everyone had had their fill; and there were always little groups of people who stayed up talking until the sun came up. Tonight the rally-goers had had their wind-down drinks, caught up with their friends, made arrangements for the following day, and had now started to leave the marquee and make their way back to their tents.

Hazel, Griff and Jonah were in the control tent; only Griff and Jonah were on duty, but Hazel had joined them to chat about potential winners for the various trophies that would be given out tomorrow evening. It was nice down here, listening to the laughter and music from further up the field; the murmur of voices passing through the gate in either direction; the giggles as someone stumbled, either through drink or just on the uneven ground... The sense that the rally was off to a great start was making everyone in the host club cheerful, and Griff and Jonah were larking about like a couple of kids, high on caffeine and relief. Griff's rally hat – a long-ribboned trilby, was hanging off the back of his chair, and Jonah's baseball cap was on backwards, and tight, making his eyes bug out as if he was having trouble keeping them open otherwise.

'What time's the first band on tomorrow?' Hazel asked Griff.

'Dunno, it's on my phone. Seven, I think.'

'Well check then,' Jonah said, 'so we can work backwards and figure out what time the awards are happening.'

Griff felt in his pocket, then shook his head. 'Left it in the van.'

'Well, what good's it doing there?' Jonah grunted.

'Almost as much good as it'd do up here, to be fair,' Griff said, grinning. 'All right, I'll get it when I've finished my coffee, then we can put it up on the chalk board first thing, before everyone heads out on the run.'

'People still up for going to Poolewe?'

'Aye. Good long ride out will set everyone up for a belting night, I reckon.'

'Lucky buggers,' Hazel said. 'I'm starting to wish I'd brought my bike. Right.' She checked the time on her own phone. 'I'm heading off now. Have a nice night duty, lads. May all your troubles be sober ones.'

Griff snorted. 'Fat chance. Have a nice sleep on your comfy sofa,' he added.

'I'd be more comfortable in my tent,' Hazel said glumly.

'There's no sofa in the office, just a couple of chairs I can push together. If I don't want a broken head I'll be better off on the floor.'

'I've got a spare air bed in the van,' Griff said. 'It'll be somewhere near the front of the back, if you see what I mean. There's a foot pump there too.'

'Great, thanks, don't mind if I do.' Hazel held out her hand, and when Griff looked at her blankly she said, 'Keys?'

'Well it's not *locked*, is it? None of us is going to go stealing it.'

'Good point,' she conceded. 'With that stupid tree painted on the side of it, no self-respecting thief would want to be seen dead in it.'

'Get out,' Griff said, throwing his hat at her.

She threw it back, and was still smiling to herself as she made her way through the gate and down the yard. Griff's van was almost empty now, and it was easy enough to find the folded air bed and the little bag containing the foot pump; she hauled it across to the portakabin with a feeling of relief that she'd have a reasonably comfy night's sleep after all. It was all very well championing the outdoor way of life and the fun of camping with mates, but when you were in your mid-thirties and had the hard floor of a makeshift building to sleep on instead of grass, it made you wonder why you'd promised to caretake the bloody site in the first place.

Earlier that evening Ade had shown up again, too, this time with his brother's boy Jamie in tow, to lock some sensitive paperwork away. Or so he'd said. It had stung a bit that he clearly still didn't quite trust her, but when he'd left he'd seemed happier. And she had to admit she didn't even blame him too much; this was his life, after all. He was bound to be both curious and concerned, she'd be wary too, if she didn't know the club as well as she did. But he had nothing to worry about, and hopefully he'd see that now and leave them alone to get on with it.

She gave a jaw-cracking yawn, turned off the light so she wouldn't have to fight her way out of her sleeping bag again, and spent a pleasantly sleepy ten minutes in the company of her Kindle before settling down to sleep. She closed her eyes just as the distant thump of musc from the marquee stopped, signalling midnight.

She was awoken sometime later, groggy-headed and blinking. The echo of the sound that had woken her was still ringing in her ears, and she reached for her phone to see the message icon flashing and the clock on the screen showing it was only a little after two a.m. She frowned and opened the message, dragging herself onto one elbow and pushing her hair back from her face when it obscured her view. It was from Griff.

Have urgent news re: your undead friend. You were right about him and your mum. Cant be seen talking to you so come up to distillery a.s.a.p. will meet you there.

Hazel's heart skipped, then raced, and she placed a hand over it in sudden panic, but gradually reason reasserted itself. She unzipped her sleeping bag and seized her jacket to keep out the chill, ensured the office door was secure, then set off up the path, her mind probing the mystery behind Griff's text. What could he possibly have found out since she'd left him that evening?

She reached the small building, and saw the shadow of the van parked alongside it as she pushed open the door. The light was already on, and she blinked against its brightness and switched off her torch, then looked around, peering into the sloping passageway that led to the cellars. 'Griff?'

There was no answer, but she couldn't have beaten him here. There was no other path, the river coursed by on the other side, and he'd have come up from the yard as she had. Suddenly uneasy, without having a solid reason on which to hang the fear, she looked around and saw a tin of paint with a bent lid on a camping table. Beside the tin was a screwdriver with a paint-splashed tip; no doubt it had been used to lever the lid off, and the chipped handle used to hammer it back on when the decorator had finished.

Hazel wrapped her fingers slowly around the grooved plastic handle and straightened again, feeling a little better. 'Griff! Don't mess about.' She took her phone out and looked at the message again. She was right about Warrender and her mum? That he'd had something to do with her death after all? A sound from behind made her jump and she turned, her breath stopping in her throat.

Leslie Warrender stood in the doorway, dressed in a black T shirt, jeans, and a cut-off denim jacket that looked too shiny and new to be anything but a prop, despite the ragged appearance of the armholes. It would have served, in the darkness, to make him look just like any other rally goer wandering off for a private place to piss in the hedge, but in this harsh light it looked ludicrous. He had an odd look on his face, and as he came closer to Hazel she held the screwdriver out in front of her like the weapon it had now become.

'What happened?' she asked, in a trembling voice. 'What did you do to my mum?'

He didn't reply but kept moving closer, and Hazel backed away, mentally mapping the layout of the cellars behind her; there was one point where the low-ceilinged passageway cut through and joined another. If she could reach that, she could circle around and be back at the door before—

'Good of him to get you up here for me,' Warrender said at last. He sounded breathy and nervous, which momentarily distracted Hazel from the words themselves. Then shock hit, and she let out a moan.

'Have you hurt him?'

'Why would I, when he's been such a help?'

'What? You're not saying he—'

'I'm not saying anything,' Warrender said. His gaze flicked briefly over her shoulder, but before she could turn she felt a movement near her leg and a hand gripped the inside of her thigh from behind. She dropped her horrified gaze to see a bike glove, and at the same time she felt a thump on the outside of her leg, and a stinging pain; another gloved hand, with the plunger of a syringe protruding from its curled fist, pressed against the outside of her thigh. She tried to twist away from her captor, but the nerves in her leg caught fire under the savage grip and she shrieked in pain. In front of her, Warrender continued his slow, steady advance, pulling her attention back to him and to the shaking tip of the screwdriver.

Abruptly she was released from whoever had administered the injection, and she staggered, trying to turn and see if it really was Griff who had done this to her; she still couldn't make herself believe it was him. But the entrance to the cellar was empty again now; whoever it was had ducked away again, into the very refuge she herself had counted on.

'What is it?' she demanded, dismayed to hear her own voice sounding so terrified and tearful. She raised it, hearing it echo off the bare walls. 'What have you done to me?'

'Sit down, love.'

'What? No!' Hazel shook her head vehemently then

241

stopped as the room tilted. 'What is it?' she asked again, and her voice seemed to come from someone else. *Am I going to die here?* 'No, no, no...'

'Sit down.' Warrender moved closer. 'You...you don't want to hurt yourself when you fall.'

It was such an absurdly concerned thing to say that Hazel wanted to laugh, but it turned into a hiccupping sob. She groped for the arched cellar doorway to steady herself, and the hand holding the screwdriver lowered, though her fingers somehow kept their grip on it. Warrender took a step forward to take it from her, but his eye caught something behind her again and he stopped. Hazel tried to make her head move to follow his eyeline, but it just bobbed on her neck like a baby's; uncontrolled, a separate part of her, unconnected to her brain.

'Sit.' Insistent, concerned.

She wanted to do as he'd said, and looked down at the concrete floor, but it undulated, making her feel sick, and one moment it seemed within reach, the next a hundred feet away. Her leg stung where the needle had gone into her thigh muscle, her stomach roiled and she tasted sour vomit in the back of her throat.

Once more. 'Sit...'

She bent over, reaching out towards the floor, and found it all too quickly, stubbing the tips of her fingers as it seemed to rush up to meet them. A voice gave a low, miserable cry, and she knew it was her own but was powerless to stop it uttering another. Tears were spilling down her cheeks, but she couldn't feel the usual sting of them in her eyes or her nose. Hands reached out – Warrender's, and whoever was with him: Griff? But she couldn't feel them, only the way they worked together to fold her to her knees, and then to guide her into a foetal position, curled up on the chilly floor. A sudden heat crept down the inside of her thighs, a combination of pressure and warmth blooming along the crotch of her jeans; part of her was still aware enough to realise what had happened, and crushing humiliation slunk through her.

Her heartbeat picked up and she tried to lift her head, hating Warrender, but, knowing he was going to be the last thing she'd ever see, wanting to see him anyway. To greedily suck the very last sensation out of this short and troubled life. She blinked blearily, trying to clear her vision, but as he stretched a hand towards her, her eyelids refused to lift again. There was a muffled conversation somewhere in the darkness over her head, a tug somewhere around the pocket of her jacket, and then nothing.

Chapter Seventeen

JAMIE ATE his breakfast slowly on Saturday morning, pondering what to do about what was stashed in his coat pocket. Mum and Mackenzie had gone off to that posh place last night, on their re-scheduled dinner, and since the restaurant seemed to be the only thing anyone wanted to talk about since the murder, he'd hoped they'd take him with them; it might have been enough to get him and Dylan talking again. Even if he hadn't been allowed to go outside and see where it had happened, he could have embellished things a bit; Dylan would never have known.

But no, Mum and Mackenzie had gone off together, all smiles and touching hands, and Jamie had been left at home with Ade, who had been unable to resist going back up to Glencoille again yesterday evening, on the pretence of tidying away some paperwork. Jamie knew perfectly well it was actually because he wanted to make sure Hazel and her friends weren't wrecking the place already, but he'd gone along cheerfully enough. They'd parked up, and Hazel had left her friends and come over right away, with her usual dark eye-stuff on, and her scruffy jeans and leather jacket. She didn't have her bike with her, because she was riding with her mate Griff in his van, but she still looked pretty awesome, and Jamie had felt important as she'd casually fist-bumped him before turning back to Ade.

'Don't worry, the place is still standing,' she'd said, heavy on the sarcasm; she reminded him a bit of his mum in that way. 'We're not going to start in with the axe-throwing and the fart-lighting until tomorrow afternoon.'

Jamie had recognised the joke, but he'd seen Ade's eyes widen a fraction before he caught it too, and he and Hazel had shared a grin at Ade's expense. Ade had crooked a finger at him to follow him into the office, and busied himself for a few minutes rummaging through paperwork and putting it away in a locked drawer. Then he'd excused himself and told Jamie to sit still and not to touch anything, and so Jamie had sat there, tearing off bits of chair-foam and flicking them towards the waste paper bin next to the desk.

Becoming bored with the target practice, he'd sighed and let his gaze wander around the portakabin. Hazel's bedroll was already there, and so was her backpack, both stashed neatly in the corner, and Jamie felt a twinge of envy. Imagine being an adult, and allowed to camp out with your mates all weekend and sleep where you liked...not even having to go to bed at all, if you didn't want to. He could hear Ade outside in the yard, talking to someone whose voice he didn't immediately recognise, and when he peeked around the doorway he saw it was Griff, with his daft hat on; Ade looked ready to talk for the rest of the evening, and Jamie heard him warning against letting anyone pee in the river – only he didn't use the word pee, of course, that was another thing grown-ups got away with – or smoke under the trees. He was waving his arms around, and

Jamie caught Hazel's words, 'we've been through this!' before he grew bored with that too.

His travelling gaze had landed on the calendar on the wall; this weekend had massive crosses on it, and Sunday had an exclamation mark and *WASH!* in huge letters. For a moment he pondered that – Ade didn't stink, so it couldn't be that unusual an event for him to have a wash – then he stopped worrying about it, because he'd just seen a cork board beside the calendar. On the board were a number of hooks, and on one of the hooks was a smart red and black key fob with an H on it. The workers' spare key for the quad bike.

Jamie had looked out into the yard again, and then back at the key. He remembered Dylan's look of utter contempt, and his skin heated up again; how could Dylan *I-shouldn't-leave-the-door-unlocked* Munro possibly call Jamie a chicken? Dylan hadn't been kidnapped by an armed American, or escaped a murderous – and barking mad – police officer in the middle of the night. Dylan was just all mouth and hot air, yet he'd managed to make Jamie feel scared and worthless nevertheless. Ethan never would have made him feel like that, he reflected, missing his friend more than ever.

But mingled with the anger and the defensive indignation was a real regret: he *liked* Dylan, even if he was a gob on a stick. He made Jamie laugh, and he'd told him about his aunt, putting his trust in Jamie to fulfil his side of the deal. Jamie's eyes were dragged back once more to the cork board. Ade wouldn't be back here again for the rest of the weekend, and most of the rally people would be out all afternoon tomorrow – Hazel had said so. A phone call to Dylan tomorrow, a quick run up the lane on the quad bike, and friendship, and honour, would be restored. No-one ever need know. And no way would Jamie even give the slightest squeak of fear, either.

He'd taken one more quick look out into the yard; Ade was further away now, peering up across the field to where some people were putting the finishing touches to a marquee, and before he'd had chance to talk himself out of it, Jamie had sprung to his feet, taken three quick steps across the office and slipped the key into his pocket. It wasn't until after he was back in Abergarry, and eating the tea Ade had cooked for him in Mackenzie's kitchen, that he realised he had no idea how either he or Dylan would get up to Glencoille tomorrow afternoon.

By this morning he had abandoned the idea of getting the key to Dylan at all, and could hardly believe he'd been so stupid as to think it was a good idea. All he wanted now was to get the damned thing back on the hook in the site office before anyone noticed it was missing. He waited until the adults were busy talking in the kitchen, then went into the hall and dropped the key into the pocket of Ade's jacket where it hung on the hook by the door. Ade wasn't stupid; he had no need of a spare, and it wouldn't take him long to work out who'd been left alone in the office yesterday, but it seemed like the best plan.

Then, just after lunch, a much better answer dropped into his lap. Mum and Mackenzie had gone into Inverness to pick up some equipment Mum had ordered with her birthday money, and Ade, who was staying all weekend, was flicking lazily through the TV channels looking for some rugby. When the landline rang, and he looked at the caller ID, his face brightened.

'Hi, Maddy, it's Ade here. Paul's gone to— Wait, slow down. What?' He listened for a moment, then looked across at

Jamie. 'No, they're out, I'll have to bring him with me. See you there. Okay.'

He ran upstairs, calling back for Jamie to get his shoes on, and Jamie got to his feet.

'Where are we going?'

'Back up to Glencoille.' The bathroom door banged closed and Ade's voice drifted through it. 'Sorry about that, but it can't be helped. You can text your mum in the car, okay?'

'Okay!' Jamie yelled back, and took the key back out of Ade's jacket pocket, with a little sigh of relief.

'I thought you couldn't go back because of the biker party,' he said, when Ade came back down and picked up the keys to his jeep.

'I know, but Maddy and I need a quick word with Griff about something. Come on, don't stand there asking daft questions.' Despite his light words, there was a tightness around Ade's mouth, and Jamie remembered the conversations he'd heard about Hazel, and that she was supposed to be staying with Maddy for her own protection. Protection against what, he had no idea, but it was clearly something important. In the meantime his relief at being given the chance to put the quad key back was enough to propel him to the jeep ahead of Ade, and scramble in without any further questions.

But the opportunity didn't look likely after all. When they turned into the yard it was disappointingly devoid of activity, with only Maddy's car, a van and a few bikes in it; there was no music – he'd been under the impression it would be some sort of scaled-down Glastonbury – and no-one was around at all, as far as he could see, let alone hoards of beefy-looking bikers like last night.

'Where's everyone gone?'

'They'll be back later,' Ade said as he shut the jeep door.

He looked tense, and Jamie wondered if someone had broken or set fire to something. Maddy must be around somewhere, but he couldn't see her.

'Shall I just wait in the office?' he asked, jumping down from the jeep. 'I won't touch anything,' he added, wondering if that made him sound guilty already.

'No, it's locked; no-one's to go in there yet. I won't be long, but if you don't want to stay in the jeep just...look at the bikes, or something.' Ade started up towards the field where the bikers were camping, and where a bigger tent than most of the rest stood just inside the gate.

Jamie blew out a frustrated breath and leaned against the jeep door. He looked around at the four or five bikes on their kickstands, but they were about as boring as they could be; no fancy, fiery paint-jobs or massive chrome handlebars. They reminded him of Mackenzie's old bike, before the crash for the most part, although one or two didn't look far off the 'after' picture either.

His eye was drawn to the space alongside the portakabin, where the muddy red and black Honda quad bike usually sat in the shelter of a clump of trees. Ade had left it back at his caravan this weekend, since there was no work going on, and Jamie sighed; it would have been fun to have sat on it for a bit while he waited, and to at least pretend he was riding it. He might even have been able to leave the key in the ignition and say he'd found it there.

An approaching car made him perk up, thinking it might be Mackenzie's, but it was just some smart-looking red Toyota that pulled into the yard and directly up to the office. A well-dressed woman got out and, to Jamie's alarm, headed straight for him.

'Where's Mr Mackenzie?' she demanded, looking both cross and worried.

'He's in Inverness, with my...oh.' Jamie belatedly realised she meant the elder Mackenzie brother. 'Sorry, I mean he's up there.' He pointed towards the large tent, where he could now see Maddy hovering in the doorway. 'What's wrong?'

The passenger door of the Toyota opened, and Dylan leaned out. 'All right, chickenshit?'

'Dylan!' The woman spared him a hot glance before turning back to Jamie. 'Do you know anything about it?'

'About what?'

'My niece, vanishing off the face of the planet,' the woman said, then shook her head impatiently. 'Never mind.'

She marched across the yard to the field beyond the stone wall, clearly dressed for a far posher place; he remembered Dylan telling him she worked in an art gallery, so she must have been on her way there now. Dylan got out of the car, leaving the door open, and wandered over.

'Mum's gone bananas,' he explained cheerfully. 'You wouldn't think my cousin was a grown woman with a life of her own.'

'What does she mean, vanished?'

'She got a phone call off that woman PI who works with your mum's bloke. Apparently Hazel was sleeping in there this weekend,' he jerked a thumb towards the portakabin.

'She was,' Jamie said, enjoying a brief moment of importance. 'I was talking to her about it last night.'

'Well she wasn't anywhere in sight this morning, and she never showed up to go on that run they were all so keen on.'

'I didn't know Hazel liked running.' Dylan rolled his eyes like a pro, Jamie thought, even as he realised he'd got the wrong end of the stick again. 'Oh, right. On bikes.'

'Aye, *on bikes*,' Dylan said, with all the scorn of one on the cusp of manhood talking to a baby. 'How else?'

'So why's your mum looking for Ade? He wasn't even here last night.'

'She's talking to them both,' Dylan said, twisting to look towards the tent. 'Here they come. Maybe I'll be able to go home now.'

'Why did she bring you anyway?'

Dylan shuffled his feet, and a faint flush touched his cheeks. 'She doesn't want me staying home on my own anymore. She was taking me in to her work with her when the PI called. *So* annoying.'

Jamie didn't answer, but to his rapidly evolving people-reading skills, Dylan's manner was a pretty good indication of who had actually made that decision. 'Well, hopefully one of them's found out where your cousin went,' he said, instead of challenging him. 'They've probably phoned her by now.'

Maddy, Ade and Mrs Munro were making their way back. Hazel's friend Griff was following, looking pale and tense instead of laid back and chilled as he usually did; clearly they hadn't found the solution yet after all. Griff peeled away from the little group and got into a neat-looking van with a picture of a tree on its side, and a moment later he was heading off the site.

'Listen, lads,' Ade said, addressing the two boys. 'Maddy and I are going to see if we can track Hazel down.'

Jamie frowned. 'Aren't you going to call the police?'

'Griff pointed out she's only been gone a few hours,' Maddy said, but she didn't look happy about the decision. 'She can't even be considered missing yet. She was supposed to be on duty in the control tent this morning, so when she didn't show up he checked in the office, but she wasn't there either.'

'Why have you bothered Mum about it?' Dylan wanted to know. 'Hazel probably just got a lift into town for milk or something.'

Maddy and Ade exchanged a quick glance, and even Dylan's mum seemed aware of what was contained in that heavy silence, but it seemed Jamie and Dylan weren't to be brought into it. Whatever 'it' was.

'I just want to be sure she's...safe,' Dylan's mum said at last.

Dylan huffed. 'Not drunk in a ditch, you mean.' It wasn't a question, and he evidently didn't feel it needed an answer. 'You can say it, you know,' he added. 'I've heard you arguing.'

'She's not had a drink since August,' Maddy said. 'I trust her.'

'We just want to find her.' Ade turned to Mrs Munro. 'Can you take the boys back to your place? We'll call you if we hear anything. Maddy, we can take your car. I'll go and see Ross, and while we're there you could call in on Breda Kelly, since they're friends.'

'I've got to be at work,' Mrs Munro protested. 'The boys will be all right here by themselves, won't they?'

'Can one of the club members look after them?' Ade looked back at the field. 'That Jonah bloke seems alright.'

Mrs Munro looked uncertain, then shrugged. 'If Hazel trusts them, then I suppose I can too.'

Ade disappeared and returned with Jonah, who looked quite pleased. 'They can help me set up for the silly games,' he said. 'The rest of the guys won't be back from the run for ages.' He turned to Jamie and Dylan. 'I've got about fifty balloons to fill with water, a tug-o-war rope to untangle and lay out, a crank to clean, and some trophies to unpack and lay out on the trestle in the marquee. Up to the job?'

'Definitely,' Dylan said at once. 'You go to work, Mum. You can call in and pick me up on the way back.'

'I'd expect you to trust me, Mrs Munro,' Jonah added. 'I'll be around at your place on Monday, with Griff and a chainsaw, don't forget.' He grinned, but somehow this joke didn't sit as well with Jamie as it should have; talk of chainsaws in remote cottages, where murder had already occurred, made him distinctly uneasy.

'Why don't you want anyone to go into the office?' he asked, after Jonah had returned to his big tent and the others got ready to leave. Again that look flashed between them, and Jamie had had too much in the way of dark experiences in the past year to misinterpret it; they wanted to preserve what might, in the worst case scenario, turn out to be a crime scene.

'It's just best if we don't,' Maddy said. 'But we'll call your mum and Paul, and get them to detour this way on their way back from Inverness and pick you both up. Okay with you?' She directed this last bit at Mrs Munro, whose hurry to be off was becoming more and more evident.

'Fine,' she said. 'Give me their address; I'll pick Dylan up after tea.' She looked at her son, as Ade took her phone and tapped in Jamie's address. 'It was always going to be a long day,' she told him, 'but at least this way you get to play with your little friend.'

Jamie didn't dare look at Dylan, but he could imagine the mortification that would be on the older boy's face. He himself wasn't overly keen on being labelled the 'little friend', but at least that part was true, strictly speaking.

Mrs Munro slammed Dylan's door for him rather pointedly, as if she'd told him a hundred times not to leave it open, then waved to the others as she went around to the driver's side. As she passed the Portakabin window, she glanced into it, then stopped and peered closer. She looked back at the gathered group with a frown.

'I can't see her jacket or her helmet,' she called. 'She *must* have gone off of her own accord then, mustn't she?'

'She came up here with Griff, in his work van,' Ade called back. 'She didn't bring her bike or her helmet.'

'She had her leather jacket though,' Jamie supplied. 'And those big boots she wears.'

'Well, she got a lift with someone else then. One of these other lot.' Mrs Munro nodded, accepting her own theory. 'She'll have got a lift with another friend.'

After a final warning to Dylan not to make a nuisance of himself, she drove out of the yard, and soon afterwards, having checked Jamie had a full asthma inhaler with him, Maddy and Ade followed in Maddy's car. The boys looked at one another, and Dylan was already scowling.

'I don't want to blow up fifty million balloons,' he grumbled.

'You were the one who said we'd *definitely* do it,' Jamie pointed out, sketching air quotes. 'We only have to stay until Mum and Mackenzie get back though. Come on.'

'No chance. You do it.' Dylan wandered over to look at the bikes. 'Where's this famous ATV then?'

'Up by Ade's caravan. The yard will be full of bikes again later, so he left it up there this weekend.' Jamie felt the key in his pocket, and was torn; on the one hand Ade had put his trust in him, and he liked Ade too much to defy him, but on the other... Despite his occasional barbs Dylan was actually pretty cool. Apart from when he called Jamie by his new favourite insult.

His mind made up, he pulled out the key and dangled it, waiting for Dylan to turn around and look. 'Want it then?'

Dylan's eyes gleamed, and he came back. 'Is that what I think it is?'

'Probably. Unless you think it's a fried egg on toast, which wouldn't surprise me.'

'Sarky. I like it.' Dylan reached out and took the key. 'Come on, then.'

'Nope.' Jamie shook his head. 'I'll tell you where it is, then you can take it up the lane. I'll just tell Jonah you've gone for a walk.'

'No way! You're coming with me. Tell him we both want a walk.'

'He'll never believe it.' Jamie felt queasy at the thought of actually being the one to take the bike. 'Go on, you go.'

Dylan's face began to twist into his old fallback expression of mingled pity and amusement. 'I don't believe you,' he said. 'You've got the key to an AT-friggin'-V, no parents around to nag, and a whole mountain to play on. And you'd rather go and blow up *balloons*?' He shook his head. 'I was right about you. Chickensh—'

'All right!' Jamie looked around to see if anyone had heard, but the yard was still empty except for the two of them. 'All right,' he repeated, more quietly. 'But he'll never go for us going for a walk.'

'Then tell him...Ade lets you ride it,' Dylan said thoughtfully, tossing the key from hand to hand.

'I don't want to drop Ade in it.'

'He's not going to know, is he? Tell Jonah you do it every Saturday, and that I'm here to look after you – and I began riding four years ago.'

'Did you?'

Dylan nodded. 'On my twelfth birthday.'

'So you know what you're doing.'

'Of course I do! Go and tell him. I'll wait here.'

Jonah looked a little doubtful, but when Jamie pointed out Dylan's credentials, and the fact that Ade had no problem with it – neglecting to mention that this was because he didn't know about it – he shrugged. 'On you go then, but don't be too long. I really could do with a hand. And some puff,' he added a little mournfully, looking at the cigarette smouldering in the squashed beer can he was using as an ashtray, and then at the pile of water balloons yet to blow up. 'I knew I should've gone on the run with the others, but such is the lot of a host club.'

'But Hazel was going to go, wasn't she?' Jamie asked. 'She's your club too.'

'A couple of us always go,' Jonah said. 'The rest have to stay back and do the donkey work. She would have been one of those, since she's not got her bike with her. And she's on the rally committee too, so that's another reason. Now get gone, or I'll change my mind.'

Jamie wondered if, deep down he was hoping for just that, and if that was why he dragged out a chair and sat down instead. 'Do you think she's okay?'

Jonah studied him for a moment, and his bearded face looked troubled, then he smiled. 'She's fine. She'll probably turn up in half an hour with fresh bacon supplies, wondering what all the fuss is about.'

'Jamie!'

Jamie poked his head out of the tent, to see Dylan waving at him from the wall. 'All *right*! Coming!'

'Go, before I change my mind,' Jonah warned, picking up his cigarette again and drawing deeply. He closed his eyes as he let the smoke out, and Jamie sniffed... it smelled sweet, a bit like the hallway in the flats back home in Liverpool, and he knew what that was, but somehow here, in the fresh air and in the middle of a field on a sunny day it didn't seem like such a bad thing. His mother would still throw a wobbly though, if she knew he'd been standing here breathing it in, so he reluctantly left Jonah to his balloons and his fragrant smoke, and went to join Dylan.

Ade's caravan was around a ten-minute walk up the lane. They passed the distillery on the way, and Jamie pointed it out, quite proud that he almost belonged to the family who owned it. 'That whisky you wanted me to nick is going to be made in there.'

'Really?' Dylan veered off the path for a closer look, but Jamie called him away.

'I want to get back before Mum arrives. The caravan's up here, look.' He led the way down a path between the trees, on the right of the lane, and after a few minutes they came to the clearing where Ade had parked his caravan until the house was built. Beside it was the familiar, but suddenly hulking-looking, Honda Fourtrax Ade had been so thrilled to pick up at auction.

Dylan went over to it, studying the dash for a moment. He seemed to be concentrating quite hard. 'This doesn't look the same as the one...the ones I used to drive,' he said, 'but they're all pretty similar once you get going.'

'The one?' Jamie repeated, and understanding swept over him. 'You've only ridden one, haven't you? You bloody liar!'

'Didn't lie,' Dylan said defensively, 'I said it was four years ago.'

'You said you *started riding them* four years ago, not that you only did it once!'

'Same difference.' Dylan sighed. 'Are you coming, or not?'

'Not!'

'Suit yourself. Don't turn around later and say I didn't offer you the chance to do something really exciting.' He climbed on, seating himself firmly in the centre of the saddle, then slipped the key into the ignition and twisted it. A green light glowed and a message marched across the display. *Hello Honda.* Dylan switched his attention to the buttons on the left hand side, and Jamie had to admit he seemed to know what he was doing.

'This is the kill switch,' Dylan said, seeing him watching. 'It's got to be in the middle, see? If I move it either side, the engine stops.' He gave Jamie a pointed look. 'It stops,' he repeated. 'So that means *we* stop. We're not going to drive off a mountain, in other words.'

'Right.'

'So are you sure you don't want a quick buzz up the lane and back? We can just go as far as that old house at the top, and do a couple of circuits of the yard. Then you'll realise how much of a baby you've been.' He gave a sudden laugh. 'You know *girls* ride these things, don't you? Ones even younger than you.'

Jamie thought about Mackenzie, and how he'd brought this very bike up to the old house, and even said how well it handled. 'Are you sure you know where the brakes are?' he asked, weakening under the older boy's bright, persuasive grin.

Dylan pointed them out. 'Front, back. Kill switch. And I just need to let go of this to slow down.' He pressed the throttle lever on the right handlebar. 'See?'

He did seem to know his stuff. Jamie took a quick breath and nodded. 'Come on then.'

'Hah!' Dylan shuffled forward slightly and Jamie climbed on behind him, sitting on the rack and grasping at the metal bars. Dylan turned the key another notch. 'Hold tight!'

The ATV was quieter than Jamie had expected, and when he looked over Dylan's shoulder he saw the boy had his thumb poised over the throttle, his other hand ready to release the brake. After a couple of jerks and blips, the bike rolled forwards and joined the path.

'Lean opposite to the way it's tilting,' Dylan called back over his shoulder as the camber of the path changed. 'We've got to balance it.'

Jamie did as he was told, and after a moment when the path evened out, he relaxed and began to enjoy himself. He found it reasonably instinctive to help balance out the tilt of the bike as they neared the house and the path curved down towards the edges, where countless years of land rovers and tractors had worn the narrow lane away. The house itself had burned years ago and was apparently due to be demolished, and the two boys cruised around the yard, staring up at the blackened, glassless windows and the sagging, holey roof.

'D'you wanna go in?' Dylan asked, twisting in his seat to look back at Jamie.

'Yeah, but not today.' Jamie looked at his watch. 'We've got to get back or my mum'll turn up, and that'll be the last time she'll let me anywhere near you.'

'Your mum sounds like a peach,' Dylan said drily. 'Come on then.'

He steered the bike to the far side of the yard and onto a grassy slope, and Jamie grabbed his shoulder. 'Not this way; we don't know where it goes! Go back down the lane.'

'It's the scenic route!' Dylan yelled back. He did something to one of the buttons on the handlebar. 'I've flipped us into four-wheel drive! Let's see what she'll do!'

Jamie sank back onto the rack, all his confidence ebbing away again, and prayed for a swift end to this nightmare. Dylan had managed reasonably well on the lane, but as they hit bumps in the grass, and found unexpected and unpredictably angled slopes, it was obvious his experience on the adventure camp course hadn't prepared him for this; Jamie's teeth clacked together regularly, and once he bit his tongue so hard he was certain he was going to spit a bit of it out. The taste of blood filled his mouth and he turned his head and spat, hoping it would fly away from the bike.

He leaned forward as close as he dared and yelled into Dylan's ear. 'Slow *down!*'

'I thought you were worried about your mummy coming back!' Dylan pressed harder on the throttle and rose to lean forward as the quad bike surged over a mound. To their right, the river, fed by the Linn of Glenlowrie, first trickled, then rushed, then roared. Jamie spared it a quick glance; the weir wasn't far away, thank goodness, which meant they were nearly back at the turning to Ade's caravan. He closed his eyes in relief, and prepared to lean as Dylan adjusted their direction, but the bike stayed on the same track. He snapped another look to his right, and his breath halted; the river widened just ahead, the bank cut deeper into the land across which they were jolting, and Dylan didn't seem to be paying attention.

'Hey!' Jamie bellowed, hitting Dylan on the shoulder again. 'Keep left! The river!'

Dylan looked, and Jamie saw him double-take, then jerk the bike to the left. The wheels smashed into a hillock and Jamie left the rack, coming back down with a bone-jarring smack, and his fingers tore loose from their grasp. Now the bike was veering back, as Dylan over-compensated, and the river bank was right beside them.

'The kill-switch!' Jamie screamed. His throat hurt with the force of it, and he saw Dylan's hand float away from the handlebar, forward, towards the yellow switch that would shut off the engine. But another jolt jerked his fingers back to grab instinctively at the brake, just as they brushed the long grass at the edge of the river. The front wheels of the bike locked up, and Jamie's initial cry of relief turned into a shriek of terror as the back end of the bike rose, taking him with it.

Everything became rushing, screaming chaos after that. He collided with Dylan on his way over the boy's head; behind him he could sense the hot, roaring nearness of the heavy ATV, even before it struck, propelling him with some force into the river.

The immediate numbness of the icy water gave way to panic that the bike was going to land on him and drive him deeper underwater, perhaps knock him unconscious... And what of Dylan? The older boy had been trapped between him and the bike as it took off; if he hadn't been thrown clear he would either be drowned or crushed. As the water closed over his head and the whining scream of the Honda died away, Jamie was absolutely certain they were both going to die.

His hands thrashed, independent of conscious thought, with minds and instincts of their own; his pinwheeling arms were slowed by the weight of the water, but still whirling as he fought to find the surface. The bike hadn't landed on him, there was no pain, but he felt his chest tighten and, for the first time, he realised the additional threat: even if he were to fight his way free of the weight of the river that had borne him away from the bank, his inhaler would be clogged and useless.

His eyes were closed so tightly that it took a moment to realise his head had broken through the surface of the water. Then he sucked in a huge lungful of air, relieved beyond belief to feel his airways expand to accept it. He was still several feet away from the bank, but when he extended his feet he could feel the stony river bed beneath them; the rocks shifted under the soles of his trainers as he half-hopped and half-swam for the side, and plunged him out of his depth again, but a quick scrabble with his toes brought him back up above the level of the water.

Gasping and blinking, he propelled himself forwards off a rock that he judged able to support him, and as it tilted away from him he seized a handful of the sharp grass that disguised the edge of the river's bank. The blades cut into his fingers, but he hung on and pulled himself into the shallower water.

Once he felt reasonably safe he was able to look around him. The quad bike lay upside down halfway down the river bank; after it had done its job of flinging Jamie clear it had crashed back down, and there was no sign of Dylan anywhere. Jamie gave a horrified moan and pulled hard on the grass, trying to pull himself out of the water, but his feet sank into the silty sand beneath him, as if the river were trying to suck him back in.

'Dylan!' His voice came out thin and high, and he coughed, trying to clear his lungs. 'Dylan!'

He felt firmer ground beneath one waterlogged trainer, and brought his other leg closer. From there he was able to pull himself along the river bank, feeling ahead with one foot and dragging the other after it only when he felt safe. It seemed to take forever, but finally he was alongside the upside-down ATV, and peering beneath it into the hollow where the sloping bank met the water.

He stopped, a sick heat filling him, followed by a chill that had nothing to do with the icy water in which he still fought for balance. Dylan's pale hand floated beside the handlebar, and his head was half submerged in the river as it swept past; his blond hair was dark now, and plastered to the visible half of a face Jamie barely recognised: slack, white, and deathly still.

Chapter Eighteen

THE SMELL HIT HER FIRST; the sour reek of vomit that climbed into her throat and joined an equally bitter taste as she unglued her tongue from the roof of her mouth. Her stomach rolled and twisted, and spit flooded into the back of her mouth... Hazel just managed to turn onto her side before a thin yellow bile came up, stinging her nose and making her eyes water as she convulsed and spat.

She almost lay back down until she realised the sheets she was looking at were caked in the vomit to which she had just added, and that she had no idea which bed those sheets were on. For a moment she simply lay there, propped on one elbow, half supported by the huge soft pillow now at her back, staring at the yellow-grey, lumpen mass and slowly coming to realise it was a miracle she hadn't choked to death. She couldn't remember rolling over to puke, but she must have, nevertheless. As she had just now. But now she was fully awake, if woozy and confused, and her heart was beating fast and heavily – she could feel it in her head and in every pulse point. It frightened her.

What frightened her more was realising she didn't recognise the room, even now she could see it all. Her head pounding with each movement, she sat up slowly and carefully, but mercifully away from the acid stink, and swung her feet to the floor. She could go no further for a minute; her head spun, and a sharp pain drove a spike into the space behind her right eye as if it meant to lever the eye from its socket.

She breathed carefully, wishing her heart would stop its lunatic crashing, and gradually found she was able to look again at the room. It was a perfectly nice one, and as her puzzled gaze took in the pleasant but generic prints on the walls, and the plain, hard-wearing carpet, she guessed it was a hotel room of some sort. There was a generously sized wardrobe, which she bet herself would be empty bar a few hangers, and she knew that if she were able to get up and go into the bathroom she'd see the toilet paper folded into points and a polite notice to re-use the towels to save the planet. *Save it? I don't think I even* belong *to it...*

The thought brought a touch of a smile to her lips, and she recognised the trembling beginnings of an overwhelming relief. When the tears inevitably came, she didn't try to hold them back; they felt cleansing and welcomingly intense. The weeping left her shaking and weak, but clearer-headed, and able to take further stock of herself and her surroundings.

The first thing she did was look for her phone, but it wasn't on the bedside table, and she wasn't wearing her leather jacket, so it must be in the pocket. She called out, in a thin and hoarse voice. 'Hello? Is anyone here?'

The silence that came back to her didn't feel as if someone was in the bathroom and trying to keep quiet; there was an undeniable air of emptiness throughout the rooms. In fact there was no sound from anywhere beyond the door either; none of the usual sounds she'd expect to hear from an awakening hotel in the holiday season. There was bright sunlight coming through the thin curtains, so it was daytime; she still had no idea how she came to be here, wherever *here* was, but she was still dressed and there was no tell-tale soreness between her legs, so she could be reasonably sure she hadn't been attacked sexually.

There was a definite whiff of urine though. Now that she'd moved away from the vomit she could smell it on herself, and thanked whatever was watching over her that, since she hadn't been raped, she would at least be able to shower. She tried to think back to last night; had she fallen off the wagon, or had she been spiked? But, if the latter, by whom? The last thing she could remember was being in the control tent with Jonah and Griff, and they'd been talking about contenders for the 'best bike' trophy. Then nothing.

Surely it couldn't have been Jonah who'd spiked her? Griff was out of the question, but... No. Jonah was quiet, but not creepy-quiet. He was just a regular bloke who had his own family and he even worked with Griff... He was just Jonah. And if someone *had* spiked her, why hadn't he taken advantage? Besides, where was he now, and why had he left her in what actually seemed like a pretty decent hotel room? It made no sense, and Hazel's head was aching too much to pursue it; if she'd fallen off the wagon she must have done a spectacular job of it, and that wasn't something she wanted to think about. She just wanted to go home and wait for the memories to return, so she knew whether or not she only had herself to blame.

She lowered her hands to her sides and pushed herself upright. Her legs held her, but the movement sent the strong stink of urine into her nostrils again and her stomach clenched. She made it across the room to the en suite, and saw she was right about the towels and the toilet rolls, but as she stripped off her stiffened jeans she saw something that took a moment to register.

Her toothbrush. In the plain glass toothbrush holder over the sink. Her wash bag on the cistern of the toilet. Hazel felt a creeping sense of disquiet and continued undressing, keeping one eye on those things as if they were figments of her imagination that might disappear at any moment. She must have put them there, so why did she have no recollection of it?

The shower was easy enough to work, and as she stepped under the blissful warmth of it she was able, for the two minutes it took to feel clean again, to put the strangeness out of her mind. The wash bag was the one she'd taken with her to the rally, and her toothbrush would have been in it. She probably hadn't actually used either of them, but it meant it was likely she'd at least come here willingly, so she must have known whoever she'd been with. Her mind kept going back to Griff and then shying away; he wouldn't have allowed her to drink, and definitely not to take any drugs.

She switched off the shower and stepped out, reaching for one of the larger towels on the rail as her feet touched the cold, tile floor. She wrapped the towel around herself before picking up her jeans and checking the pockets; just a couple of twenties and some change in the back pocket, which she put on the cistern next to her wash bag before dropping the jeans into the shower cubicle and turning on the water again. She mashed them about in it with one foot, frowning as she struggled to remember beyond the trophy discussion, and watched the denim turn from faded black to dark and shiny as the awful evidence of her lack of control swirled away down the drain. They'd take an age to dry, but at least they wouldn't stink of piss anymore.

She thought about the rally site. Where was her tent pitched? Had she fallen on the way to it, tripping over a guy rope and hitting her head? But she wasn't in a tent this time... was she? No. She was sleeping in the site office, so maybe she'd fallen on the portakabin steps?

She couldn't feel any sore spots on her head, but as she rubbed herself dry she winced at a throb in her right thigh and lifted the towel to look. There was a bruise there, on her outer thigh, and when she peered more closely she saw a tiny red dot in its centre and a flash of memory hit her: standing in a brightly lit room, a man in front of her and someone behind...

Sit down, love.

She cried out; the voice hadn't seemed to be in her head at all, but directly in front of her. It wasn't Griff's, but she associated it strongly with him, and with the bruise on her leg. The sound of her own voice echoing through this unfamiliar bathroom brought her fears crashing back and she stumbled into the bedroom as if there really was a stranger standing in the steam.

There she took one look at the congealed mess on the bed and bundled the sheets into a ball, trying not to gag again. After a while just standing in the middle of the room and trying to breathe slowly, she went to the window and pulled back the curtain, expecting to see herself looking down on some part of Inverness. What she did see just made everything more confusing.

The room was on the ground floor, and not part of a hotel at all; more likely a holiday cottage. Outside was a small, featureless yard leading onto a narrow road, and in the distance the land seemed to fall away. Beyond that was a stretch of water that could be anything, and anywhere. The road was clearly the main thoroughfare, but was pitted and rough in places, and looked as if traffic along it would be sparse. The house seemed to be alone on a long stretch of nothing, but that wasn't the cause of Hazel's dismay; the thing that drew her confused eye was the sight of her own motorbike sitting in that yard.

She backed away to the stripped bed and sat down, letting her head fall forward and covering her face with her hands. Her wet hair dripped along her arms but she didn't stop it; it was one of the more sane and predictable things she had experienced since waking. After a moment the continuing hiss of the shower penetrated the fog of her thoughts, and she accepted one thing at least: as bizarre as it was to see her bike outside, it proved she had come here willingly. It also meant that she had a way of getting home from wherever this was.

She went back into the bathroom and scooped the money off the cistern, then plucked her damp shirt from the floor and pulled a face at the crumpled heap of sodden denim still coming under the onslaught of the shower. They'd be difficult to put on, but at least they were clean now. She switched the water off, and her gaze fell on the wash bag; a peek inside confirmed it was definitely hers, and she went back into the bedroom, shaking out her shirt in preparation for putting it on. An unexpectedly brilliant idea struck her as she braced herself: sometimes places like this provided an iron for guests' use, and she could do worse than have a bash at drying the worst of the wet clothing, at least. She congratulated herself in a little whisper, but when she opened the wardrobe to check, she saw it wasn't empty after all.

Two of her own shirts and her leather jacket were hung neatly, and in the bottom were her boots and the backpack she'd taken to the rally, which now had a saggy, empty look. Her crash helmet sat gleaming on the shelf above it all; the visor was down as she always left it, and through it she could see her gloves stuffed inside.

She reached into each of the jacket pockets and checked her backpack, but her phone wasn't there. Trembling now, she went to the small chest of drawers beneath the window and pulled open the squeaking, protesting top drawer to see a clean T shirt, underwear and two clean pairs of socks. The drawer underneath held her spare jeans, folded neatly alongside her kindle and its charger. Someone was looking after her; perhaps they felt guilty? Her mind went once more to Griff, and the harder she thought about her phone, the more the connection seemed to want to click.

Griff. Phone. The rally. Her leg... Her fingers went to the bruise and rubbed there, trying to awaken it enough to bring the memory back. A shiver of chilly air brushed her skin and she dressed slowly, numb in heart but feeling physically more human with each layer she pulled on. She took her backpack into the bathroom and shoved her soaked jeans into it, not caring that they were still dripping; she didn't have the strength to wring them out. But the taste in her mouth was too foul to ignore and she found she was grateful for her toothbrush after all. That job taken care of, she dropped her washbag on top of the wet jeans and went back to the bedroom for the rest of her stuff.

The rattle of the coat hangers as she wrenched her jacket free made her wince, but the moment of normality as she lifted her crash helmet down, and her keys dropped out of it, banished the discomfort of the headache. She would soon be out of this spooky, too-neat little place. Since there was nothing but the sea in two directions, and one road, there was only one logical way to go; she'd come to a village or a town soon, or even a sign post, and then her only worry would be figuring out what had happened, and if Griff had betrayed her trust after all. She cast a last quick look around the bedroom and stepped out into the hall, feeling the weight peel away from her shoulders as her fingers automatically sifted through the keys on the small bundle to select the bike's ignition key. She discovered it wasn't there in the same moment that her gaze found the front door, and what lay in front of it.

She stopped, horror rising through her in a sickening rush and freezing her where she stood, the keys dangling from her fingers, her helmet thudding to the carpeted floor and rolling against the wall. Now she remembered everything. And now she understood why she couldn't leave after all.

The body of Leslie Warrender sprawled across the narrow hallway and up against the front door, his too-new black T shirt sticky and stiff-looking with what could only be blood. And as the memory of last night returned in all its hideous clarity, Hazel knew what had caused the wound, whose prints would be on the weapon, and who would have ensured they were the only ones that were. Her terror was matched by the anguish that Griff, who had been her friend for as long as she could remember, had lured her to the distillery with her own grief.

But what did Warrender know, that had ultimately meant he had to be killed? Had he somehow found out that *Griff* had been her mother's killer after all? Had her quiet, trusting unburdening of herself outside the Twisted Tree been the moment he'd known something had to be done? If so, then all this, including Warrender's death, was her fault. There was so much to question, to work through and to piece together, but the need to speak to someone she could really trust was over-whelming everything else.

Either Griff or Warrender had removed her phone from her pocket; she could remember feeling them do it, but it might still be somewhere in the cottage, like her other belongings, and she didn't know anyone's number by heart. A landline sat on a little table in the hall, but she already knew what she'd hear when she picked up the receiver, and she was right; a dead silence greeted her. She followed the lead to the socket, in the vain hope that it simply wasn't plugged in, but had to accept that she had no means of communicating with anyone.

As she put the receiver back she noted guest literature in a perspex rack next to the phone, and gave a hollow, hopeless laugh as she saw the address on the headed paper: a self-catering cottage called Firemore Beach View. She was up near the Arctic Convoy Memorial on the other side of Poolewe, where the Soggy Socks lot would be heading at some point today. Griff's idea of course... The grim laughter choked off, and she looked around for a clock, already trying to calculate the timings: the run was due to leave Glencoille at ten; it was a good three-hour ride, and they would have to pass by this house on their way to the memorial, meaning her presence at what would soon become a known murder scene would be witnessed by anyone who recognised her father's old Kawasaki.

A quick, panicked calculation told her that, by the time they'd stopped for their planned lunch at the Old Inn in Gairloch, they'd be passing here on the way to the memorial by about two o'clock. There was an old-fashioned clock on the cooker, and she breathed a sigh of relief to see it was still only a little after six a.m, but she had to get that bike out of the yard, and out of sight, even if she couldn't leave the cottage itself until she'd figured things out, and got some help.

Using the front door was out of the question; even if she'd been able to move Warrender's body out of the way she daren't touch it, in case she disturbed some piece of evidence that might, by some miracle, prove she hadn't killed him. She went through to the kitchen, but the back door was locked, and rather than waste time doing battle with it she went into the tidy little sitting room and examined the window. It was a sash-type, but with a secondary glazing on the inside to cut out the savage winds for any winter guests who might book the house. Something else niggled at her as that thought crossed her mind, but there was so much flying around in her head now, and all she could focus on was moving the bike. There would be time after that to search for her phone, and to work out what to do.

She unlocked the inner pane and pushed aside the half-rusted and much-painted lever that would allow her to raise the sash window. The breeze that floated in was pleasantly, though oddly, warm for the time of day, and the scent of outdoors was like a draught of energy. Hazel pushed up the creaky window and climbed onto the sill. She ducked her head out, lowered one questing boot to the ground, and was just about to slide down when she heard a car approaching along the road. With a harsh gasp she hauled herself back in and slammed the window down so hard she expected to hear a crack and then for the glass to shatter, but it held, and a moment later a car passed by and carried on out towards the headland.

Hazel raised the window once more, then she kicked the wall in frustration at her own slow thinking; the cooker's clock must have re-set when the electricity had been switched on in the early hours. When she'd been brought here. She had no idea exactly what time it really was, but the warmer air of mid-day should have been an instant giveaway.

She had to risk it. The car driver might not remember seeing anything, but the Soggy Socks lot would, and everyone who would be on that run knew her bike, too. Bikers were like that: give them a detailed description of a person or a place and they shrug and say, *yeah, maybe*. But ask who owned a black and gold painted 1984 Kawasaki Z650, with a chipped tank and scuffed footpeg, and they'd have a name out before the question mark landed. Which meant that later, when the questioning became serious, there would only be one name on everyone's lips, and that was even before they analysed the fingerprints she'd have left all over this place. Not to mention on the murder weapon.

She slid the window up again and this time made shorter work of climbing out. She pulled her shirt sleeves out to their fullest length and wrapped them around the handlebars, then pulled the clutch in and levered the bike into neutral. She pushed the bike around the side of the house, out of sight of the road, hoping she hadn't wiped away any of Griff's traces on the handlebars by covering her hands, but it was better than overlaying whatever might be there with her own fingerprints. She looked at the keyring again and noticed that it wasn't only the ignition key that was missing, the key to her shed was too; presumably when – if – she found them, they would be together.

Inside, and with the window closed, she looked again at Warrender's corpse. It hadn't yet begun to smell, but after the all-too brief spell of outdoor freshness she was convinced she could sense the quality of the air changing around him; he looked waxy and unreal, and his half-lidded eyes reflected a rogue shaft of sunlight, making her feel even more uneasy.

She stood very still for a moment, with her own eyes closed and her head pounding. She had to leave, but she couldn't do that until after she'd heard the bike run pass by, or she'd risk meeting them on the road, and who knew what Griff had told them? She was running out of time, and of people she could trust, and the thought was terrifying. The prospect of just sitting around here, waiting and wasting time, went against every instinct she possessed, but there was nothing else she could do; the road was wide open here and offered no handy hiding places along its route for some distance.

A growling in her belly reminded her it had been hours since she'd eaten, and she went into the kitchen where, with a sense of unreality laced with inevitability, she saw the fridge stocked with her favourite foods. All the things she'd have bought for herself if she'd hired the cottage for a few days... There it was again. That niggle. She stood up straight, the fridge still open and wafting chilly air around her knees. Yes, it was all about the paperwork, and the forethought.

Either Griff or Warrender must have rented this place officially, and quite some time ago, to have guaranteed it would be empty over the bank holiday. And had they done it in their own name? Unlikely. Warrender might have originally used his new name, Booth or whatever it was, but it was a fair enough bet that, no matter which one of them had originally rented it, the booking was now under the name Douglas. Her money was on Griff, who would have known exactly what kind of food she liked... The pain of betrayal began to harden into a more manageable anger.

She looked around, wondering if she ought to try and disguise the fact that she'd been here, but soon realised it was pointless; her prints would be all over the bathroom, most of the bedroom, the sitting room window, and now the kitchen... and goodness knew where else, that she hadn't even thought of. And the upchuck on the bedding. Christ... Any attempt to clean up would just make her look even more guilty; all she had now was the hope of proving she'd been abducted, and hadn't come here voluntarily.

A renewed rumble of hunger drew her back to the kitchen; while she waited she might as well have some of the food Griff had put in the fridge. But when it came down to it, she couldn't eat. As she sat down with a sandwich and a cup of coffee, the material of her jeans pulled tight against her bruised thigh and reminded her what had brought her here. All that crap about his phone being in his van, when he had really been waiting for his chance to use it to lure her up to meet Warrender... Hazel tried to swallow the nibble of sandwich she'd taken, but her throat had closed up and she put the food back down, very carefully, then swiped in sudden fury at the plate and sent it crashing against the sink. The sound was shocking in the heavy silence. She sat staring at the broken crockery without seeing it, seeing only that black-gloved left hand, gripping her inner thigh hard enough to put the nerves there into orbit, and the fist, closed around its hypodermic syringe, slamming into the same leg from the other side.

She'd kill him.

Chapter Nineteen

JAMIE REACHED out tentatively to touch the hand nearer to him. There was no movement, but when he looked closer he realised the weight of the bike wasn't pressing Dylan's head into the river bank mud, as he'd feared. Where he himself had been flung clear by the bike flipping over, Dylan had remained more or less in his seat, and the bike itself had formed a triangular space in which the older boy now lay, half in the river and half out.

'Dylan!' He grabbed at the floating hand and pulled it, hard. Dylan didn't stir, but his body shifted a little, made buoyant as the water now pushed between him and the seat. Jamie tugged again, heartened by this, but as Dylan slipped forward he realised there was a danger that he'd slide free completely, only to be swept away before Jamie could grab him; he himself wasn't a strong boy.

As if to underline this, the rock under his foot tilted as the river surged past, almost knocking him off balance, and he grabbed hold of the bike's rack on which he'd been sitting, back when he'd thought everything had got as bad as it could be...

That would have been laughable if he hadn't been so frightened.

'Dylan!' he bellowed again, as loudly as he could and directly into his friend's ear. To his relief Dylan twitched, and then again, more violently, and the next moment he was trying to lift his head free of the water, gasping, his blue eyes wide and staring around him in confusion.

'Grab hold of something!' Jamie shouted, lifting the floating hand and trying to wrap it around the handlebar again.

The fingers worked feebly, but as Dylan came back to himself properly he let out a panicked yell and grabbed the rubber grip. Jamie couldn't see what was happening on the other side of him, but he assumed something similar, because a moment later Dylan had braced himself and risen out of his prone position, while Jamie shifted onto a better foothold in order to help him.

After a great deal of shouting, shoving, slipping and grab-bing, the two boys at last managed to help each other onto the river bank, and Jamie knelt to get his breath back, his head hanging down and his wet hair dripping onto the grass beside him. Dylan staggered to his feet and gave a wail of misery, presumably as he got a proper look at what he'd done. Jamie knew he himself would be in for it as well, and probably more so. No matter how he turned it over in his mind, and tried to twist it to make it seem as if Dylan was the ringleader in all this, the fact remained that *he'd* stolen the key, he'd misled Jonah into believing Ade wouldn't mind, and then he'd actually led Dylan to the ATV. For the first thirty seconds or so, Mum would be pleased that he was alive, but it was odds-on she'd spend the next week making him wish he wasn't. He groaned and lay down, his strength spent for now.

'Jamie?' Dylan fell to his knees beside him, obviously

thinking he was injured, and Jamie felt a twinge of guilt at the worry he heard in the older boy's voice.

'I'm okay,' Jamie muttered, burying his face in his sodden sleeve. 'Let me alone.'

'I'm sorry,' Dylan said. 'I panicked. I just grabbed the brake, but it was the front one instead of the back.'

'Mum's going to brick me up in a cellar.'

To his surprise Dylan chuckled. 'Come on, wee man. We're alive, aren't we? The bike didn't go all the way into the water; they'll be able to get it pulled back off the bank.'

'I'm dead,' Jamie insisted. He rolled onto his back and stared up at the sky, while Dylan sat back and thought for a moment.

'What if no-one found out it was us?' he said at length.

Jamie gave a soft snort and gestured to his wet clothes. 'Bit of a giveaway, don't you think?'

Dylan rubbed his wet hair and then smoothed it down. Jamie was faintly irritated to see how it fell more or less naturally, while he knew his own was sticking up in true toilet-brush style. 'We can tell that Jonah bloke we found the bike here. That we've been ages because we'd been looking for it. Someone must have stolen it. See?'

Jamie sat up. 'One of the bikers?'

'Listen, if one of them went wandering up the lane last night, and they found it, then they sneaked into the office and got the key... Think about it – it could have been anyone.'

'They were probably drunk,' Jamie added. A hesitant relief spread through him. 'Right, that's what we'll say. Let's see if we can dry our clothes a bit before we go back.'

'How?'

Jamie set off across the grass, calling back over his shoulder,

'Mum always has a heater in a room when she's been decorating, to help the paint dry quicker. They've been decorating in the distillery, so there might be a heater there too.'

'So not only are you *not* a chicken after all,' Dylan said jogging to catch him up, 'you're also a child genius. Respect.'

Jamie looked at him, suspecting sarcasm, but didn't see it. 'Teamwork,' he said. 'Come on.'

'Why's it unlocked?' Dylan asked, as Jamie pushed open the distillery door a few minutes later.

'Nothing to steal. Apart from a few pots of paint and the odd chair,' Jamie added, looking around. 'Ade says it's not worth getting all the keys cut that he'd have to while it's being done up.' He peered through the gloom, but couldn't see anything in the way of a heater, not even one of those little convector ones like he had in his bedroom. There was a camping table with a paint pot on it, a few tools randomly lying around, and a bag of sugar stood open on a table next to a packet of biscuits... It was hard to believe this would soon be what Ade proudly called 'the Centerpiece of the Glencoille Experience'.

Dylan reached for the light switch, but Jamie stopped him and spoke solemnly. 'Just because you can, doesn't mean you should.'

'You got that from Jurassic Park,' Dylan grumbled. 'We could just sit for a bit, I suppose.' He was moving a little stiffly now, and kept cradling and pressing his right arm. 'We'll probably dry off pretty quickly indoors.'

He picked a spot of wall next to the space that had been kept open for the huge fireplace and sat down, drawing his knees up and locking his arms around them. He looked a lot younger now, with his hair wet and his baggy clothes shrunk onto his body, and Jamie felt more his equal than he had before. He sat on the other side of the fireplace, keeping well away from the wide-silled window, and plucked his own wet jumper away from his chest.

'It was pretty ace though, in the end, wasn't it?' he said after a moment, and Dylan let out a heavy sigh.

'The. Fucking. Best.'

They looked at one another, and suddenly they were both laughing; a kind of half-hysterical, half-genuine laughter that left them wiping at their eyes and hiccupping softly, long after the first bout had exhausted itself. Then that too fell silent, and there was only the sound of wood pigeons, drifting through the door that Jamie had propped open with a paint tin – he couldn't bear the thought of being closed in, not somewhere like this.

After a while Dylan said quietly, as if he'd known, 'Tell me about it.'

'About what?'

'About when you were trapped in the cottage up there.' He pointed vaguely in the direction of the mountain up behind the main house. 'Was it really scary?'

Jamie started to tell him, but it seemed to him that the walls of the distillery were marching a little bit closer with every passing minute. He began to shift, uneasy in the memories that only grew more terrifying as he immersed himself in the events of last summer. When he reached the part where he'd discovered his asthma inhaler was empty, he stopped talking and felt in his pocket. As he'd suspected back at the river, it was blocked and useless. He stood up quickly, feeling the chill of movement through still-wet clothes as they brushed against his skin.

'I'm going back.'

'Why? Look, I didn't mean to—'

'No.' Jamie shook his head. 'It's not your fault. I need to get my spare inhaler from Ade's office. Jonah can let me in.'

Dylan rose too, and he once again pressed at his arm. 'Remember what we said, all right? We couldn't find the ATV, so we went looking, and we found it crashed in the river.' He looked at Jamie's clothes, then his own, and his expression brightened. 'You slipped in, and I went in and got you out.'

'Sod that,' Jamie said. '*You* fell in. *I* got you out. Much closer to the truth,' he added, seeing Dylan about to protest. He started towards the door, and as he did so the light spilling from it fell on something he hadn't noticed on his way in. He bent and picked it up.

'It's a phone,' he said. 'Maybe one of the workers left it.'

'Dropped it,' Dylan pointed out. 'No-one would have left it on the floor, ya numpty. Does it still work?'

Jamie pressed the side button and the phone lit up, showing the list of missed calls and texts, but also that the phone was locked. 'Griff, Ade, Griff, Maddy, Isla,' he read aloud. He frowned. 'This must be Hazel's phone.'

'We've got to give it someone then.' Dylan grabbed it from Jamie's hand. 'She's *my* cousin,' he reminded Jamie with a scowl, when Jamie tried to grab it back. He swiped at the screen but it asked for a PIN, and he tried a few of the family birthdays he knew. 'Nothing. What was she doing up here?'

'Is there anything else of hers?' Jamie remembered what Isla had said, back in the yard. 'Her jacket or anything?'

'Nope.' Dylan pulled a bank card out of the pocket inside the phone's leather cover. 'She'll need this, but at least it hasn't been stolen.'

'What's that?' Jamie pointed to a piece of white card poking out of the slot. Dylan pulled it out and read it.

'It's a business card. Some holiday cottage on the coast: Firemore Beach View.' He turned it over. 'It's got dates on it: yesterday through to tomorrow.'

'So is that where she's gone then?' Jamie frowned. 'Come on, I'll give it to Mackenzie. He'll know what to do – he's used to this stuff.' He took the phone back and put it in his pocket.

'Why don't we call the cottage ourselves?' Dylan persisted, following Jamie out of the distillery.

'How's your phone? Because mine's probably not going to be making any more calls.' Jamie dug his phone from his jeans pocket and demonstrated, and Dylan checked his own, with the same result. His face told Jamie that Isla would be every bit as thrilled as his own mum when she found out. But Dylan's idea to explain away the situation was a good one, and if Mum thought all this was as a result of trying to do Ade a good turn, it might all still be okay.

Back at the site, some of the rally-goers were starting to return from their various rides out. Bikes were puttering into the yard, visors flipping up as the riders and pillion passengers yelled to one another and to Jonah, who was sitting on the dry stone wall watching them. He caught sight of the two boys, and after a double-take at the state of their clothes he gestured them over.

'What the bloody hell happened to you two? This is Soggy Socks, not...never mind. Go up to the marquee – Greg's waiting. You can help him mark out the tug-o-war arena and lay the rope.' He squinted as a car came through the stone gateway, and sighed. 'Talk about crappy timing. This'll be your mum, I take it,' he said to Jamie.

Jamie tensed and nodded, and Dylan blurted out the story

of the 'mysterious' quad bike theft. 'It's up there, above the weir.' He pointed up the estate. 'Jamie fell in,' he added, ignoring Jamie's fierce look, 'and I had to pull him out. But we couldn't shift the bike. Sorry.'

'Shit,' Jonah muttered. 'Where's Griff when you need him?'

Mackenzie was out of the car now, and distracted by the bikes, but Charis took one look at the boys and came over to echo Jonah's question, almost to the word. When she heard Dylan had pulled Jamie out of the river, she softened towards him considerably.

'Ade's not going to be best pleased about the quad bike,' she said, when Mackenzie joined them and she'd passed on the news. 'He was pretty generous giving the site over to the rally.'

Mackenzie looked around doubtfully at the cheerful activity in the yard. 'These sorts of people just...aren't like that,' he said. 'Besides, no-one's looking over to see if we've heard about it yet. Which they would, and they'd be looking guilty as hell.'

'Who else could it have been though?' Charis shrugged. 'I know you don't like to think it, but there's always a few bad apples.'

'Aye, I suppose.' But he still didn't look convinced.

Jamie felt a thump between his shoulder blades and looked at Dylan, who nodded at Jamie's pocket.

'Phone.'

'Oh!' Jamie pulled it out and handed it to Mackenzie. 'I found this, up in the distillery. We think it's Hazel's.'

'Well, no wonder she's not been in touch.' Mackenzie tried the same things Jamie and Dylan had, in order to unlock it, but he soon gave up. 'Look,' he said to Charis, 'you drive the kids back. I'll stay here until Ade gets back, and see if I can help him with the Honda.'

'We think Hazel might be staying in a rental place,' Dylan supplied, and produced the card he'd taken from the phone wallet. Both Mackenzie and Charis looked puzzled but deeply relieved, as Mackenzie took the card.

'I'll give it a call,' Mackenzie said. 'Thanks.'

'Just watch your shoulder,' Charis warned, taking the car keys off him. 'You don't want to go putting your recovery back.'

'It's fine.' He dropped a kiss on her forehead, and Jamie turned away in time to catch Dylan miming puking behind him. He grinned and got into the car, feeling less confident about the quad bike story now, but soaking up the familiarity and comforting smell of Mackenzie's car. Here was safety and normality, if slightly overshadowed by the potential for a row later.

Later, in fact, brought something more unexpected. Dylan's mum had arrived for her son at around six, not batting an eyelid, now that he was wearing dry clothes and with only a bruise emerging on his arm to show for his adventures. As soon as they'd gone Charis had promptly once more quizzed Jamie on exactly what had happened, no doubt making sure the story remained the same now that 'Dylan the Villain' was no longer there to influence it. She seemed satisfied, to Jamie's relief, but there was still Mackenzie to think about; he hadn't yet returned, but had called a bit earlier to say they'd recovered the quad bike, and that he and Maddy were driving out to the cottage named on the card. They'd had no answer to their phone calls.

Jamie wandered upstairs to the tiny spare room, which his mum had turned into a sort of office for her college work, and where she'd gone now to play with her new coloured filters. The walls were already plastered in blow-ups of photographs she'd taken, and even he could see she was gradually improving. Some of the images were a bit weird, but she insisted they were 'experimental', and showed she was open to new things. He hoped she'd grow out of that.

'What are these?' he asked, picking up an opened A4-sized envelope from her cluttered work table. He could see a sheaf of prints inside.

'Hmm?' She glanced over, already immersed in sliding different filters onto her camera. 'Oh, it's the photos Mackenzie asked me to get printed, from the negatives Hazel found.'

'Can I see them?'

She looked amused. 'Are you *that* bored, Jay?'

'A bit. I wouldn't be, if I had a—'

'We're not getting a dog.' Charis went back to her filters. 'Knock yourself out, lad. There's nothing interesting though; I think they only wanted it for the one on the top there anyway.'

Jamie drew the photos out and saw the one his mum was talking about. A group of three people in a row, with a building behind them that gave him a definite, but not immediately identifiable, twitch of guilt. Then he recognised it as Dylan's yard, and the building as the garage with the knocking branches. His mum still didn't know he'd gone to Dylan's; she'd have kicked right off if he'd told her that. He flicked quickly through the rest, then came back to the top one again, but this time it wasn't the building that was familiar, it was something about the man nearest the camera. With his hair blowing back, a pair of beetling eyebrows, and a distinctive mole behind his right ear... It was the bloke who'd been snooping around

Druimgalla, looking for someone who'd once lived there. Looking for Dylan's family, in other words. Maybe, specifically, looking for Hazel. It was time to come clean.

'I know him,' he said, pointing.

Charis stood upright. 'Know who?' She saw what he was looking at, and came over to take the picture out of his hand. 'That bloke, or that one?'

'The one on this end. I've...' He took the plunge, hoping this would prove important enough to take the edge off his almost-fib. 'I've been there, where it was took. It's Dylan's place.'

'What have I told you about going up there?' Charis asked, exasperation taking over her curiosity for a moment. 'That kid—'

'Saved my life, don't forget,' Jamie put in, accepting that Dylan's story worked better for this scenario. 'He's okay, you know he is. That bloke though, he was having a good old snoop around, looking for someone.'

Charis picked up her phone. 'Mackenzie needs to see this.' She took a picture of the photo now lying on the table, and added Jamie's information to the message. 'Right, if you've nothing else to add...' She stopped and tapped her phone against her lips thoughtfully. 'You said you found Hazel's phone in the distillery?'

'We went there to dry off, so you wouldn't worry.'

'How could she not know she'd left it behind?' Charis mused. 'I don't think there's even a signal up there yet.'

'It was on the floor, so she probably dropped it and doesn't even know yet.'

'Did you see anything else?'

Jamie thought for a moment, then shook his head. 'Just some paint tins and some tools. And coffee-making stuff.'

'Hmm. Mackenzie's probably still driving.' Charis made a call. 'Maddy? Can you check Mackenzie's phone for the picture I just sent?' She waited, sending Jamie a quick, distracted, on-off smile. 'Okay, yep, that's the one. Did you read the message?' She listened, staring into space, and Jamie began to feel worried about Hazel for the first time. 'D'you think I should?' his mum was saying now. 'Yeah, I thought so too. If you don't find her at that cottage, let me know.'

She picked up the photo again and stared at it, and as Jamie watched her, growing nervous again that she was going to start asking questions about the distillery, and why he was there, he saw her squint suddenly and peer more closely.

'What is it?' he asked.

She shook her head. 'Not sure.' Then she turned away and started digging around in the folder until she found the negatives again. 'Go and watch telly or something. I'll come and get tea in a bit, okay?'

'We had tea,' he reminded her; it was gone seven now.

'Supper then,' she murmured distracted once more. 'I'll be with you in a bit.'

'What are you doing?'

For a moment he thought she was going to brush him off again, but instead she beckoned him over and pointed to the photo. Not to the people, but to the garage. 'I'm having a closer look at that. As close as I possibly can. And this one too.' She held up a strip of negatives and pointed to one in the centre. 'Want to help?'

Jamie raised his eyes to hers; here was a throwback to the day they had first arrived in Scotland, last August, and her determination that *this* was the moment their lives would change, and everything would finally fall into place... Well, she had been right about the change, but it had been a pretty long and scary time before it had all fallen into place. The light that flashed in her eyes now was just the same as then, which meant absolutely anything could happen, and probably would. Jamie felt a fierce little leap of affectionate resignation, then he gave her a wry smile and nodded. 'Yeah, okay, why not?'

Chapter Twenty

SOMETIME AROUND MID-AFTERNOON, Hazel heard the rumble of bikes pass the cottage. She waited, breath held, until the noise had faded into the distance, and then pulled on her jacket. With no bike key, and no ID with which to prove ownership for roadside recovery, the Kawasaki was useless, and there was no way her pathetic funds would even get her to Inverness by taxi, let alone Abergarry, but they might get her a little way along the road at least. *If* she could find a phone box that still accepted coins. If memory served, and the leisure industry had been kind, there was a camp site a short way along the road, near the beach; there might even prove to be some helpful soul going her way with a spare seat in their car.

She'd rubbed away the excesses of her smudged and smeared eye-liner when she'd had her shower; now she made sure the last traces were gone and raked her fingers through her hair, trying to make herself look as presentable and non-threatening as possible. Then she dropped her backpack and helmet out of the sitting room window, climbed out after them and went around to where she'd left her bike.

Swallowing a surge of regret, she swung her leg over the saddle and settled into the familiar riding position, then let the bike roll down the little driveway to the road. Once she stopped free-wheeling she gave the cottage and its grisly occupant one final, loathing look before shouldering her backpack and pushing the bike along the gently undulating, but thankfully mostly flat, road to the camp site. She'd remembered correctly about that, too; wide open space either side – she'd have had nowhere to duck out of sight if she'd met the club. The people in the one car that passed her merely gave her a sympathetic look and continued on their way.

She wheeled the bike in behind the camp site's reception hut and found a coin-operated pay phone with the numbers of a few taxi firms pinned to the board. She paused only long enough to wonder if there might be some kind of search warrant out on her yet, before dialling anyway. She'd take her chances; what other choice did she have? Maddy? Ade? She'd naturally thought about them from the moment she'd known she was leaving the cottage, but had regretfully dismissed the idea. Quite apart from not having their numbers to hand, and having to use the 118 enquiry service, if Griff had made sure there *was* an alert out for her already she couldn't risk calling them either. Not yet. Not until she was safely hidden away again. Even calling the taxi was a risk, but at least this way she wouldn't be bringing her remaining friends into the firing line with her.

The taxi firm answered after a frustratingly long time, and Hazel eyed the crumpled twenties in her hand and asked how far they would take her.

'It's £2 a mile, plus £4.50 for the first mile,' the man on the switchboard told her. 'Where are you?'

'Firemore Beach.'

'Okay. Well, I reckon...Victoria Falls?'

It would be a start. A beauty spot on a Saturday afternoon would mean people passing through, and maybe a lift. She looked at her crash helmet; she could always plead an accident, or running out of petrol, and appeal to the good Samaritans among the tourists.

By the time the taxi arrived she was beginning to feel slightly more optimistic. Something about the fresh coastal air, and the chance of returning to people who believed in her, had worked on the fuzziness and the lingering headache for the time being. She sat quietly in the back of the cab, responding to the cabbie's polite, friendly questions in as few words as she felt she could get away with without sounding rude or raising suspicions. As they passed a sign to Victoria Falls, a growing roar behind them on the road made her shrink down in her seat, her heart hammering crazily as the taxi driver slowed to allow the group of returning motorcycles to flow past them like water, the riders raising their hands in thanks.

When the road was empty ahead of them she sat back up, shaking with relief that she hadn't been spotted. There was seemingly no alert out for her yet, which added to that feeling, but there was also no-one at the Victoria Falls car park, so, as the taxi took off back the way they'd just come, she hooked her helmet over her arm, hoisted her backpack again and set out towards Inverness.

Cars and vans passed her by with depressing regularity, despite her frantic waving and her most pleading, helpless expression; work vans wouldn't have been allowed to pick her up anyway, and a couple of the cars were rammed to the rooftops with camping equipment and small children, but any of the others would have had room for one woman and a backpack.

After only around twenty minutes, Hazel's bruised leg began to throb and her boots rubbed, and in keeping her mind off these swelling annoyances, she had nothing to do but dwell on the way her life had turned to absolute shit in the space of a day. She'd well and truly marked herself down as the perfect patsy; Griff had been so convincing too, when she'd said they suspected Warrender of her mother's death... She stopped, vaguely noticing she'd done it just in time to avoid blundering onto a cattle grid, but following an ugly thought that had just emerged: how long had Griff really known her father?

Had it only been since he'd left his old gang, or did it go further back? She calculated quickly; being ten years her senior he'd have been in his mid-twenties or so in ninety-eight, which was quite old enough to have attacked and killed a lone, unsuspecting woman in her home. A woman who knew him, felt comfortable with him and had even let him in – for reasons Hazel didn't want to think about but couldn't avoid now: what if she and Maddy had got it right, all of it, except the name? That actually it had been *Griff* having the affair with Hazel's mother? Griff the one who had not wanted his friendship with her husband destroyed by it, and had silenced her, either deliberately or by horrible, unthinkable accident?

Hazel flexed her tensed fingers, and crossed the road to use the pedestrian gateway past the cattle grid; she didn't trust her suddenly shaking legs not to pitch her down between the bars. *So why did Warrender have to die too?* Had he really painted the fake, or had it actually been Graeme? Always hailed as the better artist, it could easily have been him, and Hazel had to accept it, as ugly a thought as it was. He could have used his cut of the money to pay Warrender off, help him disappear, and if Griff felt guilty enough he could now be protecting Graeme's reputation. If not his daughter, she acknowledged, feeling sick again.

The doubly insulting rattle of an empty truck passing across the cattle grid behind her made her stop and stare in dismay; she'd been too preoccupied and upset to stick out her thumb to the one vehicle that was most likely to stop. The driver could have let her ride in the open back, and probably would have, if she'd had her wits about her.

'Shit, shit, *shit!*' she yelled after it as it continued up around the corner. 'Couldn't you have taken a wild *guess?*' She slapped the helmet over her arm, but all she got from that was a stinging palm, and she took a long, slow breath and re-crossed the road. It was pointless getting worked up now; it was likely to be a long and tiring night. With blisters.

The warmth of the May evening was fading, but she was hot and sweaty with the walk in leather jacket and boots; with the cool glint of blue from the loch on her left, through the trees, she trudged on, keeping behind the barrier and wondering how far she'd have to go before she found a miracle. But after only another ten minutes, she rounded a bend and there it was: scrubby trees gave way to a neatly mown grass verge, a barn-type building with a corrugated iron roof and, just ahead, the welcome site of chimneys puffing smoke into the evening sky from a cluster of buildings of mixed vintage. The yellow sign proclaimed it as the Loch Maree Hotel.

'Fishing available,' Hazel read aloud, with a laugh that sailed on a wave of relief. 'Oh, *that's* good then.' After only about half an hour's walk, here was a chance. A possibility that she could still get home without alerting the police. She chewed at her lip. How, though? She desperately wanted to call Maddy now, to find out how things lay, but she had to be somewhere safe and hidden when she did it; if she was still struggling to make her way back to Abergarry, and the police happened to check Maddy's phone for any reason, they'd both be in it up to their necks. No, she needed Maddy out there and unblemished if she was to stand any chance of getting through this.

She glimpsed someone in chef's whites clattering down the metal staircase on the side of the hotel, and her mind clicked on a gear: Breda. On a busy Saturday night there would be no opportunity for her to get away, to come and pick her up, and because she'd want to do just that it wasn't fair to ask, but if Hazel could at least *get* to Thistle, she could make any phone calls from there.

She looked more closely at the hotel, wondering if its clientele were likely to be the kind of people who'd pick up a random hitch-hiker, but it was impossible to tell. The building itself was clearly a very old one, with additional, newer, wings and out-buildings. The small-ish car park was full, as she'd expect for a May bank holiday weekend, but nothing moved in it. Then she saw her best chance – a couple of large, touring motorbikes leaned companionably beside one another next to the path that led towards the loch: a BMW and a Honda Gold-wing, both with large panniers, and doss rolls bungeed to the back. She didn't recognise either bike, which didn't mean for certain that they were nothing to do with the Soggy Socks rally, but it was a reasonable bet, particularly at a time when the site back at Glencoille would just be coming to life.

A police car shot past the hotel on the main road, heading back the way Hazel had just come, and, a few seconds behind it, a plain black van going at a similar speed. Word was probably out, then. Her heart picked up a quicker beat, and she tried to tell herself she was being paranoid, that whoever had booked the cottage in her name had doubtless booked it for the whole weekend, and so no-one could possibly have found the body yet... But it was no good. Griff would obviously have called in an anonymous tip-off, and Hazel had compounded her guilt by fleeing the scene, just as he'd hoped. Played right into his hands once again. A very quick search of the area would reveal her bike too, even tucked away as it was.

'You fucking *idiot!*' She sat down on a large rock, pressing her hands to her eyes, as if by blocking out the evening light she could pretend none of today had happened. But eventually she had to raise her head again, so she could keep an eye on the two touring bikes. Presently her patience was rewarded, as two bikers in matching full leathers emerged from the hotel; Hazel was just about to stand up and hail them, when they began unstrapping their sleeping rolls and unclipping the panniers and she muttered another curse. Not moving on then, staying over. She waited until they'd taken their gear back inside, then wandered over and made a mental note of one of the number plates.

Two minutes later she was at reception, and delivering her helpful message: 'Sorry to disturb you, but there's a bike outside with its lights on. I'm worried the battery'll go flat before the owner realises. Registration? Yes, of course...'

She went back outside and waited. After a few minutes one of the tourists came out again and squinted over at his BMW. He shook his head and was about to turn away, so Hazel called out and stopped him.

'I'm really sorry,' she said, gesturing to her helmet. 'I need a massive favour, and who better to ask than a fellow biker?'

He looked around; a short-ish, bald man in his early sixties, sweating in neck-to-ankle red and white leathers, and with a matching bandana swinging loosely around his neck. 'Favour?

What kind of favour?' His accent put him squarely in New York. 'And what's with the subterfuge?'

'It's tricky,' Hazel said, coming a little closer. 'I didn't want to put you on the spot by asking you in public, but it's really vital that I get to Inverness, as soon as possible.'

'Where's ya bike?'

'My boyfriend left me behind.' It seemed more plausible than that she'd managed to lose her own key.

'Why the hell'd he do that?'

'Please,' she said, 'it's a long story. Can you get me across the bridge, at least?'

'That's gotta be an hour each way.' He scowled. 'Can't you get a cab?'

'I don't have any money, or my phone. Dave has it all. But I'll be able to transfer cash to you as soon as I get back.' She fumbled at her neck and unclasped her chain. 'Here,' she said, with rising desperation, 'this is solid silver – my dad gave it to me when my mum died so I'll want it back, but if you can get me to an address in Inverness I can pay you there and then.' Breda would be able and happy to help with that, she was sure. 'Please,' she added, but her spirits dropped as the biker's expression remained closed. Then, after another searching look, he relented and gave her a comforting pat on the arm.

'Okay, miss. Never could deny a damsel in distress. Let me just go tell my friend.'

'Thank you,' Hazel breathed, and returned to sit on her rock again. She entertained the cold and fleeting thought that he was going to call the police instead, but after a few minutes he returned, while his curious friend watched from the hotel doorway. Hazel found her gloves in her backpack, and gave both men a brilliant smile of thanks as she pulled them on.

'I can't thank you enough.'

'I'm not taking you to this Dave, am I?' her saviour said as he put his helmet on. 'He sounds like a real asshole.'

'Oh, he is.' Hazel slipped onto the seat behind him and fastened her chin strap. 'The worst. And no, I'm not going to him. Can you take me to Thistle? It's a restaurant on—'

'Sure. I know where that is.' He waved to his friend and pressed the ignition; a moment later they were on the road back to Inverness, and the relative safety of the crowded city.

She slid off the bike in the alleyway behind Thistle, and while the biker waited she made her way to the yard behind the kitchen, and then through the wooden gateway to the covered outdoor area. A few people spared her a curious look, but generally she felt comfortingly anonymous as she pushed open the door to the passageway. She knocked loudly at the kitchen door, aware of the noise level in there, and waited, holding her breath and rehearsing what she would say when she saw Breda. But she didn't say any of it; she just took one look at the immense relief on Breda's face and burst into tears.

Somehow, still wrapped tightly in her friend's arms, she managed to gasp out her embarrassing request for money, and heard Breda click her fingers at someone. 'Don't worry, love, we'll see that gentleman's looked after.'

'My necklace,' Hazel hiccupped, remembering. 'Don't let him drive off with it.'

'That lovely thing from your da?' Breda rubbed her back as if she was a child. 'Of course, don't worry. We'll make sure you get it back.' She gently eased Hazel back to arm's length. 'What do you want me to do?'

'I need to get hold of Maddy, or Ade. And I need some-where to wait.'

'I'm sure I can fit you in for a meal in the restaurant if you'd like?'

'No, I need to...stay out of sight.'

'This all sounds very intriguing.' Breda was frowning now. 'Can you not tell me anything more?'

'I've not done anything illegal, I promise.' Hazel's heart sank at the growing suspicion on her friend's face. Not that she blamed her. 'If you give me the Glencoille number, I can call Ade from here and be out of your way.'

'He won't be at work this late though, will he?'

'No, but his mobile number's on the outgoing voicemail message.'

'Ah, grand.' Breda nodded. 'I didn't think of that.'

'Can I wait here until he comes?'

'I suppose you could wait in my office,' Breda said, but she still didn't look happy about it. 'Do you promise we're not going to be getting a visit from the police? Only—'

'I promise. Unless...' she hesitated, 'unless you call them,' she said quietly. 'But I swear to you, I've not done anything wrong. No matter what you might hear over the next few hours,' she added.

Breda considered her for a long, painful moment, then sighed. 'All right. For the sake of Linda's faith in you, I believe you.'

'Thank you.' Hazel fought back tears of relief, and was about to follow her out towards the office when she became aware of a pressing need; the memory of urine-soaked jeans made her shudder. Never again. 'I need the toilet first,' she said. 'Would that be okay? I'll be quick.'

'Of course.' Breda gestured to the door of the WC.

'Come to the office when you're ready. Tell you what, I'll call Glencoille for you while I'm waiting, shall I, and get that number?'

Hazel made quick use of Thistle's smart, gleaming facilities, and as no-one came in, she then used the sink to wash the sweat and tear stains from her face. As she patted her skin dry on a handful of paper towels, she caught sight of herself in the mirror and had to stare very hard to convince herself that she was real, alive, and here in Inverness; so much had happened in just a few hours, it was hard to anchor herself in her own body again.

How quickly things had turned around since waking up this morning in the middle of nowhere; confused, dazed, sick and terrified. She pressed the heel of her hand against the bruise on her thigh, and her heart hardened further against her erstwhile friend and self-styled 'protector', Dave Griffin. Now she was back, and she knew what he really was, he'd be wise to keep his distance.

Paul had offered to drive Maddy's car, since Charis had taken his, and Maddy had readily accepted; she was too tense now to concentrate on mundane things like other road users, like the group of bikes that had overtaken a taxi, on their side of the road, a few minutes ago. She turned the business card over and over in her fingers as the Corsa carried them out towards the Arctic Convoy Memorial. 'I just don't get why she'd have booked this place, on this weekend' she said, not for the first time. But a quick phone call to the booking agency had confirmed it, when Maddy had pretended to be Hazel herself. They had to accept that, for whatever reasons she might have had, Hazel had planned to leave the rally on Friday night and tell no-one about it.

'It's her phone that bothers me,' Paul said, frowning. He was subtly rolling his left shoulder as he drove, and flexing his fingers on the wheel, but as soon as he saw her looking, he stopped. 'It was so bloody weird, the kids finding it like that.'

'Aye, it was.' It was in Maddy's pocket, and as much as she'd tried, she'd had no more luck than anyone else getting into it. 'She'd have come back for it the minute she realised she'd left it, even this long distance. And what the hell was it doing in the distillery anyway?'

'Yeah, I don't—'

'Stop!' Maddy braced her hands on the dashboard, as Paul slammed on the brakes and brought the car to a slewing stop, diagonally across the road.

'Jesus!' he exploded. 'What is it?'

'Go back,' Maddy urged, 'up to the camp site we just passed.'

The engine whined as they backed up to the entrance to the camp site, and they had barely stopped again before Maddy was out of the car and running into the car park. 'That's her bike, isn't it?'

Paul followed, and needed no more than a quick glance. 'Aye, I'd know it anywhere.' He grasped the handlebars and pulled the bike upright, then rocked it backwards and forwards for a moment, his head cocked, listening. 'She's not out of fuel. D'you think she's staying here, instead of the house?'

'Maybe it's a decoy.' Maddy was baffled, but starting to question how well she knew Hazel after all. 'She certainly didn't want anyone to know about the booking,' she said, 'and we wouldn't have found out, either, if she hadn't left her phone. I wonder who she was meeting?'

'Hey!'

They looked up to see a cross-looking young man, glaring at them from the doorway of the reception hut. 'That yours then?'

'A friend's,' Maddy called. 'Do you know where she is?'

'Nope, we found it lurking behind the office and had to move it back out here where it belongs. If you see your friend, you be sure and tell her there's a fine for leaving a vehicle on the field!'

'We will,' Paul called out, in a friendly voice, then turned to Maddy. 'This is all wrong. I don't like it one bit. Come on.'

They stopped outside the single-storey holiday let, with the painted slate beside the front door: *Firemore Beach View*. It was a standard type of cottage for a casual coastal tourist; whitewashed cob walls and a neat little front yard, probably only one bedroom, a basic kitchen, and costing the earth to rent over the bank holiday weekend. Why had Hazel done it?

Maddy got out of the car and walked up the path, hearing Paul following her, more slowly. When she turned, he was looking at the dry dirt in the yard.

'Tyre marks,' he said, pointing. 'Going right around the back.'

She nodded. 'Window's open a crack.' She stepped up to it and peered through, seeing the pin-neat little sitting room beyond. She bent and shouted into the inch-high gap between window and sill. 'Hazel?' She didn't really expect a reply, all things considered, but was still disappointed when only her own voice echoed back to her.

Paul pushed at the front door. 'It's not locked,' he said, 'but there's definitely something stopping it from opening.'

'Stop then,' Maddy said, her insides giving a sudden twist. 'Just...stop pushing.' She took a deep breath. 'What if it's her? What if it's Hazel?'

Paul's face was unusually pale when he turned to her, and he joined her beside the window. He bent and listened for a moment, then got his fingers beneath the window frame and shoved it upwards. 'You'd better go,' he said quietly. 'I'm sorry, but you're smaller, and—'

'It's fine. I'll do it.'

'I'll go to the back door – just go straight there and let me in.' He didn't say, *don't go looking*, but they both heard it.

Maddy nodded mechanically and lifted one leg over the sill, bending at the waist to duck through the gap. Paul had been right to send her; he'd never have fitted that broad frame through here without doing himself some damage, and helping Ade to pull the quad out of the river had already given him fresh pain lines around the mouth.

Maddy crossed the sitting room and pulled open the door, but before she could locate the kitchen and, presumably, the back door, she saw the cottage's sole, gruesome occupant. The breath left her in a rush of horror, but that immediately gave way to relief that it wasn't Hazel. There was a faint, sweetish smell lingering in the hall, and Maddy pulled her jumper up over her nose and hurried through to the kitchen.

'It's locked,' she called, seeing Paul's silhouette on the other side. 'Don't for God's sake try to break it down, either. Not in your state.'

'Is she... Is it her?' he called back, in a lower voice.

'No, it's Warrender. I'm coming back out.'

Sliding out into the fresh air again made her realise how strong the smell had been. It wasn't quite stomach-turning, not yet, but it wouldn't be long. 'We've got to call this in.'

'Aye.' Paul had his phone out already. As he spoke to the despatcher, Maddy's own phone rang; she glanced at the screen, ready to kill the call if it didn't look important. But it was Nick.

'I'm giving you the heads up.' He sounded as if he was walking fast, and his voice was low, and hard to hear. 'We've had to seal off the distillery at Glencoille. We think it's a murder scene.'

Maddy's head swam again. 'There's a body?'

'No, but there's a potential murder weapon, and I just wanted to let you know we're looking for your friend Hazel. I hear you've got her phone?'

Maddy clapped a hand over her pocket, as if he could somehow see it bulging there. 'Who told you that?'

'Mads, listen.' Nick had presumably got far enough away from his team now to allow him to stop and to speak normally. 'This is serious. We need that phone.'

'Do you think Hazel's killed someone?'

'Where is it?'

Maddy looked across at Paul, who'd finished his call. 'Come out to the Firemore Beach View, the other side of Poolewe,' she said quietly. 'We've just called in a dead body. His name's Leslie Warrender, and he first died in 1998.'

Chapter Twenty-One

MACKENZIE SAT in the car with a tight-lipped Maddy at his side. They'd watched in near silence as the forensics team erected their small tent by the window, the suspected point of exit, and taped off the area; Warrender's body had eventually been taken away, but crime scene examiners were still walking in and out, taking measurements and photographs. Mackenzie and Maddy had been unceremoniously shunted aside, but Mackenzie was under no illusion that they would be allowed to go home anytime soon; there would be statements to make, questions to answer, and then the same questions again, but asked by different people. He knew the drill, all too well.

In the meantime, Charis would be waiting for him, and he took out his phone now to update her. 'I still don't know how long I'll be,' he said, looking across the road at the bobbing lights around the cottage. 'Could be an all-nighter, so don't wait up.'

'Okay. I'll miss ya though.' Her voice was warm, as always, but there was something else there that made him wonder if he wouldn't actually have been a bit of an unwanted distraction.

'So, what are you up to?' he asked, as casually as he could manage. 'Anything interesting?'

'Not really. Just...messin' with the photos Hazel gave you.'

'And?'

'And nothing. Yet.'

'Yet?'

'Just get yourself home when you can, Mackenzie. I think I might have something useful for you when you do.' She paused, and he knew she'd say no more on the subject tonight. 'Tell Maddy I hope they find Hazel, and that she's okay.'

He passed on Charis's message, but Maddy just nodded. She'd given Hazel's phone to the police, and had retreated to her car as soon as Nick and his team arrived, but Nick kept looking over at them, and his expression was both wary and suspicious. Mackenzie didn't like it.

He looked up and into his rear view mirror as a fresh set of headlights approached, slowed and pulled in behind him, then died. 'It's Ade,' he said, opening his door. 'Maybe now we'll find out what went on at Glencoille.'

Ade climbed out of his jeep and came over, shoving his hands into his pockets to keep off the coastal chill. 'Christ,' he said, looking at the activity by the cottage, then ducked down to greet Maddy through the car window. 'How are you holding up?'

'I'm okay.' She got out, looking restless and anxious. 'What an almighty mess.'

'What happened?' Mackenzie asked Ade.

Ade appeared ready to launch into it, then looked over at the cottage and his expression darkened again. 'Tell you what, you tell me yours and I'll tell you mine.'

'They won't want us talking,' Maddy pointed out, and sure

enough an officer broke away from the group and started in their direction.

'I've already been questioned,' Ade called to her. 'My alibi's been checked out.'

'I'm sorry,' she said, 'but we're going to have to ask you to return to your vehicle.'

'In that case can you get on and ask your questions so we can go home?' Mackenzie said, knowing he sounded irritable and not really caring. He recognised the officer as DC McAndrew, who'd questioned him and Ade last year. She'd been okay back then, but she looked mightily pissed off now; presumably she had a life to get back to as well.

'You've got a habit of finding dead bodies, Mr Mackenzie.'

'Occupational hazard,' he said apologetically.

Her gaze went to Ade, and she sighed. 'You *again*?'

Ade held his hands up. 'Look, I wasn't even here when he found War...the body.'

McAndrew frowned. 'What did you call him?'

'His name's Leslie Warrender,' Mackenzie said, 'not whatever any ID you've found on him might say.'

McAndrew eyed him closely, then turned back to Ade. 'In your vehicle for the moment, sir, if you don't mind? I'll see what I can do about your interview,' she added to Mackenzie, and gave Maddy a perfunctory nod before rejoining her team.

The interviews, conducted in the back of a police car, were short and centred mainly on why Mackenzie was so convinced the victim's name was Warrender, though the police didn't volunteer an alternative. They took all the details they could get, and when it was Maddy's turn he could see from her expression that she knew full well every word she spoke was driving Hazel deeper into the dirt. But there was nothing else to do now, except tell the truth.

When they were released, they followed Ade's jeep for ten minutes down the road to the Loch Maree, a fishing hotel he sometimes used. They sat together in the cool, fragrant dark, on the raised grass verge, and Maddy told Ade what she had found in the guest house.

'He's been stabbed in the chest, but that's all I know,' she said. 'There was no murder weapon.'

'No, that's because *they've* got it.' Ade jerked a thumb back along the road. 'They're already looking for Hazel,' he added quietly. 'I'm sorry.'

'I know, Nick told me, but that's all he said. Why do they want her? What do they think killed him?' She blew out a breath as Mackenzie put his hand on her arm.

'We've told him our part,' he said. 'Let him tell his in his own time, aye?'

'Okay,' Ade said. 'Dave Griffin went to send her another in a fairly long string of "where are you?" texts, and found one he'd supposedly sent her before. He swears he didn't send it though, and he hadn't noticed it right away, not until he scrolled back through their conversation thread. It said something about having urgent news about her mum, and asked her to go to the distillery. It was sent just after two o'clock this morning.'

'So he lured her up there,' Maddy said, frowning.

'Or someone did. I was there when the police found a Doc Marten footprint, in the plaster dust by the window seat, in her size.'

'But that's because she sat there when we were talking!' Maddy said. 'I remember how she brushed the dust off and sat there while we waited for Paul. Didn't she?' She turned to Mackenzie, who nodded.

'Best make sure you mention that if they question you again, then. Although...' Ade sighed, and looked reluctantly at them both in turn. 'They also found a screwdriver, covered in blood.'

'*Could* that have been what killed him?' Mackenzie asked Maddy. 'You saw him.'

Maddy looked ill. 'It could have been, I suppose.'

'So,' Mackenzie said, his voice heavy with regret, 'from the police point of view it ticks all the boxes. Means, motive *and* opportunity.' He shook his head, perplexed. 'But if he actually died in the distillery, how the hell did she get him all the way out here? And why?'

'They won't have been able to identify any fingerprints yet,' Maddy said, her voice sharp now, 'so can we stop talking about her as if she's done it?'

'I think the point is that it's unlikely,' Ade said. 'I mean, how, and why, have got to be pretty basic questions the police will ask, and there's no sane answer to either. And forensics can tell when a body's been moved after death, can't they?'

'Playing devil's advocate though,' Mackenzie said, giving Maddy an apologetic look, 'Maybe she had help. Maybe Griff *did* text her, but knowing that message is going to show up on her phone, he's pre-empting the question. Like all those smart-arses who think they're being clever by reporting their car missing before anyone discovers the crime they committed with it.'

'Where's Hazel's phone now?' Ade asked.

'They've got it.' Maddy said. 'No doubt they've unlocked it and are going through it with a fine-toothed comb as we speak.'

'And they know she's the one who booked that place?'

'Presumably. It was easy enough for me to find out, and I doubt they'd have wasted any time, the moment Paul called it in. If the booking was made on that phone, she's in big trouble.' Maddy kicked impatiently at the wall with her heel. 'We've got to find her before they do. She was probably walking if she left the bike at the camp site.'

'Not if Griff was helping her,' Ade pointed out. 'If he used his van to get that body up here, and now he's framing her for it, he could have dropped her and her bike anywhere.'

'If he's only framing her, that's sort of a good thing,' Mackenzie said quickly, seeing Maddy's stricken expression. 'It means he likely hasn't...you know.'

'Killed her?'

'Aye.' They all stood up and he turned to his brother. 'I'll get back and see what Charis is being all mysterious about, Maddy can relieve her dad of babysitting duties, and you can drive back along this road and call in at one or two places on the way. See if anyone saw Hazel, or helped her; it might help us find where she went when she left here. Maybe start with this place.'

'Okay.' Ade cleared his throat and gave Mackenzie a pointed look, which he interpreted to mean could he please push off for a minute. He obliged and walked back to Maddy's car, resisting the urge to look over his shoulder. But when he got back behind the wheel he saw them in the rear view mirror; her head lowering tiredly but naturally to Ade's shoulder, and his arms wrapping themselves very slowly around her, almost reluctantly, as if he still wasn't ready to accept his feelings were worthy of her, and he wanted to give her the chance to run.

She didn't.

———

Arriving home, Mackenzie was surprised to find Charis still up. She had a glow about her that he recognised very well; he'd once had it himself.

'Oh aye,' he said, a little drily, 'what have you found, then?'

'Is Maddy with you?'

He blinked. 'Why on earth would she be?'

'Well, you know, you're working a case together. Can she come over?'

'No she can't, she needs to sleep! She's got a five-year-old, don't forget.' He looked beyond her, at the open kitchen door. On the table he could see papers spread out, and he went through to investigate. 'What are these?'

'Blow-ups of some of the other photos,' she said. 'From the negatives in the envelope.'

'And?' He started sifting through some of them, and stopped. 'What's this?'

'It's a painting. A photo of one, at least. Well, half of one. Well, not quite—'

'Hang on!' He turned to her and took her by the upper arms, looking down into her upturned face. She looked ready to explode with the need to tell him what she'd found. 'Start again,' he said, smiling despite his tiredness and the worry that gnawed at him.

'Right. That there,' she pointed, 'was taken on the same camera roll as the one with the Douglases and Leslie Warrender. But it was taken inside the garage, look. You can see the edge of the window, along there.' She indicated on the photo.

'It looks to me like a rough sketch of that Cathedral thing that Warrender faked. Doesn't it look like it to you?'

'I didn't know you'd seen it.'

'Takes about a second to look up,' Charis said. 'So it was painted up there, where Hazel's parents lived.'

'By Warrender.'

'No,' Charis said, and now she looked prouder than ever. 'By—'

'Hazel's dad?'

'By her mum. I'm almost sure of it.'

Mackenzie frowned. 'How can you tell?'

'Because there are pictures of her dad's canvases too, on the same roll.' Charis sifted through the print-outs on the table and placed two of them side-by-side. 'Look. His painting, we know that, because it's already signed. This is how his palette looks, and how he lays his brushes down: on the bottom, in the little channel there. Solvent for cleaning his brushes on the ledge underneath the easel.' She pulled the first photo closer and laid it beside them. 'Yvette's. Smaller easel, set lower down. Colour palette on a little table at the side, with the brushes and the solvent jar. Jam jar,' she added, pointing to Graeme's easel again, 'not pint pot.'

Mackenzie looked at the pewter tankard on Graeme's two photos. 'We don't know he always used those,' he said slowly, reluctant to burst her bubble, 'but if we could find Hazel we could ask her.' He drew her close and felt her hands slide around his waist. 'You've been busy, and brilliant,' he murmured against her hair, and she held him tighter. Over her head he let his gaze drift across the photos she had spent so long developing and studying, and thinking about.

'She probably told Warrender she was going to come clean

to Ross,' Charis mumbled into his sweatshirt, around a yawn. 'And that's why he killed her.'

'Aye, sounds likely. Warrender made some pretty good money out of this deal; if Ross found out he hadn't even painted it, he'd not have got a penny, and if Yvette had an attack of the guilts after Silcott died, they'd all have been right in it. There's a hell of a motive for them both.'

'Where are you going?' Charis looked up as he eased away from her and picked up his keys again. 'This can wait, can't it?'

'Nope. I'm going to see Patrick Ross. I need to know if he knew about this.' He took out his phone and took pictures of the two easel photos.

'You're going to Inverness? *Now?*'

'I'll not be long, and anyway this could be important for Hazel. Go up to bed, you've earned a bloody good sleep.' He kissed her goodbye, thoroughly enough to let her know how much he'd have preferred to stay, then went back out into the chilly night.

He called Maddy, hoping he hadn't interrupted a continuation of that tender and very private moment he'd witnessed outside the hotel, but she was alone. He told her what Charis had found, and couldn't help grinning at her predictable response.

'She's...tenacious.'

'Get over yourself, Clifford. She's got a good brain.'

Maddy chuckled. 'Fair enough. Has Ade got hold of you yet?'

'No, did he find something?'

'Aye. A biker staying at the Loch Maree Hotel punched him in the face and split his lip.'

Mackenzie fell silent in astonishment. 'He what?' he managed at last.

'Called him every name under the sun, refused to tell him where Hazel had gone, but said she was better off without a bully boy like him, and that if he hung around asking any more stupid questions he'd ram a—'

'Okay, okay,' Mackenzie said hurriedly. 'I get the gist. Is Ade okay?'

'Seems to be. They got into it a bit though, I gather, before the bloke's mate intervened, then all three of them were thrown out of the hotel. Bikers weren't best pleased, but Ade's back out looking for Hazel now.'

'What the hell was it all about?'

'As near as I can fathom it, Hazel told this bloke she'd been abandoned in the middle of nowhere by her boyfriend, and had begged a lift across the Kessock Bridge. Beyond that, no idea.'

'So she made it back as far as Inverness then; that's something. She might get a lift back to Abergarry from there.'

'We've got to find her before the police do.' Maddy sounded deeply worried now. 'The evidence is stacking up, and she needs to be prepared.'

'Shit. Nick's been a bit more forthcoming than usual, then, has he?' Mackenzie settled behind the wheel of his car and fitted the key in the ignition. 'What's he said?'

'Fingerprints on the screwdriver, and in the blood on it as well. The boot print at the scene's been matched to the ones in the yard around the office, and in the rally's control tent, and they've lifted prints from all over the rental cottage. Like, *everywhere*. And vomit. Quite a lot of it, all over the bedding.' Her voice was tight. 'He's pretty sure it's all going to turn out to be hers, and it won't take long to check, since she's already on file. It's probably already come through and he's too busy to call me back.'

'Or doesn't want to deliver the bad news,' Mackenzie said grimly.

'Aye, more likely.' Maddy sighed. 'The vomit makes me wonder if she didn't maybe go back to her old ways at the rally, and then lose it when she saw Warrender. Why else would she have been so sick?'

'I keep coming back to that message from Griff, but he's got an alibi for the night Linda Sturdy died. And so's Hazel. So... we can assume Warrender *did* kill Linda, as we thought. Maybe Griff considered him a threat too, and did something about it? Or it might have been revenge on Hazel's behalf, when she told him Warrender probably killed her mother.'

'If she didn't react to the knight in shining armour act the way he expected, and threatened to tell the police...' Maddy paused, and he could imagine her nodding as she thought it through. 'They're genuinely good friends,' she said, 'so he'd naturally want to avenge her loss. But for that same reason, he wouldn't want to go as far as killing her, just to protect himself. Setting her up for the murder instead would be the next best thing, so it sounds plausible I suppose. What are you doing now, anyway?'

'I need to know if Ross had any idea that Yvette actually did the painting, and if she got paid for it.'

'Can't that wait until the morning?'

'It could, but this way I can keep an eye out for Hazel too. She's more likely to be hitching when it's dark.'

'Pick me up on the way,' she said immediately. 'I'm too wired to sleep.'

'Nope. Not a good idea. Tas needs his mum awake and with it, not snoring over breakfast.'

'I do *not* snore!'

He grinned. 'Get some sleep, Mads. I'll call you in the morning.'

Hazel checked the clock for the millionth time and tried to work out how long she'd been here. It had been hours, and there was still no word from Ade. Breda had told her, tearful with regret, that it had been too late to get the necklace back; when they hadn't returned with money after a few minutes, the biker had taken off with it. But that blow had been only one more in a long, long day, and no doubt she would mourn its loss properly later, but for now all she wanted was to see a friendly face. Breda had left her in the office, with another admonition to stay out of sight, and after an hour she had brought in a tray of the most delicious food Hazel had had in ages.

After she'd eaten, Hazel folded her arms on the desk next to her crash helmet, then rested her head on them and closed her eyes. The thought of being home, or even at Maddy's and in Tas's too-short little bed, brought her an overwhelming sense of longing. She imagined her dad in his familiar pose; crouched beside the Kawasaki, looking at her over his shoulder and shaking his head at her predicament, but maybe smiling too, at the way she'd handled it so far. She wasn't aware she'd drifted into sleep until the door clicked open and Breda came in again.

'He shouldn't be long now,' she said, passing Hazel a bottle of spring water. 'I told him you're safe, so he knows there's no immediate hurry.'

'Why's he taking so long?' Hazel croaked, wiping her sleep-swollen lips. She twisted the lid off the bottle and took a long, satisfying drink.

Breda busied herself stacking the used plates back on the tray. 'He's...having trouble getting away just now.'

Hazel thought her friend seemed to be finding it difficult to meet her eyes. 'What is it?' she asked. 'You're looking a wee bit shifty.'

'Not at all.' Breda smiled, but it was definitely a little strained-looking. 'He said he'll be here just as soon as he can. He's a bit tied up with his brother, apparently.'

'Can he call Maddy instead then?'

'Um, it's difficult,' Breda said, and now Hazel was certain.

'Tell me what's going on,' she said, hardening her voice, and Breda looked trapped and didn't answer for a moment. Then she sat opposite Hazel and sighed.

'Why don't *you* tell *me*, love?' she said, still quiet, but now sympathetic rather than evasive. 'Ade said something about a... a murder?' She looked away as she spoke the word. 'There's even talk that the police might be looking for you. I feel as if I'm not just keeping you safe here, but...well, all right, yes, *harbouring* you.'

Hazel could feel the flush staining her skin, and knew Breda had noticed it. 'I'm sorry to have brought this to your door,' she said, with an effort and through a rapidly tightening throat. 'I promise you, I didn't kill anyone.'

'It's right what he said then? That the police think you did?' Breda's eyes were wide with dismay.

'It's a long story, but I promise I'll tell you all of it, as soon as Ade comes and we can get it all sorted out.'

Breda looked as if she wanted to ask more, but in the end she just let out her pent-up breath and shook her head. 'Just as you like. Showing up here like that... I knew there was something, but I never for one minute...' She let her words trail away again, her expression still shocked. 'Sit tight. I'll see if I can't hurry your man Ade up a bit.'

'Can I call him?' Hazel's hand reached for the phone, but Breda stopped her, clearly embarrassed.

'I'm sorry, love. I don't believe this rubbish, not for a minute, but if the police have been talking to your friends already, and if this office phone's recorded as making phone calls like that at this time of night... Well, it'd bring the business into disrepute. And I'd get the sack if it came out that I was hiding you as well. You do understand?'

'Your mobile then?' Hazel saw the indecision melt into embarrassment, and nodded. 'Not fair, I'm sorry.' She gave Breda a shaky smile. 'Thank you for believing me, anyway. I'd have been lost without you.'

'I'm glad I was here. At least I can keep you safe, if nothing else.' Breda picked up the tray. 'There's another thing though, now this has come up.' She looked even more uncomfortable now. Mortified even, and Hazel grew alarmed.

'What is it?'

'My assistant manager has come on duty. He's likely to come in here at some point, and I can't risk him seeing you.'

'Do you want me to leave?'

'Lord, no! This is the safest place for you, right enough.'

'You'd better lock the door,' Hazel said, guessing what she was trying to say, and only glad it was something that could be easily fixed. 'Then he'll have to come to you for the key, at least.'

Breda slumped in relief. 'Exactly. Hopefully you'll be gone back to your home before that becomes an issue. But Max, God love him, has a habit of sneaking in to pinch my ciggies, and... well. You understand.'

'Better tell your chef not to set fire to the place then,' Hazel

teased. She handed Breda the packet of cigarettes from the in-
tray on the desk. 'Hazel Flambé is off the menu for tonight, tell
him.'

'Oh, there's the window in an emergency,' Breda said, too
earnest and worried to appreciate the attempt at light-hearted-
ness. 'I'd not leave you otherwise. And if Ade isn't able to get
away in the next hour, I promise I'll leave work and drive you
back home myself.'

'Thank you. Hazel closed the door behind Breda and
listened to the key turning in the lock. She tested the window,
which was indeed unlocked, and since they were on the ground
floor there was no more drop here than there had been at the
holiday cottage. Feeling better, she went back to sit at the desk,
where she considered what Breda had told her.

Ade and the others were being questioned about Warrender, which meant Griff knew for sure now that she'd left the
cottage, and was no doubt putting the next part of his great, but
unexplained, framing plan into action. And which one of them
would the police believe: a respected local businessman, or a
convicted criminal?

She took stock of anything that might fall in her favour
versus everything that might incriminate her, but it was a piti-
fully small comparison: there was the bruise on her leg, and
when she'd been to the toilet she'd still been able to see the tiny
prick-mark on her pale skin, but she could easily have administered the drug there herself. Likewise the bruising could have
come from anywhere, and Griff had been wearing a glove so
there would be no way to match the bruises against his fingers.
But she wasn't about to give up, and perhaps trying to preserve
evidence, rather than destroying it, might go some way to
convincing them of her innocence. At least buying her some
time before they charged her.

She emptied the bottle of spring water into the plant by the window and, praying Breda wouldn't remember something and come back, took up a position behind the door, dropping her jeans and pants. She didn't manage much, and wished she'd thought about it before she'd used the restaurant toilet, but it should be enough. She screwed the lid back on tightly and tucked the bottle into her backpack; a little insurance in case her body managed to process the remainder of whatever drug Griff had given her before she could be tested. She needed everything she could get now.

Chapter Twenty-Two

PATRICK ROSS WOKE in darkness and briefly panicked when he saw Julie's half of the bed was empty, then he recalled the cocktail event she'd gone to in Edinburgh with her friends. Maybe her arrival home was what had wakened him. He sat up in bed and listened again, but it was a knock at the door, not a key in the lock, that had dragged him from his sleep. It came again, impatient, and after a glance at the clock to see it was a little after two o'clock, Ross's heart skipped in sudden fear as his mind woke up properly. Was it a coach crash? A fire at the gallery?

He seized his dressing gown and hurried down the stairs, his feet wanting to slow down, just so he could avoid hearing whatever terrible news this early Sunday morning had brought him. He snapped on the hallway light and braced himself, but when he pulled open the door, all he felt was a huge swell of anger.

'What the *bloody* hell are you doing here?'

Mackenzie looked genuinely surprised, then apologetic. 'I know it's late,' he said. 'Can I come in?'

'And if I said no?'

Mackenzie shrugged and gave him an annoyingly charming smile. 'I'd remind you what you've got to lose.'

Ross stared at him a moment longer, fighting for words, then stood aside. Mackenzie stepped over the threshold, and Ross looked out into the yard, hoping to see the lights of an approaching taxi dropping Julie back home, but the only lights were from Inverness in the distance. Mackenzie looked wide awake and practically humming with energy as he stood in Ross's hall, or maybe that was only in contrast to the way Ross felt; woozy-headed, bemused, and dog-tired now that the rush of fear-fuelled adrenalin had passed off again.

'Do you know who painted *Florence Cathedral*?' he asked.

'Fabrizio Mercanti,' Ross grumbled. 'What's this, *Mastermind*? My specialist subject: annoying fucking questions?'

'I meant the fake,' Mackenzie said, his voice even. Then he held up a hand. 'No, in fact, let's get the important stuff out of the way first. Do you have any idea what's been happening over the past twenty-four hours or so?'

'I've been working at home, drafting advertising copy for the summer exhibition.'

'So you've not heard about the abduction of that young lady, the one *you* brought to Warrender's attention?'

Ross's mouth went dry. 'God, no. Have they found her? Is she all right?' He went into the sitting room to pour a drink, and Mackenzie followed but refused the offer. The glass stopper rattled against the neck of the decanter as Ross replaced it and turned back to Mackenzie. 'Well? Is she okay?'

'Hard to say, but you'd better hope so,' Mackenzie said. 'She got away from the place where she was taken, but we don't know where she is now. We *think* she made it back to Inverness, but we don't know any more than that.'

'What happened? Was it Warrender?'

'We think so. But we can't ask him, because he's dead.'

Ross stared numbly at his drink for a moment, before raising his eyes to Mackenzie's. The investigator's jaw was rigid, all pretence of friendly, apologetic charm gone now. The eyes were hard, and Ross was uncomfortably aware of the rugby-player frame and above average height.

'Dead,' he repeated. He tried to figure out how this could be bad for him, and he couldn't. 'So, no blackmail,' he added, before he could stop himself.

'And there's your motive,' Mackenzie said, his voice dangerously soft in comparison to the hard lines of his face and body. 'And have you got an alibi, Mr Ross? *Working from home* won't really cut it, you know. Can your wife vouch for you?'

'She's away,' Ross said slowly. Oh, this could be bad for him, all right. 'There's nothing to say I killed him, Mackenzie. Nothing at all. You said it yourself: all he has is a fake painting.'

'And where is that, I wonder?' Mackenzie leaned on the door, his head tilted. 'If he was telling the truth, and he really does have someone back in France just waiting for a missed call before it all comes out—'

'He doesn't. Didn't! He couldn't have.' Ross scowled and swallowed half his drink in one gulp, for once wishing he didn't keep the really good stuff locked away in his office. 'Look, Mackenzie, I have a feeling you know I didn't do this, so why don't we stop *pissing about*, as you like to say?'

'All right, let's get back to my original question. Do you know who painted *Florence Cathedral*?'

Ross sighed. 'Leslie Warrender.'

'Wrong.'

Ross stared at him perplexed. 'You're not going to tell me it was that girl's father, are you?' He frowned, remembering. 'She told me he was an artist, so maybe she was hinting?'

'She told you?'

'When I came up to see the Glencoille plans. We talked briefly about art, and she said her dad was a natural.'

'I see. But no, it wasn't him, either.'

'*Her* then?' He shook his head, feeling stupid. 'No, she'd have only been a kid.'

'Her mother.'

Ross frowned and rubbed at his temple to stave off the incipient whisky/tiredness headache that was in no way being helped by this news. He thought back to the conversation in the portakabin office, but it was hazy. There had been some sarky comment about the print of the snooker-playing dogs, which he'd absolutely deserved, and she'd said loads of relatives on her father's side had been artists. Had she said anything about her mother? He couldn't remember... Yes, she had.

'She said her mum dropped out of uni,' he said slowly. 'And that her dad was the artist. I'm sure of it.'

'Dropping out of uni doesn't erase a person's talent, Mr Ross. I'm sure half the people you exhibit have never taken part in a degree show in their lives. Probably more than half.'

'I know that,' Ross snapped. 'But my point was that she was praising her father's talent, not her mother's. What makes you so sure it was the mother who painted this one?'

Mackenzie took his phone out and navigated for a moment, before holding it out. 'Scroll right,' he said. 'Compare and contrast: Yvette Douglas and Graeme Douglas.'

Ross did so, and he saw immediately that there was little point in questioning it further. 'That shit,' he breathed.

'Aye. So the assumption we have to work on is that Douglas knew his wife had painted the picture. He also must have realised later that, when she was killed, it would have been to shut her up.'

'You don't think he killed his own wife?'

'No.' Mackenzie looked grim. 'We think Warrender did it. Made it look like a burglary, then got Douglas to help him fake the boat accident.'

'And Douglas would have done that?'

'He might have if he didn't know yet why he was doing it.' Mackenzie shrugged. 'He probably thought he was helping him escape *you*.' He took back his phone. 'Warrender only came back because he knew Douglas had died, and there was no-one else who'd expect to see him.'

'He came back because he'd heard about Christie's.'

'What?'

Ross poured himself another drink. 'One of the reasons I was looking for an investment opportunity was due to a particularly large windfall at auction. He'd heard about it, and that's when he made his move. He definitely knew about it,' he added, seeing Mackenzie's doubtful look. 'He mentioned it when we spoke, knew roughly the amount, everything. *That's* what brought him back, I'm sure of it. Maybe he only felt safe to come back because of Douglas though.'

'You're probably right, in that case.' Mackenzie went back to leaning on the door with his arms folded, and now he was frowning. 'Presumably your auction thing would have been in the art magazines and so forth, and being an artist he'd have kept up with all the news.'

'All the best ones,' Ross agreed, not without a certain sense of pride.

'So how did he know about Graeme Douglas?'

Ross didn't have an answer to that. 'He wasn't well known

enough to make the art circulars, and unless it was some tragic accident, or murder—'

'It wasn't.'

'Then I've no idea, sorry. But that's not my problem, frankly.'

'Then let's go back to what is.' Mackenzie tapped the phone in his pocket. 'Now we know Yvette Douglas painted your *Florence Cathedral*, and if I believe your story, you gave the money to Warrender, not her.'

'Well, of course I did.'

'I wouldn't mind betting that what he passed on to her was a good deal less than you gave him.'

'Without question. I know the man.'

'So, the thieving little shite deserved all he got, wouldn't you say?'

Ross put down his glass, feeling the trap closing. 'I didn't kill him,' he said, in as steady a voice as he could manage. 'I had plenty of reason to, but I didn't. I can't pretend I'm not glad *someone* did, though.

Mackenzie held up his hands. 'I'm not saying you did. I'm just trying to help the person they're accusing of his murder.'

'Which is who?'

'Doesn't matter.'

'What time was it? And where was he killed?'

'Sometime in the early hours of yesterday morning, in the Glencoille distillery.'

Ross's chest loosened, and he let out a slow, relieved breath. 'I drove my wife to the coach station in time for a six o'clock departure yesterday morning. Which meant I was here, with a witness, until at least five.'

'I told you, I'm not—'

'Saying I did it,' Ross finished for him, and shot him a glare.

'You can say that as often and as loudly as you like, Mackenzie. I feel better for knowing I have an alibi.'

'Do you have one for April 1998, when Yvette Douglas was killed?'

'Ross's mouth fell open. 'What?'

'Well, you say you didn't know she was the one who'd done the painting,' Mackenzie said, in reasonable tones. 'We've only got your word for that. She would have been a danger to you, wouldn't she? What about your wife? She'd have wanted to protect you. What about William Kilbride?'

Ross shook his head at all these questions. 'What's he got to do with it?'

'Just opening the floor to ideas.' Mackenzie sighed. 'Look, okay. We're pretty sure it was Warrender who killed her, since he had the biggest motive, but right now we just want to help someone who's likely to be arrested at any minute for killing *him*.'

'This girl who works for Ade Mackenzie,' Ross guessed. 'Yvette's daughter.'

Mackenzie shrugged again. 'Warrender abducted her, with help, and now he's dead. So either it was her, or whoever was working with Warrender. We think that might be Dave Griffin.' His eyes turned flinty. 'Who *you* arranged to meet at the Burnside the other night.'

Ross's heart pinched again, and he realised there was no sense denying it. 'I just... I had an impatient moment,' he confessed. 'I didn't go. I changed my mind about the whole thing, realised how stupid it was.'

'But Griff went there anyway, since you were so kind as to provide a location for him.' Mackenzie shook his head, a fleeting look of contempt crossing his face, replaced by dawning realisation. 'When I confronted him he made out he only wanted to beat the sod to a pulp for killing Yvette Douglas, but...what if what he *really* wanted to do was to come to some kind of financial arrangement?'

'Such as?'

Mackenzie sounded as if he was unravelling his thoughts as he went. 'Maybe he'd agreed to help Warrender get Hazel out of the picture,' he mused, 'just in case she knew who he really was. In return for a cut of the blackmail money. Then...he kills Warrender, frames Hazel for it, and plans to collect the money from you, as arranged. Only now he gets all of it.' He had begun pacing as he spoke; now he stopped and faced Ross. 'And I watched him go. *Shit!*'

'Hardly your fault.' Ross wanted to beat Mackenzie up with his mistake in the same way Mackenzie had blamed him, but he knew, deep down, it was nothing like the same thing. Twice now he'd led danger to Hazel Douglas's door, and he desperately wanted to put it right. 'Where is she now? Hazel, I mean?'

'I told you, we don't know.' Mackenzie resumed his prowling of the room. 'She was left in a rental cottage out on the west coast, with Warrender's body. We know she got out, and that she made her way back as far as Inverness, or at least the Kessock Bridge. After that we're assuming she's hitched a lift back to Abergarry, but no-one's seen or heard from her yet.'

'Does she have any family or friends she could call? It'd make more sense for her to lie low for a bit, until she can get her head straight. Not to mention she must be exhausted.'

'She won't be able to trust her friends now,' Mackenzie said bitterly, 'probably not even us. And her only family lives out in the sticks.' He stopped and swivelled to face Ross. 'And *you know her.*'

'Out in the sticks?' Ross frowned. 'Are you talking about Isla Munro?'

'She's Hazel's aunt. Yvette's sister.'

'Jesus.' Ross swallowed hard. 'It *must* be connected, mustn't it?'

Mackenzie was looking taut and worried, now he'd worked out Griffin's involvement. 'We can dig up the details later,' he muttered. 'Right now I just want to find Hazel and make sure she's safe.'

'Thistle!' Ross blurted. When Mackenzie raised his eyebrows, he went on, 'We had dinner there a week or so ago. Me, Will Kilbride and your brother. He brought Hazel with him to take notes, and she and the manager got on really well. She might have gone to her for help.'

'The Irish woman? Breda Kelly?'

'That's her. She was a friend of Linda Sturdy's, and she and Hazel got talking after dinner. Swapped numbers, I think, or at least talked about it.'

'Right.' Mackenzie pulled open the door. 'Don't call anyone, not even Isla. We don't know who we can trust right now.'

'But you think you can trust me?' Ross couldn't resist asking. 'I could have the girl holed up here, and be sending you on a wild goose chase, for all you know.'

He didn't know whether to be pleased, relieved or insulted when Mackenzie's smile returned as he gave Ross a brief once-over and shook his head. 'Nah.' He turned back to the door, and his voice sharpened again. 'Who's that?'

Car headlights swept the yard and rippled across the dimpled glass in the door, and Ross relaxed. 'It's just Julie. Can I tell her?'

'Up to you,' Mackenzie said, taking out his own car keys.

He pulled open the door. 'One thing I do believe about you is that you feel like shit for putting Hazel in danger. Am I wrong about that?' He turned thoughtful, appraising eyes on Ross, who shook his head.

'No. You're not wrong. I hope you find her,' he added.

'Thank you. If you hear anything, you know how to reach me.' Mackenzie raised a hand and threw a quick greeting at Julie as she climbed, a little tipsily, from the taxi.

'Good trip then?' Ross asked, amused despite everything, as his wife walked ultra-carefully across the drive to meet him at the front door. 'You can't still be drunk, not after a four-hour bus drive.'

'The only way to avoid a hangover on a coach,' Julie said gravely as she hooked her arm through his, 'is to keep drinking.' She looked up at him quizzically. 'Why are you up, anyway? And what was that man doing here?'

Ross guided her into the kitchen and switched the kettle on. 'Brace yourself,' he said. 'It's been a day and a half already.'

Mackenzie slowed down for a roundabout on the edge of town and left his brother a voicemail message. 'Wherever you are right now, go straight to Thistle; Breda's on her safe list, so there's a good chance she went to her for help.' His right foot pressed down harder as he hit the dual carriageway. 'I'm worried who else might have worked that out though,' he added grimly. 'Griff, for one. I'll explain later. Look, I've just passed the retail park at Inshes, so I'm nearly there, but she'll need someone she knows and can trust, and she hardly knows me.'

He ended the call and drove the last ten minutes to the restaurant in tense silence, trying to avoid triggering speed cameras. The restaurant was still lit up inside while the night's clean-up was under way ready for early breakfasts, but the outdoor string lights and the garden spotlights were all off now, and the small car park was empty but for a few vehicles in the staff spaces. Mackenzie's relief was short-lived, however, as he crossed the car park and saw that one of these was a white van with a stylised tree painted on the side, and *G&M Garden Services* printed neatly beneath it.

His gut tightened and he rattled the locked restaurant door in frustration. When no-one came, he went around to the yard behind the kitchen and found two members of staff in cleaning uniform emptying bags of kitchen waste into large bins.

'I need to see Miss Kelly, if she's around,' he called as he came up the path. 'Please, it's urgent.'

'Sorry, mate,' one of them said, 'haven't seen her for a bit. But I might be able to find Mr Russell. Wait here.'

Mackenzie studied the yard while he waited, picturing Warrender hovering by the back gate that he himself had just come through, checking Linda Sturdy was alone before taking a bottle from one of those plastic crates...

'Paul?'

'Max, thanks for coming out. I need to see Breda. Is she still here?'

'Aye, I think she's in the office.' Max beckoned Mackenzie into the passageway. 'What's happened?'

'Is she alone?'

'As far as I know. She said she had paperwork to catch up on, so that she could come in later tomorrow.' He led the way through the restaurant, to a door on the far side, and then into another small corridor.

Mackenzie kept craning his neck for a sight of Griff, but he saw only tired restaurant staff running down the final few minutes of their long shift. 'Did you see anyone else come in?'

Max shook his head and turned the handle of the office door. 'Locked,' he sighed. 'She must have gone after all. I'm sorry to have—'

'Max?' A voice behind them made them both turn to see Breda, a covered cup of coffee in one hand and a key in the other. 'What do you want?'

'Mr Mackenzie wanted to see you. I told him you were working late.' He nodded at her coffee cup. 'Good idea, I could do with a fuel injection, myself.'

Breda glanced at the cup, as if she'd forgotten she was holding it, and a wary look came across her face. 'What can I do for you, Mr Mackenzie?'

'It's about Hazel Douglas,' he said. 'We think...we're *hoping*, she might have come to you earlier tonight. Have you seen her?'

Breda seemed about to deny it, glancing back into the restaurant as if she expected them to believe Hazel was in there, then she looked more closely at Mackenzie and let out a heavy sigh. 'Yes, she did. This is for her.' She nodded at the coffee cup, then gestured for Max to leave them. When he'd gone, throwing a curious look over his shoulder, she spoke in a low, faintly embarrassed voice. 'I didn't really know if I could trust either you or your brother,' she confessed. 'I'm afraid I told her a little white lie until I felt sure.'

'Lie?'

'I told her I'd called your brother. Just so she wouldn't panic, you know? I wanted to get a feel myself, for whether you were truly on her side. I believe you are.' She slid the key into the lock, but paused before turning it and leaned close to the door.

'Hazel, love, I've not got Ade with me yet, but his brother's here, okay? You're still quite safe.' She raised her eyebrows at Mackenzie as she made this promise, and he nodded, hoping he looked as sincere as he felt, and casting another look around for Griff.

'Ade's on his way too,' he added through the door, and when there was no answer Breda shrugged and opened it, then stopped dead. The first thing Mackenzie was aware of was the window standing wide open, and as the early morning breeze was pulled in by the opening door, the curtains flapped, knocking over a small plant pot. The second thing he noticed was the prone form of Dave Griffin next to the filing cabinet, then the dark spill of blood on the carpet around his head and the familiar crash helmet on the floor beside him.

Breda drew a shocked, whistling breath, and turned to Mackenzie, her expression dark. 'I think it's finally time we called the police, don't you?'

Chapter Twenty-Three

Hazel only became aware that she was crying as she reached the end of Ness Walk and turned onto the bridge. Her right bicep throbbed as she raised it to wipe angrily at the tears that had begun to blur her vision, but there was only one destination in her mind now: the railway station. She crossed over the river and made her way tiredly up through town, wondering what Breda's reaction would be when she found Griff, and if things could possibly have turned out any other way. It was hard to see how, though. She supposed it had been inevitable; since the moment she'd realised who had betrayed her they had been on this collision course, and now it had finally happened. It played across her blurred eyes like a strip of silent, black and white film, only turning to hideous colour in the very last second.

After she had stashed her urine sample away in her back pack, she had dozed again, while she waited for Breda's shift to finish, and although it was a thin, unsatisfactory sleep, she had awoken feeling clearer in her mind. Perhaps it was the last of the drug leaving her system, perhaps just her own natural resilience kicking in. She grew restless; the longer all this went on, the guiltier she looked, and she went to the window and opened it wide so she could lean out and inhale the night.

In the distance she could still hear cars and sporadic horns from across the river; late-night taxis and travellers; Saturday night/Sunday morning party-goers; laughter, singing and arguing. Such familiar sounds opened a door onto memories that were both joyful and hateful, and Hazel drew her head back inside, already missing the feel of the night air on her skin. A key in the lock made her sigh with relief, and she picked up her backpack, more than ready to go now. But it wasn't Breda who came in.

Hazel froze as Griff stepped through the door, his gaze travelling around the office even as his hand swept the door closed. Her heart locked up tight, and her first, instinctive surge of happiness at seeing him crumbled as the memory of what he'd done took its place. She stepped back and her hand fumbled for the first thing to hand, which was the telephone handset on the desk. She flung it, as hard as she could, feeling the muscle in her right arm wrench painfully, and as Griff stumbled back, taken by surprise and with his hands raised to protect his face, she grabbed her crash helmet.

Again she felt her arm quiver with the force she put behind the swing, but the pain in her fingers was worse, as the helmet smashed into the side of Griff's head and was yanked from her grip by the impact. Griff stumbled and put out a hand to steady himself, but his vision must have been impaired, because as she watched, in rising horror, his fingers missed the edge of the filing cabinet for which they flailed, and instead his head came down on the corner of it, snapping up and back, and then he crashed to the floor and lay still.

The spreading blood began soaking into the carpet immediately; Hazel felt her stomach clench, and the meal Breda had provided rose into her throat as she lurched away. She kept it down this time, somehow, and stumbled to the window once more. She slid out, no longer appreciating the cool breeze on her hot face, only seeing again Griff's head, jerking savagely as it hit the cabinet. And the way the blood had sprayed as he fell.

* * *

She came to the traffic lights by the Inverness Town House and paused, swiping at her eyes again. What right did she have to cry? Until now she'd held tightly to the fact that she hadn't done what she'd soon be accused of doing; she'd killed no-one. She was all too painfully aware that it was no guarantee against her being convicted of it, but *she'd* have known she was innocent, at least, and that might have helped in some small way. Her own integrity would have been intact.

But now she was exactly what they thought she was. It didn't matter that Griff had tricked her, drugged her, and, almost worse, allowed her to think she'd escaped, while in reality a return to her former life was impossible. It didn't even matter that she had friends like Breda, Maddy and Ade ready to fight her corner. All that mattered was that Griff was dead, and that she'd killed him.

She looked to her left, where just a couple of streets away the railway station waited, and made her feet move, trying not to think about everything she was leaving behind: those same friends she had found; her new life; the job she loved now, and the one that had been promised; her aunt; her cousin... All those years she had spent fighting her way out of the hole into which she'd fallen when her mother died, and then again when she'd lost her father... It had all come to nothing and now she had fallen into a new, even deeper one. There would be no question of community payback this time.

As she emerged onto Academy Street, and the railway station was directly ahead of her, she was almost running, and experiencing a strange and disturbing sense of elation. It was time to bring all this fear and uncertainty to an end. To stop fighting what she could never beat. She marched across the forecourt and into the station, hearing those special sounds of late night travel all around her, and a couple of minutes later she was standing at the desk of the Transport Police.

'I think you're looking for me,' she said. 'My name's Hazel Douglas. I've just killed someone.'

The questions seemed endless. It had been at least an hour before someone had actually bothered to tell her that Griff was in fact alive, and in a critical condition in Raigmore Hospital. Hazel had accepted the news numbly at first, trying not to be blinded by sudden hope that things might yet work out after all. It wasn't as if the bastard would own up. But at least she was back to knowing she wasn't a murderer, and she'd been right; it *did* help. A little, at least.

Knowing Ade and his brother were both waiting outside was comforting too, despite the hopelessness of her situation. As yet she hadn't been charged, so she'd had no reason to request legal representation, but she knew from experience that that moment was getting close now. She'd been examined by a doctor, and had handed over the spring water bottle with her sample, and all she could do now was answer these questions and hope that Griff had fucked up somewhere down the line.

The female detective sergeant was familiar, and Hazel remembered she'd been one of the officers who'd broken the news of Linda's death a hundred years ago, up at Glencoille. It turned out she had also spoken to the Mackenzies on a couple of occasions, and over separate issues. She had seemed open to their pleas on Hazel's behalf, but Hazel had no idea if any of it had yet been followed up. Or whether it would be. She wished Maddy were there. Or Breda. More than anything she wished her father were there.

One of the more damning, and hard to dismiss, counts against her was the string of photos she had apparently uploaded to the bike club's rally page in the early hours of yesterday morning: gleeful captions such as: *why slum it in a tent when you can sneak away to a secret paradise!* accompanied by shots of an immaculate guest house bedroom, her wash bag and toothbrush on a sparklingly clean toilet cistern, and her helmet, back pack and leather jacket in the wardrobe. The same shirt that she now wore was pictured hanging alongside her jacket, and it didn't matter how many times Hazel protested that she hadn't had her phone, the photos had been found on it; she couldn't prove she hadn't uploaded them herself before returning to Glencoille to kill Warrender.

'But why would I draw attention to the place?' she demanded. 'How stupid would I have to be to splash photos of what I know will be a crime scene all over social media?'

'Perhaps you didn't know that, at the time,' DC McAndrew said. 'It's hardly the point, is it? You were there; *that's* the point. Maybe you'd forgotten you'd already posted the photos when you decided it would make a good place to stash a body, while you went for help to dispose of it.'

'I *never* post photos on that site. Check back. It's not my style.'

'We're checking everything,' McAndrew assured her. 'I want to talk again about the text message from David Griffin.'

Hazel struggled to keep a lid on her temper. She'd told her story so many times she began to disbelieve it herself. 'You've checked my phone,' she said, for what felt like the hundredth time. 'I got the text from Griff. He knew we suspected Warrender of killing my mother; he knew that would get me there.'

'Mr Griffin was brought in for questioning yesterday, when you went missing,' McAndrew said. 'He actually volunteered the information about the message.'

'That doesn't mean he didn't send it!' Hazel covered her eyes in frustration. 'Drawing your attention to it would be a great way to make himself look innocent, don't you think?'

'I do think, yes.' McAndrew paused, then looked down at her hands. 'Remind me, Miss Douglas, didn't *you* hand yourself in?'

Hazel subsided, annoyed with herself for walking into that trap. 'That's different. I knew I was being set up for killing Warrender. I knew there'd be a warrant out for me.'

'It's in no way different.'

'It was a bigger risk, for starters.'

'That's certainly true, although Mr Griffin seems to be suffering for what he did.' McAndrew folded her hands on the table. 'Now. Tell me again what Miss Sturdy said when she found the photograph of the man you claim was Leslie Warrender?'

338

Maddy sat up, momentarily disorientated at finding herself on a sofa. She pushed aside the crocheted blanket, pressed the heels of her hands to her eyes and looked around, relaxing as she recognised Paul's front room. Paul's and Charis's now, she reminded herself, lowering her feet to the floor. Daylight was streaming through a narrow gap in the curtains, laying a thin, bright bar across the carpet, and from the kitchen Maddy could hear talking and the clatter of plates.

There was no way Maddy had been going to stay at home last night, knowing Charis was working on the case, and to be fair Charis had coped remarkably well with her visitors' sudden arrival in the small hours; she'd only rolled her eyes the once before giving in and opening the door wider. Tas had enjoyed his little adventure too, he'd been immediately carried, still drowsy and wrapped in his own duvet, straight up to bed in the room Ade was staying in. As the hours marched on towards dawn, Charis and Maddy had talked everything through surprisingly amicably, pooling what they knew, until Charis had eventually pulled the blanket out of the ottoman and told Maddy to grab forty winks on the sofa before it all kicked off again.

'You up then?' Charis shouted, as Maddy jerked the curtain wider with a rattling sound. 'Gettin' toast if you want some, and then I want to show you something.'

'Great, thanks!' Maddy went upstairs and used the bathroom, finishing her wash by rubbing a fingerful of toothpaste over her teeth, in the absence of any forethought last night. She joined Charis, Jamie and Tas in the kitchen, and bent and hugged her son, relishing the feel of his warm, soft skin against her cheek, then smiled at Jamie.

'Thanks for putting me up,' she said to Charis, accepting a cup of coffee with a grateful sigh. 'What is it you wanted to show me?'

'Look at this.' Charis sifted through the blown-up photos they had been looking at while they talked everything through last night. She pulled out the most familiar one, just as the landline rang, and she grabbed a pen and circled part of the picture, pushing it across the table to Maddy before she went to pick up.

'Hello?' She paused, and a warm smile crossed her face. 'Hiya. How's it going?' She listened for a minute and murmured some sympathetic words, then looked over at Maddy. 'How'd you guess?' she said wryly. 'Here she is.' She passed the phone across and went back to her side of the table. 'Give him back after,' she warned, and Maddy briefly raised her eyes to the ceiling.

'Paul? What is it?'

'Hi, Mads.' His voice was cracking with tiredness. 'Listen, it's not Griff who abducted Hazel, I'm sure of it.'

'How sure?'

'I'm at Raigmore now. He's still not great, and I wasn't allowed to talk to him, but your brother was, and he says Griff's in a total mess about Hazel, and he doesn't think Griff's in any fit state to be acting.'

'Right, that makes sense,' Maddy said slowly, her eyes on the photo. A familiar and very welcome sensation was uncurling inside her, and she remembered again why she loved this work so much. 'Because *I* need to talk to *you* about Breda Kelly.'

'Breda?' Paul sounded baffled. 'What about her?'

'She lied about knowing the Douglases, and Warrender. She knew them all right.'

'Christ! How do you know that?'

'She's in the photograph with them,' Maddy said, shooting Charis a fiercely triumphant grin, which Charis returned along with a little victory dance that made both boys snort with laughter and cover their mouths.

'What are you talking about?' Paul said. 'She isn't. I've seen it.'

'There's a reflection in the garage window, Paul. She *took* the photo. Charis has done a brilliant job cleaning it up, and we expected to see Griff, but it's definitely a much younger Breda.'

'Text me a copy of the cleaned-up one,' Paul said, the tiredness in his voice gone now. 'I'll get the police to look at it while she's there, so they can ask her about it. If she lies again, they'll be all over her.'

'She's at the station?'

'Aye. She was brought in when we found Griff. She's not under suspicion, but they're still talking to her about why Hazel was locked in her office. This could be *very* interesting, actually, particularly since she messed up the Linda Sturdy crime scene too.'

'Maybe that was more deliberate than she led us all to believe then.' Maddy frowned. 'I mean, when you think about it she could easily have slid out the back a few minutes earlier than she said she did; it's that busy in there – who'd notice the exact time?'

'Right.' Paul sounded grimly pleased. 'I'll talk to Nick. Where's that photo?'

'I'll send it now.'

For a moment the line was quiet, then he spoke again, and this time there was a smile in his voice. 'I knew you would, you know.'

'Knew I would what?'

'Go straight around to see Charis, once I told you she was working on something. You said you were too wired to sleep. I should have listened.'

'She was pretty surprised to see us,' Maddy said, looking over at Charis again, but Charis was once more poring over the prints, squinting and comparing.

He laughed softly. 'I'll bet.'

Right,' she said, 'we'll keep trying to put stuff together at this end. Let me know what happens.'

'I will. I'll head back to the station now. Ade says hello, by the way. He's knackered, and just heading back now, but he's taking a detour.'

'Where?'

'Somewhere up near Glencoille. It's a long story; I'll tell you when I get back.'

The call ended, and Maddy put down the phone, mystified. 'Charis, will you be okay with Tas if I pop out for a bit?'

'No problem,' Charis murmured, lifting up a string of negatives. 'I'm just gonna keep playing for a bit.'

'Great. Thanks.'

Maddy grabbed her car keys and a slice of dry toast, and left her to it; within ten minutes she was sitting in her car at the junction where the end of Abergarry met the narrow, winding road to Glencoille.

She didn't have to wait more than half an hour before Ade's jeep crawled up to the junction, and she got out and waved. Ade pulled over, and Maddy climbed in without an invitation.

'I come bearing news,' she said, and pointed up the hill. 'Don't let me keep you, though. I can talk as we go.'

Ade threw her a look but shifted back into gear, and soon they were away from town and climbing. Maddy told him about the photo and watched his eyes widen, and his expression darken, as the implications sank in. 'All that time she was being Hazel's friend,' he muttered, shaking his head. 'All those supportive little touches... What a bitch.'

'I think she genuinely liked Hazel,' Maddy ventured, 'but her own agenda was too big to let that get in the way.'

'Which was?'

'It's only a theory at the moment.' Maddy took a moment to get it straight. 'Okay, Charis and I think that Breda and Warrender were working together. That she's the one who brought Warrender back, telling him Graeme Douglas was dead and that it was safe to put the squeeze on Ross. Who,' she added, 'had that money from Christie's burning a hole in his pocket. Warrender would have known about that too, since he'd have kept up with that side of the news. Once Breda knew the money was on its way, she used Warrender to help her abduct Hazel, and then killed him herself, leaving Hazel to carry the can.'

'Why though? It's a big leap from blackmail to murder.'

'Not that big, when you're talking two million quid.'

'Hmm. She did know about the bike run out to the memorial,' Ade said thoughtfully. 'We were talking about it that night we all had dinner. She could have booked the cottage in Hazel's name.'

'Aye, but it wouldn't have been free at such short notice.' Maddy shook her head. 'Personally I think it was *first* booked a long time in advance, under Warrender's new name. Booth, is it? If she was in touch with him she'd have known that.'

'Fair enough, but how would she have known the club was taking the run out there that weekend?' Ade slowed to take a turning that led them beneath a canopy of leaves that dappled the road with filtered early morning sunlight.

'Apparently they do it every year,' Maddy said. 'It wouldn't be hard to look through the club's Facebook posts and find that out. Your chat at dinner would have just confirmed it.'

'Devious.'

'Certainly is.' Maddy shook her head. 'The more I find out, the less I can work out whether to applaud, or rip the bitch's head off. Where are we?'

'Somewhere behind Druimgalla.' The jeep had stopped, and now Ade got out. Maddy followed, seeing a pathway running down alongside the densely packed trees, separating them from what was evidently private land, and fenced off.

'Paul and I were going to come up here yesterday afternoon, until events overtook us a bit.' Ade shoved his hands into his jacket pockets. 'Come on.'

'Come on where?'

'We're going for a little walk, to see if we can't find out a bit more about what the esteemed Dr Booth was up to.'

They followed the pitted, uneven path, until they came to a clearing where, sure enough, a nylon tent was pitched off to the side. In the centre of the clearing was a circle of small stones surrounding the burned-out remains of a fire, and a pan turned upside-down on the grass to dry.

'*This* is where he was staying?' Maddy wanted to laugh, but she couldn't; the hours she'd spent on the phone and in person, cajoling, begging, certain that eventually she'd find out which guest house he was staying in...and all the time he'd been hiding away up here.

'Turns out it's very close to where Hazel's aunt lives,' Ade said, dropping to one knee to unzip the tent. 'Paul and I found it on the map; it's just at the end of this patch of forest.' He peered into the tent, and the way he wrinkled his nose made Maddy grin. 'Stinky bastard.'

'Well, the shower facilities leave a bit to be desired,' she pointed out, looking around the clearing. 'D'you think he was using Isla's place then? Is that what this is about?'

'It's possible.' Ade reached into the back of the tent and brought something out. 'This looks like it's borrowed, don't you think?'

'A plastic tub? He could have brought it with him.'

'Could have, but unlikely. He bought the tent here in Scotland; the packaging's still in here. Why would he have bothered with a plastic tub?' Ade backed out of the tent and stood up straight, looking relieved to be out in the air again. He opened the tub and took a closer look at the remains of what had been inside, then gave it a tentative sniff. 'Some kind of stew, I think. I reckon we'll find this belongs to Mrs Munro. Shall we go and have a chat?'

They arrived, after another ten minute walk, at the back of Druimgalla and climbed over the fence, but before they could cross to knock on the door, Ade's phone rang.

'It's Ross,' he said, surprised, and his thumb rose to kill the call, but instead he put the phone on speaker as Maddy came closer. 'Hi, Patrick.'

'I can't get hold of Mackenzie,' Ross blurted. 'Can you tell him something?'

'I can get a message to him, aye, but he's still in Inverness just now, and I'm...not.'

'Tell him it's Breda Kelly.'

'We know. He's on it.'

Ross let out a heavy sigh. 'Thank God.' His voice dropped to a calmer register. 'I had no idea she was related until Julie told me.'

'Related?' Ade and Maddy swapped bemused looks.

'You said you knew.'

'Related to who?' Ade demanded. 'Come on, this is important!'

'She's Andrew Silcott's daughter.'

Maddy's forehead went tight, but she had another of those relieved, uncurling sensations as the story began finally rolling into place. 'Are you positive?'

'My wife knew her mother.' He sounded wretched now. 'It's so stupid! She even mentioned it before, but I didn't twig.' He sighed. 'We got talking when she came home from her day trip early this morning. I told her what had happened to Hazel, but that we thought she was okay, that she'd gone to find Breda Kelly to get help. Julie said she was glad, that Breda was lovely, and didn't I remember how nice her mother was? I said I didn't know her mother, and she told me it was Amanda Silcott.'

'Shit!' Ade stared at the sky, while Ross continued.

'Amanda reverted to her maiden name and moved back to Ireland after the divorce, but Breda stayed with her father. When he died she moved to be with her mother. She took Amanda's name, Kelly.'

'Why did your wife never say anything?' Maddy broke in.

'Why would she?' Ross was indignant. '*She'd* no idea any of this was going on! I certainly hadn't told her anything about the bloody painting!' He paused, then asked cautiously, 'Who am I speaking to?'

Maddy told him. 'Well, there's Breda's motive for screwing you over, Mr Ross,' she added. 'You helped kill her dad.'

'Jesus,' Ross said, in a small voice. 'She never gave the

slightest hint. She came to my *birthday* party! She must have delivered that cursed bloody card.'

'And it's her motive for killing Warrender too,' Ade said. 'We were barking up entirely the wrong tree.'

'But at least we'd eventually got to the right forest,' Maddy said. 'Pun intended. Right suspect, wrong motive.' She walked away, pulling out her own phone. 'I'm going to let Paul know.'

She could hear Ade behind her, ending the call with Ross, while she explained the news to Paul. 'If we can get her nailed for Warrender's murder, they'll have to let Hazel go,' she said. '*Then* we'll have time to start working on why Warrender killed Yvette Douglas.'

'I'll speak to Nick,' Paul promised. 'Hopefully this'll be enough to actually arrest her. On suspicion, at least.'

'Do you know how Hazel's doing?' Maddy asked.

'She's just had her six-hour review, but they're obviously still holding her.' His voice changed, as if he'd moved somewhere else, and was now so low she had to concentrate hard to hear him. 'Nick says she's doing okay; she's being co-operative and telling them everything she can think of. Her urine sample shows traces of Ketamine, and she's got a nasty set of bruises on her leg, but it's not conclusive.'

'He's telling *you* all this?' Maddy shook her head. 'He must be serious about leaving the force, then.'

'He's keeping me well informed, aye. I'll pass on what you've told me about Breda, and let you know what happens.'

Maddy looked up as the front door of Druimgalla eased open cautiously and Dylan Munro poked his glossy blond head out. 'We've been spotted,' she murmured. 'I'll call you later.'

'Spotted? Who by? Aren't you with Charis?'

'No, I came up with Ade, to check Warrender's tent, and now we're pretty sure he had a connection to Isla.' Her gaze went to the garage, and another question took a step closer to its answer. 'There's every chance the painting's been stashed here, at Druimgalla.'

Ade had crossed the yard to the front door, where Dylan was looking sick with worry, and Maddy ended the call with Paul and followed. She was puzzled by the boy's extreme reaction; surely he didn't know about all this too?

'Is your mother about?' Ade asked him.

'She's in the kitchen.' But instead of moving back to let them in, Dylan stepped outside and pulled the door closed behind him. 'We didn't mean to do it,' he muttered. 'It was just an accident. It wasn't Jamie's fault. Please, don't tell my mum.'

'*Jamie*? What was an accident?' Maddy had the horrible, but thankfully fleeting thought that somehow this boy and Jamie had been involved in Warrender's death. 'What did you do?'

Dylan faltered, and his gaze went from her to Ade and back again. 'Nothing. Come in.'

Maddy and Ade exchanged a look and followed the boy into the kitchen, where Isla greeted them without surprise. Her face, even paler than her son's, was lowered, though she looked up briefly, saw the plastic tub in Ade's hand and looked away again.

'It's right then, what they said on the news? He's dead?'

'Aye. I'm sorry.' Maddy said quietly. 'Were you very close, then?'

'No, not really. But he was going to give me a share.' She looked as if she thought she'd said too much, but the time for lies was past now. As was the time for misplaced sympathy, and Maddy's voice turned hard.

'A share of the blackmail money, you mean?'

Isla flinched, then nodded. 'He knew I worked for the

348

gallery, and when he told me what Ross had done, and how it had resulted in my sister's death, I felt justified in—'

'Hold on. Why would he have told *you* about that?' Maddy looked at Ade as she took a seat opposite Isla, but he appeared equally mystified; why would Warrender have deliberately incriminated himself if he hadn't needed to?

Isla looked at them as if she thought they were idiots. 'Well...because of what happened. Why else?'

Ade slid into the seat next to Maddy. 'Why don't you tell us exactly what he told you?' he said, and when his voice turned this deceptively soft he reminded Maddy more than ever of his younger brother. 'We've got as long as it takes.'

Isla looked at them both in turn, and then at Dylan, standing by the door. 'Come in, love. You're old enough to hear this.' She turned back to Maddy and Ade, lowering her gaze to her linked hands on the table in front of her, and she remained in that position for the time it took to tell her story. 'It was just before Graeme's birthday,' she said. 'The big four-o. Leslie said he'd come round to see Yvette while Graeme was away in Stirling, to help her plan his party.'

Chapter Twenty-Four

Druimgalla. April 1998

LESLIE WARRENDER KNOCKED at the door, turning over ideas for his friend's birthday, and what he could do for it in the space of a couple of weeks. He could hear the radio in the kitchen, turned right up... He thought he knew why; he had been doing the same lately. Trying to drown out the accusations in his own head.

The front door was unlocked, as ever. He fixed a smile in place and went in, hoping the daughter wouldn't have left for school yet, so he and Yvette might both be able to find the disguise they still needed, every day, just to appear normal. His luck was out, and his mind immediately dropped all its attempts to focus on Graeme's fortieth; it went instead to the one thing he had been desperate to forget about: the shocking, public death of Andrew Silcott last month. Yvette would want to talk about it for sure, now that they were alone for the first time since it had happened. She would want to know how the hell they were supposed to live with what they'd done, and he had no idea what to say to that. They just...had to.

He took a deep breath and went into the kitchen, where Yvette was still in her bright yellow dressing gown, a slice of toast in one hand and a butter knife in the other. She put them both down as Warrender came in, and her face lost all expression.

'Go away, Leslie.' She pushed her dark hair back from her face, and he could see her hand was shaking; he was glad she'd put the knife down.

'I came to talk about Graeme's party,' he said in a low voice. 'Can't we do that, at least?'

'Party?' She stared at him. '*Party?*' She turned away, her hands braced on the edge of the sink. 'After what we've done,' she went on, 'how are we supposed to talk about beer and music?'

'Hazel's at school, isn't she?'

'Yes, but—'

'All right then.' He pulled out a chair and gestured for her to do the same. When she didn't, he hung his jacket on the back of it and sat down anyway. 'We'll talk about the other thing.'

'We can't—'

'Sit down, Yvette,' he said quietly. 'Please?'

She did, and her fingers knotted around each other on the table in front of her. 'It's our fault,' she said, her voice barely above a whisper. 'Breda's father is dead, and it's *our fault.*' She hissed this last, and glanced at the door as if she expected Hazel or Graeme to have come home unexpectedly.

'We didn't know it would happen,' he began reasonably, wishing he could take comfort from it. 'It was just...a money thing. And a talent thing. You were so much better at that style than me, despite everything.'

'Despite dropping out of uni to get married, you mean?' Yvette gave a brittle laugh. 'Oh, it's all right, I could just paint my pretty little flowers and leave the important men to their important work.'

'Don't.'

'You came to me,' she reminded him. '*You* were the one with the bright idea. The one who broke into Silcott's house and stole the bloody thing! Why didn't you at least warn me you were going to do it? Just showing up here one night with it, and telling me what you wanted me to do? That was...' She shook her head, clearly lost for words.

'You didn't have to,' he reminded her.

'Oh, right!' Yvette's blue eyes flashed. 'I was supposed to turn that sort of money down, was I? After you pointed out how I was ruining Graeme's life? Cramping his creativity by forcing him to teach instead of paint, just so he could afford a daughter he didn't even want?'

'He did want her,' Warrender said, feeling wretched. 'I'm sorry I said that. I was just desperate.'

'I *know* he wanted her!' Yvette slammed her hands on the table. 'I don't need you to tell me that! But you convinced me that turning down that commission would have been another nail in his coffin. Just one more way to bring him down.' She gave a short, bitter laugh. 'Well, do you know what? I was wrong. This isn't *our* fault, it's yours. All of it.'

'No-one could have known Sturdy would go fucking...*insane* on that Silcott moron,' Warrender said, his own temper building now. 'The man was an idiot! Clueless about art, and we took advantage of that. We're both to blame, and you know it.' He didn't believe it himself, not for a minute, but if the guilt had pressed heavily on him when it was shared, he knew he wouldn't be able to stand against its full weight. 'You could have spoken up at any time.'

She was staring at him now, wide-eyed with disbelief. 'How dare you,' she breathed. 'Get out.'

'Yvette—'

'Just go! And you can tell Graeme you're double-booked for his birthday.'

Warrender hesitated, but rose to his feet. She would see sense someday, but it was probably just a bit too soon. 'Look,' he said, 'I'll come, and I won't mention this again, okay?'

'Oh, let him come to the party, Yvette.' The voice in the doorway brought them both up short. Breda Silcott stood there in her habitual grey sweatshirt and black leggings, her long hair twisted up in a towel from the shower. Her voice was soft, and her smile wide, but her eyes were glittering in an unhealthy way. 'You two carry on with your plans,' she invited. 'I'm just going to get some breakfast.'

'Breda,' Yvette began, and her face had turned pale. 'How long have you—'

'Been listening?' Breda came into the kitchen. 'Not long, don't worry. Certainly not long enough to have heard you call my recently deceased father a moron.' She flashed her unnerving smile at Warrender. 'Tea, anyone?'

'What are you doing here?' Warrender asked her. She'd been known to hang around the Douglases like a bad smell, but he'd always thought that had more to do with Graeme than with his wife. It explained why Yvette had looked nervously at the door earlier, though.

'She was upset,' Yvette muttered. 'I met her in town

yesterday and brought her back here to talk. We drank, and she stayed over.'

'And now I know why you were so kind to me,' Breda said, with a savage, tearful little grin. '*Guilt*, pure and simple. Between the two of you, you killed my dad. For money.'

'It wasn't like that,' Yvette began, but Breda whirled on her, the towel falling off and her wet hair cascading onto her face. It made her look like some furious creature from mythology.

'*You* put that club in Matthew Sturdy's hand, you stinking little bitch. You robbed him of everything, for whatever pathetic reason you had, which had nothing to do with *my* family! You didn't care what he did about it. Not as long as you got your blood money!'

She grabbed the butter knife and advanced on Yvette, who shoved her chair back and stumbled away from the table, her feet sliding in her backless slippers. 'Stop it, Breda, you don't know what you're doing.' She flung a look at Warrender, who stood frozen in place. The butter knife was small, and not sharp, but he had no doubt it could do some damage nevertheless. Yet he just couldn't move.

Yvette broke her own paralysis and kicked off her slippers ready to run, but Breda flung the knife into the sink with a clatter. 'Don't be fucking stupid,' she said in a heavy, defeated voice. 'Piss off, Leslie. Yvette and I need to talk.'

Warrender looked at Yvette, who pulled her dressing gown more tightly around her, a flimsy armour against Breda's grief and anger. 'Shall I go?'

'Aye, go.' Yvette picked up her drink and went into the sitting room, and Breda followed her, without the butter knife, Warrender was relieved to note. He thought they looked calm, both of them, ready to talk it through. Yvette was good with words; Breda would soon understand it had all been just a terrible mistake, with unforeseeable consequences.

'And the party?' he ventured.

'Do what you like.' Yvette shut the sitting room door in his face, leaving him standing in the hall feeling half lost, half relieved. It had been nightmarish every time he'd seen Breda Silcott; the funeral had been the worst, of course, but perhaps now she'd aired her fury they might begin to move past it. The party might even be the new starting point, as long as she kept her mouth shut around Patrick Ross.

He heard raised voices in the sitting room and pulled open the front door; clearly the 'moving past it' point was a way off yet, and he didn't want to stand here and listen to this. He went out to the garage and spent a few minutes looking over Yvette's canvases, wondering again why, with a talent like hers, she was content to paint such comparatively bland works. After a few minutes of looking over the paintings stacked against the wall, he gave up his pointless musing and went back out to his car, but with the key in the locked door he hissed in annoyance as he remembered his jacket, still hanging on the back of the chair in the kitchen. For a moment he considered leaving it there, then realised it would look dodgy if Hazel came home from school and found it, or worse still, Graeme returned from the pedagogy symposium he was attending. There never had been anything between himself and Yvette, but she was a good looking woman, and Graeme was bound to suspect. He sighed and went back indoors.

Passing the front room again, he paused to see if he could hear what they were saying, but there was only silence. He imagined them sitting opposite one another, each looking angry and hurt, and was mightily relieved to be this side of the door. He grabbed his jacket from the kitchen and made his way back down the hall, but was startled to hear a crash from the sitting room. Surely things hadn't come to a fight after all?

Knowing he'd regret it, but never dreaming just how deeply, he opened the door, and as his brain absorbed the scene, his vision tilted and swam. Yvette lay on the sofa, her bare feet dangling over the arm, her dressing gown gaping and the terry-towelling belt around her neck. Her face was discoloured and mis-shapen, and as his gaze locked on it, his peripheral vision caught movement from the other side of the room. He dragged his head up and around, to see Breda opening the bureau and pulling out one of the drawers. She had already overturned the magazine rack and flung a plant from the window sill onto the floor, and as she became aware that Warrender had returned, her face lost all its hectic colour.

'Wait,' she said, her voice tight. 'We need each other.'

'Do we hell!' He was surprised he was able to speak; just looking at Yvette – or what she had become – was making his heart stutter and his skin tighten. He swayed on his feet and grabbed at the back of the sofa, trying to breathe slowly.

'Listen,' Breda said, abandoning her assault on the furniture and coming closer. Warrender tensed, but didn't step back. 'I'm assuming Patrick Ross gave you a decent payment to help him screw Matthew Sturdy out of his life's savings.'

'I gave it to her.' He nodded at Yvette, and Breda barked a single, harsh laugh.

'You're not telling me you gave her all of it, or even half.'

He shrugged. 'I'm telling you nothing.'

'I can give you more. And I can help you...disappear. *If* you keep quiet about me being here today.'

'Disappear?'

'Die. In an accident.' She arched a brow at the sudden look

of fear he knew had crossed his face. 'Faked,' she said patiently, 'rather like that beautiful *Florence Cathedral*.'

'But...why?' he managed.

'This is clearly a burglary,' she said, looking around and, he was sickened to see, not even flinching at the sight of Yvette. 'House up here, out of the way and with no nosey neighbours... It's inevitable, wouldn't you say? Yvette came into the room at the wrong time, poor love.'

'Christ, you're cold.'

'I'm focused,' she corrected him. 'I'll go to my mother's in Ireland, and you, or rather Leslie, will lie unlamented and undisturbed at the bottom of the North Sea. Meanwhile, somewhere in Europe, there's a brand new PhD in Art History on the scene.'

'And that's it?'

'That's it. Over. For good.' She folded her arms. 'Or do we go through the whole mud-slinging business of blame and counter-blame, and ruin us both?'

'How can you just work it all out like that, after...after this?' he gestured at Yvette, and the chaos in the room.

'Like I said, I'm focused.' Breda nodded at the back of the sofa. 'I'd start with wiping that down, if I were you. Not that it matters too much, since you're a friend of the family. But maybe you grabbing like that won't come across too well if someone spots it.'

'Then what happens?'

'You get yourself an alibi, and I'll be in touch about the other thing. For now though, you just stand ready to be a pillar of support for your best friend.' She gave him a sympathetic look, her head tilted in mock sorrow. 'He's just lost his wife.'

'So it *all* started with Breda,' Maddy said, into the silence that followed. 'And it ended with Warrender.'

'You're saying she killed Leslie as well?' Isla asked, her voice hoarse now.

Maddy nodded. 'And Linda Sturdy, though we're going to have trouble proving any of it.'

'I'll go to the police,' Isla said, looking at Dylan. 'I'm so sorry for all the secrets.'

Dylan didn't answer; he was still subdued, but now the direction for it had changed, and he wouldn't face his mother. Instead, he turned to Ade and took his moment. 'I stole your quad bike,' he said bluntly. 'It was me and Jamie, and we pitched it into the river. Not on purpose,' he added, and the earnestness of that made Maddy want to smile so she turned away. When she looked back, Ade was scowling, and she put a hand on his arm.

'We can talk about this later, aye?' She got up and crossed to the back door. 'I take it the painting's in your garage then?'

'No,' Isla said, rubbing her face with both hands, half her attention worriedly on Dylan after his own confession. 'It's at the gallery.'

'Seriously?'

'Hidden in plain sight, and all that, or at least, in the basement.' Isla gave her a grim smile. 'Even if I despise Patrick Ross for what he did to my family, I have to admit that working for him has its perks.'

Ade frowned. 'So Warrender parked up there in the forest, then brought the painting to you here so you could take it in to work with you?'

'No, it was never here. Well, not since Yvette painted it. He had it couriered directly to the gallery.'

'Bold move. Wasn't it a risk that Ross would notice?'

Isla shook her head. 'We've got a summer exhibition coming up; we're getting work delivered all the time from artists who can't be here in person until the exhibition itself. I've just been left alone to get on with it, since Patrick seems to have had...other things on his mind.' The flicker of a smile appeared and was gone. 'Poor bloke, eh?'

The coldness in her voice gave Maddy a little shiver. 'Right, I'm going to call my partner,' she said. 'Let him know what's going on.'

She took her phone out into the yard, leaving Ade to take up the issue of the quad bike if he chose to, but she had a feeling he wouldn't; Dylan was too much like himself, and Jamie was practically his nephew. There might be repercussions much later, but this wasn't the time. Unfortunately for both boys, their mothers were less likely to be so understanding.

'Paul, hi. You ready for this?'

―――――

Mackenzie went out to the entrance of the police station, where Hazel had been brought after she'd given herself in to the transport police. Maddy had told him that Isla was on her way in to make a statement before she was pulled in, which might go some way towards mitigating any charge that might arise from her involvement. He'd reluctantly agreed to wait for her, so she wouldn't be alone, and, desperate to be heading home after a long, worrying and fraught night, he sat out in the fresh air and kept an eye out for a red Toyota pulling into the car park.

He had passed on the information about Breda Kelly, or Silcott, or whatever the hell she called herself, and he'd been like a cat on hot bricks ever since, waiting for news; now there was even more to tell Nick, but he wouldn't want to keep being called out to the desk, away from the investigation. It could wait until Isla arrived. Mackenzie tried not to look at his watch, and instead mentally counted the time it would take to descend from Druimgalla to Abergarry, and then to reach Inverness. Even on a Sunday, and in light traffic, it was a fair old drive so he'd bought the strongest coffee he could find, and now he took it onto the grassy area at the back of the car park near the entrance.

After an hour of fighting to stay awake, he got up and wandered down past the bicycle racks, following the path as far as it would let him before he reached the official vehicle park at the end. When he went back there was still no sign of Isla Munro's car, so he reluctantly came to the decision it was time to go in and pass on the information himself. She'd had her chance.

He had actually come close enough to the entrance for the automatic door to slide open, before a nasty niggling sensation crawled up his spine; he swore, looked at his watch, and ran back to his car, angry with himself for wasting so much time. It wasn't even as if he'd been thinking this case through during that time either, he'd been too busy dwelling on his own future, on Charis, and Glencoille. He called Ross as he reached the car, and threw his phone on the passenger seat while he drove at speed out of the car park, aware he might be storing up trouble for himself again with speeding fines, but this time not caring.

'Meet me at Waterfront,' he bellowed, as soon as Ross answered. 'Now!' He stabbed blindly at the disconnect button and turned his attention back to the ugly thought that had propelled him back to his car: there was no way in hell that someone in Isla Munro's position would voluntarily set herself up for a possible custodial sentence. Apart from it being a terrifying prospect for anyone, there was Dylan to think about, and by all accounts the lad was already a tear-away-in-training. In care he'd be in danger of being swallowed up and lost forever, and she'd already seen what it had done to her niece. She would have driven straight to the gallery instead and was probably even now engaged in destroying the only evidence that linked her to both Leslie Warrender and Breda Kelly. Once that was gone, the whole thing could fall apart, relegating Yvette's murder again to the realms of the unsolved.

The drive from the police station to the gallery would take under ten minutes on a good day; Mackenzie estimated he was there in a tad over five. He didn't bother to park legally, he was pretty sure he'd be clobbered for some part of this flight sooner or later, anyway. It would probably take Ross another five minutes or so to get here, but there was no time to waste hanging around for him, either. Mackenzie tried the front door of the gallery, which, as he'd suspected on a Sunday, was locked. He stepped back and looked either side, but there was no break in the buildings along this road; they were all joined together as far as he could see in one direction, and right to the end of the terrace in the other.

'Shit!' He ran to where an access lane led him past several parked cars and into the narrow road that ran parallel with Ness Walk. A further short jog brought him to a small entranceway that seemed to correspond with the rear of Waterfront. Hoping he was right, he went in, his gaze falling immediately on a red Toyota Yaris parked haphazardly beside a set of steps leading downwards. He placed another call to Ross, planning to tell him to call Isla, but there was no reply, and he shoved his phone away with another grunted curse, before it had rung out more than twice.

He went to the top of the steps and looked down to see a drop of around eight feet to a sturdy metal door. Closed. Mackenzie slid beneath the iron railing to save time, hissing a curse as he wrenched his left shoulder and felt the old pain flare across the top of his chest. He took a moment to breathe it away, then raised his right fist ready to hammer on the door, but at the last moment he changed it to a polite knock instead.

'Isla? It's Paul Mackenzie.' He somehow managed to speak with an easy, friendly tone. 'Can you let me in a sec?' He waited, holding his breath, and a minute later there was a loud, metallic clunk and the door opened a few inches. 'Hi.' He gave her his cheeriest smile. 'Maddy called me and asked me to see you're okay about giving your statement. She didn't want you to be alone.'

'I'm on my way,' Isla said. 'I just needed to...pick something up. I'll be out in a minute.'

She tried to push the door closed again, but Mackenzie had already smelled it: the sickly-sweet smell of petrol. He rammed his boot into the gap between door and jamb, biting back a shout as the metal edges of both ground into his foot.

'It's okay,' he said, leaning on the door with his right shoulder and keeping his voice even. 'We'll make sure you're looked after. I promise.'

'Go away!' Isla hissed, dropping all pretence now. She pushed on the door, but evidently realised she was no match, and instead stood back and let it open fully.

Mackenzie stumbled into the cool, dry storage space beneath Waterfront. Canvases were stacked against three of the walls, wrapped in bubble wrap and protected with extra tape on the corners, but against the fourth wall, where the door presumably led to stairs up to the gallery itself, only one canvas was opened; the brown paper was torn away from one side of it, showing the corner of *Florence Cathedral*. A red plastic petrol can lay beside it on its side, still leaking liquid that puddled around the painting and crawled greasily up through the paper.

Mackenzie spoke quietly. 'What are you doing, Isla?'

'Isn't it obvious?' She strode over to the can and picked it up, clearly ready to continue her work.

'I mean, why the petrol? Why not just take a Stanley knife to the stupid thing?'

'Because I don't want to just destroy that!' Isla jabbed her finger at the painting, and her voice rose, becoming unsteady and shrill. 'I want to destroy all of it! Most of all I want—'

'To destroy Patrick Ross,' Mackenzie said quietly. 'I get that. He's all that's left of it now, except Breda, isn't he?' As he spoke, he eyed the fire extinguisher on the wall beside the gallery door, wondering how long it would take him to reach it, and if it would be too long. A fire down here would spread fast; one extinguisher wouldn't be anywhere near enough once it took hold. He noticed it was a water-based extinguisher in any case, so any attempt to douse a petrol trail would just spread it around and make it worse.

Isla followed his gaze, and she sounded tired now. 'Get out, Mr Mackenzie, and you can pretend you were never here. I won't tell anyone you knew about it. They'll assume it was an insurance job, I expect.'

'You've not taken it too far yet,' he said reasonably. 'Come with me and give your statement, and we can work out what to do.'

The whole situation was throwing back horrific echoes of trying to talk doomed widow Donna Lumsden into surrendering to armed police, but she had chosen to feign an intent to kill instead, and had drawn police fire anyway. He couldn't let that happen again; even if there were no police, in sparking that fire Isla would destroy herself almost as completely as Donna had. And there was no guarantee either of them would make it back to the door and out to safety, either. She must know that.

'Come on,' he urged. 'Dylan and Hazel are both waiting to talk to you.'

'Go away,' she repeated dully. 'You won't change my mind just by throwing names at me. Ross deserves everything he gets.'

The door to the gallery rattled and jerked open, and Isla instinctively backed away from Mackenzie, her feet knocking the legs of a row of stacked easels and sending them clattering sideways onto the basement floor. She gave a startled cry at the sound, and whirled to look at Patrick Ross, who was staring at her in astonishment. Mackenzie had time to remember that no-one had told the man about his director's involvement, before Ross breathed in the smell of petrol and his gaze fell on the red can in Isla's hand.

His eyes flew wide, and he lunged at Isla and grabbed at the can, in the same moment that she hauled it back and swung it at his head. Ross stumbled back, retching as the remaining petrol dowsed his face and hair, and Isla dropped the can and reached into her pocket, bringing out a cheap, clear plastic lighter. She pushed the small black lever on its side, opening it up to its fullest, and thumbed the wheel.

The flame leapt and Mackenzie moved forward, his movement as unthinking as Ross's wild grab for the petrol can; he seized hold of Isla, pulling her away from Ross; if they lost the paintings, too bad, but if Ross was within range of that flame he'd go up like a rocket. The lighter fell to the ground and went out, and Isla let out a cry of frustration and stooped to pick it up. Mackenzie also made a dive for it, but from the corner of his eye he saw a swift movement, and twisting to look up, he saw Ross bringing the fire extinguisher around in a clumsy arc, aiming for Isla's head.

He rose in alarm to stop the canister before it could connect with the stooping woman, and, stepping forward into its trajectory, he took the brunt of the awkward but surprisingly powerful swing. The bottom edge struck his left arm, and a ferocious, sickening pain smashed its way up into his healing collar bone and shoulder; his fingers went numb, and even as he dragged in a couple of deep breaths he knew that he'd missed his chance to prevent Isla picking up the lighter. It was still at her feet, too far away for him to reach even if he'd had any feeling in his fingers to pick it up, and hadn't been fighting the blooming black flowers at the edge of his vision.

There was a dull clang from somewhere close by, and Mackenzie heard Ross swearing as he bent to retrieve the extinguisher he'd dropped. Isla was now desperately flicking the wheel of the lighter again, her eyes brimming with furious tears, and Ross was just staring at her in frantic denial.

'Stop her then!' Mackenzie gasped, incredulous at the man's helplessness. He pressed his free hand to his shoulder, praying that one stupid move hadn't set him back months in his recovery, and the movement sent a wave of all-too familiar pain across the top of his chest. He swallowed a groan, flexing his fingers to try and regain some feeling as he stumbled forward to where Isla now stood among the most precious and valuable of the covered canvases – those genuine pieces of art that were simply being stored here. As he and Ross watched, the lighter flared and Isla's white face was lit eerily by the flame that leapt high and bobbed about, dangerously unpredictable. She bent and touched the lighter to the corner of one of the paintings, but the bubble wrap simply melted and failed to catch, and Mackenzie, seeing there was still a chance, lurched towards Ross instead.

'Give it to me!' He grabbed the extinguisher and yanked out the pin, aiming the hose at Isla's hands rather than the feeble, dying flame at her feet. The force of the water blew the lighter out of her grasp and sent it spinning harmlessly away to land against the metal external door, but Mackenzie barely had time to breathe a sigh of relief at the near miss before he heard Isla give a shout of rage, and he turned to see her launching herself at Ross.

The gallery owner, having been transfixed by the potential loss of his priceless collection, half-turned towards her as she reached him, trying at the same time to step away, but fell backwards onto the floor, and his eyes turned frighteningly blank as his head bounced on the concrete. Isla was astride him in seconds, one hand drawn back and her rigid fingers ready to claw at his face, and she let out another shout as Mackenzie seized her arm from behind her. She wrenched free with surprising and alarming strength and drove back with her elbow, catching him hard in the stomach. When he drew his next breaths they were laced with a deep, spreading ache that momentarily eclipsed even the pain in his chest, but as the feeling began to return to his numbed fingers he was able to seize both of Isla's arms and, after another brief struggle, he finally dragged her away.

She wriggled in his grasp, stamping backwards onto his feet and shins, and throwing her head back into his body, and his rapidly waning strength almost failed him as the pain was re-awoken just as it had begun to subside a little; he felt a growing fear that, despite his size, he would be unable to hold her after all. Ross was gazing up at them both in semi-dazed fear, but as Mackenzie finally wrapped both his arms around Isla, keeping her pinned, he was able to scoot himself backwards until he came up against the door jamb.

'Keep hold of her, for Christ's sake!'

Mackenzie, still breathing hard and with difficulty, spoke harshly, directly in Isla's ear. 'Stop it! Isla! Stop! Come on...'

She subsided all at once, as if finally accepting that her cause was a hopeless one, but Mackenzie didn't trust her enough to release her just yet. She was drawing deep breaths in which he could hear the thin, high whistle of unspent fury, and every one of his nerves was on high alert, waiting for her to re-launch her attack. Eventually he felt the tension drain from her body, but he still gave Ross time to move into the short stair-well, putting the doorway between them, before he slowly loosened his grip.

She stepped away from him, glaring at him aggressively as if he'd been the one to strike her. 'You had no right to stop me,' she said in a breathless, furious voice. 'He deserves to lose it all.'

'Ross didn't kill your sister.' He indicated the forged Mercanti with his good arm. 'Nor did that, or any of the others,' he added, hoping to appeal to her common sense now. 'Breda Kelly did that.'

'Breda Silcott,' Isla corrected him flatly, and Mackenzie saw Ross come back into the room, his eyes wide. He gave a minute shake of his head, and Ross clamped his mouth shut on what looked like a hundred questions.

'Aye, her,' Mackenzie said. 'So, do you want her to pay for what she did?'

'Don't patronise me! Of course I do!' Isla hesitated, then gave a sigh so deep and heavy it had to hurt. 'But I don't want to go to prison, and leave Dylan—'

'You nearly left him anyway, and for good,' he reminded her, looking at the pool of petrol. 'You don't know whether any of us would have got out if you'd lit that.'

'Of course we would have.'

Mackenzie left it; his chest and shoulder hurt too much for him to find the strength to argue, and he was still shaking at how close they'd come to being trapped in here and burning to death. He bent over as a spell of dizziness threatened to take him away, and breathed through it, one hand pressed against his shoulder, the other braced on his thigh. He was vaguely aware that if Isla chose this moment to renew her assault on Ross, the gallery owner would be on his own. But it seemed she'd accepted the sense of backing off now, and she kept her distance.

'I won't press charges about this, Isla,' Ross said, presumably feeling generous, but Isla looked at him with contempt.

'You need to worry about your own prison sentence.'

'What?'

'You're in this up to your neck, Ross,' Isla said, with undeniable satisfaction. 'As soon as I give my statement, we're both on borrowed time.'

'Aye, it's all tied in now,' Mackenzie admitted, as an aghast Ross looked to him for support. 'We can't get Breda for any of this without passing on the full history of her and Warrender, and her connection to the fraud.' He shrugged, then immediately wished he hadn't, and swore brightly. 'What we can do,' he went on, 'is give the police every bit of information they ask for, and hope they'll appreciate it enough to go easy.'

'Fuck's sake, Mackenzie.' Ross scowled. 'You said I wouldn't—'

'That all changed with the Breda Kelly thing. But what do I know, anyway? I'm not a police officer.' Mackenzie gave him a thin smile. 'In fact, as of right now I'm not even a PI anymore. And d'you know what else?' He shared a look of contempt equally between them. 'I'll take my chances with a demonically possessed quad bike any day, over so-called educated bastards like you two.'

Chapter Twenty-Five

HAZEL WALKED SLOWLY BACK across the hospital car park to Paul Mackenzie's car, exhausted beyond belief now it was finally over. For her, at least. Griff still had a long way to go, and speaking to him just now in his hospital bed, Hazel had been struck by the way he'd looked, stripped of his vibrancy and his smile; he'd seemed smaller, a lot older, and most disturbing of all, just...*ordinary*, when she knew in reality he was anything but.

He'd forgiven her, he'd said. He understood. Knew that the swipe with the crash helmet had been designed only to allow her to escape, and that she couldn't have foreseen the consequences... But all the while he'd been reassuring her there had been another look in his eyes. Not wariness, and certainly not fear, but a deeper sadness that she hadn't trusted him. That she could have believed, even in the extremity of her terror, that he could have done something like that to anyone, let alone her. How could she make him understand how, once the 'evidence' had clicked and the certainty had sunk in, there had been no escape from that? There had been no-one to tell her to stop, to think, and to think again. No-one to reason with her, and to guide her towards a different conclusion. She'd been utterly alone.

So yes, he had a long way to go, and, to regain his unquestioning friendship, so did she.

Mackenzie had spotted her crossing the car park, and had got out of his car and lifted a hand, lowering it again instantly with a wince. She quickened her step, knowing he was as keen to get back to his loved ones as she was to her friends, and gave him a grateful smile as he opened the passenger door for her. She slumped in the seat with a sigh of relief, and Mackenzie got back behind the wheel, moving a little stiffly, and turned the ignition key. Hazel frowned slightly; all he'd said was that Isla had resisted going to the police, and that he'd had to restrain her from hurting Ross, so he must have wrenched his shoulder quite badly in the process.

'So. Home?' he asked.

'Home.'

He shifted the car into gear but didn't do anything further for a moment, and when she looked at him she saw he had closed his eyes and was controlling his breathing. 'Do you want me to drive?' she asked worriedly. 'Come on, swap over. You're in no state.'

He opened his eyes again and shook his head. 'Definitely not, you've been through a lot worse. This'll settle down again in a minute.' He sent her a sudden smile, as charming as it was unexpected. 'If you can put up with the odd filthy word, we'll be fine.'

She smiled back. 'I think I'll cope.'

She hoped he wouldn't want to discuss what had

happened, but he seemed to understand her need for quiet, and the car purred out of the car park with no further talk between them. At the junction, where they waited to turn right, she looked to her left, towards the police station, and tried to imagine what was going on there now; what Breda Kelly was saying, or not saying. What Isla was saying or doing, and if she was all right. She knew only too well what the woman was going through, and she wouldn't have wished it on anyone.

It had been a gruelling night of questions, and then a long, long wait to find out if they had enough to charge Breda with Warrender's murder, and therefore let Hazel go; when the decision had finally come down, Hazel had locked herself in the toilet and sobbed. Not the same silent, barely acknowledged tears that had blinded her as she'd walked to the station to hand herself in, this time she had actually, properly sobbed as she had in the cottage, and with the same cleansed but raw feeling when the tears had subsided.

Maddy's brother had accompanied Hazel out of the station, but instead of vanishing back inside to continue building the case against Breda, he had sat in the back seat of Mackenzie's car and told them all they had on her. Hazel still didn't know if he'd been allowed to do that, and Maddy had made such a song and dance about him being straight down the line, but he hadn't seemed to care anymore.

'It's not just about Warrender now,' he'd said. 'As soon as we got the info about Breda's past it all slotted together, and, thanks to Isla's statement, she's being questioned about your mother's death too. All things coming together, however slowly, it's looking promising.' In the rear-view mirror Hazel saw him rub his hands through his hair and yawn. 'Christ, I could do with forty winks.'

'It's been a hell of a night,' Hazel said, feeling the ache of fatigue in her own bones.

Mackenzie twisted in the driving seat. 'So what *do* they have right now, to hold her with?'

'Abduction, for starters,' Nick said. 'The holiday cottage booking was made on your own phone, Hazel, but all via text. Any idea how that might have happened?'

'None. When was it made?'

'Twenty-Third of April, around nine p.m.'

'The day after Charis's birthday,' Mackenzie put in, and Hazel breathed out slowly.

'That's the night I had dinner with Ade, Ross and Kilbride, at Thistle. My phone was in my jacket pocket for most of it, and our coats were taken from us at the door.'

Nick raised an eyebrow. 'Your phone's not locked?'

'That's a point. Yes it is, so I don't...' Hazel swore softly and closed her eyes. 'She "bumped into me" during our bike club meeting at the Twisted Tree and gave me her number. I'd have had to unlock it right in front of her.'

Nick nodded. 'Okay, well, ample opportunity for Booth to have cancelled the original booking, and her to have immediately made yours. I know it's not ideal, but we're working on the rest; at least this is something we can charge her with so we don't have to let her go. The staff at Thistle say she didn't stay for clear-up on Friday night, due to a sprained wrist, so she has no alibi for the time you were taken, Hazel. And,' he added with a satisfied little smile, 'no sprained wrist either.'

'She was the one who told your Max to re-schedule mine

and Charis's birthday meal,' Mackenzie mused. 'That would have been right after you had lunch with her,' he added to Hazel. 'She was already making her plans then, fixing it so that anyone else you might have tried to call that night was harder to reach than usual.'

'We talked about my favourite foods at that lunch too,' Hazel remembered. 'The same type of food the fridge in the cottage was stuffed with, that Griff knows I like. She was so sly. I can't believe I fell for it. So many lies.'

Nick started, and his hand went to his jacket pocket. 'I almost forgot this.' He took out a clear plastic bag and passed it forward between the seats: Hazel's silver necklace, last seen disappearing into the pocket of her American saviour-presumed-thief.

'Breda said he'd...' She shook her head. Of course she had. Feeling an almost childlike trembling of relief and joy at having the essence of both her parents with her again, she fastened the chain around her neck. 'Have they got anything on her for Linda?' she asked, letting the silver lump fall back into place beneath her shirt.

Nick pulled a face. 'That's a bit tougher. We know she did it, but she'd been questioned and ruled out, since she had no motive. Her blood had already contaminated the scene when she cut herself on the broken bottle. Supposedly trying to revive Linda.

'Well now you know she *did* have a motive,' Mackenzie added. 'She'd planned to kill Warrender all along, to protect her secret. She might even have been the one to draw him back here, with that in mind. But he couldn't resist testing the waters with that interview. It would have worked,' he added, 'but when Linda saw that photo it changed everything.'

Hazel frowned. 'What difference would that have made?'

'Easier for Kelly to kill someone who's already dead,' Nick said. 'But all eyes would have been on Warrender once word got out; he'd have been on the police radar right away.'

'So better not to have to try and hide him,' Mackenzie said, 'but to let someone else take the blame for the whole thing.'

Hazel let her head fall back against the headrest. 'Christ! *Why* did Linda have to tell her she'd recognised him?'

'We're only assuming she did,' Nick pointed out. 'But it's a safe assumption, given it would have been playing on her mind. It's a motive to work on, anyway. Claire – DC McAndrew that is – questioned Max about Kelly's movements up to fifteen minutes before she found the body.'

'And?'

'He'd gone in to her office, to pinch a cigarette out of her pack before she went outside and took them with her. She was due a break in about ten minutes, and they were still there on the table, so he had assumed she was still working.'

'It would have been crazy busy in there,' Mackenzie said. 'Easy to have slipped out early.'

'We questioned a couple of the people Linda was having dinner with,' Nick said. 'Linda had gone to use the bathroom between main course and dessert, and that was the last time any of them saw her. But she'd emptied her bladder at time of death.' He gave Hazel's shoulder an apologetic squeeze, but carried on, 'and there was a considerable amount at the scene. She must have been waylaid by someone to go out and have her smoke first, instead. That could only have been Breda Kelly.' He sighed. 'But if she wasn't out there long enough to smoke, she wouldn't have been there long enough to chat, and to find out about the photo. If we can't place her at the scene, we have no motive.'

'Breda could've smoked one of Linda's fags,' Hazel mused. 'She probably wouldn't have liked it though.'

'Why not?' Mackenzie asked, but it was Nick who supplied the answer, sitting forward, and grabbing at the backs of both front seats.

'Menthol!'

'Aye,' Hazel said. 'Not everyone's cup of tea, but any port in a storm.'

A flicker of a memory made her close her eyes, trying to make it fit her train of thought. She'd been shown the crime scene photos of both Warrender and Linda, while they'd still been hopeful of shocking a confession out of her, but she'd had nothing to confess. The photos though... What was it about them? The back of Linda's jacket, wet at the shoulder where she'd leaned against the wall; it *suggested* she'd been turned towards someone, talking, but that wasn't enough. It could have been anyone. What else? There was obviously the broken glass; there was a bloodied footprint, later attributed to Linda herself; then looking slightly further away, a numbered tag beside Linda's bag, and another beside the single menthol cigarette butt, half-submerged in the puddle near the kitchen door... Hazel drew a sharp breath and her eyes flew open.

'The bin!'

Mackenzie blinked. 'What?'

'The bin thing, on the wall outside the kitchen.' Hazel's heart began to beat faster, in sudden, hopeful excitement. 'It's pretty big, probably hasn't been emptied in a while... Can you get DNA off a cigarette after this long?'

'Too fucking right, you can!' Nick was already pushing open the door and pulling out his phone. 'You two get off home. I'll call you later.'

Mackenzie had waited for Hazel to fasten her seatbelt. 'I take it you want to go to the hospital first?'

'No.' She'd sighed. 'It's the last thing I want, after what I did. But I think I should.'

His expression was grave, but sympathetic as he pulled out of the parking space. 'I do too.'

Now, as Mackenzie's car negotiated the winding road back towards Abergarry, Hazel alternately dozed, remembered, tried to forget, hated herself, and told herself she'd done nothing wrong. By the time they reached Maddy's house she was a wreck. Her eyes burned with tears shed with her face turned towards the window, unremarked upon by Mackenzie, but she'd seen how he had kept stealing worried glances at her as he drove. She was grateful for his silence, and when they arrived outside Maddy's house it took a minute or two for her to bring herself to get out of the car and go inside.

When she did, she realised she had a welcoming committee, and almost broke down all over again, but she was immediately enveloped in a hug, and with a heartfelt cry from Maddy. 'Thank God you're out! I can't believe that bitch!' She pulled back and gave Jamie an apologetic look. 'You didn't just hear that.'

Hazel found herself smiling properly, for the first time in what felt like forever, as she looked around Maddy's sitting room. 'I can't tell you how it feels to be here with you lot.' She threw a look at Ade, who had taken Maddy's hand and drawn her to his side. 'Even you.' She gave their linked hands a pointed look, and Maddy just shrugged.

'Some things you just can't argue with.'

'I find that hard to believe,' Charis put in, earning herself a warning look from Mackenzie even as she put her arms around him with deceptive care and looked up at him with naked worry on her face. His frown melted at that look, and a whole silent conversation seemed to pass between them as his lips curved into one of his rare smiles.

'So where are we up to?' Maddy asked, patting the sofa beside her. 'What's the latest with Isla?' She looked at Dylan, who was sitting uncharacteristically quietly at the table with Jamie.

'She's still at the station,' Hazel told him, 'but I'm sure she'll be home soon.'

He seemed happy enough with that, but the truth was, she herself knew only that Mackenzie had brought Isla in, and that she'd given her statement, but that for some reason they were still keen to talk to her.

Mackenzie went out into the kitchen to make 'the strongest coffee in the known universe', and Charis looked over at Jamie. 'Why don't you take Dylan upstairs for a bit?' she suggested. 'You can take turns reading stories to Tas.'

Both boys looked mutinous at the prospect, but Charis insisted, and when she heard the bedroom door close she turned to Hazel. 'I didn't want Dylan to hear this, but Isla didn't just resist going to the police, she tried to destroy Waterfront.' She explained what Mackenzie had told them while Hazel had been visiting Griff, and Hazel stared at her, dismayed.

'Oh my God, poor Dylan. And poor Isla. Mackenzie didn't mention anything about that. Is he okay, by the way?'

'He's fine, just a bit sore.' Charis gave the closed kitchen door a look of exasperated affection that Hazel knew was masking something much deeper. 'I'll be dead happy when he can stop doing stuff like that, though.'

Maddy's phone rang before Hazel could reply, and she stood up so she could dig it out of her jeans pocket. 'Nick? Hi. Just a sec.' She shouted for Mackenzie, then put the phone on speaker and propped it against the remote control rack on the coffee table. 'We're all here; what've you got?'

'We found the cigarette,' Nick said, and Hazel answered the puzzled looks around her with a triumphant grin that was mirrored on Mackenzie's face. She indicated to the others that she'd explain later; it was good enough news in itself, but she couldn't suppress the wild hope that Linda had passed that cigarette to Breda, instead of offering the packet; it would put them both out there at the same time, and expose Breda's lies.

'What about the DNA?' she asked. 'Have you found Breda's on it?'

'Too soon, yet,' Nick said. 'But it was the only menthol butt in there, and it was buried pretty well so'd probably been there for a couple of weeks. It's looking good,' he went on, his tone turning careful now. 'Listen, Hazel, I don't want you to get your hopes up, because we still have to confirm Breda's DNA.'

'But?'

'But Linda hadn't been out there long enough to smoke two cigarettes before she was found, her dinner friends confirmed that, and they say she wouldn't have anyway...'

'And?' They all leaned forward towards the phone, sensing the tension at the other end.

'And Linda's shade of lipstick's on the butt we found.'

Charis drew a quick breath. 'So...she what, smoked half of it, then passed it over?'

'Possibly,' Nick said, still sounding very careful. 'We can't get ahead of—'

'Bugger that!' Hazel's smile was so broad now it was beginning to hurt. 'Kelly's DNA'll be on there, along with Linda's. We know it will!'

'Would that be enough for the Procurator Fiscal if it was?' Maddy asked.

'Together with everything else, I'd say we'll be charging Breda Kelly with at least two murders by morning. Possibly three.' Nick sounded tired but satisfied now, and he ended the call promising to keep them updated. Maddy retrieved her phone and put it away before hugging Hazel once more.

'I hope they get her for your mum too,' she murmured.

Mackenzie nodded. 'If Isla does the decent thing, they will. She might even just give it all up and confess. She might as well.'

'What decent thing?' a low, worried voice asked from the doorway, and they turned to see Dylan, with Jamie at his shoulder, both looking confused and suspicious. 'Come in, Dyl,' Hazel said quietly. 'We'll have a little chat about your mum.'

Much later, after full dark had fallen, Nick came to Maddy's house instead of calling her. Everyone was still there, talking endlessly over what had happened and what might have happened; they were operating on a severe lack of sleep, but a strange, hyper-awareness had fallen over them. Hazel felt she was seeing things with more vivid clarity than ever, and all the hundreds of tiny things Breda had said and done had slotted into place and created a picture of such deviousness she wondered how the woman functioned day to day. The pressure of living with, and perpetrating, such lies and violence must be immense.

'DNA's a match,' Nick said quietly, as Maddy reminded him of his nephew sleeping upstairs. 'They're charging Kelly with Warrender's murder, and with Linda's.' He gave Hazel an apologetic look. 'Your mother's is going to take either a confession or some new evidence, I'm afraid.'

'I'm going to keep looking,' Hazel said grimly. 'It'll be there.'

'But at least the woman who killed her is going down,' Dylan said. 'She'd better be, anyway.'

'I'm confident they'll get a conviction.' Nick looked at Maddy, then Mackenzie. 'You've all done an amazing job on this; you should be proud. We're grateful, believe me.'

'How things have changed,' Mackenzie said wryly. 'The police thanking me for something.'

'Not bad for your last case,' Maddy said, and when he looked at her she offered him a sad little smile. 'Aye, I know you've made up your mind. I won't try to persuade you to stay, but I'll miss you, you great lump.'

'You're not going to be a PI anymore?' Jamie looked bitterly disappointed. 'That sucks.'

'What will you do?' Hazel asked Mackenzie. She'd come to rate him highly, in the short time she'd known him, as an investigator as well as a friend. It was disappointing to find out he was packing it all in.

'I'm joining the family firm,' he said, sending his brother a quick smile. 'The Mackenzies of Glencoille, wasn't it?'

'It was.' Ade raised his coffee cup in salute. 'Welcome aboard, *gille beig*.'

Mackenzie snorted. 'I warned you about that.'

Hazel turned to Maddy. 'What does that mean for the agency? Will you have to shut down?'

'God, no. I'm not ready for that yet.' Maddy shook her head. 'You don't want the job, do you?'

Hazel laughed. 'Not on your nelly. I'm going to be assistant manager up at Glencoille, remember?' She gestured to Ade and Mackenzie. 'Someone's got to keep these lads in check.'

'I can't believe you want to give it all up,' Charis said, sitting up from where she had been resting against Mackenzie's good side, and looking at him quizzically. 'Don't get me wrong, I'm relieved, and I know you'll love being part of your family's business. But...won't you miss it?'

'Miss what?' he asked, amused. 'Sitting around in my car at four in the morning, hoping to catch an insurance cheat out jogging?'

'Well, yeah,' Charis conceded, 'but what about the other stuff? The stuff that balances all that out? Like...working something out that answers all the questions. Like discovering stuff that makes all the little bits fit together? It's...such a *buzz!*' She shook her head and smiled. 'Remember when I got that kid to talk to me last year? Lumsden's daughter? That was a *major* clue and it pretty much solved everything, you can't deny that. And yesterday,' she went on, 'looking at them photos and spotting Breda in the reflection – it made me want to run around screaming... What?' She flushed as she seemed to realise she was babbling, and that all eyes were on her. She turned to Jamie. 'What?' she said again.

He sighed. 'You're going to do it, aren't you? You're *actually* going to do it.'

'Do what?' Charis looked genuinely puzzled, then her eyes widened. 'Work with *her?*'

'No, she's not,' Maddy said quickly, then peered more closely. 'Are you?'

'Well,' Charis turned her face up to Mackenzie. 'I don't know. Am I?'

He slid an arm around her shoulder and pulled her against him. 'I have no idea. Are you?' The resigned look he gave Maddy, over the top of Charis's head, made everyone laugh, including Maddy.

'You'd have to apply for the job, like everyone else,' she warned. 'No favouritism.'

'You worked very well together in the past, Mads,' Ade said, ignoring the dig in the ribs. 'Rescuing the lad there,' he pointed at Jamie, 'and this stuff with the photos. You could save yourself a lot of interview time and advertising money.'

Silence fell over the room.

'Trial period,' Maddy said firmly.

'Shame you'll have to re-brand again,' Hazel said, picking at her flaking nail polish.

'Re-brand?'

'Well, you won't be Clifford-Mackenzie anymore. I could run you up some designs for new business cards and suchlike though. I'm sure Ade won't mind me using the office software.' She flashed him her most charming smile. 'Not once I'm assistant manager.'

'I suppose,' Ade said darkly. 'As long as you do an absolutely brilliant design for Glencoille first.'

Nick's phone blared; he shot a guilty look towards the ceiling and the sleeping Tas, and snatched it up before it could go off again. 'DS Clifford.' He listened for a moment, thanked the caller, and then let out a huge sigh as he put his phone in his pocket.

'She's confessed.' He looked at Hazel. 'All three.'

Hazel blinked rapidly, but the tears wouldn't be held back. She lowered her face into her hands, and time blurred for a while. She was aware of movement in the room, of Nick rising to leave, of people murmuring their goodbyes, and of doors opening and closing. Someone's phone went, and there was more muffled conversation, but none of it mattered now.

Eventually she sat up straight, and found herself alone in Maddy's sitting room. She sniffed and wiped at her eyes with her sleeve before going in search of someone, finding Maddy and Ade in the kitchen.

'How are you feeling?' Maddy asked. She looked red-eyed and exhausted, but very, very happy, and Hazel saw that same quiet happiness on Ade's face. She allowed herself a smile of her own.

'Fine, thanks. Where's everyone?'

'Kids are in bed, Nick's gone.' Ade pointed at the window, to the darkness of the small back yard. 'Paul and Charis are out there, and they're doing some serious talking. Have been for some time. Let's just say you might not be needing to re-brand the agency after all.'

'She's told him not to leave?'

'Oh, he's definitely leaving,' Maddy said, 'and Charis will be taking his place, but I'm pretty sure we're still going to be called Clifford-Mackenzie.'

The penny dropped, and Hazel laughed. 'That's very nearly the best news I've had all day.'

'Then you'll be ready for the next bit,' Maddy said. 'Nick called again after you left. Ross is still being questioned over the fraud, but will probably get off with a suspended sentence. And,' she smiled and squeezed Hazel's arm, 'Isla's been cleared. She's exhausted and a bit emotional, so she's going straight home. We'll drop Dylan home to her tomorrow.'

Hazel couldn't speak for a moment. She just nodded and bit her lip hard; no more tears... God, no more. She'd shed enough in the past two days to make up for all the years she'd held them back.

'I thought I'd leave it to you to go up and tell Dylan,' Maddy said gently. 'They're in my room.'

Hazel went up and tapped lightly on the door, but there was no reply, and when she pushed open the door she saw Jamie sitting on the bed reading. The wild-boy-in-the-making was fast asleep at his side, looking five years younger than his age, and almost unbearably innocent. Jamie had looked up from his book as she'd knocked, and now raised a finger to his lips like a protective parent; Hazel nodded and backed out.

'Can I borrow your car, Mads?' she asked, going back into the kitchen. 'Just for a couple of hours.'

'What for? You need to sleep.'

'Aye, and I will. But first I want to go and see Griff.'

'It's late,' Maddy said gently. 'You could fall asleep at the wheel, and then what good would that do?'

'But I need to—'

'He's your friend.' Maddy guided Hazel into the sitting room and sat her down on the sofa. 'I know you think he hates you, but he doesn't. He couldn't. Go to sleep, hen.' She braced a cushion against the arm of the sofa and patted it. 'There's plenty of time. All the time in the world now.'

Hazel obediently rested her head on the cushion and heard the back door click, then murmuring voices, and the immediately hushed exclamations of congratulations from the kitchen. She closed her eyes, letting the voices of her friends wash over her, and felt a smile creep across her face as those voices followed her down into deep, blissful sleep.

Maddy glanced into the sitting room on her way to the front door a little later, then pulled the door closed quietly. She looked back at Paul with a smile. 'She's a fan of yours for life now,' she murmured. 'You'll never be stuck for great advice on how to maim people.'

He gave a short laugh. 'I'll take that, though to be fair I'm less in need of that now than I was before.'

'How's the shoulder?'

'Easing. It'll be fine.' He saw her sceptical look, and smiled. 'I promise. And I'm going to be looked after to within an inch of my life, you know that.'

'I know.'

Outside, they saw that the sun was just beginning to paint the sky with the first splashes of pink. Maddy looked up at it and smiled. 'I love this time of day. Even Abergarry looks nice.' She turned back to see that Paul's focus wasn't on the sky at all, but on the end of the path where Charis was leading a sleepy Jamie to her car. His face was no longer tired, and carried a quiet contentment that strangely suited him. It softened the hard angles and made him look younger and infinitely more approachable.

'You're definitely doing the right thing, retiring from Clifford-Mackenzie,' she said, and he looked down at her. 'Not that you won't be missed, at least a little bit,' she added, and hoped he understood just how much.

'Good to know. By the way, don't feel pressured.' He nodded towards where Charis was now ushering Jamie into the back seat. 'You were put on the spot a bit back there, but if you don't want to work with her you only have to say.'

'I wouldn't dare.' Maddy said, and laughed softly. 'Jamie would kill me, for starters.'

'Aye, he would. He's as excited as she is, and I'm pretty sure he's now *this* close to getting that dog he's been banging on about.'

'Well, her first exciting job can be fixing that wonky bloody sign on the door.'

He chuckled. 'I'll make sure I send her along with her tool kit on her first day. With her name stencilled on it, of course.'

There was a long silence between them then; the shifting of their working relationship into its new place in their memories. In sudden, unexpected panic, Maddy almost asked him to change his mind, just so things could stay the same, but they wouldn't anyway. Everything was changing now, and it remained to be seen whether it really was for the better.

'You've got a good one there,' Paul said, and when she turned he was looking back up the path, to where Ade stood outlined in the doorway. 'He might be older than God, and ugly as sin, but he'll do you right.'

'He's dreadful,' she agreed, feeling the warmth inside her glow a little brighter as Ade lifted a hand. 'He'll take a lot of knocking into shape.'

'Mackenzie!' Charis hissed across the quiet street. 'I'm knackered. Are you coming or what?'

'Another pearl,' Maddy murmured reverently, and yelped as he tugged her ponytail. 'Go on then, before she wakes the whole neighbourhood.'

He moved off down the path, but when he reached the gate he stopped and looked up at the mountains that surrounded their town. Mountains which had claimed the lives of people he'd loved, and in which he had only recently been able to find some kind of peace again. When he looked back at Maddy, he was smiling.

'It's been good, Mads, really good. But I think it's going to get better for all of us now.'

Maddy nodded and watched him cross the street and join Charis by the car, then she turned to go indoors. He was right; the Clifford-Mackenzie agency might be changing the shape of what it had been, but there was another new Clifford-Mackenzie partnership in town now. The Mackenzie part of that one held out his hand and drew her indoors, closing the door on the brand new dawn. For now.

The Clifford-Mackenzie Crime Series

Crossfire

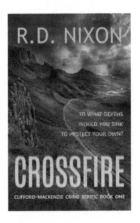

To what depths would you sink to protect your own?

Hogmanay 1987
A prank robbery has fatal consequences.

Five Years' Later
Highlands town Abergarry is shaken by the seemingly gratuitous murder of a local man. The case is unsolved.

Present Day
Ten-year-old Jamie, while on holiday in Abergarry with his mum Charis, overhears a conversation. To him, it is all part of a game. But this is no game and the consequences are far more serious than Jamie ever imagined.

Old wounds are about to be reopened.
Struggling PI team Maddy Clifford and Paul Mackenzie and find themselves involved by a chance meeting. How deeply into those wounds will they have to delve to unravel the mystery?

Available from Amazon.

Praise for *Crossfire*

'Without a doubt, one of the most exciting books I've read!' Shelley Clarke

'Crossfire has stormed into second place in my personal rating system.' Jane Clements

'I loved this book. So many twists and turns which kept me guessing'. H. McLeod

'A gripping mystery.' Yvonne B.

'Nixon can write, no doubt about that!' Johnny Nys

'Beautifully written and an excellent, intricate plot.' Linda

Fair Game

It's autumn in Abergarry

The nights lengthen, the weather turns, and the atmosphere darkens as the community is rocked by a brutal roadside murder: a loan shark's 'bag man', Craig Lumsden, is found bludgeoned to death in his car in the early hours of the morning.

The season for murder

The case seems simple enough. and the fingers quickly point to the most obvious suspect. But things are rarely as simple as they seem...

A murder that's too close to home

Too close for comfort, and definitely too close for complacency for private investigators Maddy Clifford and Paul Mackenzie. Delving into the case brings at least one of them face-to-face with danger... Will life in Abergarry ever be the same again?

Praise for Fair Game

'R.D. Nixon has given PI team Maddy and Mackenzie another intricate plot to investigate. *Fair Game* is beautifully written with a chilling sense of evil throughout, and twists and turns all over the place. Strong, realistic characters, an enticingly atmospheric setting and plenty of suspense make for a five-star read.' Linda Huber, bestselling author of psychological thrillers

'Flawless writing, incredibly true to life characters and a great plot. I think this author has got to be at the very top of British crime writers.' H. McLeod

'Well, I can confidently say that I have found a new author to add to the 'buy anything they release without needing to read the blurb first' list. This book was absolutely great.' Kerry Young

Acknowledgments

I'd like to say a huge 'thank you' to **Rebecca** and **Adrian** at **Hobeck Books,** for giving me the chance to share the Clifford-Mackenzie stories which have been running around in my head since the early 90s. Thanks to my fabulous and patient editor, **Sue Davison,** and to **Jayne Mapp** for the absolutely stunning artwork she has created for this series.

Additionally, my gratitude goes to everyone who's taken the time to write and post online to tell me how much they've enjoyed the books, and to the book bloggers who've been so generous in their reviews; the crime writing community is filled with such kind souls!

My thanks, of course, to my family and friends who have steadied me when I've wavered, and supported me when my foothold has been uncertain. You have helped me more than you know.

Thank you to everyone who has bought or read these books. We will leave these characters to their new lives for now, but I'm already sensing a return at some point – if only to make sure Maddy and Charis are still on speaking terms...

Whatever happens next, and wherever my writing leads, I hope you'll come with me.

About the Author

R.D. Nixon is a pen-name of author Terri Nixon, who has been publishing historical drama and mythic fantasy novels since 2013. The initials belong to her two sons, who are graciously pretending not to mind.

Terri was born in Plymouth, UK. She moved to Cornwall at the age of nine, and grew up on the edge of Bodmin Moor, where her early writing found its audience in her school friends, who, to be fair, had very little choice. She has now returned to Plymouth, and works in the university's Faculty of Arts, Humanities and Business. She is occasionally mistaken for a lecturer, but not for long.

Bad Blood is Terri's third crime novel in the Clifford-Mackenzie series. The first novel, *Crossfire*, was published in July 2021 and *Fair Game* followed in March 2022.

Hobeck Books - the home of great stories

We hope you've enjoyed reading this novel by R.D. Nixon. To find out more about R.D. Nixon and her work please visit her website: **www.rdnixon.com**

The Macnab Principle, and many other short stories and novellas, is included in the compilation *Crime Bites*. *Crime Bites* is available for free to subscribers of Hobeck Books.

Crime Bites includes:

- *Echo Rock* by Robert Daws
- *Old Dogs, Old Tricks* by AB Morgan
- *The Silence of the Rabbit* by Wendy Turbin
- *Never Mind the Baubles: An Anthology of Twisted Winter Tales* by the Hobeck Team (including all the current Hobeck authors and Hobeck's two publishers)
- *The Clarice Cliff Vase* by Linda Huber
- *Here She Lies* by Kerena Swan
- *The Macnab Principle* by R.D. Nixon
- *Fatal Beginnings* by Brian Price
- *A Defining Moment* by Lin Le Versha
- *Saviour* by Jennie Ensor
- *You Can't Trust Anyone These Days* by Maureen Myant

Also please visit the Hobeck Books website for details of our other superb authors and their books, and if you would like to get in touch, we would love to hear from you.

Hobeck Books also presents a weekly podcast, the Hobcast, where founders Adrian Hobart and Rebecca Collins discuss all things book related, key issues from each week, including the ups and downs of running a creative business. Each episode includes an interview with one of the people who make Hobeck possible: the editors, the authors, the cover designers. These are the people who help Hobeck bring great stories to life. Without them, Hobeck wouldn't exist. The Hobcast can be listened to from all the usual platforms but it can also be found on the Hobeck website: **www.hobeck.net/hobcast**.